END GAME

END GAME

(Fallen Empire, Book 8)

LINDSAY BUROKER

Illustration Copyright © 2016 Tom Edwards
TomEdwardsDesign.com

ISBN: 1542643384
ISBN-13: 9781542643382

FOREWORD

This is the final novel in the Fallen Empire series, and I would like to thank you for sticking around and spending so much time with my characters. I hope you enjoy this last installment (it's the longest of the books by quite a bit!). I do have some ideas for spinoff series, so look for more adventures in 2017, but in the meantime, please enjoy this last ride with Alisa, Leonidas, and the gang.

Before you start in, please let me thank some more folks for sticking with me through all these books: my editor, Shelley Holloway, and my beta readers, Sarah Engelke, Rue Silver, Cindy Wilkinson, and Walt Scrivens. Also, my thanks to Tom Edwards for the cover design for all the novels in the series.

Now, please jump into the story…

CHAPTER ONE

The stars stretched across the view screen, bright, majestic, and beautiful. Neither Alisa nor Jelena were looking at them as they munched their dinners. Instead, they watched the holodisplay on Alisa's netdisc, as Andromeda Android hurled evildoers out of her path while rescuing Delgottan cheetah kits from a mafia lord intent on skinning them for their luxurious furs.

"I think I've been in those sewers," Alisa said, pointing at the display. "These take place in Perun Central, don't they? Andromeda better watch out. There are massive sewer cleaning automatons that can squish you if you're not careful."

"*Mom,*" Jelena said, throwing her an aggrieved look. "I haven't seen this one before."

"So I should be quiet?" Alisa popped one of Beck's grilled zucchini slices into her mouth.

"Dad says you're not supposed to talk during vids. *Especially* when the hero is pulverizing the bad guys."

Dad.

Alisa suddenly struggled to get the zucchini down. She had been enjoying her daughter's presence in NavCom, even if Jelena was uninterested in hearing about her mother's exploits, but having her mention Jonah filled her with sorrow. And guilt. She had not been thinking about her late husband often enough, especially these last couple of months. Even though she had been understandably busy, she wondered if forgetting to think about him was a betrayal. Had Alisa moved on too quickly? Had she fallen in love again too quickly? If Leonidas had not come into her life, she never would have gone looking for anyone else so soon. She still hadn't figured out a way to explain her feelings about him to Jelena. Of course, it had been less than a week since she had been reunited with her daughter. Alisa's body still ached from having all those rocks dropped on her, despite the painkillers she was on, and despite the nanobots that had swum around her system for days, repairing bones and tissue.

"Dad was particularly aggrieved when you talked while he watched documentaries of the original colonists collecting plant samples and building survival huts," Alisa added, trying to encourage the conversation. Even if it roused feelings of guilt within her, they *should* talk about Jonah. They both needed to.

Jelena rolled her eyes. "I know. His vids were *so* boring. He watched that one all the time when you were gone."

While Alisa tried to decide if there was condemnation in that statement, an implication that she'd been gone far too long and Jelena had been forced to endure far too many documentaries, the end credits rolled on the cartoon. Jelena stood up, her mostly empty plate in hand.

"I'm done. Can I go back with the Starseers?"

Jelena still wore the black robe she had been wearing the day she arrived. Alisa vowed to shop for her as soon as they had a chance. She admonished herself for not having thought to do it ahead of time, though she worried Jelena might prefer that robe to normal children's attire. Alisa *had* returned the jacket she'd found in Jelena's room on Cleon Moon, but if her daughter ever wore it, it was under the robe.

"Again?" Alisa asked, careful to keep any disapproval out of her voice, even if she couldn't help but be hurt that Jelena was spending more time with the Starseer refugees than with the mother she hadn't seen in a year. "I thought I could show you how to pilot the *Nomad*, now that we're out of the asteroid belt."

Jelena wrinkled her nose toward the control panel. "I have to learn more things. *Useful* things. So I can help get Thorian back."

Alisa wanted to point out that being able to pilot a ship *was* useful, but she wiggled her fingers toward the hatchway. "Go ahead, but wash your plate on the way through the mess hall. Don't just leave it on the table again."

That earned another nose wrinkle, but also an, "All right," before Jelena sprinted out of NavCom.

Alisa watched her go, the robe flapping around her ankles, her ponytail swaying on her back. She told herself not to feel rejected. This was what kids did. They fled their parents to do fun things. She just found it unnerving that Jelena's "fun thing" was spending time with people in black robes with creepy mental powers.

No, she had better not think like that, she told herself firmly as she turned to check the sensor station. Jelena was reading minds these days. Alisa did not want her to find anything but love and acceptance in her thoughts. *Jelena* wasn't creepy. And neither were most of the Starseers. Just the ones who kidnapped children. And brewed beer.

I heard that, Abelardus thought into her mind from wherever he was on the ship.

Oh? Are you monitoring my thoughts constantly, or were you simply bored and needed entertainment?

I saw your offspring sprinting through the corridors and thought I would check on you.

Because you were worried about me or her?

I worried you might be having lurid thoughts about your cyborg, and I was going to remind you that Jelena has developed rudimentary telepathy.

I already figured that out, but thanks for the tip. Alisa did not comment on cyborgs or luridness. She had barely seen Leonidas since Alejandro had pronounced her well enough to return to work—and pilot the *Nomad* someplace where they could find a regeneration tank for the more seriously injured Ostberg, who was still in sickbay. Leonidas had been staying in his cabin, much as he had when Alisa first met him and he'd wanted nothing to do with her because he was a loyal imperial soldier and she wasn't.

She wondered what he would say if she visited him and asked if he wanted to watch a vid.

Better knock first, Abelardus said. *Your horny cyborg is making up for lost time. Are you watching?*

Trying not to, but he can be noisy when he's thumping against the walls. My cabin is next to his, you know.

Alisa grimaced, less at the comments and more at the thought that Leonidas was alone with his dreams and lust instead of with her. But with a telepathic daughter, Alisa didn't feel comfortable engaging in a relationship with him, not until there had been more time to acquaint Jelena with the idea of her mother having a love life with someone who wasn't her father. Hells, Alisa would have been hesitant to have perfectly acceptable marital sex with Jonah now that Jelena could read minds. How awkward.

Starseer children tend to learn about the birds and the bees at a young age, Abelardus informed her dryly.

I bet. After confirming that there weren't any ships within sensor range, Alisa reached for the comm. She wanted company, but not his. "Leonidas?"

A moment passed without a response. Maybe he wasn't in his cabin, after all.

"Yes?" he replied.

"There's not much going on right now, so I can break away from NavCom. Do you want to do some sparring? I believe my armor has been in its case long enough to mostly repair itself." The day before, she'd had Mica work on the dents too large for the case's facilities to handle. She did not yet know how they would find Tymoteusz, asshole kidnapper of Prince Thorian—among other crimes—but she wanted to be ready when they did.

Leonidas hesitated again before answering. "I don't think that would be a good idea."

"You don't? I thought you agreed that I needed practice in the armor."

"You do. I'll program a few training scenarios into the hover pads, and you can practice on them."

Alisa scowled at the comm panel. She didn't want to spend time with *pads.* She wanted to spend time with him. Even if they weren't going to be lovers for a while, did that mean they couldn't be together at all?

"It'll be easier that way," he said quietly.

"Are you thinking of Jelena?"

Maybe he was worried about telepathic eight-year-olds too.

"I'll let you know when the routines are programmed in," Leonidas said and closed the channel.

Alisa scowled again, feeling lonely despite all the people on her ship right now. All of the cabins were being used—she had cleaned out her mother's old cabin to loan to Admiral Tiang, and Jelena now, of course, occupied the one Alisa had reserved for her since the beginning—and the Starseers they had picked up on the station, along with the ones that had been aboard since Arkadius, were still camping out in the cargo hold.

She grabbed her plate and headed to the mess hall, hoping she would find Beck or Mica or Yumi to chat with, and also hoping she wouldn't find anyone unappealing, such as Alejandro or—even worse—Durant. She had caught Durant sitting in with Yumi's sister and several other Starseer women, the children's tutors. Durant was the last person Alisa wanted involved in Jelena's education. She wasn't even sure she approved of the other people—that Lady Westfall was definitely snooty. As Jelena's mother, shouldn't Alisa decide who could teach her daughter what? But she felt so out of her element when it came to Starseer things that she had no idea how to gauge the effectiveness of one tutor over another, and the Starseers had a tendency to stop talking whenever Alisa walked past. Either that, or they started exchanging looks in a way that made her believe they had switched to telepathy.

"Evening, Captain," Beck said when she walked into the mess hall.

Alisa faltered one step in. There were boxes everywhere. She could barely *see* Beck.

"Uhm, Beck?" she asked.

"Just preparing an order, Captain. I tried to pack everything in the cargo hold, but the Starseer kids kept accidentally knocking my boxes over with their boisterous minds. I *think* it was accidental, but the mess hall seemed safer."

"Er, yes." Alisa picked her way down an aisle between segmented boxes filled with bottles of a brownish red sauce. "For whom are you preparing an order?"

For the last few weeks, they had been fleeing the Alliance, the empire, android treasure hunters, and rogue Starseers. When had he had the time to receive an order?

"Chef Terra, a caterer out of Sherran Moon." Beck turned and poked his head over a stack of boxes, his bleached blond hair swaying with the movement. It was in need of cutting and a reapplication of dye—his dark roots were showing. "You said we're heading to Aldrin, right? To drop off Ostberg on one of the moons?"

"Yes, it's the closest planet to the asteroid belt that isn't Alliance-controlled, and the moons offer several medical options, even if we avoid Cleon Moon, which I plan to do. Alejandro approved."

"Good. Might I suggest Sherran Moon?"

"Because you have cargo to drop off there?"

"It just so happens that I do. And they have medical facilities, if you don't mind paying by the hour as well as the service. Isn't that convenient?"

"Terribly convenient. If Alejandro says Sherran Moon works, that's fine with me." While she was looking for a clear path to the sink for her dish, Alisa noticed a plate of sandwiches and cookies on the table. Jelena's empty plate was also there, though Alisa couldn't blame her much for not having maneuvered through the box maze to find the sink.

"That's for Admiral Tiang." Beck nodded toward the sandwich plate while loading more bottles of sauce. How had he had time to *make* all those? And where had he been storing all these boxes and bottles? And the ingredients for filling them? "Do you want to deliver it to him, Captain?"

"Deliver it? I don't remember room service being mentioned on the *Nomad's* passenger transport flier."

"I thought you promised Tiang a luxury experience when you were negotiating his fare."

"Even if I did, I'm fairly certain captains and pilots aren't supposed to deliver food."

"I can do it, but I thought you might want a chance to spy on him."

Alisa flushed. Did the entire ship know that she had eavesdropping tendencies?

"Have you been by his cabin lately?" Beck continued.

"Not for a few days." Alisa recalled that Tiang had been borrowing some of Alejandro's medical equipment and setting up a lab of sorts. He hadn't explained what he was working on.

"You might want to."

"Do you know what he's up to?"

"No idea. But it's *involved*."

"Hm." Alisa picked up the plate of sandwiches. "Should there be any vegetables on here? I'm not sure sandwiches and cookies are a balanced meal for a brain surgeon." Or anyone, she amended silently.

"There are pickles on the sandwiches. That's all he'll eat. Trust me, I've tried more nutritious fare. Everyone wants sweets. Did you like the maple-cinnamon grilled sweet potato chips? They were wonderful, weren't they?"

"They were." Alisa headed back to the passenger cabins with the plate. Even if her thoughts had been geared more toward Jelena these last few days—and how she could get rid of the majority of her passengers and return her life to normal—she *was* curious what Tiang was up to in his cabin. So, delivery it was.

As she passed Leonidas's hatch, she thought about knocking and dropping off a sandwich. Tiang was a skinny sixty-year-old man—did he truly need *three* sandwiches? But she wanted to respect Leonidas's privacy. If he wanted company, he could come find her.

"Yes?" came Tiang's muffled voice when she knocked at the hatch.

"Delivery," Alisa said.

The hatch opened, and steam—or was that smoke?—flowed out.

Startled, Alisa stepped back. "Admiral?"

Tiang appeared in the hatchway wearing a red suit and a helmet. He peered blearily at her through the faceplate, looked down at the plate, and after a glance back into the cabin, where a ventilation fan had just started to whir, he stepped into the corridor. He closed the hatch behind him.

"Good evening, Captain."

"Is that one of the hazardous-material suits from sickbay?" she asked, gaping at him.

"It is, yes."

"Are you wearing it for any particular reason?" Alisa eyed the closed hatch. He wasn't doing something dangerous in there, was he? Something that might leak out and affect the rest of the ship?

"It's comfortable and stylish?"

"If that was a question, I think the answer is no."

"Ah." Tiang reached for the plate. "Is that for me?"

Alisa stepped back, taking it with her. "Yes, it is, and you can have it if you tell me what you're doing in there."

"Research."

"Research that could endanger the entire ship?"

"Hm, only those with Starseer blood most likely, and only if there's a breach, which there shouldn't be. I'm taking suitable precautions."

"Half the people on this *ship* have Starseer blood," Alisa said. Including her. Even if it hadn't manifested into any Starseer talents.

"Yes, and I am taking precautions, as I said." Tiang's fingers twitched toward the sandwiches, or maybe toward the stack of cookies. "Captain, I'm quite famished. May I have that plate?"

"Does Alejandro know what you're up to in there?"

"He does. We brainstormed this together a couple of weeks ago. After our first encounter with the rogue Starseers, which did not go overly well."

"You're doing something that could help a future encounter go more well?" Alisa wished there wouldn't be any more encounters, but she had promised Jelena and Leonidas that she would help them find Thorian. She never would have thought she'd see the day when she was risking herself and her ship to search for the only heir to the Sarellian Empire, an empire she absolutely did not want to see reestablish itself.

"I hope that will be the end result, yes."

She waited to see if Tiang would elaborate. He did not. He merely gazed forlornly at the plate.

Alisa sighed and handed it to him. "Carry on then. Just be careful. We don't want anything contagious or hazardous escaping your cabin." Especially not now that her daughter was on board.

"I agree, Captain." Tiang pushed the hood of the suit back and accepted the plate. He only managed one bite of a sandwich before grabbing a cookie.

A faint beep drifted down the corridor from NavCom.

"I better check on that," Alisa said, giving him a curt wave. It sounded like the comm panel rather than the proximity alarm, so she didn't sprint back to the pilot's seat, but she had sent out messages and set up sys-net alerts, hoping to discover where Tymoteusz had gone after kidnapping Thorian.

"Tell Beck thank you, Captain," Tiang called after her.

She glanced back, intending to tell him that he could share the message himself, but Tiang was already stepping back into his cabin—laboratory.

"Odd man," she muttered as she swung around the corner and into NavCom.

She slid into her seat and pulled up the incoming message. Unfortunately, it wasn't from any of the sources she had contacted. Even more unfortunately, it was from Cleon Moon. There wasn't anyone in any of those domes that she wanted to talk to, and it made her uncomfortable that a message would show up when the *Nomad* happened to be on the way back to the area. Maybe that White Dragon simpleton they had left in charge of his family's wrecked dome had realized he hadn't gotten a good deal.

She started to tap on the message to open it, but saw that it wasn't addressed to her. It was for Leonidas.

Alisa leaned back in her seat. She could only think of one person on Cleon who might want to get in touch with Leonidas, and it was quite possibly her least favorite person on the moon.

She reached for the internal comm. "Leonidas? Can you come up to NavCom, please?"

Yes, she could have routed the message straight to him, but Beck hadn't been incorrect in identifying her nosy streak. She wanted to know what this was about.

A moment later, Leonidas ducked into NavCom, wearing his gym clothes, as usual. He had a towel over his shoulder, and sweat gleamed on his forehead. Alisa suspected that if Abelardus had heard thumps coming from his cabin, it'd had to do with working out rather than anything more carnal, especially if it had been during the day.

"I didn't realize that programming those hover pads required physical effort," she said, trying a smile. After talking to him earlier, she wasn't sure he wanted to see her or would appreciate being called up here.

He returned the smile and lifted a hand, as if he might stroke her hair, which he often did when he visited her here, but he lowered it and cleared his throat. "I wanted to run through the program myself to ensure it would be suitable."

"Thoughtful, thank you." She turned toward the comm panel, telling herself that almost-touch didn't sting. *She* had been the one who said they needed to give each other some space while she figured things out with Jelena. He was doing what she'd asked, nothing more. "You have a message from Cleon Moon. We're close enough that I think you can get a live connection."

She waited for him to point out that she could have sent the message to him in his cabin.

"Cleon Moon?" Leonidas eyed the comm panel warily.

"It could be fan mail. Maybe some footage of you slaying genetically engineered dinosaurs got out, and there are now thousands of women swooning over your manliness."

"I disabled the cameras that tried to follow us," he pointed out, not commenting on his manliness.

"As I recall, you crushed one between your hands as if it were a candy wrapper."

"Which disabled it, yes."

He sighed and touched the message button. The *Nomad's* old console did not have anything so fancy as holo technology, so the face of the sender appeared on the built-in monitor. Alisa had no trouble identifying the woman, even in two dimensions.

"Solstice," she groaned.

"Greetings, Colonel Adler," the tawny-haired woman said, smiling in her sultry way. Even though the video only showed her from the neck up, she had the look of someone lounging on an expensive couch while a robot served her Cloud Killers with fancy olives on a stick. "I've missed you," she added.

"So," Alisa said, "it *is* fan mail."

She watched Leonidas out of the corner of her eye, wondering if he would find the mafia leader attractive now that he was of a state of mind— and body—to notice such things. She trusted that he would not act upon such an attraction, even if he did, but she had to apply some effort to tamp down feelings of worry. Unfounded feelings, she told herself.

Leonidas only grunted in response to her comment.

"As you'll recall," Solstice went on, the message pre-recorded, "you owe me a favor." She waved a hand, perhaps to indicate the dome or the moon. "Things have grown rather chaotic of late, and with my husband across the system on business, I'm in need of assistance."

Alisa could imagine just what kind of assistance she needed, but she kept the thought to herself.

"Nothing too onerous, I assure you," Solstice said. "And I may even have some information for you. I've recently acquired some media stations on other planets, and the news has been interesting of late. You and your ancient little freighter are even in it, did you know?"

"Maybe I should be watching more than cartoons up here," Alisa muttered. Had the Alliance let out news of the staff and the rogue Starseers?

"Do comm me when you get a moment, Colonel," Solstice said. "Is there any chance you're heading this way? Soon?" Her face changed from sultry to imploring. "I truly need your help."

Alisa frowned. *That* plea would likely work better on Leonidas than a sexual one, even now that things had changed for him. He was noble to the core, and she doubted he could resist a woman—or even a man—asking for help.

"We are going to one of Aldrin's moons, aren't we?" Leonidas asked, meeting her eyes after Solstice disappeared from the monitor.

"Yes, but not that one."

His eyebrows arched. "I could contact Solstice and ask if there are regen tanks in any of the medical facilities within her dome."

"Beck has about a million crates to drop off on Sherran Moon," Alisa said, glad to have an excuse to keep them away from Cleon.

Leonidas tilted his head. "I imagine CargoExpress has facilities on Cleon Moon. A mafia presence hasn't been known to keep them out of lucrative metro areas in the past."

"It would cost Beck a fortune to send all those boxes via a carrier. And we *are* a carrier. It's silly to hand our freight off to someone else."

Leonidas sighed. "What if I pay for it? I *do* owe the woman a favor, whether I want to be in her debt or not." He waved at the now-blank monitor.

"Leonidas," Alisa groaned, dropping her forehead into her hand. "It could be a trap."

Or, more likely, Solstice wanted another try at getting Leonidas into her bed. Still, the trap angle seemed like a reasonable argument.

"She lent us her ship and assisted us in getting Beck out of the White Dragon dome."

"I haven't forgotten, but she only did that because of you. Because she wanted you to owe her a favor. Just like this." Alisa lowered her hand and gazed up at him, willing him to understand that nothing good would come of this. "She runs a *mafia* organization. We can't trust her."

"I agree, but if I can repay the favor without impinging on my honor or endangering anyone here, I would prefer to do so and not have to worry about it again going forward."

"Can't you repay favors *after* we find Thorian?"

His face darkened. "We don't know where Tymoteusz took him, and all those Starseers in the cargo hold have been unable to figure that out. I've asked. Several times."

She hadn't realized he had done that.

"They say the staff is either too far out of range or that Tymoteusz has found a way to hide it somehow," Leonidas said. "Solstice has connections. She may be able to find information that we can't. It's not as if I can ask the remnants of the empire for intel. They're further behind on all this than we are." From the frustrated way he spoke the words, Alisa wondered if he had already tried to ask the empire. "And the Alliance surely won't give me information. I assume they won't give you information either."

"I'm hoping to hear back from Tomich, but I'm not holding my breath." Of the various comm messages Alisa had sent after recovering from her injuries, only her sister-in-law Sylvia had responded. She wanted to know when they would return to Perun so she could see Jelena again. Alisa wished she had the answer for that.

"I don't like the idea of working with the mafia," Leonidas said, "and I also do not trust her, but as I said, she may be a good resource for this."

Alisa glowered at the stars on the view screen. She wasn't sure he was right, but she also wasn't sure he was wrong.

She tapped the comm for sickbay. "Alejandro, are you there?"

"Where else would I be?" came his prompt response.

"I thought Tiang might have talked you into helping out in his mad scientist laboratory."

"I have a patient to monitor."

Ostberg. Alisa closed her eyes. She owed him something, something more than paying for a slot in a regen tank. The kid had helped them numerous times, and the chickens loved him. From what she'd heard, he had parents out there who loved him too. Parents who had sent him to be tutored by Starseers, not to traipse around the system in a freighter putting his life in danger.

"Can you look up the facilities on Cleon Moon and see if anything there would be suitable for his needs?" Alisa asked.

"Cleon Moon?" Alejandro asked distastefully. "I thought we were going to Sherran."

"We can go there first, if that's the best place, but Leonidas thinks that Solstice may be able to get us information on Thorian's whereabouts."

"Does *he* think that, or does his penis?" Alejandro growled.

Leonidas's eyebrows flew up. Alisa was surprised by the comment, too, if only because she didn't remember Alejandro being around when they had met with Solstice—and when she had draped herself all over Leonidas's armor.

"Unless Tiang's surgery was more cutting edge than I realized," Alisa said, "I don't think his penis is capable of thought."

"Tell me about it," Alejandro muttered. A couple of thunks sounded, followed by a huff and a sigh. "There are facilities we can use on Cleon Moon," he said. "But if there are any delays to my patient being healed or to us finding Thorian, I will object strenuously. Probably with drug-filled injectors."

"It *has* been nearly two days since you stabbed me with one of those."

"To my lament, I assure you."

Alisa closed the channel and waved to the comm panel. "Tell her we're coming, if you wish."

She rose, intending to give him privacy for the conversation, as much as her nosy brain did not want her to.

"Alisa?" he said softly, a puzzled furrow to his brow.

"Yes?"

"Thank you for defending me on that matter." He glanced toward his lower half. "I don't believe there is any sexual interest motivating me, but I admit that isn't something I've had to watch out for in some time."

"I'm glad to hear it." She was *relieved* to hear it, even though she hadn't truly thought he was interested in Solstice. She just hated the way that woman oozed up to him with her aggressive flirting. "I'll let Beck know that he better pad those boxes, since a less reliable freight hauler is going to deliver them for him. But maybe he can pay for extra special handling. Since you're footing the bill." She winked at him and turned toward the hatchway.

Leonidas caught her before she took more than a step, slipping his arm around her from behind.

"I miss you," he said softly, and kissed the side of her neck.

"I miss you too." She thought about flinging the hatch shut, wriggling around in his grip, and kissing him passionately, but the sound of Starseer children laughing drifted up from the cargo hold, reminding her that they were not alone on the ship—even when they were.

Leonidas dropped his arm and stepped back.

"Cleon Moon, here we come," Alisa said, heading toward the mess hall. She lowered her voice to mutter, "Hope this isn't a mistake."

CHAPTER TWO

Alisa stood on the walkway overlooking the cargo hold, her forearms draped on the railing. Lady Westfall, the headmistress of the Starseer school, what remained of it, was standing in the middle of a circle of cross-legged young students, Jelena included. They had to be communicating telepathically, since none of them had said anything out loud since Alisa arrived ten minutes ago. Several tools that looked like they might have been borrowed from engineering had been floated up into the air, some with ease and some with wobbles followed by clanks back to the deck.

"I longed for this kind of experience when I was a girl," Yumi said, walking up the steps to join Alisa. She had just fed the chickens—the flock had grown to thirty or forty, and their improvised coop now took up a larger corner of the cargo hold.

"I just wanted a dog," Alisa said, and glanced at the time display on a wall panel. The *Nomad* was less than six hours from Cleon Moon, and she hadn't gotten much sleep last night. She'd had dreams rooted in jealousy rather than logic, and she'd woken with the distinct impression that nothing good would come of seeing Solstice again.

"I wanted a dog too," Yumi said. "And to be able to communicate with it telepathically, so I could send it chasing after any bullies that bothered me."

"Sounds like you were a needy kid."

"I won't deny that."

"Are you enjoying getting a chance to spend time with your sister?" Alisa asked.

"Very much so. At first, I thought we had little in common, but she also finds science of interest. I've been showing her some of my breathing exercises. I'm trying to keep her busy so she doesn't follow Abelardus around the ship and gaze adoringly at him."

"You wouldn't approve of them as a match?" Alisa would be tickled to have Abelardus firmly interested in someone else.

"I'm not sure he's aware of her interest. She's not very good at flirting. Even though she finds him attractive, he often irks her when they actually talk, and she ends up insulting him."

"I can assure you that won't deter him if he realizes she wants to share a bunk with him. She should just say something blunt. She seems reasonably good at blunt."

"Perhaps."

Mica walked out of engineering wearing a scowl. Yumi waved to her, and she waved back curtly as she stalked over to the group of young Starseers. She leaned past a boy's shoulder and snatched a torque wrench out of the air.

"I wasn't done with that," she growled, and stalked back to engineering.

Jelena's head turned to follow her. As soon as Mica disappeared through the hatchway, three different tools floated out and across the cargo hold. They settled down in the middle of the circle.

"Where'd my spanner wrench go?" came Mica's growl from engineering. Jelena smirked.

"*Jelena*," Westfall said, frowning at her.

"What?" Jelena asked innocently.

"I believe your daughter may be a troublemaker," Yumi whispered.

"Can you see the shock on my face?" Alisa made a circle with her finger pointing at herself.

Yumi peered at her. "No, I mostly see tension. You're reunited with your daughter now. Doesn't that make you happy?"

"Of course, it does."

Yumi's eyebrows drifted upward.

"Can't I be tensely happy?" Alisa scowled as Durant walked out from under the walkway, where the Starseers had their blankets and meager belongings spread, and stood behind the students with his arms folded over his chest. He had better not be teaching them his loathsome, kidnapping ways.

"Can I interest you in one of my compounds?" Yumi asked.

"No."

"I still have some of the Bliss that I made the last time we were on Cleon Moon collecting samples. Perhaps you and Leonidas would like to—"

"*No,*" Alisa said, looking toward Jelena, hoping she wasn't paying attention to her mother right now. She carefully kept Leonidas out of her thoughts. "I appreciate you trying to help, Yumi, but right now, we can't... can't."

Yumi looked to the children, then back to Alisa. "Ah. Well, if at some point in the future, you change your mind, let me know. If you don't wish to experiment with chemical substances, I could also guide you in a relaxing meditation."

"I'll remember that." Alisa wondered what Leonidas would think if she took his hand and walked him to Yumi's cabin for a group meditation session.

"No," spoke a male voice under the walkway. "I have none of my gear—*or* my files, thanks to you. We're not researching anything right now. Go help the captain with something."

Bravo Six came into view and walked up the stairs, his android features as bland as ever. He still wore the eye patch that Mica had supplied him with to hide the missing eye.

"Greetings, Lady Captain," he said, stopping next to Alisa. "Do you have any tasks that I might work on?"

"Your old owner isn't pleased with you?" Alisa had expected Bravo Six to go back to working for the Starseer research scientist who had employed him on Sepiron Station. The man was one of the refugees now camped below.

"Not at this moment. I failed to copy all of our research files from the database before the station was destroyed."

"Were you supposed to do that?"

"My last order came from the station commander. I was to assist Bravo Seven in defending the station from intruders." Bravo Seven— had that been the one Leonidas tore to bits? "I believed that order took precedence, and since I had not been ordered to collect the data, I did not think to do so. This was a failing. I did not know the station would be blown up, but I should have thought to make copies of our research files regardless."

"We all make mistakes." Alisa clapped him on the arm, though she doubted androids were capable of being reassured. "If you need a project, you could go over the news feeds I've been collecting. We're trying to figure out where Tymoteusz and the other *chasadski* went. Any sightings or snippets of data on their whereabouts would be helpful."

"Understood, Lady Captain. I shall begin on this endeavor."

"Good. Thank you." Alisa watched him head toward NavCom. "Maybe we can find a replacement eyeball for him on Cleon Moon. Do you think there are any android creation and repair facilities there? Solstice had a number of models in her compound."

"I don't know, Captain," Yumi said quietly, and looked past her shoulder.

Alisa turned and jumped—Durant had come up the stairs and stood only a few feet away.

"What do you want?" she asked, thinking of the last conversation they'd had, the one where he'd called her a grub who couldn't effectively raise a Starseer daughter. He'd also blathered about the empire returning, about people lying in wait, ready to rise again with Prince Thorian at the head of their movement. She'd promised to space him if he didn't leave at the next stop. Unfortunately, there hadn't been a next stop yet, not unless one counted the hidden asteroid base that Tymoteusz had destroyed. Maybe she could dump him into a dinosaur-filled lake on Cleon Moon.

His eyes narrowed. He was probably monitoring her thoughts. She smiled. Let him.

"Your daughter has a tendency toward stubbornness and irreverence," he said.

"Imagine that."

"Because of her superior Starseer genes, she could be a suitable mate for Prince Thorian, but she should learn to be refined and obedient."

"I'm quite positive those traits aren't encoded in her superior genes." Alisa wondered if Durant would see it coming if she punched him. "Is there a reason you're talking to me? Because I would prefer you didn't."

"Proper behavior rarely has a genetic component. Her unruliness is a result of her upbringing. As her mother, you should ensure she has better manners. She must be appropriately disciplined. As the prince's mate, she would be expected to attend important imperial functions, social and political, as well as birthing children who must be raised carefully since they will have the potential to have great power."

"Would you stop trying to set my eight-year-old daughter up with a ten-year-old boy? Not only is it creepy to talk about her birthing children right now, but the odds of her still liking the same boy in ten or fifteen years are pretty low. And you're certainly not going to arrange any marriages. Who do you think you are, anyway? The empire is gone, and we don't even know where Thorian is right now."

"We will find him," Durant said firmly. "All shall pass as I have planned."

"Uh huh."

"It is good that you assigned the android to search for the staff."

"Someone here has to do it. Your people don't seem to have a clue."

"No." Durant's forehead furrowed as he gazed toward his camp. "Almost immediately after Tymoteusz left the asteroid base, the staff disappeared from our awareness. Even those with the strongest senses can no longer feel it. He may have discovered a way to muffle it."

Muffle a staff? Alisa imagined a bag being pulled over the orb on the end of it, and knots being tied around the stick part.

"Captain?" Leonidas spoke over the comm. "You better come to NavCom. There may be trouble."

"So soon?" Alisa muttered, remembering the "tax collectors" that had come after her ship the last time they approached Cleon Moon. She hadn't expected to encounter anything like that until they were closer to orbit.

She turned away from Durant, but he spoke again as she started toward NavCom.

"You should use your parental influence to ensure she's an appropriate candidate for the future emperor when the time comes," he said.

"You should tie that robe around your face and gag yourself," Alisa said over her shoulder, not stopping.

"I don't understand your recalcitrance. As her mother, you will be ensured a position of luxury and ease. A modern ship, if you wish. You would want for little and demands on your time would be few once Jelena reaches childbearing age."

Alisa ground her teeth. If she'd had a stun gun at her waist, she would have shot him.

"If you don't wish to take on this responsibility, then I will—"

Alisa had reached the end of the walkway, but she whirled and glared at him. "You stay away from her. You're a delusional madman, and you're not going to discipline her or anyone else." She shuddered, wondering what kind of discipline Durant might have already inflicted on Jelena—since she still seemed herself, she hoped that meant the man hadn't had time for anything of the sort as he'd been kidnapping children and fleeing from planet to moon to station.

He lifted his chin and met her glare. *You do not have the power to stop me,* he spoke into her mind. Along with the words came the image of her lifting a stun gun and pointing it at his chest, only to have the weapon torn from her grip and held up in the air where she could not reach it.

"Wanna bet?" she growled, forming an image of her own, her opening the cargo hatch as Leonidas hefted Durant over his head and hurled him out of the ship. He tumbled thousands of feet, his black robe flapping in the wind, and plummeted into a lake. A T-rex promptly swam out and ate him. Alisa had no idea if T-rexes could actually swim, but she liked the vision, so she kept it firmly planted in her mind.

Durant sneered. *The cyborg will not strike against me. He was loyal to the empire long before he met you.*

"You're not the empire. You're a delusional kidnapper."

I want the same thing as he does, the empire to return to power and Thorian to lead it there.

Tired of arguing with the idiot, Alisa turned and stalked away. Even though it worried her sometimes that Leonidas *was* loyal to the old empire—and Thorian—she knew he wouldn't side with Durant over her for anything.

Alisa passed through the mess hall, the table still surrounded by boxes, and entered NavCom, where Beck and Leonidas were pointing at the view screen and having a discussion. Alisa couldn't yet see what they were pointing at, thanks to their broad shoulders blocking the way.

"Do you think I have time to add more insulation to the cargo I'm preparing?" Beck asked. "You know, before I have to jump into my armor and defend the ship? I don't want all my bottles getting broken in a battle."

"They can intercept us in less than twenty minutes if they so choose," Leonidas said.

"Maybe I can insulate *some* of the boxes. What are the odds that they'll be scared away by our new e-cannons?"

"A warship has twenty e-cannons, a dozen ship-rated blazers, and a reinforced hull and redundant shield generators."

"So the odds are low," Beck said.

"Very low."

Alisa was on the verge of clearing her throat, but Leonidas turned sideways so she could enter NavCom—and see the view screen. A hulking white Alliance warship was framed in the center, the distant green gas giant, Aldrin, just visible behind it. A glance at the sensor display showed several other ships in the area.

"Is that the same fleet we encountered in the asteroid belt?" Alisa asked. She supposed it was foolish to hope that Commander Tomich might have escaped whatever trouble he'd been in, acquired a fleet, and come out to help her.

"I'm not sure," Leonidas said. "I was unconscious when that fleet showed up."

"Wish I had been. Talking to that Admiral Agosti was about as fun as chewing on rocks." Alisa stepped past the men and sat in her seat.

"The warship has positioned itself in our path."

"I can change our path," she said, but it wouldn't matter if the ship wanted to catch up with them. Warships had speed; seventy-year-old freighters did not.

Leonidas tapped at the sensor station controls. Alisa started to ping the ship to get an identification, but her comm panel lit up with an incoming message first.

"Captain Marchenko of the oft-beleaguered and unfairly harassed *Star Nomad* here," she said.

"Captain," came the humorless response. "This is Admiral Agosti. I understand that you *still* have Admiral Tiang aboard your ship."

Alisa sighed. When Agosti hadn't given pursuit after Sepiron Station had been destroyed, she'd hoped some superior of his had told him to leave them alone.

"We haven't yet reached a port that has enticed him to want to leave my ship," Alisa said. "You're more than welcome to comm him and discuss the situation with him. Again."

"We know you have him drugged, or you've otherwise coerced him to want to stay aboard." The admiral's voice lowered to a mutter. "It's not as if there's another reason an officer would stay aboard that floating junk barge."

Alisa glared at the comm. Why were people going out of their way to irk her today?

"Yes, we're coercing him with cookies. He adores my chef, and that's why he's staying."

"As nice as it is to be adored," Beck said quietly, "I have a feeling I better hurry if I want to get my boxes insulated before a battle starts." He trotted back toward the mess hall. Apparently, crates of broken sauce bottles would not impress a client.

"Tell Tiang that someone wants to talk to him," Alisa called after him. She turned back toward the comm. "Any chance Admiral Hawk has joined your fleet since the last time we spoke, Admiral?"

"*Senator* Admiral Hawk is busy on Arkadius and is not active duty anymore."

"Senator?" Alisa mouthed. Had there been an election while she had been busy dodging asteroids? "Well, how about Commander Tomich?"

"No."

She sighed over her shoulder to Leonidas, who was standing behind her, as if to protect her from Agosti. She appreciated his presence, though it wouldn't do much good as long as this confrontation was limited to comm chatter.

"You *will* give us the admiral back," Agosti said. "Even though we have superior forces and can take him physically, we are willing to offer you something of value in trade."

"Like what?" Alisa muted the comm. "If they're offering deals, that means they don't want to fight us, right? Maybe our e-cannons are scarier than Beck thought."

"Unlikely."

"Maybe *you're* scarier."

He wasn't in his crimson combat armor yet, but he could loom imposingly even without it.

All he did was arch an eyebrow in response.

"Enable video transmission, Captain," Agosti said.

Alisa toggled a button, curious about what he wanted to show her. "Done."

A moment later, Agosti's pompous face appeared on her monitor.

"I was hoping you'd show me something more enticing," Alisa said. "Supplies for my ship, perhaps. Or supplies for my chef. He's going through a lot of ingredients in preparing an order for an important client."

"Should you be goading an admiral?" Leonidas murmured.

"It's not as if kissing up would do any good."

"Have you ever tried it?"

"Well, no, but I've never tried shooting myself in the foot, either, and I'm sure nothing good would come of that."

The display on the monitor changed. Agosti's face disappeared, and a room or a cell came into view. A person lay on a built-in bench, the only furniture in view. His black robes contrasted sharply with the white walls, and Alisa's mouth sagged open as she recognized the bearded face.

"Stanislav," she whispered.

Was he alive?

His eyes were closed, and he wasn't moving, but they wouldn't be keeping his corpse locked in the brig, right? Bruises darkened one side of his face, and who knew what injuries lay under the robe, but the fact that he seemed to be alive gave her hope. She had assumed him dead, dead before she had decided if he was a decent person or not. Dead defending the ship's airlock so that she, Leonidas, and the doctors could escape Sepiron Station.

Without taking her gaze from the monitor, she muted her end of the transmission and switched to the internal comm.

"Abelardus, come to NavCom, please," she said.

"As you can see, Captain," Agosti said. "We have something that is of value to you. We are open to a trade."

Coming at once to do your bidding, my demanding Captain, Abelardus spoke into her mind.

Just see if that's really Stanislav over on the warship, will you?

What? One second.

Alisa un-muted the outgoing channel. "Something of value to me? A Starseer? I've already got plenty of those." She wanted Stanislav back, of course, but it might be better not to let them know he mattered one way or another to her. Otherwise, Agosti might try to bargain for even more than Tiang's return.

"Yes, I'm aware of that," Agosti said, his voice chilling several degrees. Ah, that might be the real reason that he was hesitant to bring his warship closer and force a boarding. "I am authorized to trade this man to you in exchange for the admiral. We will send a shuttle over to your airlock for a simultaneous exchange."

"Tiang," Leonidas said, and Alisa turned in her seat.

Tiang stood outside of the hatchway, looking as if he didn't particularly want to come in. He had changed out of his hazardous materials suit. Good. Alisa didn't know what Agosti would have made of that. Maybe he would have thought she was forcing Tiang to juggle bars of radioactive material while she kept him drugged.

"It seems your leave is up," Alisa said. "The Alliance wants you back."

"But Captain, I've set up my lab, and I'm progressing in my work, and I can't take it with me. There won't be any Starseers on the Alliance ship."

"There's at least one," she muttered, waving at the monitor.

Stanislav disappeared from the display, and Agosti's face returned.

"Your decision, Captain?" Agosti asked.

"That Starseer is a lot of trouble," Alisa said, waving for Tiang to come forward. "I'm not sure I want him back."

"Our records show that he's your father."

How had they figured *that* out? Had Stanislav told them? "And you think that negates my statement?"

A grunt sounded. Leonidas had risen to his feet and picked up Tiang, bringing him through the hatchway and depositing him in front of the vid pick up.

"*Really*, Colonel Adler," Tiang protested, "I hardly think this manhandling is appropriate, given the recent favor I've done for you."

"Admiral Tiang," Agosti blurted, relief in his voice. Had he thought Alisa had done away with him since the last time they spoke? "Are you injured? High Command is very worried about you. As is your daughter."

"You didn't even send her a message?" Alisa muttered.

"Actually, I did." Tiang frowned at Agosti's image. "I told her where I went. She shouldn't be worried."

"Unless she's in the camp that thinks you're drugged."

Tiang took a deep breath. "Admiral Agosti, I am engaged in a research experiment presently, as this ship seeks to find the Staff of Lore and the one who used it on Arkadius. Perhaps you would be willing to work with the captain. Since she has the loyalty of the Starseers, it makes sense to work with her."

Alisa kept from coughing at the word "loyalty," but barely.

"We don't work with criminals, Admiral," Agosti said. "Prepare to leave that ship. We're readying a shuttle to retrieve you."

Tiang tried to step back but bumped into Leonidas's chest. "I can't go at this time."

Agosti's already deep frown deepened. "*Drugged*," he whispered to someone to his side.

Alisa dropped her face into her hand. Maybe she should have Leonidas carry Tiang to the airlock and force him to rejoin the Alliance. Only the implication that Tiang was working on something that might help them deal with Tymoteusz and get Thorian back kept her from issuing that order right then.

That is Stanislav, Abelardus spoke into her mind, *but he's unresponsive.*

Unconscious from his wounds? Or had the Alliance inflicted *further* wounds on him in the last couple of weeks? Her fingers curled into a fist.

They may be drugging him to keep him from using his powers. He's strong enough that they couldn't keep him in a cell if he didn't wish it.

"Will you do the trade or won't you, Captain?" Agosti asked, now looking at her instead of Tiang.

Tiang huffed and stuck his fists on his hips.

"I need a day to think about it," Alisa said. More like, she needed a day to try comming Hawk and Tomich again. *Senator* Hawk. If he'd just been elected into that position, he might have been too busy to check on the message she'd sent him before. Or rather, the message she'd sent for him through his wife's comm. She had no idea if either of them had checked those messages. With Arkadius busy rebuilding Laikagrad, it would be understandable if they hadn't. Alisa needed more people high up in the Alliance chain of command that she could contact.

"I see," Agosti said coolly. "It appears that you are en route to Cleon Moon. If you change your mind, we will be in the area."

The monitor went black. Alisa had expected more of an ultimatum—do the trade now or never. The reasonableness worried her. Maybe Agosti was planning some raid to retrieve Tiang and thought he would have the opportunity to do it when the *Nomad* was down on the moon.

She turned to face Tiang. "Can't you go back to them, let them check you out to see that you're not drugged, and then talk to someone about staying?"

"I doubt they'll let me come back to my lab even if they see that I'm not drugged. They'll think I'm being influenced by Starseers or something silly."

Alisa sighed and shooed him toward the hatchway. Leonidas stepped aside so he could depart.

"We could force him to leave," Leonidas said.

"That crossed my mind, but not only do we owe him a favor—" she waved toward Leonidas's head, "—whatever he's working on could be useful in getting Thorian back. But Stanislav would be useful for that too." Not only that, but she hated the idea of leaving him in the hands of the military. Who knew what they would do to him, especially since he had been the one to keep their people from boarding the station and getting whatever it was they had wanted there.

"True," Leonidas said.

"Ideally, I'd like Stanislav back, *and* I'd like to keep Tiang, so he can work on whatever medical weapon he's creating. Is that too greedy?"

"The Alliance believes so."

"That's because they're being asteroid kissers."

"I will not disagree." He smiled slightly, probably because she was denigrating the Alliance. She would have to denigrate the empire later, just so he knew she wasn't switching sides.

Alisa punched in the last contact information she had for Tomich. If he was still back on Arkadius, or wherever they had been holding him when they'd taken him off his ship, it would take a while to reach him.

"Tomich," she said, recording a message, "it's your favorite freighter captain again. If you have any sway with anyone right now, I would appreciate it if you made an offer to your superiors for me. If they will give Stanislav Schwegler to me with no strings attached, I'll tell you where Tymoteusz and the Staff of Lore are. Just you. I want you out here to deal with, not this obtuse brick, Admiral Agosti. Marchenko, out."

"Has something changed in the last hour?" Leonidas asked curiously. "Have you learned where they are?"

"No, but that message will take a while to get back. I figure we have a day or two to find out where Tymoteusz and the staff are."

"Ah. Then we had better hope that Solstice can, indeed, offer us some intelligence on the matter."

Alisa was hoping Bravo Six would come up with the answer and that they wouldn't need anything from Solstice, but she couldn't bet everything on that. She tapped the controls, adjusting the *Nomad's* course to pointedly go *around* the warship while continuing on to Cleon Moon.

CHAPTER THREE

Alisa helped Alejandro load Ostberg onto the hover board that Ostberg had used to carry Durant onto the *Star Nomad* in the very dome they were once again inside. When they had approached the entrance, the air traffic controller had not stopped them or even commed Alisa to say hello. Even though Alisa knew Leonidas had sent word that they were coming, the ease with which they had flown in made her nervous. As had the fact that Solstice had not, when he asked, been willing to disclose the nature of the favor she needed over the comm.

A squawk came from the corridor outside sickbay. Several chickens had escaped the coop and were monitoring Ostberg's progress. Alisa hoped they wouldn't try to follow him to the medical facility.

"It'll be good for the kid to be able to rest somewhere without all that *bawking*," Alejandro grumbled.

Alisa brushed Ostberg's shaggy blond bangs away from his closed eyes. He'd woken a few times in the last few days, but had been in enough pain that Alejandro had knocked him out again. She wished she had thought to trim his hair while he had been unconscious.

"Have any of the Starseers gotten in touch with his parents?" Alisa asked, glancing toward the hatchway.

Abelardus stood there with his staff—he and a couple of the others were going to escort Ostberg to a hospital and glower fiercely to ensure he received proper treatment. Alisa suspected money would do more to ensure proper treatment than glowers in the dome that Solstice's mafia family ran, but she didn't know how much of that the Starseers had. They certainly hadn't been paying her much for their passage and all the food they were eating. She didn't mind feeding the children, but the adults tended to irk her more often.

"Yes," Abelardus said, "but we weren't able to tell them where he was being taken for sure until now, so it'll be several days before they can get out here. But I'm sure they'll come."

"Is someone going to stay with him until they get here?" Alisa knew she should let the Starseers worry about him—his parents had apparently signed him up willingly to be tutored by them—but after having him aboard for the last few weeks, she felt responsible for him. He'd even helped them escape those treasure-hunting androids in the asteroid belt.

"I'll ask," Abelardus said. "Do you know yet how long we'll be on Cleon Moon?"

"Too long."

He lifted his eyebrows.

"I don't know," Alisa said, "but I don't think this is the kind of place where you want to leave your wallet and shoes sitting on a chair unguarded while you snooze in a regen tank."

"You think the highly trained medical staff would rifle through his belongings?"

"When the medical staff is owned by the mafia, yes. And I don't think we know much about how trained they are."

"Maybe the chickens can come along and watch after him."

"Maybe your brother can go. He owes Ostberg for watching over *him* when *he* was unconscious." Normally, Alisa wouldn't have volunteered Durant for anything regarding protecting minors, but Ostberg had been loyal to him for some reason. She assumed he was less of a worm suck when he was with other people. Besides, she wanted him off her ship. This seemed as good a place to leave him behind as any.

Abelardus squinted suspiciously at her, but all he said was, "I'll ask him."

Alisa stepped back as Alejandro navigated the hover board through the hatchway, barely making it without scraping the jamb. The chickens protested vehemently as the strange object floated out. Wings flapped, and feathers flew.

Alisa stepped out into the corridor to follow and almost ran into a red-armored shoulder.

"I'm heading out to meet Solstice," Leonidas said, nodding to her.

He hadn't invited her to go along. What would he say if she announced that she would accompany him?

"In full armor?" Alisa tapped his red forearm as Abelardus and Alejandro continued toward the cargo hold with Ostberg. "Is that because you anticipate trouble in the city or because you want to look good for Solstice?"

"Does my armor make me look good? I thought it made me scary."

"Solstice seems oddly immune to being scared. Maybe because she has all those androids around to act as bodyguards. I assume she's never seen what you can do to androids. Once she collects a few of their body parts off her roof, she may grow warier."

He grunted and turned toward the cargo hold.

"Leonidas?" she called, stopping him. The others had disappeared, leaving them alone in the corridor. "What do you think I should do about Stanislav? And Tiang?"

"Leave the hatch locked in case the Alliance comes after Tiang in the next two hours. I'll try to make this meeting as short as possible."

"I was thinking more about a possible rescue mission."

"For Stanislav? Or are you positive I'll need rescuing from Solstice?"

"For Stanislav. You *better* not need rescuing from her."

"You're not thinking of storming aboard a heavily armed and patrolled Alliance warship, are you?" Leonidas asked.

"No, I was thinking of *sneaking* aboard a heavily armed and patrolled Alliance warship."

"It's hard to sneak aboard a warship in space. There's not a lot out there to conceal your approach."

"My plan is still in the formative stages."

"Let's see what Solstice wants first," he said, heading toward the hold. "Maybe she'll have the information you promised the Alliance that you have, and be willing to trade."

"*Let's*? As in, let *us*? Am I invited along?"

Leonidas paused and looked down at her. "I assumed you would come whether I invited you or not."

"You did? Because you think I'm the kind of woman who wouldn't be confident enough to let you go off to meet another woman unsupervised?"

"Because you're nosy and will burn with curiosity if you can't come."

"Oh. Well, that's true." She held up a finger. "Wait here. I'll get my stun gun."

Alisa ran back to her cabin, in case he was, despite his words, entertaining notions of leaving without her. If Solstice was up to something dodgy, she wanted to be there to help Leonidas out of whatever spider web she entangled him in.

"Sure, that's it," she muttered, grabbing her holster with her stun gun and multitool off the back of her desk chair. "It has nothing to do with being nosy."

She found Leonidas waiting in the cargo hold next to the open hatch. The ramp was extended, and Alejandro, Durant, and Abelardus were heading down with Ostberg's hover board. Durant carried a bag over his shoulder, as well as his usual staff. Alisa didn't bother to repress a surge of glee that he was leaving. Maybe she would get lucky and never see him again.

Such an inhospitable host, you are. Abelardus looked over his shoulder at her.

Alisa might have replied, but Jelena and two boys ran out from the Starseer camp and waved after the men.

"Goodbye, Erick," Jelena called. "I'll feed the chickens!"

Erick? Was that Ostberg's first name? Alisa tried to remember if she had known that.

Tut, tut, Abelardus told her. *Inhospitable* and *unobservant.*

I'm sure he would have told me his first name if he wanted me to use it. Keep insulting me, and I'll take off before you come back.

And deny me the honor of riding around in a dilapidated freighter that clanks every time it turns to port?

The Nomad *does not clank.*

It does if you're down in the cargo hold while it's in the air.

Alisa frowned. She might have to check with Mica about that.

I would miss Beck's cooking, Abelardus said, still speaking to her, even though the group had turned onto the busy dock promenade and nearly disappeared from view.

Who wouldn't? Alisa replied, before whistling from behind distracted her.

Beck was using a hand tractor to bring the first of his boxes down to the cargo hold.

"You better let Leonidas slay some dinosaurs while we're here," he told her. "This is going to be a big CargoExpress bill."

Alisa started to ask Leonidas how he felt about that, but a tug at her sleeve turned her focus in another direction.

"Where are you going?" Jelena asked, frowning at Alisa's faded flight jacket.

"Hopefully to get information on where Tymoteusz is. On where *Thorian* is."

"Can I come? I can help."

Alisa shook her head. "It'll probably be dangerous. You stay here with the others." She waved toward Beck rather than the Starseers. She preferred having Jelena spend time with people she knew and trusted, even if they couldn't teach her special Starseer things. "I bet Beck will let you help him get his order ready for pickup."

"Whoa, Captain. You sure know how to entice a kid with excitement." Beck winked at Jelena.

Alisa wished Leonidas would try to befriend Jelena, too, but he was standing in his armor, his back to them as he gazed out toward the promenade. A crimson statue on her deck. Jelena might have rejected any overtures of friendship he made anyway. So far, since she'd witnessed Alisa kissing Leonidas in sickbay, she'd gone out of her way to avoid him.

"I figured you'd have some cookies in one of those boxes," Alisa said, "and that she could use her mental powers to lift one from its spot."

"Mom," Jelena said sternly. "This is serious. I can help. I can find out things when people are thinking them. Ask Lady Westfall. I'm getting really good!"

Lady Westfall walked away from the group of Starseers—they had stopped their tutoring session when the children ran off to bid Ostberg farewell. Gray-haired and prim looking, she headed toward Alisa and Jelena. Alisa held back a grimace. Between piloting the ship and spending the first few days in sickbay, she hadn't said more than a handful of words to the woman since she boarded. Of course, the woman hadn't gone out of her way to say anything to Alisa either. Still, she ought to sit down and have a conversation with her eventually, especially if Westfall was the one choosing her daughter's curriculum. But this wasn't the time.

Leonidas's helmet swiveled toward her. He didn't say anything, but she probably needed to hurry up if she wanted to go with him. Was that the right thing to do? Could she truly help with Solstice, or would it be better to stay here with Jelena?

"Come, Jelena," Westfall said, extending a hand toward the camp. "Your telepathy skills are rudimentary. We will work on them while your mother is gone."

"My skills are good. This morning, I talked the chickens into walking in a circle for treats. I can help." Jelena stepped back from her and turned imploring eyes toward Alisa. "Why can't I come help? You're not taking a Starseer, and I could help if the lady you're seeing knows anything she doesn't tell you."

Alisa didn't point out that she hadn't told Jelena they were going to see a lady. Her telepathy skills seemed just fine.

"You'd take Erick," Jelena said. "He's told stories about how he got to blow stuff up and help with bad androids."

"He's older." And tall enough to pass as an adult. Alisa had thought him closer to eighteen than fourteen the first time they met.

"A Starseer might be useful to you in an interview," Westfall pointed out.

"But not an eight-year-old one," Alisa said, starting to feel ganged up on.

"No. An adult."

"You don't need an adult," Jelena said. "You need me. Thor's my friend."

"I know he is," Alisa said, resting a hand on her shoulder. Jelena looked at it sulkily. "I'm glad he's your friend and that you care."

Westfall frowned at Jelena, and it looked like some silent communication passed between them. Jelena crossed her arms over her chest, hunched her shoulders, and stomped over to join the adults. Leonidas was still watching, and Alisa flushed. Watching tantrums, even if this had been a reserved one, might not do much to endear him toward the idea of fatherhood. Would he rethink his plans for a family?

"I wouldn't mind Young-hee's help if she'll come," Alisa said, when she noticed Westfall still standing there, looking like she had something to say.

"Good," Westfall said. "Come, children," she added, waving the other boys away from the hatch. "We have studies to attend to."

"I hope you don't mind," Alisa murmured to Leonidas. "She made a good point. Someone with telepathy might be useful."

"More useful if she weren't wearing Starseer robes and announcing what she is," Leonidas said, nodding toward Young-hee.

She grabbed her staff and headed toward them.

"They don't seem to do incognito," Alisa said.

"It's more that none of us have spare clothes," Young-hee said. "Tymoteusz did not give us time to pack before taking over the temple. *Chasadski* are rude."

"I've heard that."

Leonidas nodded at Young-hee and started down the ramp. Jelena was looking at them, so Alisa waved toward her as she headed out. Jelena hesitated, and Alisa thought she would ignore her, but she waved back grudgingly.

Don't get hurt, Mom, her voice sounded in Alisa's mind.

I'll try not to. Alisa kept her response short since she didn't know if Jelena could hear her words the way Abelardus did. Was that a more advanced skill?

Of course I can hear them. I told you, I'm good. Don't listen to Lady Westfall. She never admits anyone is good.

Sorry, she hasn't given me a report card, so I don't know how to gauge your goodness.

Mom, Starseers don't get report cards. Amazing how the exasperated tone of a kid could come through a telepathic link.

Never? What if I request one? So I have something to hang on the fridge in the kitchen.

I could draw you a picture for the fridge. Like I used to do.

Something about the answer made Alisa think that maybe she *should* ask for a report card. She shouldn't wash her hands of Jelena's Starseer education, just because she knew so little about it.

A picture of us would be nice, she replied.

Dad too?

Yes.

"Alisa?" Leonidas asked from the promenade.

We'll talk later. Thank you for staying with Westfall. Alisa hurried down the ramp.

"Sorry," she told Leonidas and Young-hee. "Didn't mean to delay you. Important report card discussion."

"Someone is waiting for us." Young-hee pointed past people striding along the docks with shopping bags or hover boards full of supplies to where two androids in black uniforms with silver piping, Solstice's house colors, stood waiting.

From the way Leonidas was staring at them, they had been sizing each other up for a minute or two. As soon as Alisa joined him, he strode straight toward them.

"Maybe I should have worn my armor," Alisa murmured.

"The blue stuff?" Young-hee asked. "Why didn't you?"

"Last time, Solstice's androids insisted that I leave my weapons before going into her compound. I figured the rules wouldn't have changed." Alisa didn't mention that Leonidas hadn't been asked to remove *his* weapons and armor on their previous visit. Solstice had been trying to recruit him for a security position, so he'd gotten the friendly treatment.

"Then I suppose it's a good thing all I have is this trusty walking stick," Young-hee said, leaning on her staff as she walked at Alisa's side.

Alisa snorted. "Good luck getting an android to believe that. I haven't found them to be very gullible."

The androids did not say anything as Leonidas approached, but they parted to walk beside Alisa's little group. To *surround* her little group. Maybe she should have brought Bravo Six for extra support, even if he wasn't a combat model. But she wanted him to figure out where Tymoteusz was. Someone had to give her a lead.

"No, sir," one of the androids said when Leonidas tried to turn down a street, apparently not on the approved route back to the compound.

Leonidas's eyes narrowed behind his faceplate, but he obeyed the android's redirection.

At the halfway point, two more androids appeared out of the crowd and joined the group, making Alisa feel hemmed in.

You know I can't read their minds, right? Young-hee asked silently.

I know. I'm assuming we're being taken to meet Solstice. And you can read her mind.

Understood. Did you bring any of my sister's drugs?

Should I have? Alisa still had some of the compound that could make it difficult for Starseers to control people, but she hadn't expected to meet any of them in the dome. As far as she knew, her ship was the only place collecting Starseers.

She has other useful things, Young-hee said, sounding slightly bemused.

Have you sampled some?

We meditated together last night. While sampling. My mother wouldn't approve. Young-hee slid Alisa a sly smile, appearing pleased at this streak of rebelliousness. She was, Alisa recalled, only in her early twenties.

I won't tell her.

The four-story compound with its drab cement walls came into view at the end of the street, and Alisa withdrew her comm unit. One of the androids watched her. To make sure she didn't pull out a weapon? Or would he object to communication?

"Mica?" Alisa asked quietly, keeping an eye on him.

"What?"

"You sound cranky."

"You commed me to tell me that?"

"No, it was an observation."

"Starseer kids keep floating my tools out of engineering and hiding them. Can't you bring them some hoops or balls to play with?"

"They're not dolphins. Listen, I wanted to let you know that we're being escorted to Solstice's compound by androids."

"Because you're special?" Mica asked.

"That's one possibility. The other is that Solstice doesn't trust us."

"No? I thought Leonidas made her sensitive places tingly."

Young-hee tripped and planted her staff to catch herself.

"Maybe it's a good thing you have a walking stick," Alisa observed.

"Definitely," Young-hee murmured.

"How long do we wait without hearing from you before planning a rescue?" Mica asked. "Keep in mind that the crew member most likely to be able to carry out a rescue is currently wearing an apron and instructing the CargoExpress woman on how to stack his boxes."

"If I haven't checked in in four hours, get concerned."

"How many androids are flanking you now?" Mica asked.

"Four."

"Six," Leonidas corrected, nodding toward one side of the street behind them.

One that Alisa hadn't noticed before was following them about twenty feet back. She peered through the pedestrians and ground vehicles toward the same spot on the other side of the street and spotted another one.

"Six," Alisa agreed.

"I'll start practicing my concerned look now."

"Thanks, Mica. You're indispensable."

"I know I am."

The gate to the compound opened as they approached it. The gloomy gray building, which looked more like a bunker than a residence, had not changed. Alisa eyed the top-floor windows, remembering that Solstice's huge art-filled quarters were up there. Tinted forcefields kept her from seeing anything inside.

The androids closed in, marching her group up the steps, through the double doors, and into the foyer. Two more androids waited inside.

"These are not the limited resources of a woman in need of a favor," Alisa told Leonidas.

"You don't think so?"

"What can you do for her that eight androids can't do? And no, this isn't the time to make jokes about large cannons."

He blinked, and she wondered if he had forgotten his first big attempt at sexual innuendo.

"Jokes aren't on my mind now," he said.

"Remove your armor and weapons," one of the androids said.

"All of us?" Alisa asked.

"All of you."

"Hm." She reached for her stun gun and handed it to the closest android. She hadn't expected to be allowed to bring it in, regardless.

Leonidas did not move.

"Your combat armor is not permitted for this meeting," the android told him. He also gave Young-hee's staff a pointed look. "Nor is your weapon."

"This is just a walking stick," Young-hee tried.

"You are wearing a Starseer robe. It is highly likely that you are carrying a Starseer foci staff, a tool capable of enhancing mental powers and generating an electrical current that can be used independently as a weapon or a shield."

"I told you they weren't gullible," Alisa muttered. "Is Solstice putting together an army for a reason?" she asked them as Young-hee sighed and leaned her staff against the wall.

Leonidas hadn't moved yet. None of the androids answered Alisa.

"Solstice asked me here for a favor," Leonidas said. "If she wants a favor, she can come down here and ask me about it."

"You are required to remove your combat armor and all weapons," the android said.

"No."

Alisa eased a couple of steps away from Leonidas. If he ended up in a fight with eight androids, she did not want to get in his way. Nor did she want to get in the way of an android being hurled down the hallway.

The android that had been giving orders moved several paces down the hallway and tapped a comm unit.

"Can you handle this many in your armor?" Alisa whispered.

"No," he replied, never taking his eyes from that comm unit. With his enhanced hearing, maybe he could hear both ends of the conversation.

"Then maybe it's best to comply for now. If we have a battle right here and don't get to talk to Solstice, we won't find anything out." Alisa looked at Young-hee, wondering how much she could do in a fight with a bunch of androids. She had seen Young-hee hurl someone across a library with her mind once, but she wouldn't be able to tinker with the mind of anything with a computerized brain.

"There shouldn't *be* a battle," Leonidas said.

Alisa wasn't so sure. What if this request for a favor was a ruse? Maybe the Alliance had made a deal with Solstice to set a trap for Leonidas. But why would the Alliance be after him now? He had no more idea of where Thorian was than anyone else did. And Alisa was the one who had kidnapped Tiang and was drugging him, or so they seemed to think.

"Understood, mistress," the android with the comm said.

A *click-thunk* noise came from behind Alisa. The doors locking.

"Nullify the cyborg and remove his armor," the android said.

CHAPTER FOUR

Alisa was still processing the android's order when Leonidas spun around. He slammed his shoulder into one of the locked doors, striking it like a battering ram. Though they were made of something far sturdier than wood, a thunderous crack filled the hallway. He rammed the door a second time, and it flew open, cement splintering and metal warping. But the time it took to assault those doors cost him. Three androids leaped onto him, gripping his armor, and the others also charged toward him.

"Outside, Alisa," he barked, whirling to face his attackers.

The uniformed security androids swarmed over him, and Alisa could only stumble back to the wall as a boot almost took her in the eye. Leonidas hadn't managed to move the fight away from the door, so she didn't know how she could escape, even if she wanted to abandon him.

Young-hee pressed her back against a wall, her eyes wide.

"Try to knock them away from him," Alisa told her, her hand dropping instinctively to her belt where her stunner had been, but there was nothing there. One of the androids had set it on that desk. It wouldn't have done anything against them anyway. *She* couldn't do anything against them. Why hadn't she worn her armor, damn it?

She watched with horror as Leonidas stumbled, dropping to one knee under the assault. He hurled one android down the hall so hard that he flew all the way to the far end, but the others tore at him with their great mechanical strength. An ominous snap sounded—a piece of his armor breaking?

"Young-hee," Alisa urged.

She didn't seem to be doing anything.

"Not that I'm doing anything either," Alisa muttered, thumping her fist against the wall.

Then an idea came. She couldn't do anything to help with the androids, but maybe she could stop the person giving them orders. Especially since they were all focused on Leonidas, deeming her a non-threat.

Alisa circled the fight, ducking a leg that flew out, a leg that was no longer attached to its body. For a moment, she thought Leonidas might somehow come out ahead, that he would survive long enough to tear the androids into pieces, but another snap sounded. Leonidas roared in anger— or was that pain?

With her heart in her throat, Alisa made it to the table. None of the androids were paying attention to her. She snatched the stun gun and sprinted down the hallway toward an elevator. She knew from her last visit that it would take her up to the top floor, Solstice's lair.

Alisa felt like she was abandoning Leonidas and Young-hee, since she hadn't warned them, but she hadn't wanted to warn the androids either. As it was, before she reached the elevator, she heard boots pounding on the marble floor behind her. The doors to the elevator stood open. As she flung herself into the car, she glimpsed one of the androids racing down the hall after her. She slammed her stun gun against the button, mashing it repeatedly, certain her swift pursuer would reach her in time to stop her.

When the doors shut and the elevator lurched into motion, she let out a relieved breath. If she could make it to the top floor, she might have a chance of surprising Solstice—of stunning the damned bitch. How *dare* she set Leonidas up.

A thump sounded against the doors, and Alisa's relief was short-lived. Leonidas would have the strength to force those doors open. An android would too. But maybe he would have orders against destroying elevators in the compound where he worked.

A wrenching sound filled the car, and it lurched to a stop. Alisa pitched against the back wall with a curse. The lights went out, save for the control panel, which informed her that she was halfway between the second and the third floors. That wouldn't do.

She jabbed buttons, trying to open the doors. She had to climb out and find some stairs. It wouldn't take that android long to run up here.

The buttons flashed but otherwise ignored her. She pulled out her multitool, flicked on the light, and looked for an access panel in the ceiling. A square light panel was the only thing up there.

A boom echoed through the building, and that panel shivered. Had Leonidas brought grenades?

Something above the car groaned, and the floor shivered.

Hoping Leonidas and Young-hee were all right, Alisa flicked the laser cutter out on the multitool. She had to jump to reach the light panel with it, so all she managed was a slash before landing again. Feeling like an idiot, she jumped several more times, trying to cut out the panel. Another groan came from above. She imagined plummeting back to the ground floor and landing in the android's arms. Maybe the car would land *on* the android.

Alisa kept jumping and cutting. The ceiling panel tumbled free so abruptly it startled her, bouncing off her shoulder before she could get out of the way. Wires dangled down from a hole in the ceiling, and a dark shaft rose above it.

A shout sounded in the hallway outside—whether from the second or third floor, she couldn't tell. She stuffed her multitool in its holder and jumped, wishing for the augmented power of her armor. Without any grace, she pulled herself through the hole and onto the top of the car. Memories of the last elevator shaft she had climbed came to mind. That one hadn't had a cable, only tiny rails to grip, tiny rails she had only been able to climb with the help of her armor. Luckily, this less sophisticated model had a cable.

A wrenching squeal came from below. The elevator doors.

Alisa scrambled up the cable in the dark, not waiting to see the android run into the car. Grease and grit caked her palms and made the climb hard, but fortunately, she did not have to go far. Unfortunately, the doors on the fourth and final floor were closed. She reached for her multitool again, thinking the lick of the laser cutter might cause them to open. Her fingers brushed the stun gun first, and she snatched it and shot at the doors. She didn't expect it to do anything, but hoped for more luck.

A slash of light entered the shaft from below. Still hanging from the cable, she peered down as an android peered up at her through the hole.

"Damn it," she growled and fired at him.

The stun gun wouldn't have damaged an android, but maybe the darkness kept him from recognizing her weapon. He leaped back out of sight. Alisa fired at the elevator doors again. She was halfway to holstering the stun gun and grabbing the multitool when a sickly bleat came from the doors. One of them jerked, then opened.

Light entered the shaft, bright enough that Alisa couldn't see anything in the room outside. She would have waited for her eyes to adjust, but the android stepped back into the car below her. Cursing again, she swung her legs out and flung herself through the open door.

She landed in a crouch, pointing the stun gun ahead of her. Just as she spotted Solstice—that damned woman was lounging on her sofa and drinking from a glass, the same as she had been last time—a dark figure appeared in her peripheral vision.

Alisa sprang forward as a pair of arms reached for her. She ran toward Solstice, hoping to reach her, press the stun gun to her neck, and use her as a shield for protection. But the dark figure reached Alisa first, catching her and hefting her into the air as if she weighed nothing. She snarled and tried to turn her weapon on her captor, but her arms were pinned painfully to her sides, and it was all she could do not to drop the stun gun. She doubted it mattered. She could tell from the faux skin of the fingers wrapped around her arms that an android held her.

It walked her forward, her legs dangling a foot above the floor.

"That was moderately entertaining," a woman said. It wasn't Solstice.

Alisa hadn't had time to notice the second woman in the room, this one also lounging with a drink. Silver-haired and pale-skinned with a simple blue earstar, she regarded Alisa blandly. She wore simple trousers and a wrap in contrast to the dress with the plunging neckline that Solstice had on. Of course, she also looked to be thirty or forty years older than Solstice, so maybe plunging necklines were no longer flattering.

"Captain Merchant-something, wasn't it?" Solstice asked Alisa, making no move to wave for her android to put her down.

"Marchenko," she growled.

"The cyborg looks to be out of juice," the second woman remarked.

"What?" Alisa wrenched her neck to look in the direction of her gaze, toward the walls that had, the last time she had come, displayed videos of people being eaten by dinosaurs in those dreadful swamps. Today, the internal security camera footage was on display, including a view of the hallway Alisa had left. Young-hee was nowhere to be seen. Leonidas was...

Alisa gulped.

He was down on the floor, shattered marble tiles under his body, unmoving androids sprawled around him, many with limbs ripped off. But two other androids stood over him, forcibly removing pieces of his armor. He wasn't doing anything to fight them—he wasn't moving at all. Was he unconscious? Not dead...he couldn't be dead. They wouldn't be bothering to take off his armor if he was dead.

Hoping that logic proved true, Alisa turned a scowl on Solstice.

"Any chance you'll pay for my androids and my broken doors?" Solstice asked the older woman, her tone dry. Callous.

As ridiculous as it was, Alisa felt stung on Leonidas's behalf. Solstice had been draping herself all over him before, determined to recruit him—if not bed him—and now she wasn't even worried that he was unconscious. Maybe worse.

The silver-haired woman waved an indifferent hand. "Send me a bill. You'll come to the meeting? Your husband is invited, too, of course, though I've always gotten the impression that you run more of the family business than he does."

"Just the important business." Solstice smirked.

Alisa, still watching Leonidas for a hint of movement—a hint of *life*—barely noticed. Maybe she should be paying attention to what the women were talking about, but all she could do was grimace and wince as pieces of his armor were pried off. Finally, he lay unmoving on the floor, in nothing but the fitted T-shirt and underwear he wore underneath.

"No wonder you kept in touch with him," the older woman said, her tone dry this time.

Solstice threw her a startled look. "*Ms. Henneberry.*"

"I'm not dead, dear."

One of the androids picked up Leonidas, looking ridiculous as he balanced Leonidas's big, muscled frame over his shoulder. He headed toward the camera, in the direction of the elevator Alisa had taken, though that was presumably out of order now.

"He is nice looking, isn't he?" Solstice said. "Do you want to sample him before we get rid of them?"

Get *rid* of? Alisa stared at the women, suddenly much more invested in the conversation.

"No, he's dangerous," the silver-haired woman—Henneberry—said. The name sounded somewhat familiar, but Alisa couldn't place it. Maybe because she was busy being distracted by her impending death. "They both are. Trust me, I know. They've cost me a lot of money."

"Uhm," Alisa said. "Who are you?"

Neither woman bothered looking at her.

"Don't you have plenty?" Solstice asked dryly.

"Only because I'm not in the habit of throwing it away, usually."

Alisa? Young-hee's voice whispered in her mind. She sounded far away. *I'm outside the compound. The gates almost shut in my face, but I was able to break one and escape.* She hesitated. *I'm sorry I ran. But he told me to, and I wasn't able to do much against the androids. I can't—couldn't concentrate when they were right there, and I was in the middle of the fight.*

Understandable, Alisa thought. Young-hee only would have been cap-tured if she had stayed. *Do you have a comm unit on you?*

No. But I can get in touch with my people without going far. I don't think—wait, I thought too soon.

What?

Two androids just came out the wrecked gate. I think they may have been sent to look for me.

Get back to the ship. Let Mica know what happened. If you and your friends could stage a rescue, we may be in a position to appreciate it. Leonidas was no longer vis-ible on the camera, but Alisa thought of his unconscious form draped over the android's shoulder and tried to share the image with Young-hee so she would know how much trouble they were in.

I…see. I will.

"Money means little anymore," Henneberry said. "What matters is cre-ating a dynasty."

"You don't think you've done that already?"

Henneberry snorted. "Nothing that will last once my squabbling chil-dren and grandchildren are done with it." For the first time, she looked at

Alisa, as she stroked her chin thoughtfully. "You tried to deny me that staff, but in the end, I shall have something better, an alliance with the person who has it."

"That's lovely for you. I'd love to talk further about it, but I have a hard time concentrating when I'm dangling in the air." Alisa looked down. "Also, my fingers are going numb."

Henneberry kept stroking her chin, no hint of sympathy in her expression. She looked like someone contemplating the death of a pest. Alisa liked it better when the woman had been ignoring her, though she was starting to get an inkling of who this was, at least insofar as it related to her.

"You're not the kind of person who likes to deploy android treasure hunters, by chance, are you?" Alisa asked.

"I thank you for the drink, Solstice," Henneberry said, once again ignoring Alisa. She set down her glass and rose to her feet.

Alisa flexed her own feet. Maybe she could get a nice kick in if the woman walked past.

But Henneberry headed for a back door rather than toward the elevator, perhaps because the elevator was inoperable. Casually, as she walked by Solstice's lounge, she said, "I want that one dead. And her brawny friend too."

"Of course, Ms. Henneberry," Solstice said.

Alisa couldn't keep from gaping at her. She wasn't surprised that Solstice would kill *her*, but Leonidas? Just like that? Like he meant nothing to her?

Solstice sipped from her drink, ice rattling in the glass. An android detached himself from a guard position and escorted Henneberry to a back door. Solstice touched the diamond-and-gold earstar hooked over her helix.

"Beta Seven?" she asked. "I told you to bring the cyborg up here, right?"

Judging by her frown, an answer did not come right away. Alisa hoped Young-hee was doing something to fiddle with the workings of the security androids, even though she knew Ostberg would have been the better Starseer when it came to machines and computers.

"Beta Eleven," Solstice said.

"Yes, ma'am," the android gripping Alisa by the arms said.

Solstice pointed at her. "Kill h—"

A boom rattled the building, and a gout of fire spewed forth from the broken elevator doors. The android dropped Alisa and threw itself toward Solstice, dragging her to the floor and covering her protectively. The two other androids in the room raced for the elevator shaft.

Alisa found her feet and darted for cover behind a display case, the art-filled shelves inside rattling. Another boom erupted, this one not as loud and from the other direction. Something slammed into one of the androids, lifting him from his feet and hurtling him back several meters. The other one whirled toward the door that Henneberry had gone out. The airborne android exploded before his feet touched back to the floor.

What in the suns' fiery hells had that been? A rocket?

The android still by the elevator shaft dove to the side as another rocket hurtled through the air, buzzing as it passed near Alisa's hiding spot. This time, the android was fast enough to move out of the way. The rocket slammed into the back of the elevator shaft and exploded. A shockwave hit the android, hurling him to the side, even as the floor quaked underneath Alisa.

Debris flew out into the room, hammering the furniture and ricocheting off the display case. She pressed her back to it and kept her hands up to protect her face as other cases crashed down all around her. Smoke hazed the massive room, but she saw Solstice shouting and trying to squirm out from underneath her android protector. Alisa's battered eardrums couldn't make out the words.

The smoke near the back door swirled as a figure strode into the room. The android protecting Solstice jumped to his feet. Alisa patted herself, hoping to find her stun gun, but it had fallen to the floor in the chaos.

The smoke-shrouded figure raised its arm and fired a huge weapon. The android tried to leap away, but the rocket caught him in the shoulder with enough force to send him spinning. Solstice flung her hands over her head. The rocket exploded in a blast of fiery orange and yellow. Alisa's display case toppled, and she sprang away as it crashed to the floor. Other furniture slammed down all around her, statues and ceramics shattering as they struck down.

The android's arm and half of his torso hit the floor, and the rest of him tottered and fell backward like a dead tree toppling in a windstorm.

Solstice lifted her head, but could only stare as the figure strode out of the smoke. The haze cleared enough for Alisa to make out a fitted T-shirt, bare legs, mussed hair, and a rocket launcher the size of a small vehicle.

"Leonidas," Alisa rasped, smoke trickling down her throat and making her cough.

He flicked his fingers in acknowledgment, but his focus remained on Solstice. She tried futilely to scramble away, but he caught her and one-handedly hoisted her into the air. As someone who had recently received the same treatment, Alisa smiled in appreciation.

"Better add a few more androids to the repair bill you're sending that woman," Alisa said cheerfully. "And an elevator shaft."

She picked her way through fallen furniture and shards of ceramic toward Leonidas. She wanted to give him a hug, but that would be awkward when he was holding an enemy in one hand and a rocket launcher in the other. There were cuts and bruises on his face, and his T-shirt was ripped in several places, but he appeared far fitter than he had in that video footage.

"Colonel Adler," Solstice said, her voice remarkably calm considering she was dangling a foot above the floor. "It's good to see you again."

He grunted and looked around the room, as if searching for a hook or something to hang her from.

"I hope you'll forgive me for luring you here under a pretext," Solstice said, trying to twist in his grasp so she could beam a smile at him. "I had little choice in the matter."

"I'll bet," Alisa muttered. "Who was that woman who wanted us dead?"

Leonidas looked at her, his eyebrows drawing together. He must not have run into her in the hall. Too bad. Alisa would have liked for her to be hanging on a hook somewhere.

"Beatrice Henneberry," Solstice said, as if that should answer all questions.

Again, Alisa thought the name familiar, but she couldn't place it. Was it one of the mafia leaders?

Leonidas did not appear any more enlightened than she.

"It sounded like it might be the lady who owned Captain Echo's ships," Alisa said. "Someone trying to get ahold of the staff for a private collection, perhaps."

Solstice rolled her eyes. "She's the founder, majority shareholder, and current CEO of CargoExpress, you idiot. What kind of business woman doesn't keep abreast of the economic news?"

"One that spends a lot of time being harassed by the mafia." Alisa scratched her jaw. So that was Captain Echo's wealthy owner. Now that Solstice had shared the intel, she did remember hearing the name in the news over the years, usually in stock reports. CargoExpress was a large and frequently traded company, so fortunes were made and lost on the rise and fall of its stocks. She looked at Leonidas. "I suppose it's too late for you to look into an alternate carrier for Beck's shipment. I don't believe I want to support that woman's business anymore."

"I would check," he said, "but one of the androids stepped on the inside of my helmet and damaged the comm." He narrowed his eyes at Solstice, as if breaking his armor was a greater crime than trying to kill him.

"I am sorry about that, Colonel," Solstice said. "I would never have betrayed you, but in a recent chat with Ms. Henneberry, it came out that I knew you, and that she was rather put out with all the meddling you and your captain have done." She flicked a hand dismissively at Alisa. "She applied some pressure, and I have no wish to make an enemy of the woman, so I let myself appear to comply."

"*Appear*," Leonidas said, looking down at his near-naked state.

Alisa hoped his armor would be repairable.

"I wasn't truly going to have you killed," Solstice assured him.

"When that elevator blew, you were in the process of giving that android an order to kill *me*," Alisa said.

"Well, of course. You're mouthy and annoying."

Alisa propped a fist on her hip. The only redeeming part of that comment was that it caused Leonidas to glare ice daggers at Solstice. He must have tightened his grip on her, too, because she squirmed.

"Ow, argh, Colonel, love, would you mind putting me down, please? So we can discuss this in a civilized manner?"

"Colonel Love?" Alisa mouthed. "Did your superiors ever address you so, Leonidas?"

"None that are left alive."

Leonidas took pity on Solstice, or, knowing him, felt guilty about hurting her, and lowered her to the floor. Though he must have felt confident in keeping her from escaping, he patted her down for weapons before letting her go. Probably not a bad idea. Alisa wouldn't underestimate her.

He found a couple of vials that she kept in her bra, withdrew them, eyed the bluish green liquid inside, and set them on a high shelf out of her reach.

"Really, Colonel," Solstice said, adjusting her bra, "I was imagining your touch being less brusque."

Alisa did not want to dwell on Solstice imagining Leonidas's touches. Instead, she said, "The CargoExpress woman is associated with the mafia?"

"Not at all," Solstice said. "Oh, she does business with all of us, the same as everyone else—who doesn't need packages delivered, after all?—but she doesn't have ties to any of the mafia families. I believe she was an orphan actually, and that her business and fortune are entirely self-made."

"Then what are these meetings about?" Alisa looked to Leonidas. "While I was here, dangling from an android's grip, she and her husband were invited to a meeting. It sounded like a lot of the mafia heads were. It also sounded like it might have something to do with the staff."

"So amazingly observant you were, Captain," Solstice said, "for a woman who was on the verge of being killed. Colonel, love?" Solstice pointed at the couch she had been sitting on earlier, which now lay on its back with soot coating half the cushions. "Will you set that upright for me? I need to sit down. My home is in terrible disarray, and I feel fraught."

This time, Alisa rolled her eyes. She hoped Leonidas would ignore the request, but, without setting down his rocket launcher, he hefted the couch into the appropriate position.

Solstice smiled, watching the play of his leg and arm muscles as he lifted the substantial piece of furniture. Alisa couldn't resist another eye roll.

"Thank you." Solstice approached the couch and made a *hmm* as she eyed the sooty cushions.

"I'm not dusting for you," Leonidas said.

"No? Not even when you were the one who left my home in such disarray that the cleaning robots are too alarmed to come out?"

"We shouldn't stay," Alisa told Leonidas. Solstice's calm made her think she had backup on the way. Would someone in the mafia-equivalent of a police station have heard the explosions, or have been warned when the androids didn't report in? There could be troops heading into the building even now.

"I'd be quite delighted if you left, Captain," Solstice said. "But Colonel, let's talk." She sat down and patted the cushion beside her. "I feel bad for the ruse I was forced to enact. I am, however, delighted that you've returned. My offer of a security position is still open, in case you were wondering."

"Yes, he stays up nights, worrying about whether your job offer is open," Alisa said.

Leonidas walked to her side instead of joining Solstice on the couch. He stood close and patted her back, lifting an eyebrow. Alisa wasn't sure what the gesture meant, but had a feeling it might be a silent chastisement for being petty. Given Solstice's rudeness in trying to kill her, Alisa did not believe she deserved chastisement. Still, she was pleased that he stayed close and didn't rush to lower his hand.

"Are you all right?" he asked quietly.

"Yes. I apologize for running and leaving you back there. I was hoping to burst in here, which I did do, and stun the masterminds responsible for the ambush, which I did not do." She spotted her stun gun among the debris and pointed to it. "Ah, yes. There it is."

"I *wanted* you to leave. That's why I forced open the door." His tone turned dry. "The *outside* door. You were supposed to go out, not in."

"I couldn't have stunned anyone from outside." Alisa was glad when he didn't point out that she hadn't managed to stun anyone from inside either. "Young-hee went out. She's clearly a less obtuse partner."

"Clearly."

Remembering that Young-hee was on the way back to the ship to gather reinforcements, Alisa patted Leonidas and left his side. She needed to find her comm unit. It, too, had fallen out somewhere in the chaos.

"Since I did lure you here with deceit," Solstice said, resting her elbow on the back of the couch and ignoring Alisa as she grabbed her stun gun and poked around for her comm device, "I won't punish you for the destruction you've done to my home. Especially if you set some more of my furniture upright." She waggled her eyebrows at Leonidas, smiling not at his face but at his pectorals.

"And we won't punish *you* for trying to kill us," Alisa said, "if you tell us all about this meeting to which you've been invited." She found her comm unit and dusted it off as she mouthed to Leonidas, "See if she knows about Thorian."

She almost said Tymoteusz and the staff, but believed that he cared more about the boy.

Leonidas nodded at her. Alisa moved away to use her comm. Solstice would be far more likely to give information to him than to her, and as much as she liked snooping, she suspected that information would more likely come out if she was out of earshot.

"Mica?" she asked, comming the ship.

"*Captain*," came Mica's prompt and exasperated response.

"That's me. We were in trouble—"

"Yes, I gathered that from the Starseer who collapsed on the deck in front of me, followed by the security androids that tried to board our ship."

"Er, *did* they board the ship?"

"Not yet, but only because we closed the hatch. I've got Bravo Six in NavCom in case we need to fly, but I doubt we're getting out of the dome without that woman's permission."

Alisa grimaced at "that woman," who was sitting on the couch, thrusting out her chest as she spoke to Leonidas, her gaze skimming up and down his body as she did so.

"I hope you weren't planning to leave without us," Alisa said. "I don't think Solstice is going to lend us a ship again."

"We thought we could pick you up on the way out. And not pick up the others. I gathered you wouldn't mind leaving Durant."

"I wouldn't, though I've gotten used to Abelardus, and wouldn't mind keeping him around. He's useful now and then."

"If you say so. Look, what do you want us to do? Right now, the androids are milling about outside the ship, but I wouldn't be surprised if more showed up with blowtorches and tried to cut their way in."

"Stand by for a few minutes. Leonidas is having a chat with Solstice."

"Oh? Is he making her sensitive places tingly?"

"Even as we speak."

"And that's not bothering you?"

"She can tingle all she wants. He's mine."

Leonidas looked over, his enhanced ears apparently allowing him to listen to two conversations at once in addition to hearing at great distances. Alisa thought he might raise an eyebrow at her claim, but his eyes closed partway in a look that seemed to convey agreement. It made *her* sensitive places tingle a bit.

"Have you heard from Alejandro or Abelardus?" Alisa asked, hoping the fiasco here wouldn't affect Ostberg's treatment.

"Not yet. I'll check on them."

"Thanks, Mica. Out."

Leonidas left Solstice on the couch and joined her.

"Did you get what we needed?" Alisa asked, watching Solstice as he approached and wondering if he'd heard the part about the androids guarding the ship.

"I got…something. I'll tell you back at the ship. We may not want to linger in the area."

"No kidding."

"I don't think Solstice will bother us further, but if Henneberry is still in the city, she may not be pleased if she finds out we haven't been executed."

"I don't think her feelings on the matter are fair, considering that her androids attacked *us. Twice.*"

"The second time, they were just following us."

"So they could steal what we found. That's unacceptable."

Leonidas wrapped an arm around her shoulder. "Let's find my armor and get out of here."

"You don't want to roam the city like that?" She slipped an arm around his waist, patting his butt in the process.

"Not particularly, though I may have to, since those androids damaged my armor as they tore it off me."

"How did you get away from them? And where did you find that?" She pointed to the rocket launcher he hadn't relinquished yet. He seemed fond of it. Maybe he would start taking it to bed with him.

"They cracked my faceplate and gassed me. I let them think I'd inhaled a lot of it and was more unconscious than I was."

"So you were only *partially* unconscious when I saw you on the camera, androids tearing pieces of your armor off like wolves digging into a scaled rothrat?"

"Something like that. I'd spotted the cameras in that hallway and thought I should wait to free myself until I was in a blind spot. As for the rocket launcher…" He hefted the giant weapon—the barrel was long enough that it would drag on the floor if he didn't carry it just so. "It was in a closet with cleaning supplies."

"The natural place to store a weapon."

"In a house run by a mafia woman, I imagine so." Leonidas glanced toward the shelf where he had set those vials, then nodded toward the back door. "Shall we head out? That way should be unblocked."

"Yes, I understand the elevator is out of service."

Leonidas patted the rocket launcher, and they headed for the back door.

Solstice narrowed her eyes as they passed, perhaps because they were walking side-by-side, Leonidas's arm still around Alisa's shoulder. She thought about squeezing his butt when Solstice would be sure to see it, but decided that would be petty. Butt squeezes should be for private fun, not to show off possession.

"Don't forget my offer, Colonel," Solstice called after them.

"I won't," he said without looking back.

"Security chief?" Alisa asked. Now, more than ever, Solstice probably wanted him in charge of city security, or maybe her personal security, since her resources had been decimated.

"I'll tell you that when we get back too," he said quietly, eyeing a wall-mounted camera as they passed. "You may actually want to take advantage of it."

"If Solstice is offering, I doubt it."

"We'll see," he said.

CHAPTER FIVE

Alisa paced as she waited for everyone to file into the mess hall, a mess hall that was clear of boxes now. Unaware of the schemes of their CEO, a couple of CargoExpress representatives had come by to pick up Beck's packages for delivery. She hoped Leonidas hadn't had to pay a fortune for it, since he and his armor had suffered so ignobly due to the whims of the company's founder. At least he could afford to be generous. Alisa didn't pay him much for his security officer position, but he'd made out when he turned in those dinosaur heads the last time they had been on Cleon Moon.

Yumi and Mica walked into the mess hall together, sharing sly grins about something, and Alisa waved for them to sit down. Mica had a netdisc in hand and was poking at a holodisplay, taking some notes. Or maybe that was a sketch. She seemed to be drawing.

Beck was already in the mess hall, whistling to himself as he perused notes in a recipe program open on his netdisc. Young-hee had also joined them. Even though she was much younger than the Starseers tutoring the children, it seemed she had been pushed forward as the representative of the group, the person officially given the job of dealing with the grubs.

Leonidas leaned against a bulkhead, his bruises having swollen significantly since leaving Solstice's compound. Alisa wanted to kiss them and bring him an ice pack, but she also wanted to throttle him a little, since he hadn't yet shared the details of what he'd learned from Solstice, saying only that he might as well tell everyone at once, because she would probably want to include the rest of the group in her decision-making. It excited her to hear that there were decisions to be made. That was promising. She'd also lost some of her exasperation with him when he had pulled her into an alcove before they reached the docks and given her a kiss that had left her *more* than tingling.

"Something I don't dare do on the ship anymore," he'd said sadly when he let her go with obvious reluctance.

"I know. I'm sorry."

"Don't be sorry. Just find a place where we can be alone together when this is all over."

"It'll be easier if we can get Jelena to like you. You could be more… fun."

"I'm afraid to be around her at all when thoughts of you pop frequently into my mind."

"Oh," she'd said, realizing why he might be spending so much time locked in his cabin. Unfortunately, she didn't have a solution for that. All she could think to do was to dose him with Yumi's qui-gorn powder, but she wasn't sure how well that actually worked for keeping Starseers out of people's heads. Abelardus had still been able to communicate telepathically with her when she'd taken a dose on the hidden asteroid base. Granted, she hadn't known how much to take. Perhaps a bigger dose would have done more.

"Were you able to board the *Nomad* without trouble, Captain?" Yumi asked as Alisa continued to pace. "Earlier, Mica showed me footage of security androids standing outside the hatch, contemplating a way in."

"Yes," Alisa said. Those androids had been gone by the time she and Leonidas returned. As much as she detested Solstice, the woman had seemed willing to forgive Leonidas for destroying half of her compound and security team. It must be nice to be so handsome and desirable that women forgave such grievances. "We're just waiting for Abelardus and Alejandro." Mostly Abelardus, she amended silently, not caring if Alejandro made it to the meeting. She was glad, however, that they had reported in, saying they'd successfully gotten Ostberg into a regen tank and paid for his treatment. Leonidas had, she'd learned, footed the bill on that as well. She *would* take him off alone somewhere when all of this was over. He deserved to be loved, not locked away like a forest troll.

You need not wait any longer, Abelardus announced into her mind. *We are arriving now. Fanfare would be acceptable.*

There are some cookies on the table. Will that do?

Are they the white-and-black checkered ones?

I'm not sure. They're new ones, I think. Frosted. Beck made some to give to the CargoExpress people to help ensure they wouldn't jostle his packages overmuch.

Some people would just stamp fragile *on the boxes.*

Beck is special.

In many senses of the word.

Don't be insulting, or I'll let Leonidas eat the cookies. We had a battle. That always makes him hungry.

Actually, he had been busy taking care of his armor and hadn't yet ravaged the cookie plate. Alisa hoped his case would be able to repair the damage the androids had done to the pieces. She vowed to wear her own armor the next time they went into a potentially dangerous situation. She should have been able to do more than run into an elevator and get herself captured.

"Disgraceful," she muttered.

"How much pacing you're doing?" Mica asked, looking up from her sketch.

"No, captains are supposed to pace."

"Well, can't you do it somewhere else? You're disturbing the chickens." Mica pointed to two that had escaped from their coop and were plucking at a pile of corn that someone had mounded in a corner of the mess hall.

Alisa was surprised the whole flock wasn't up here. "They don't look disturbed. They look fat."

"Several people have taken up the slack and are feeding them now that Ostberg isn't able to," Yumi said. "Do you have a preliminary blueprint yet, Mica?"

Alisa halted her pacing and frowned suspiciously at them. Alejandro and Abelardus walked in, but she barely noticed.

"Blueprint for what?" Alisa asked.

"Your new aquaponics system, of course," Mica said.

Yumi beamed a smile. "For the ducks and geese."

"And fish," Beck said.

Alisa groaned. Hadn't she been firm enough when she'd said they wouldn't be adding a pond to the *Nomad*? What kind of freighter had a duck pond in it?

"Isn't that the kind of thing you're supposed to check with the captain about before building?" Alisa stared at Mica, feeling betrayed. She'd known Beck and Yumi had been lobbying for this, but she hadn't thought Mica would get involved in something so frivolous.

"I haven't built anything yet," Mica said, holding up the holodisplay. "It's a drawing. In air. That's all."

"*Yet*," Alisa said, her mind snagging on that one word.

Alejandro sighed noisily. "You told us to hurry back for an important discussion, Captain. Surely *this* is not the topic."

"Fish are important," Beck said. "Especially when they're perfectly grilled and drenched in a white sauce."

Abelardus smirked across the mess hall at Alisa. *Are you ever alarmed that this is the crew that's supposed to obtain the Staff of Lore and save the galaxy from certain oppression and destruction at the hands of your uncle?*

Actually, this is the crew that was supposed to get Jelena back, and it did. It's wonderful.

"Is there room for a viewing window so we can see the fish swim?" Beck asked, leaning over Mica's shoulder.

"A *window*?" Mica said. "This isn't an amusement park attraction."

Abelardus's eyebrows twitched.

Mostly wonderful, Alisa amended and turned imploring eyes toward Leonidas. "Would you like to share the information you learned now?"

"Before the divisive window debate is settled?" he asked.

"You know, I don't think your sense of humor is any less inappropriate than mine. It just comes out at different times."

"Perhaps." Leonidas nodded once and walked to the head of the table. "According to Solstice," he said, making it clear from his emphasis that she might not be a reliable source, "the wealthy Beatrice Henneberry, owner of CargoExpress, is assembling many well-off entrepreneurial colleagues, as well as the heads of many of the more powerful mafia families, in a location that has not yet been disclosed, at least not to Solstice."

Alejandro opened his mouth, probably to ask, "So what?"

"Tymoteusz is coming to the meeting."

Alejandro's open mouth sagged open further, and he didn't say anything.

"What?" Beck asked, pushing his recipe holodisplay to the side. "Why? And who's in charge of whom?"

"Apparently, Tymoteusz and his people have decided that the few dozen rogue Starseers he can influence won't be enough to take over the system, even with the help of the Staff of Lore. He reached out to Henneberry, perhaps others, in the hope of creating a wealthy and powerful group that isn't beholden to the empire or the Alliance. He wants their people and resources, and he's offering a chance for them to position themselves in more advantageous places when the government is reordered. Naturally, he intends to get rid of the existing Alliance and also the remnants of the empire."

"Naturally," Yumi murmured, frowning at the table.

"What more advantageous position could the owner of CargoExpress need?" Beck asked. "That woman must have a gazillion tindarks and probably owns a few moons and planets too."

"A place in history is what Solstice said," Leonidas said. "Henneberry wants to be one of the founders of what could become the next empire, or its equivalent. A government that could last for centuries and affect every person living in our system."

Alisa took a seat at the table, rested her elbows on it, twined her fingers together, and pressed her chin against them. Tymoteusz had been daunting enough to deal with when it had just been him, the staff, and however many of his people were on that ship of his. Even though the staff could deliver terrible damage, it hadn't truly seemed that much more powerful than any other super weapon that current technology could come up with. Something to worry about, yes, but not something that would change the course of history. This, however, was alarming. With all those wealthy, powerful, and influential people, the odds of taking over the system seemed far more in his favor. And she could imagine just what kind of government would arise to service the needs of mafia families and business tycoons. By the suns, it might even be worse for the average citizen than the empire had been.

Leonidas had finished talking, and Alisa noticed that everyone was looking at her.

She closed her eyes. This wasn't her fight, and it hadn't been from the beginning, but somehow, here she was, at the center of it all. Again. Because she had promised to retrieve a little boy. Because she had helped pull that stupid staff into this dimension. Because the man threatening to take over the system was her uncle. Hells, why couldn't she just run freight, teach Jelena how to fly, and have sex with Leonidas? She had simple desires. Shouldn't the universe be willing to oblige simple desires?

"What are you thinking, Captain?" Yumi asked.

"She's contemplating sex currently," Abelardus said.

"*Captain*," Alejandro said in a scathing tone.

Alisa gave Abelardus a flat look.

"There may have been something about running freight too," he said. "While having sex."

"If I were paying you, I'd fire you." Alisa sighed, letting her gaze shift back toward the table. "Does anyone have any ideas? It seems like we might want to sneak into this meeting."

"With a tracking device," Mica said.

Alisa lifted her eyebrows.

"If Terrible Tym shows up, that wouldn't be necessary, but if they meet up somewhere around here and then fly to his location, they could lead us to him."

"And where Tymoteusz is, Thorian should be too," Alisa said.

"Buying a tracking device would be easy. I can do that here and modify it for our needs."

"So long as one of us is able to get in and stick it in a remote corner of Henneberry's ship?" Alisa asked.

"Presumably, that would have to happen. Unless you could talk Solstice into doing it."

"Doubtful," Leonidas said. "Solstice didn't sound like she planned to go to the meeting. She didn't know where it was being held or when. This could be next week or next year."

"I would think that Tymoteusz would want to cement alliances sooner rather than later. Even though he's proven himself capable of handling everything we've thrown at him so far..." Alisa looked over at Young-hee, who winced. "He must feel vulnerable. He has to sleep, right? And currently, all he has is that ship, as far as we know. And it's not a big ship, so he can't have that large of a crew on it with him. Leonidas, do you have any idea if Henneberry was *starting* on Cleon Moon as part of her mafia-recruiting trip? Or was this a last stop? Did she already have a bunch of people lined up when she approached Solstice?"

"I don't know, but I got the impression that Solstice hadn't been given a lot of time to contemplate her decision."

"She hadn't made it yet?"

"No. She likes her dome; she's not sure she wants to have to worry about ruling an entire system."

"Hm." Alisa wished she had asked more questions while dangling from that android's grip. Not that either woman would have answered them or even acknowledged her. "Yumi, can you poke around on the sys-net and see if you can find the name of Henneberry's flagship and where it's parked right now? I assume she's not taking public transit around the system. If it's right here in this dome, that would be handy."

"I'll see if I can find it, Captain," Yumi said. "I'll recruit Bravo Six to help. He's excellent at searching news sites and tabloids."

"I'm sure his creators are so proud of him. Leonidas?"

"Yes?"

"Can you get in touch with Solstice? I'm assuming she slipped her private contact information into your undies while we were there."

"She gave it to me the last time we were here." His eyes closed to slits. "Undies were not involved."

"No? How disappointing for her. After she personally accepts your call, as I'm guessing she will, please inform her that she *is* interested in ruling the system and that she definitely wants to go to that meeting."

"You want me to tell her what she wants?"

"Yes," Alisa said. "She owes us a favor now."

"How do you figure that?"

"You didn't kill her."

"By that reasoning, every person I haven't killed owes me a favor."

"Sounds logical to me. And convenient. Maybe we should let people know." Alisa beamed a smile at him, which he did not return. Ah, well. "Yumi will try to find out where her ship is currently, but it'll be a lot easier if Solstice can tell us where and when the meeting will be held."

"I have no doubt about that. What I doubt is that Solstice will tell me."

"Don't underestimate your charms."

Abelardus made a noise between a snort and a cough. "His what?"

"Charms." Alisa leaned over and patted Leonidas's left and right pectoral muscles. "They're prodigious."

"I may gag," Abelardus said.

"That would be mature."

"Ah." Beck held up a finger. "I might gag a little too."

"See what you can do, please," Alisa said, smiling at Leonidas again. Where was Stanislav now to subtly influence people to go along with her way of thinking? "In the meantime, I have something else I need to plan."

She slid off the bench.

"Something exciting and dastardly?" Abelardus asked.

"How to get my father back from the Alliance."

CHAPTER SIX

Alisa slid into her seat in NavCom and checked for messages, hoping that Tomich had responded while she had been gone. Her heart quickened. A couple of messages had come in, and one *was* from him.

"Marchenko," he said, a star-filled porthole behind his head. Wherever he was, it was back on a ship. Alisa decided to find that promising. "I'm en route to a new mission, so I don't have time to say much, but I want to warn you: this isn't the time to irk the Alliance. Something huge is going on out there, and if you stay out of trouble, they may forget all about you. That's all I can say. Tomich, out."

"Huh." Alisa leaned back in her seat and fiddled with her braid. Something huge. Could the Alliance have gotten wind of the mafia meeting? Would Tomich have been sent out to investigate that? He wasn't intel; he was a pilot. But maybe an intel team needed a high-ranking pilot to fly them somewhere. Or maybe his "something huge" had nothing to do with Henneberry and her meeting. Maybe Tomich was off on a unicorn hunt. Either way, the warning implied that this wouldn't be a good time to storm—or sneak—aboard an Alliance warship to rescue Stanislav.

"Mom?" came Jelena's soft voice from the hatchway. Behind her, the corridor had dimmed for the night cycle. They should both be sleeping, though Alisa did not know if she could with so many thoughts racing through her mind.

"Come in." Alisa waved her daughter to the co-pilot's seat.

Jelena pushed herself into it. She had grown a lot since the last time they had been together, but her feet still dangled above the deck. She kicked them in the air, thumping her toes rhythmically against the base of the console.

"Anything I can do for you?" Alisa asked.

"We're just sitting here." Jelena waved to the view screen. It currently displayed the promenade behind the ship, the foot traffic dwindling as night fell in the dome.

"Yes, we had some business here. And we had to drop Ostberg off for medical treatment."

"I know, but that's done now, right?" Jelena eyed her, the "Why aren't we leaving right away to look for Thorian?" unspoken.

"He's in a regen tank, yes. And Durant is with him."

"Durant." Jelena's face screwed up in distaste.

Alisa frowned at her. "Did he do anything…I mean, I know he kidnapped you, but did he hurt you in any way, or…" Maybe she should have already asked this, but it was an uncomfortable conversation to have.

"Nah, but he's stupid."

Alisa snorted. "I won't disagree."

"He keeps saying how I need to learn to be a lady. Which sounds super boring. And like you can't say what you want. And then he talks about the empire, like I'm going to work for it. And like Thorian is going to work for it. We're just kids, Mom. He's weird."

"The empire fell—that's the reason I fought for all those years—and the Alliance is in charge now, so you and Thorian would have a hard time finding work if you were determined to be employed by the empire."

"Yeah." Jelena swung her legs some more. Thump, thump, thump. Did she even know that Thorian was the prince? Had anyone ever told her? Had Thorian? Maybe she knew but didn't care, or didn't quite get what being a prince meant. "Do I have to pay attention to him?"

"Who? Durant?"

"Yeah."

"No, I'd prefer it if you didn't."

"*Good.*" Jelena sounded truly relieved.

Maybe Alisa should have told her that days ago.

"Do I have to pay attention to Lady Westfall?" Jelena smiled slyly.

"Uh, probably so." Alisa would hold back on giving a firmer answer on that until she'd had more of a chat with Westfall. Or until she could find someone else to tutor Jelena. Abelardus had offered at one point, but that had been when he thought he and Alisa would have babies together. She couldn't imagine him being a teacher and role model to a little girl. Stanislav…She trusted him more now, since he'd sacrificed himself—or had believed he might be sacrificing himself—to save the rest of the ship. Could she imagine him teaching Jelena? Would he be interested? He had seemed curious about her, but would that translate to caring about her?

"Who's Stanislav?" Jelena asked.

Reminding herself that her thoughts were an open page to her daughter now, Alisa said, "My father and your grandfather."

Jelena's face scrunched up. "I thought you didn't have a father."

"Technically, everybody has or had a father, but I didn't know who mine was until recently. Your grandmother never told me about him."

"Why not?"

"I'm not sure. They parted ways before I was born. Maybe she thought it wasn't important. It sounded like she never saw him again after that. Since she's gone, I'll probably never know."

"Is he like Grandpa Yuri?" Jelena asked.

Alisa snorted. "Nobody's like Grandpa Yuri," the man who owned eight sets of spectacles, since he constantly lost them, usually perched atop his own head. "Your dad comes—came—from a long line of quirky people." Maybe that should have informed her that he had Starseer genes, even if he had never told her.

Jelena pulled her legs up into the seat, wrapped her arms around them, and rested her chin on her knees. "I miss Dad."

"I know. I do too."

Jelena squinted sidelong at her, as if she didn't fully believe that, and that hurt.

"I know you saw…something," Alisa said, wincing at her clumsy tongue. "I know you saw me with Leonidas. That doesn't mean I don't still love and miss your father."

"Whatever," Jelena muttered.

"He was a wonderful man. I'm glad he had you and that you had him while I was gone. And…I'm sorry that I wasn't there with you for so long. When I signed on to help the Alliance, I didn't imagine I would be away for years."

Jelena shrugged a shoulder.

"Do you want to talk about Dad at all? Or…how things went in the end?" Alisa didn't truly want to hear the details of that horrible day from Jelena's point of view, or from anyone's point of view, but maybe it was a story Jelena needed to tell. Maybe it would help her.

"Nah. I already did that with Thor. He lost both of his parents, you know."

"I'd heard that, yes." Alisa's first thought was that a fellow child wasn't an appropriate person to talk to about one's problems, but maybe he'd been easier for her to trust and befriend than the adult Starseers. And Alisa hadn't been there, so who else would she have spoken to?

Jelena nodded, as if she'd heard the thoughts and agreed.

"It's all right, Mom. I know the Alliance was important to you."

Alisa wanted to explain that the Alliance should be important to Jelena, too, but what could an eight-year-old care about the government? Had Alisa cared one whit about it when she'd been that age? Hells, she didn't think she had even cared at eighteen. Not until the Perun Arcade Massacre had happened, and she had lost her best friend. Alisa hoped that the war and fighting were truly over now and that Jelena wouldn't have to lose a best friend. But she thought of Thorian and grimaced bleakly.

"Can we get a pony?" Jelena asked.

"Er, what?"

"This ship is dented, and burned, and ugly, but it's *huge*. Like a farm. And it already has chickens. And there might be ducks."

"There won't be ducks," Alisa said firmly, though even she was starting to doubt that. Wasn't the captain supposed to be the absolute ruler and decision maker on a ship? How had this aquaponics scheme come so far along? And could an aquaponics tank truly be of use to a duck? Didn't they need beaches and grasses and slugs and all the things that went around a *real* pond?

"What about a horse?" Jelena asked.

"The Nomad isn't *that* big. And it's not ugly either."

"It's like living in a dented metal box."

Before Alisa could argue that statement, Jelena rushed on.

"But it's a *big* box. Much bigger than our apartment. I'm sure there's room for a horse. She could have a stall in engineering!"

"She?" Her daughter had already determined the sex of her horse? How long had this speculation been going on?

"A stallion would be too rowdy."

"I don't think Mica would care to share engineering with a horse, rowdy or otherwise. But listen. After we get Thorian, we can head over to Upsilon Seven. There's a whole continent there that's dominated by grasslands, and they raise snagor and horses. There's always cargo to pick up to run to or from there, and there are tons of riding facilities. My mom took me there when I was about your age." As memory served, it had been because she had been making an argument very similar to Jelena's. The *Nomad* was big. Why couldn't it have a horse? When she had been musing on the topic, she hadn't decided on the horse's sex. A lack of forethought, perhaps.

"Can Thor come?" Jelena asked.

"If he's allowed to stay with us for a while, certainly."

"Why wouldn't he be allowed to stay?"

"A lot of people have designs on him."

"What does that mean?"

"I don't know. It's complicated."

Knowing her answer wasn't satisfactory, Alisa braced herself for more interrogation. But Jelena grew distracted. She turned in her seat, peered over the backrest, and shrank down.

Alisa followed her gaze. Leonidas stood in the corridor, half turned, as if he'd spotted Jelena in there with Alisa and had decided to leave. But he'd been spotted. As quietly as he walked around, he couldn't hide from a Starseer.

"I don't mean to interrupt." He lifted an apologetic hand.

"It's fine," Alisa said, though from the worried look Jelena wore, she might not agree. How could Alisa make it so that Jelena wasn't afraid of

Leonidas? Especially when he was avoiding them? Not that she could blame him, if he was having lustful thoughts of Alisa around her telepathic daughter. "Did you find out anything from Solstice?" Alisa asked, trying to push down thoughts that might make Jelena uncomfortable by sticking to business.

"Yes," Leonidas said. "Solstice said we should lie low and not get involved. She let Henneberry believe that her wishes had been carried out and that we're dead. If we're spotted wandering about, that could cause Henneberry to lose trust in her."

"Everyone wants me to lie low. I'm not good at that."

"I've noticed." He smiled slightly.

Jelena frowned, and he lost his smile. Great, what fond—or lustful—thought had he been having that she'd seen? Maybe Alisa should talk to Young-hee and ask her to have a chat with Jelena. Hadn't she mentioned that it was considered rude for Starseers to pry into the thoughts of those who weren't enemies intending to do harm? Maybe children didn't learn that until later.

Leonidas cleared his throat. "Solstice also said, when I pressed her for the location of the meeting, that Henneberry is looking for a caterer."

"A caterer? As in an outfit that delivers food to a party?"

"Fresh and fancy food, yes. Solstice said there should be a bulletin out there somewhere—apparently, most of the local catering companies aren't eager to work for mafia meetings, so Henneberry hasn't had many nibbles yet."

"Oh, Leonidas," Alisa breathed, her mind filling with visions of Beck turning kabobs on his grill. "This could work perfectly for us."

"Hoping for anything to work perfectly might be overly optimistic, but I thought it might spur ideas for you."

"I'll tell Beck right away to start thinking up ways to turn himself into a legitimate catering company—or at least a company that *appears* legitimate. Maybe Yumi can help with that, create him a sys-net presence."

"I'll leave you alone to plot." Leonidas glanced at Jelena, who was still frowning at him, and inclined his head toward her. "Both of you."

"Wait," Alisa blurted, though she didn't know what to say next. She knew she couldn't make Jelena like him overnight, but she needed to find a way to get the ball rolling in that direction. Otherwise, they would feel awkward around each other indefinitely. "Jelena?"

"Huh?"

"I'd like your opinion on something. A couple of weeks ago, Leonidas and I were discussing ways that he could appear less scary to people."

Leonidas's expression turned a little suspicious as he regarded Alisa. Funny how often people gave her such looks.

"He's too big," Jelena said, though that wasn't the opinion Alisa had hoped to hear.

"That's not his fault. His mom made him eat his spinach when he was a boy."

Jelena also turned a suspicious look on her, probably knowing that Alisa was trying to make her laugh and make the situation seem less serious, make Leonidas seem less scary. Even if Jelena was suspicious, she wasn't able to keep from responding.

"He ate too much then," she said.

"He does that a lot. You should see him demolish a plate of brownies."

Jelena looked at Leonidas, as if she had never considered that a big, brawny cyborg might eat brownies, but she kept most of her face hidden behind the backrest.

"I told him he should paint his armor pink, so that it wouldn't be as alarming to people," Alisa said. "What do you think about that option?"

Leonidas simply stood there while this chat went on, not contributing anything, maybe not daring. He seemed willing to be the topic of the debate though. He even slouched against the bulkhead, perhaps trying to appear less intimidating. Less *big*. At least he wasn't in his armor now. He was wearing socks. Who could be alarmed by a man in socks?

"He'd be *scarier* in pink," Jelena said.

"You think so?"

"For different reasons, perhaps," Leonidas murmured.

"What if he wore stickers on his armor?" Alisa asked.

Leonidas's lips flattened at this suggestion.

Jelena's face screwed up in what was sure to be a rejection, but then she asked, "What *kind* of stickers?"

"Andromeda Android?" Alisa suggested.

"Maybe."

"What do you think, Leonidas? Will you consider going into battle with an Andromeda Android sticker on your fanny?"

"I'd rather be Beck's assistant caterer," Leonidas said.

Alisa grinned, amused—and pleased—that he'd learned just how her mind worked and knew she was already concocting a catering plan.

"Well, that's definitely going to happen," Alisa said, "so I guess stickers could happen, too, eh?"

"I'm going to bed," Leonidas said. "Goodnight, Alisa. Goodnight, Jelena."

He walked away. Hurried away, was perhaps the more appropriate term.

Well, at least Jelena hadn't been the one to flee the room.

"He's weird," she said.

Alisa tried to decide if that was better than being scary.

Jelena turned around in the seat again. "Will you tell me more about Stanislav?" she asked.

She sounded more intrigued by the idea of having another grandfather than by having a Leonidas. Oh, well. They had to start somewhere.

"Absolutely," Alisa said, and started telling the story of how she'd found out about him and about how she had Starseer genes.

She hoped she wasn't getting her daughter's hopes up about a grandfather that she would never meet.

―――――

Alisa curled her armored fingers into fists and punched the hover pads floating in the air in front of her, their engines humming softly, little puffs sounding as they whirred about. She connected with one, but the other zipped away too quickly. A small indicator on the side of the one she'd hit showed the force of her blow. The one that had evaded her circled, trying to get behind her. She whirled, almost overcompensating, thanks to the speed the armor gave her, and slung another punch. She missed by embarrassing inches, and the pad zipped in and smacked her in the helmet. She lunged for it, now swatting instead of punching, trying to grab the thing and wring its little padded body.

"I thought that armor would make you more of a warrior, not less of one," Mica said. She was walking around engineering, running tests and recording results.

"The armor isn't what's vexing me. Leonidas programmed these things to harass me."

"Harass you or challenge you?"

"I think the difference in those definitions is in the eye of the beholder. Also known as the victim."

Alisa dodged another attack. She shouldn't complain. Beck and Yumi had found the posting for the catering gig and applied. If their fictitious company was hired, Alisa might need every bit of extra training she could get. Catering for one's enemies sounded like an activity that would be fraught with complications.

"Have I told you how delighted I am that you're grunting, straining, and complaining with me here in engineering?" Mica asked.

"Six times now, yes. But I could read between the lines that you were lonely in here by yourself." Alisa ducked as one of the pads zipped toward her helmet again. "Halt program," she said, needing a break. Sweat bathed her skin. Even though the air suckers kept moisture from dripping down and off her chin, she itched to simply drag her sleeve across her face, but she couldn't do that with the helmet on.

"You just didn't want to practice out in the cargo hold in front of the Starseers, and there isn't anyplace else on the ship large enough."

"You know me well. I—" Alisa paused as Yumi jogged into engineering wearing a distressed expression.

"Has trouble found us?" Alisa unfastened her helmet.

Thanks to the warnings from multiple directions telling her to lie low, she hadn't yet flown the *Nomad* away from Solstice's domed city. Her sensors informed her that the Alliance warship was still up in orbit, along with several other Alliance ships. Alisa figured it was too large to enter the dome, and she felt safer down here than she would up in the sky. But that could all change if they sent shuttles down with teams of soldiers to "rescue" Tiang.

"Mm, trouble has found *me*." Yumi looked to Mica first, then threw a hesitant glance at Alisa.

Alisa thought about leaving so they could talk. Yumi probably hadn't expected to find her here. But if this trouble could affect the ship, shouldn't she know about it?

"Nosy, nosy," she muttered to herself.

"Captain?" Yumi asked.

"Nothing. What's your trouble? Can I help?"

"As long as you keep the cargo hatch door shut and locked."

"Oh, I've been doing that since Durant left." Alisa clasped her hands behind her back, waiting curiously to see if she would get more details.

Yumi chewed on her lip.

"You better tell her," Mica said. "It's not like she kicked Beck off when she found out the White Dragon was after him. Twenty seconds after he signed on."

"I'm not worried about being kicked off. I don't think." Yumi closed her eyes and took a few deep breaths, her lips moving as she muttered some mantra or prayer.

Surprised, Alisa looked toward Mica, hoping for more of a clue. She had never considered herself unapproachable and threatening. Even if she was dressed in her combat armor, it was sexy blue armor, not scary red cyborg armor. Though perhaps she should look into cartoon decals for her butt, just in case.

"I don't want to be trouble," Yumi said, opening her eyes. "I got a message from…an old acquaintance."

"The one with the palace and the yacht?" Mica asked.

"Seven yachts," Yumi said.

"Yumi," Alisa said, "I had no idea you made drugs for the rich and famous."

She meant it as a joke, but Yumi's expression grew bleaker.

"*Do* you make drugs for the rich and famous?" Alisa asked more seriously.

"That wasn't my intent. In fact, my hobby started more out of curiosity. As I told you, I used to hope there might be a way to awaken my Starseer genes so I would develop their powers. As a result of that interest, I grew quite educated on a number of topics related to nootropics and started doing freelance research for a pharmaceutical company. That paid the bills, but my first love is teaching. I truly *am* a science teacher."

"I believe you."

"About four years ago, I got a tutoring job. For this acquaintance. He was clearly someone who could afford tutors for his three children—they already had four other tutors for various subjects—and since I was between jobs, I thought it would be a pleasant adventure. He said he was a real estate developer and had earned his fortune that way." Her lips thinned. "I later learned he was the son of a mafia lord."

"Oh?" Alisa was more interested than horrified in the revelation. Was it possible this mafia prince had sent Yumi a message because he was in the area? Perhaps in the area for a certain meeting? "I do seem to remember you looking over your shoulder and flinching a bit when you first came on the *Nomad*," Alisa added.

"Er, you noticed that?"

"Pilots have keen observation skills."

Mica snorted.

"Was this fellow the reason?" Alisa asked. "For your hasty addition to my passenger manifest?"

"Can you call it a passenger manifest when you only had two people on it at the time?" Mica asked.

"Absolutely. And I had three. Leonidas wasn't working for me then."

"He wasn't your passenger either. He came with the ship."

Alisa waved away the unimportant distinction. She wanted to hear more about the mafia prince and if he'd been invited to Henneberry's meeting.

"I was fleeing from him," Yumi admitted. "From his people. Who were looking for me. As I said, he hired me to tutor his children, but over the course of that first year, we became somewhat close, and he learned of my freelancing and my esoteric knowledge of mushrooms, plants, and the like. He grew interested, and asked me to make some compounds. I did, including a couple of originals. He passed them around to a few colleagues—at the time, I didn't know anything about his mafia connections, as he presented the image of a responsible businessman. All of the public data about him, at least under the name I knew him by, verified what he'd told me."

"Yumi, I'm not going to condemn you for working for the mafia."

"No, but I condemn myself," she said sadly. "For being naive. For not figuring it out and getting out of there sooner. But I was fond of the children, and…" She shrugged. "It doesn't matter now. When I finally did leave, he'd made quite a bit of money and some new connections by peddling and sharing my drugs around. I never told him how to make it or left any records. So when he ran out, he came after me. I fled to Dustor, figuring nobody would think to look for anyone there, but as it turns out, that's a popular hiding spot, and all the bounty hunters know it."

"I can imagine." Alisa remembered the unwashed miscreants living in the junk cave where she'd reacquired the *Nomad*.

"When I saw that your ship was leaving and heading to imperial territory, I thought my odds of getting lost might be good there, and that the mafia probably didn't have a huge presence on Perun. En route, it occurred to me that an old freighter flying around the system and never staying in one place for long might be a better place to live than on a planet. And after a while, when nobody caught up with me, I thought he might have forgotten about me."

"Until now?"

Yumi nodded. "I just received a personal message from him, sent locally. His yacht, the *Meritorious*, is in orbit around Cleon Moon. He said he's here on business, but he'll be coming for me too."

"If he tries, he'll get pecked to death by forty crabby chickens," Mica growled. "And a crabby engineer."

Yumi smiled slightly, but did not appear reassured.

"I'd point out that kidnapping people is against the law," Alisa said, "but it probably isn't here."

"No police will stand with me against him," Yumi said.

"Well, we will."

"Thank you, Captain, but I don't wish to get the ship in trouble. I'll start packing and look for transport—"

"The hells you will," Mica said. "You're staying right here."

Alisa nodded. "Besides, it's not as if this ship isn't already in trouble. Your mafia man and the Alliance can compete with each other to see who comes knocking on our door first."

"Captain?" Beck poked his head through the hatchway. "We've got a problem."

"The mafia or the Alliance?" Alisa asked, wondering if someone was *already* knocking at the door.

"It's the catering gig."

"Good news?"

"We're hired."

Alisa clenched a fist. "Excellent news."

"But we don't have long to pull everything together. The meeting is in less than three days. I don't know…" Looking daunted, Beck pushed a hand through his dyed hair.

"We can do it," Alisa said. "We'll just get started right away."

"Such optimism," Mica said, shaking her head in a pitying manner.

"I know you love it. Beck? Just tell me what needs to be done, and I'll get you the people you need to make it happen."

"Including Leonidas?" Beck asked.

"Of course."

Beck looked faintly horrified. "The one time I asked him to chop nuts for me, he turned them into nut flour."

"Someone needs to carry trays, right? He would be excellent at porting things for you."

"So would a hover board."

"I promise, he'll be an excellent assistant," Alisa said, "and so will I."

"Just so long as he keeps his charms to himself," Beck muttered as he walked out, still wearing that daunted expression.

Alisa swatted Yumi on the arm. "Did you truly think *you* would be the one to bring trouble to this ship?"

"I didn't," Mica said.

CHAPTER SEVEN

Alisa stood at the counter in the kitchen, a knife in hand and several stalks of celery on the cutting board in front of her. Leonidas, similarly equipped, held the position beside her, and six Starseers were lined up to the left, including Young-hee, Abelardus, and the adults not involved in tutoring the children. Alisa was fairly certain the cranky, white-haired one at the end was the research scientist who had berated Bravo Six. Now, he could do something useful.

"This is called the rolling chop," Beck said, demonstrating from the end of the counter. "Hold the knife like you're shaking someone's hand, not like you're going to kill them." He shot Leonidas a pointed look.

"How come he mentions not killing people every time he instructs us on a knife technique?" Leonidas murmured to Alisa.

"It's a mystery." She nudged him with an elbow. Surely, he must have noticed all those addenda had been directed toward him.

"Beck?" came Yumi's voice over the comm.

He set down his knife and headed for the panel. "Here."

"It's official: the Personal Touch Catering Company has been retained. Henneberry's chef wants to look over a prospective menu for the approximately three hundred and fifty people."

"I'll be right there to talk to him," Beck said, and jogged out of the kitchen.

"Hope Yumi's routing that call through a few nodes, so it can't be traced to the *Nomad*," Alisa said.

"Yumi knows what she's doing on the sys-net," Young-hee said as she worked on some carrots Beck had given her.

"I know," Alisa said, though she felt nervous. "She's the one who made it look like Beck's business had been around longer than a day. Somehow, she added a bunch of reviews on different sites, appearing to date back for several years."

"I didn't know her experience as a science teacher had taught her how to commit fraud," Leonidas said.

"She has a wide and varied background," Alisa said. "Beck was also able to get a testimonial for the company from his buddy Chef Leblanc. He was kind of wistful when he told me about it, like he wouldn't mind if his catering outfit truly existed. Are you supposed to be pulverizing that celery?"

"It's not pulverized. He said to slice it thin. It's thin."

"And flat." Alisa looked in the direction Beck had gone. "I hope this works out and that they're not pulling a ruse on us even as we're pulling a ruse on them."

"If it helps, we believe we've located Henneberry's ship in orbit," Young-hee said. "Martya and Nyarai and I have been looking. They have good range when it comes to sensing everything from artifacts to what people are thinking."

"Would any of you be able to sense the thoughts of someone chatting with Beck on the comm?" Alisa asked.

"Not generally, but if that person happened to be on the ship we were monitoring…"

Alisa waved toward the exit. "Why don't you go hover nearby while Beck talks to that chef, then?"

Young-hee and two of the Starseer women hustled out of the kitchen.

"I think they just wanted to get out of cutting things," Abelardus said, waving a knife. "Do any of us truly need to do this? Won't all the chopping be done before we take the food to its destination? And then we just set up a buffet and some plates?"

"Probably, but I'm sure Beck will need help with the preparations before we go. We have to look and perform like a legitimate catering company while we're there. The last thing we want is for them to figure out who we are before we get to snoop around."

"Or after," Leonidas murmured.

"If Tymoteusz is there for the meeting, maybe even aboard Henneberry's ship, we might find a way to get Thorian right there. Then the *after* won't matter as much."

"I don't think we'll be that lucky."

"You're such a supportive cheerleader."

"I'm practical," Leonidas said.

"Was it your practicality that convinced Solstice to chat to Henneberry about catering needs?"

"More my wheedling. She wasn't as certain that she owed me a favor as you were."

"Did you point out how you could have killed her and didn't?" Alisa asked.

"That didn't seem like a tactful thing to mention."

"Tactful? Leonidas, I've never heard anyone say imperial cyborgs are known for tact. They're known for making living things dead and flattening buildings and spaceships with their bare hands. Also celery." She poked one of his limp slices with her knife.

"Glad to know I have such a flattering reputation."

Alisa grinned and squeezed his arm. "Just be glad some women are drawn to men with such reputations."

Abelardus coughed. "I'm certain Beck didn't mention that there would be cooing and canoodling in his class."

"Yes, but while the teacher's gone, the students will rebel," Alisa said.

"I begin to see why Durant has been lamenting the recalcitrance of your daughter."

Beck jogged into the kitchen before Alisa could respond to that.

"Everything's finalized," he announced, lifting his arms in the air. "They've accepted my menu and sent us a deposit to buy food for the gig."

"Were the Starseers able to tell if it's the *right* gig?" Alisa asked.

"Everything seems legitimate, and Beatrice Henneberry herself sent the deposit."

Alisa grinned at Leonidas. "And you had doubts."

"Who, me?"

"There is one obstacle," Beck said. "Henneberry's ship will be flying out of orbit for the meeting, so we'll need to deliver the food on our private catering shuttle."

"Do we have a shuttle?" one of the Starseers asked.

"That's the obstacle."

———

Alisa stopped pacing in the cargo hold long enough to check the camera turned toward the docks for the sixth time. As soon as Beck's food order arrived, she could take off. They had been in Terra Jhero for three days, long enough for enemies to have pinned down the *Nomad's* location. And that made her nervous.

Once they had their catering supplies, they could prepare the food in space. They could later transfer the finished dishes to the shuttle she hoped Leonidas, Mica, and Bravo Six were even now locating—Six was along to fly the craft back if they found something. The team had left early that morning, stopping at an electronics boutique to buy a tracking device along the way. Leonidas had mentioned using his dinosaur money to rent a shuttle, and Mica had mentioned using his brawn to forcibly acquire a shuttle. Alisa didn't know which method to vote for. Renting anything on this moon would likely cost a fortune, and two-thirds of the shuttles had probably been illegally acquired anyway. She well remembered the tax collectors that had accosted her ship on its first approach.

A cargo van trundled down the promenade with vegetables painted on the side. Alisa reached for the cargo door hatch, assuming that was their delivery.

Actually, Abelardus spoke into her mind, *that's trouble.*

How so?

Footsteps clanged on the walkway above, Abelardus walking out with his staff and a frown. They were alone in the cargo hold, since the Starseers had taken their lessons up to the rec room that morning. Jelena was with them, as usual.

"There are twenty people in the back of that truck," Abelardus said.

"And no vegetables?" Alisa frowned at the monitor. The truck was still coming, trundling slowly along since crowds of people thronged the promenade.

"Oh, there's a bunch of food back there, too, but I don't think the armed men and women are there to keep the produce fresh."

Alisa clenched a fist. "We *need* that produce." They had exactly thirty-six hours before their catering shuttle was supposed to dock with Henneberry's yacht, and it would take time to fly out of orbit to the meeting spot—they were still waiting for coordinates on that.

"The produce is there for the taking," Abelardus said. "I just think you might have to do more than sign for it to get it."

"Can you tell whose people those are?" Alisa asked, imagining a kidnapping team here to collect Yumi.

"They're not wearing uniforms, but I think they're soldiers."

"Soldiers? Not mercenaries?"

"I don't know. Nothing about the way they're straddling those piles of cabbage heads tells me the difference. Some of them are in combat armor though. Maybe all of them."

"Twenty people in combat armor?"

"At least."

Alisa groaned. She had a feeling they would be better off keeping the hatch shut and ordering food from another grocery service, but if those men had come prepared for a kidnapping, they might not find a closed hatch much of a deterrent.

"Round up any of your people who think they can convince a bunch of soldiers to unload groceries instead of guns," Alisa said, jogging for the stairs. "I'll grab my armor and comm Leonidas." She glanced toward engineering, wishing she hadn't sent Mica away on the shuttle errand. She could have come up with some nice explosives to thwart intruders.

"And to think," Abelardus said, "I didn't believe there had been enough excitement of late."

As Alisa dug her comm unit out of her pocket, he added, "I have more good news for you."

"What?" She passed him on the walkway without slowing.

"Ostberg's parents arrived, so he's in good hands now. Do you want me to call Durant back to the ship?"

"Absolutely not," she said, running into the corridor. "Leonidas?" she spoke into her comm as she went. "We need you back at the ship as soon as possible."

"What's wrong? We're across town, making a deal on a shuttle."

"Is it really a deal," came Mica's voice in the background, "when the current owner is on the ground under your foot?"

"That's the current *possessor*," Leonidas said, "not the current owner. This is an imperial shuttle—look at the markings."

"I'm sure this poor fellow stole it fair and square."

"Get that shuttle and come over here as quickly as possible," Alisa said, running through the mess hall and toward her cabin. "Beck's grocery delivery came with armed men."

"Be there shortly," Leonidas said and closed the channel.

Alisa ran into her cabin and threw open her armor case. She was halfway dressed when Jelena poked her head in.

"Is there going to be a *battle*?" she asked, her eyes round as she looked at the pieces of armor going on.

Alisa's gut clenched at the idea. Being boarded and having to fight had been alarming before, but now that her daughter was onboard, she had so much more to lose.

"I hope not," Alisa said. "I'm hoping the Starseers can convince the men who want to ambush us that they prefer peace to war."

"I can help."

"Yes, you can. From inside the rec room with the other children. I'm sure Lady Westfall can direct you on how to help." While staying in the back corner with the lights off and the hatch locked, Alisa amended silently.

Jelena curled her upper lip.

"I'm surprised she isn't keeping you all in there now," Alisa added. If Abelardus knew there was trouble, the rest of the Starseers must also by now.

"I escaped," Jelena said. "To check on you!"

"Thoughtful." Alisa jammed her feet into her boots.

"And to help."

"Very thoughtful." She grabbed her helmet and strode for the hatchway. A distant clang sounded. Their delivery truck driver knocking on the hatch?

"I'll come with you."

"You can come with me as far as the mess hall." Where she would deposit Jelena firmly in the rec room and hope Westfall, indeed, had plans to keep the children safe. She felt guilty foisting her daughter off on someone else, but Jelena had been so independent since she returned that it seemed normal rather than strange. "Want a ride along the way?" Alisa asked, trying to head off the objection that appeared to be forthcoming. "I'm extra strong in my armor."

"Really?"

Alisa crouched and waved to her back. "Grab on."

Jelena slung her arms around Alisa's neck and wrapped her legs around her waist. Though she was in a hurry, Alisa did a few jumps—careful not to hit her head on the ceiling—and then sprinted to the mess hall at top speed. This resulted in a peal of laughter from Jelena, one that secretly delighted her.

Westfall stood in the mess hall by the rec room hatchway, her arms folded over her chest, and one foot tapping on the deck. She frowned when Alisa ran into the room.

Alisa refused to look sheepish. She deposited her load and said, "I'd appreciate it if you watched my daughter. We'll try to keep the trouble to a minimum."

"I *was* watching her. She ran away."

"No, I *sneaked* away," Jelena said.

"She needs more discipline from her mother," Westfall said.

"We'll work on it when life returns to normal," Alisa said.

"Alisa?" Abelardus called up from the cargo hold. "We're ready to deal with our guests."

"Stay with Lady Westfall," Alisa told Jelena. "No more sneaking today, all right? But if you can help from within the rec room, I'd be more than happy to have that assistance."

"Oh? Lady Westfall, what can we do to help?" Jelena ran past her and into the rec room, where the other children waited at the game table, watching the exchange curiously.

"We'll monitor from in here." Westfall headed inside and locked the hatch.

Good.

Alisa jogged into the cargo hold to find the hatch still shut and Abelardus and Beck standing next to the controls. Beck wore his full armor and had a rifle slung across his chest. Abelardus had his staff. If they were going to fight with twenty armored soldiers, they would be drastically outmatched, but Alisa allowed herself a smidgen of hope when she spotted Young-hee, Martya, and Nyarai in the shadows under the walkway.

"Groceries instead of guns?" Alisa asked them as she came down the stairs.

"We'll do our best," Young-hee said. "I've touched the minds of a few of them. Someone promised them a fight, and they seem eager for it."

"Can you make them eager to deliver cabbages instead?"

"They're less excited by that prospect. It goes against their orders and their natural tendencies."

"What are their orders? Can you tell?"

"They're here for Tiang," Abelardus said.

Ugh. Alisa hadn't even seen Tiang all day. As far as she knew, he was still locked in his mad scientist lab.

"It's hard to convince people to do things they completely don't want to do."

"But not impossible, right?" Alisa asked. "I've seen Stanislav make weapons officers fire on their fellow ships." Stanislav who was drugged and stuck in an Alliance brig at the moment. She should have been making plans to rescue him instead of waiting for something to come of her messages to Tomich.

"He's powerful," Young-hee said.

"You are too. I've seen you hurl your own people around." Alisa gripped her shoulder lightly, careful of the strength from her armor, and smiled at the others. "I know you can do this."

"We'll try."

"Let them know there are cookies available to delivery people who bring in our goods without causing any trouble," Alisa said. "Oh, and just try to target whoever is in charge. If they're soldiers, they won't do anything without their squadron sergeant or whoever came along giving the order."

Young-hee blinked. "That's a good point. And obvious. I hadn't thought of it."

"Good. Try that. And the cookies." Alisa jogged over to join the men. "Beck, we have cookies, right?"

"If Leonidas didn't eat what was in the jar this morning."

"There are eight children on the *Nomad* right now, and you're automatically blaming him for missing cookies?" Alisa peered at the monitor to find the grocery truck backed up the *Nomad's* ramp, its large rear door not yet rolled up. Crates full of fruits and vegetables were painted on that door. So innocuous looking, as was the man in overalls standing next to the exterior comm panel, frowning as he waited for a response. He tried knocking again.

"Leonidas has a bigger mouth than any of those children," Beck said. "Bigger everything."

"He is a big man," she agreed.

"If that was a comment about sexual anatomy, I didn't need to know that information."

"You two have bled and fought together. I thought you already knew everything about each other's anatomy." Alisa reached for the comm panel.

"We didn't do it naked," Beck muttered.

"This is Captain Marchenko," she said to the person standing outside. "Can I help you?"

"We've got your order," the man said, sounding exasperated.

"Excellent! Please roll up the door of your truck, and we'll get our cargo hold loading equipment ready to receive you."

"We need you to open your hatch."

"Which we'll happily do as soon as you open your truck and we can see the goods." She looked to Beck. "Right?"

"Happily," he agreed.

"This is a mafia-run city, after all," Alisa said. "We figure it's wise to see our cargo before inviting people into our ship."

The man tapped a green earstar and muttered something too softly for the comm to pick it up. He listened for a moment, then raised his voice.

"If you don't want your food delivery, we can find someone else who does," he said.

"Of *course* we want it," Beck said, rushing to speak before Alisa could. "It's in there, right?" he whispered to Abelardus.

"Under the soldiers, yes," Abelardus whispered back.

"They better not be crushing my peppers and star pods with their boots."

"Is there some reason you can't open the door and show us the goods?" Alisa asked innocently. "It should only take a moment, and then I'll be happy to open our hatch."

"Fine, fine," the man snapped, then turned away from the camera to mutter again.

Long seconds passed.

"Are they doing something crafty?" Alisa asked Abelardus.

"Hiding."

"Craftily?"

"No, but well enough that we won't be able to see—"

On the video display, the truck door rolled up. Crates of fruit sat next to boxes of fresh meat and piles of potatoes and cabbages. Alisa squinted but couldn't see any soldiers.

"They're there," Abelardus said.

"Open your hatch," the man outside said. "If there are any further delays, I'll be forced to charge you another delivery fee."

"Another? There was a first one?"

"There were a first three. As you pointed out, this is a mafia-run moon. We deal with taxes, you know."

"Yes, I've met some of the tax collectors." Alisa thought she caught movement in the very back of the van behind that potato pile. Was that the gleam of a helmet? At least she had delayed the inevitable. She hoped Leonidas and Mica were on their way back. "Opening the hatch now," she told the man and closed the channel. "Young-hee? Have you got the sergeant picked out?"

"I believe so. Ready."

Beck stopped Alisa before she could reach for the hatch controls. "I'll do it. Why don't you and Abelardus take cover behind the stairs?"

"I don't think it's appropriate for us to hide while you take the brunt of the fire if the mind manipulation doesn't work."

"Yeah, it is." Beck waved toward the interior of the ship. "Your little girl is up there."

Alisa hesitated, wanting to point out that since she had combat armor now, she shouldn't be hiding, but if trouble rolled through the hatch along with that truck, she could shoot well enough from behind cover.

"Thanks, Beck." She clapped him on the shoulder and jogged for the stairs. She waved for the Starseer women to gather behind them too.

Abelardus stayed with Beck, who shrugged and hit the controls.

The hatch thunked open, and Alisa tensed, expecting the soldiers to stream out immediately. Instead, the truck backed farther up the ramp, clearing the top of the hatchway by a foot. It rolled into the cargo hold, and the chickens, which heretofore had not been making a fuss, erupted in a group protest.

At first, there wasn't any movement in the back of the truck, aside from a single potato that rolled from the top of the pile to the bottom. Then someone spoke.

"You heard me," a man said from behind the food crates. "Get this cargo unloaded."

"Er, Sergeant?"

"I said do it." A soldier in green Alliance combat armor came into view, a rifle hanging from a strap across his chest. But his hands were full of bumpy sacks of root vegetables, not weapons.

"The others are confused," Young-hee said. "We're working on soothing them, making them believe their sergeant didn't crack his head on the casks of whiskey. Westfall and the others are helping."

The sergeant jumped down from the truck, his movements mechanical, less fluid than those of an android. He walked the sacks over to where other food crates were fastened in the cargo hold. Soon, a few more men came out, carrying sacks or boxes. One operated a hand tractor and moved the potatoes en masse.

"It's working," Alisa breathed, hardly able to believe it. The men acted more like automatons than human beings, and seeing people's minds manipulated always made her uneasy, but in this case, if it would save lives, who was she to complain?

Yes, have faith in my people, Young-hee spoke into her mind. *By the way, that sergeant is expecting cookies.*

I'll hand deliver them personally if all that food makes it to a safe harbor.

Alisa watched with delight as the men continued to move crates. The chickens clucked cheerfully, too, perhaps smelling some fresh corn.

Next to Alisa, sweat gleamed on Young-hee's forehead, and the other women wore expressions of utter concentration. Alisa had the sense that it wouldn't take much for things to unravel, and she silently urged the soldiers to hurry with the unloading.

She activated the comm inside of her helmet. "Admiral Tiang? Are you in your cabin?"

Several seconds passed, along with a thud and a grunt, before he replied, "Yes, Captain."

"Your people are here to pick you up, just in case you want to go with them." She didn't want to lose him, but she also knew these soldiers would eventually drive outside of the Starseers' influence and realize that they hadn't accomplished their mission.

"*Go?* I'm in the middle of a crucial step. Captain, I'm so close. Tell that Admiral Agosti that I'll be happy to join him as soon as I've perfected my experiment."

"They're almost done, Captain," Beck said, his voice coming over her comm. He was whispering, too, dumbfounded as he watched the armored soldiers delivering his vegetables.

"I see that," Alisa said. "You'll have to thank our Starseers with a special meal tonight."

"I'll be preparing about three hundred special meals tonight. Not expecting to get any sleep."

"Well make it three hundred and ten, eh?"

He snorted. "Might as well. I—"

A shadow fell across the cargo ramp, and Alisa winced, imagining some of Solstice's law enforcers zooming in at an inopportune time. But whatever made the shadow did not land, at least not in sight. The soldiers continued offloading the truck until a clunk sounded above the cargo hold. Alisa frowned up at the ceiling. Had something struck them?

It's Leonidas and Mica, Abelardus told her. *There were no docking slots open, so Bravo Six landed the shuttle on the roof.*

"Oh," she said. *Of course.*

Alisa turned on her comm, intending to tell them that they did not need to charge to the rescue, but a clang came from the cargo ramp as Leonidas landed on it. He was in full combat armor with his biggest rifle in his hands. All of the Alliance soldiers swung in his direction.

Problem, Abelardus said into her mind as Alisa said, "Stay out there, Leonidas."

But seeing him broke the spell. Shouts filled the cargo hold, and the soldiers dropped what they were carrying and snatched up their rifles.

"Run, Leonidas," Alisa said. "The Starseers are handling—"

The squeal of blazer fire cut her off as all the soldiers opened up at once. Some stood their ground and fired, and others ran for cover behind the grocery truck. Most of them shot at Leonidas, but a few swung rifles toward Alisa too. The spell was definitely broken.

"Get back," Alisa shouted to Young-hee and the others as she lunged out from behind the stairs. She wanted the soldiers aiming for her, not the Starseers. She didn't know if the women could all make protective barriers the way Abelardus could.

Blazer fire slammed into her shoulder, and she abruptly stopped worrying about anything else except staying alive. Leonidas charged into the cargo hold, shooting at the men he could target without risking catching anyone else in the crossfire. Others, he bowled into, using his sheer power to knock them out of the way. Blazer fire tagged his armor, bouncing off, for now.

Alisa fired at those targeting her, but she did not truly want to hurt anyone, especially not Alliance soldiers. "Abelardus," she yelled. "This would be a good time for mind play."

It's always a good time, he told her, and a second later, three armored soldiers flew through the hold and slammed into one of the bulkheads.

"Find the admiral," the sergeant yelled. He ran toward the stairs—and Alisa.

She fired at his chest piece, then flung herself into a roll to avoid *his* fire. A crimson beam bounced off the staircase railing. Fortunately, Young-hee and the others had moved into a corner, behind some of the freshly deposited food crates. They were safe, for the moment.

As Alisa jumped to her feet, whirling to fire at the sergeant again, he growled and sprayed blazer bolts in her direction. The armor made her fast, but his made *him* fast too. Until his rifle was torn from his hands by a mental attack. It flew up and landed atop the food truck. He paused, gaping toward it, and Alisa took advantage. She sprang at him, rotating and slamming a side kick into his chest.

He flew back, as if a battering ram had struck him rather than a boot, and smashed into the side of the grocery truck. He left a dent as he slid down it. Unfortunately, the blow did not deter him for long. He lifted his arm to fire at Alisa with his built-in blazers.

She dove toward him, rolling to advance under the bolts. Before he could adjust his aim, she came up and sprang for him. Instead of bothering with her built-in blazers, she relied on her unarmed combat training. She hammered punches and kicks at him, hoping the armor would give her the speed and the strength to dent his. She aimed for seams instead of the usual centerline targets. Seemingly startled by her ferocity, he tried to jump back to give himself space, but his back thumped against the side of the truck.

Shadows fell across them, making them both pause. Three of his men had climbed atop the truck to avoid Leonidas. They sprang from it to the walkway, bypassing the stairs. Beck had planted himself at the bottom of the steps to keep soldiers from advancing into the ship, but these three made it past him. He cursed and turned, as if to run up after them, but two soldiers near him waded into him, keeping him there.

Realizing they were after Tiang, and that their search of the ship might take them to the rec room, Alisa renewed her attack against the sergeant with intensity. If she took their leader out, the others might falter.

Her fists flew, and she barely felt the impact as they hammered into his chest plate. She threw an uppercut that took him in his armored chin, her fist landing hard enough that it knocked his head back. It clanged against the side of the truck. Before he recovered, she chopped her open hand down on his faceplate. A faint crack reached her ears. She lifted her hand to strike more blows, but the sergeant was hurled to the side even as she swung.

She scrambled back, afraid she would be swept away too. She couldn't tell which Starseer was responsible, but the man hurtled through the air, legs over head, as if he were doing cartwheels. He landed on the cargo ramp and rolled down, joining a pile that already had ten men in it. A few were trying to struggle to their feet, but having the sergeant crash onto them discombobulated them further.

"Let's get them *all* out there," Alisa said over her comm, as she turned toward the stairs, prepared to chase after those other three soldiers. "Then we can shut the hatch and take off."

We have *been working on that,* Abelardus spoke dryly into her mind, as another armored man spun through the air and out the cargo hatch.

One of the men Beck had been facing dropped to the ground, but the second one still hammered him. Leonidas had leaped up to the walkway in time to head off those three soldiers and was engaged with all of them at once, crowding the narrow space.

Since nobody else was charging at her, Alisa shifted so she could aim at Beck's opponent without risk of hitting him. She popped one of her blazers out of her suit and fired at a seam on the man's back. It was hard to sustain the pinpoint fire with him boxing with Beck, but she did her best. Sooner or later, his suit would light up with a warning about the damage he was taking…

The man yelled something, his helmet muffling it, and launched himself at Beck instead of turning toward Alisa. They went down, wrestling, limbs entwined, and Alisa had to stop firing. Up on the walkway, one of Leonidas's opponents went sailing through the cargo hold. He landed a few feet shy of the ramp, and she started toward him, thinking to roll him out before he could recover. Some of the soldiers who had already been knocked outside found their feet and ran up, trying to get back into the ship, but Abelardus leaned against the wall nearby, watching the spot. An invisible barrier kept the men from getting inside. Mica and Bravo Six had made their way into the ship at some point—Alisa glimpsed them following the wall and running to engineering. Maybe Mica had some grenades in there.

A truck door slammed behind Alisa. She turned, raising her arm to fire, but she was too slow. Two soldiers sprang from the cab and crashed into her.

She went down hard, her elbow clunking into the deck. She tried to lift her legs, to kick the men off her, but one already had her pinned.

"That's the captain," he barked.

A gauntleted hand clasped around her neck. Her armor protected her, but warnings flashed on her display, and something in her helmet groaned as he squeezed.

"Use her for a trade," the second man said. "Her for Tiang."

"She should die," the one with his hand around her neck growled. "*Traitor.*"

Again, Alisa tried to buck them off and roll away, but they were both on her, the strength more than matching hers.

"Abelardus," she called, hoping he was still leaning against the wall on the other side of the truck. Could he see her predicament? "Little help! And I am *not* a traitor."

Her suit groaned again, and a faint hiss reached her ears. If that neck armor gave away, she would be dead in an instant.

She twisted again, this time only trying to get her arm up. She fired, hoping to angle the beam toward her assailant's suit. His rage-filled face filled her vision, and at first, she thought her aim went awry, that she was burning through the ceiling instead of him, but then surprise flashed in his eyes, and he glanced to the side of his helmet, observing some reading. Hoping he was distracted, Alisa tried to get her legs up again.

This time, she managed to free one knee and ram it into the soldier's hip. It jostled him, but he kept his grip on her neck. She rammed him again and twisted. His hands slipped, but the second man reached in, a large gauntleted palm gripping her faceplate, as if her helmet were a forceball, and he was going to use it to hurl her across the hold.

A blur of red flashed through her half-blocked vision, and the man gripping her helmet let go as he was hefted from the deck. The one still pinning her shouted a startled curse. Finally, Alisa had her distraction. She got both legs under him and pressed them into his chest plate. She rocked and thrust upward with all of her armor-enhanced strength.

The soldier flew straight up, past the top of the truck, nearly reaching the ceiling. Alisa leaped to her feet as Leonidas threw his man through the hatchway. Abelardus must have lowered his barrier, because the soldier sailed through, crashing into his fellows before they could make headway into the ship.

Alisa's attacker landed on the deck three feet from her and bounced. She lunged in and grabbed him as if he were a doll. Grinning maniacally, she hefted him into the air over her head, the servos in her suit groaning but giving her the strength for the movement. As Leonidas had done, she pitched her man toward the hatchway. He didn't fly as fast or far, but he landed with enough velocity that he rolled toward the ramp. Maybe a Starseer gave him a nudge, because he continued onto and down it, joining the pile of men at the base. A huge pile of men.

"That's all of them," Leonidas called. "Close her up."

The ramp raised slowly, since there were still men on it. Someone must have given mental shoves, because they all toppled off. The hatch closed, locking the Alliance team out.

"Abelardus?" Leonidas propped a fist on his hip and looked at Alisa.

"What?" she asked.

"When you needed help, you called for Abelardus instead of me." Judging by the distaste on his face, this was an inexcusable faux pas.

"Only because the last I saw, you were fighting three men at once up there." Alisa waved toward the walkway, but all of those men were gone now, thrown out with the rest. "He was leaning against the wall, like he was looking for a cigarette to smoke."

"Really," Abelardus said, strolling around the back of the truck to join them. "I was using my prodigious mental talents. Some of us use our brains to fight and not our beefy muscles." He sniffed disdainfully at Leonidas.

Mica and Bravo Six walked out of engineering, Mica holding what appeared to be grenades, and the android gripping a crowbar. Mica looked toward the closed hatch, a hint of disappointment in her expression. Sorry to have missed the battle?

Leonidas put an arm around Alisa's shoulder and turned his back to Abelardus.

"Whenever you need me, I'm there for you," he said quietly. "No matter what I'm doing."

"I understand. Thank you. Next time, I'll make sure to cry out for you when I'm being squished to death."

"Excellent. If, for some perplexing reason, I'm not able come to you, cry next for Beck."

"Oh, I see. You just don't ever want me to ask *Abelardus* for help."

"He's not reliable," Leonidas said.

"I heard that, Beefy," Abelardus called from the end of the truck.

"Also," Leonidas said, not turning back toward him, "don't expect me to obey orders to run away."

He raised an eyebrow, and she recalled that she had yelled that when he first leaped down from the roof of the ship. She'd hoped she might avert the battle if she acted quickly enough, but she could understand his unwillingness to leave her in a questionable situation. And she appreciated that.

"Not when you're in danger," he added.

"It seemed like a good thing to suggest," Alisa said, wondering if she should bother explaining that the soldiers had been under Starseer control until he showed up. No, it didn't matter now. And she had been the one to frantically comm him and tell him to come as soon as possible.

"I will never run and leave you alone with twenty enemy soldiers." He looked at the food crates, his brow crinkling. "Even if they were in the process of unloading your groceries."

"I don't want Alliance soldiers to be enemies," she said with a sigh and leaned against his shoulder. "I'm tired of having so many enemies."

"I know." He patted her shoulder.

"Sergeant Kapoor?" a tinny voice came from someone's comm.

Alisa spotted an abandoned helmet and walked over to it.

"This is Captain Marchenko," she said. "If you're looking for the head of your ambush team, we've decided not to allow him access to my ship."

A banging came from the closed cargo hatch. They would need to take off soon, before the soldiers could come up with another plan to get in.

"Marchenko," the man on the other end growled. Was that Admiral Agosti again?

"I offered to let Tiang go with your team, but he wasn't interested. Why don't you come down here personally to talk to him? I'll guarantee your safety. At least in my ship. I don't have any control over the dome here."

The growl that came through was inarticulate, and then the channel clicked off.

"How am I ever going to get that man to like me?" Alisa asked.

"By giving him his admiral back?" Leonidas suggested.

"Trust me, it's crossed my mind, but Tiang doesn't want to go."

"So make him go. It's not as if they want to torture and interrogate him for state secrets. They just want to put him to work."

"But apparently not the work he wants to do."

"You don't sign on to the military to do the work *you* want to do. You do the work the outfit needs."

"I'm not sure if that's true for medical research admirals."

"It's true for everyone," Leonidas said, his voice stern. He wasn't backing up Admiral Agosti, was he? "You don't get to run off when you don't get the assignment you want."

"Well, he's doing the work I want him to do—I think—so I'm going to let him stay here as long as he likes."

"That man is going to be severely disciplined when they get him back, if they ever figure out this is his fault and not yours." Leonidas lowered his arm. "I wonder what that will look like. Admirals don't usually need to be disciplined."

"He's not like other admirals."

"Oh, I know."

Leonidas's gaze shifted upward, toward the walkway and the corridor. A small, black-robed form crouched there, looking down with wide eyes. Jelena.

Alisa grimaced. How had she slipped away from her tutors again? And how much of the battle had she seen? Her gut squirmed at the idea that she might have been that close, somewhere she could have been trampled by men in heavy armor, or cast aside and injured, as if she were nothing but some obstacle.

Alisa strode toward the stairs, unfastening her helmet as she went.

I only came at the end, Jelena blurted into her mind, shrinking against the bulkhead.

Alisa had reached the walkway, but paused, startled by the words and also the fear that came with them. Was Jelena afraid of *her*? She'd only intended to be stern, maybe to send her to her cabin as punishment for disobeying.

You're scary in that...that blue thing, Jelena thought, and shared an image of Alisa, as she appeared from her eyes, tall and fierce in her armor, anger stamped on her face.

Alisa lowered her helmet and took a breath, trying to paste a calm expression on her face. And into her heart.

So is he, Jelena added, sharing an image of Leonidas pummeling soldiers, breaking their helmets, hurling them across the cargo hold as if he were an android rather than a man. From Jelena's perspective, he seemed even taller and more imposing.

Alisa continued forward, her helmet dangling from her fingers.

"All right," she said, though it stung that Jelena saw Leonidas—and even her own mother—as scary because of the armor and the fighting. "You're not in trouble." The Starseers had been a part of the fight, too, standing in their ominous black robes and waving their staffs. Why didn't Jelena see *them* as scary? Alisa did. Maybe because Jelena was used to them now? Or because she was *one* of them? "But let's take you back to Lady Westfall for now. Or do you want to come up to the cockpit with me? I'm going to fly us..." She wasn't sure where yet. If she left the dome, she would be an easy target for the warship, but if she stayed here in the docks, those soldiers would return with blowtorches. "Somewhere."

"I'll come with you," Jelena said, tentatively lifting her hand.

Alisa clasped it gently, and they walked toward NavCom together.

"Did Westfall let you out because the battle was over?" she asked. "Or did you sneak out?"

Jelena smiled slyly up at her.

"I see."

A soft clang sounded behind her, Leonidas following at a distance. Alisa smiled over her shoulder at him. She should have told him that she appreciated his help. She would later. And she'd also have to figure out how to get him out of his armor and into a position where Jelena would find him less intimidating.

"Nobody's staying to help me unload the groceries?" Beck called plaintively.

Alisa assumed Young-hee, Abelardus, and the others were leaving too.

"We need to get started cooking right away," Beck added.

"Leonidas will help you chop celery after he changes out of his armor," Alisa called back.

"Never mind. I don't need help."

Alisa grinned at Leonidas as he turned toward the crew cabins. She caught a few faint words. "Pickiest cook I've ever met."

CHAPTER EIGHT

Terra Jhero had a junkyard. It was only five miles from the docks, and Alisa doubted it would take the Alliance long to locate her freighter parked in the back corner, but she hadn't had the option of flying far. As she had been reminded as soon as she'd taken off, Bravo Six had piloted the newly acquired twice-stolen shuttle back to the *Nomad* and, with Leonidas in a rush to get inside to help, parked it on the freighter's roof. Her ship had protested mightily when she had taken off with it still there, but several of the soldiers had returned by that point, so that had seemed more plausible than sending Bravo Six outside to move the craft. After lifting off, it had been a slow balancing act to get it even the few miles to the junkyard, and Alisa imagined they had been quite the sight to the passersby below, people wondering if the shuttle would pitch over the side and land on them. But freighters were designed to haul cargo; nobody had ever specified that the cargo had to be on the inside.

"You're clear," Alisa called up the ramp and into the hold, waving to Leonidas in the cab of the delivery truck.

At the rumble of the vehicle's engine, a rat scurried out from under the ramp and toward a pile of debris stacked nearby. The furry black creature was the length of Alisa's forearm and had fangs that reminded her of the dragons in the marshes outside the dome. It wasn't the first rat she'd seen since landing. She would hate to be stuck here at night.

Leonidas drove the truck out, pointing it toward an uncluttered spot in the junkyard. Alisa had already moved the shuttle off the roof, finding a mostly bare spot to park it. A couple of plastic chairs might have been sacrificed since nobody had rushed out to clear the area for her.

Mica, who stood to the side of the ramp, readying cans of spray paint, said, "So, we're returning the stolen truck—sort of—but we're keeping the stolen shuttle?"

"Somewhere, a poor grocer is lamenting that his truck was hijacked by a bunch of Alliance soldiers," Alisa said. "As soon as we're done here, I'll send a message letting him know where he can find it. As for the shuttle, I didn't *tell* you to pick up a stolen one and not pay for it."

"Leonidas made that decision. He seemed affronted that an imperial shuttle had made its way here without an imperial pilot or master."

"Was he in command of your shuttle acquisition mission?" Alisa asked.

"I figured I was just there to make sure the thing could fly."

"I only ask because a few weeks ago, you were pointing out to him that the chief of engineering outranked the chief of security."

"You never verified that. We were left to wonder."

"I'm still waiting for a chart to be posted somewhere in the ship," Leonidas said, joining them, the truck parked against the wall of the junkyard.

"I think Mica likes to keep things flexible," Alisa said, "so she can be in charge when she wants to be and not in charge when she wants to foist the responsibility on someone else."

"Uh huh." Mica waved one of the spray cans she'd prepared. "Who's helping me paint? I've got the materials printer working on stencils, so artistic skills won't be required."

Alisa looked at Leonidas. "I believe she's implying that she doesn't expect such skills from either of us."

"She hasn't seen my needlepoint."

"Neither have I. When do I get my gift of a battlefield dotted with wildflowers?"

"You two are an odd couple," Mica said and tossed a can of white paint to Alisa. "Let's lay down a base—we can't show up to a mafia event with black imperial paint smothering the catering shuttle." She lifted a can toward Leonidas. "You staying and helping?"

"I've been forbidden from assisting in the kitchen," he said.

Mica tossed him another can.

"I suspect we'll get more helpers soon," Alisa said. "People who couldn't master the rolling chop or find that working with Beck isn't to their tastes."

"He better not be a tyrant," Mica said. "The children are in there helping."

"The last I saw, he was only letting them carry things. Jelena and two boys were arguing over who got to play with the hand tractor. Abelardus was encouraging them to eschew such mundane tools and use their minds."

"Abelardus used the word eschew?" Mica asked, lowering a mask and setting to work on the shuttle.

"Perhaps not that exact word. Did you get a chance to look at that tracking device you two bought?"

"It's already modified."

"Excellent."

"But its range isn't infinite. We'll have to stay close to the ship you stick it in if we don't want to lose them."

"I expected as much."

Alisa and Leonidas moved around to the front of the shuttle and also started painting.

"Is Tiang helping with the kitchen work?" Leonidas asked.

"I don't think Tiang knows there *is* kitchen work. Or that his people came and tried to forcibly remove him from my ship."

"We're fortunate that none of those soldiers were killed. If the Alliance keeps trying, it may be impossible to prevent deaths." He looked at her sidelong as he sprayed white paint over the black. "Is keeping him here worth that? Especially when he could be traded for Stanislav?"

"Well, I *have* known him longer than I've known Stan." Alisa smiled, but it was a poor joke, and she knew it. Leonidas's mouth didn't so much as twitch. She lowered her can and sighed at the hull of the shuttle. "I hate to say this, but I don't trust the Alliance in this instance. I don't trust *Agosti*. He's proven himself to be…"

"Intractable? Dense?"

"An asshole."

"Ah. Of course."

"An intractable, dense asshole. I don't trust him to actually make the trade if I agree to it. And I know it's horrible to be thinking about tactics above people, but Stanislav has already faced Tymoteusz and lost. As have we. Maybe I'm being delusional, but I very much want what Tiang is cooking up in his cabin to be a brilliant way to defeat the *chasadski*."

Before Leonidas could comment on her delusions, her comm unit beeped.

"Marchenko," she answered. She kept hoping Tomich would get in touch again. She'd sent a response to his message, one urging him to find Stanislav and try to get him released, so he could help against Tymoteusz. She hadn't mentioned the mafia meeting, though she'd thought about it. But this time, she didn't want the Alliance bursting in—so far, they hadn't done anything to fix her problems when they had done that. They'd usually ended up shooting at *her* instead of at the true target.

"Captain," came Tiang's voice. "I'm in need of a *chasadski* Starseer."

"I don't have any stored aboard."

"I need to conduct an experiment to see if I'm on the right heading with my research, and I don't wish to use any of our ally Starseers."

"I'm sure they appreciate that. If we're able to capture any of Tymoteusz's people, I'll be certain to save one for you."

Leonidas returned to spray-painting the hull.

"I had hoped to have this tested and prepared for dissemination the next time we met Tymoteusz," Tiang said. "Perhaps someone here might volunteer...for the greater good."

Alisa scowled at her comm unit. "I forbid you to do medical experiments on any of our passengers. Even Abelardus."

"Then I am at an impasse, Captain."

"You'll just have to do the best you can without running experiments on people." A rat scurried about at the edge of Alisa's vision. "Can't you use animals? There are plenty of rats out here."

"Rats don't have Starseer genes."

"So take some of that blood you got from Ostberg and inject it into a rat."

"Really, Captain. You lack even the most rudimentary understanding of—well, hm. Maybe if I...Let me look something up."

He didn't close the comm, so Alisa left it open as she went back to painting the hull.

"You may be lucky he didn't do experiments on you while he was performing your surgery," she told Leonidas.

"I don't have Starseer genes, so I'm certain I'm not of interest to him."

"A cyborg with telepathy and telekinesis would be a scary thing to contemplate."

"Indeed."

As it was, Alisa still didn't know how she would manage to make Leonidas less scary for Jelena. He was being aloof instead of friendly. Even though Alisa understood his reasoning—Jelena would be horrified if she peeked into his mind and caught fantasies of him having his way with her mother—it made it all the more difficult for her to gain familiarity with him.

"Captain?" Tiang asked.

"Yes, Admiral?"

"Please bring me some rats."

"*Bring* you?"

Leonidas snorted.

"Six or eight should suffice."

"Admiral, I don't know if you saw it in the brochure, but there's no room service aboard this freighter."

"None at all? I am paying quite a bit. I believe you promised me a luxury experience."

"A luxury *dining* experience," Alisa said. "Not a luxury lab-rat-specimen retrieval service. And I'm positive you've eaten your fare in cookies already."

"I'm looking at the original brochure now," Tiang said.

"*Is* there a brochure?" Leonidas murmured.

"The original fliers I made back on Dustor are still in the system. They were appealing enough to entice Alejandro and Yumi to show up."

"I never saw those."

"That's because you had already barricaded yourself aboard. Obviously, you knew without ever seeing a brochure that you would be experiencing a sublime and luxurious experience on my ship."

His eyes closed to slits. "Were I young and immature, I'd be spray-painting you right now."

"Please, don't. I have a dearth of clothing as it is."

"The paint is water soluble," Mica called from around the corner.

"Hm." Leonidas's eyes narrowed even further.

"Captain," Tiang said, "I really could use those rats. I'm not young enough and spry enough to catch them."

"I'll have someone get on it right away," Alisa said, "but only because I'm expecting whatever potion you're creating to perform miraculous miracles against our enemies."

"Potion? I'm not a witch, Captain."

"Leonidas," Alisa said, closing the comm and tucking it away. She hefted her can of spray paint, suspecting she would need it for self-defense purposes momentarily. "Would you be a good security chief and collect six or eight rats?"

He pointed his paint can at her, but hesitated to fire first. Noble to the end. Alisa didn't hesitate.

His enhanced reflexes *almost* got him out of the way of the spray, but the nozzle was set to a wide distribution. She grinned as she caught his elbow.

Unfortunately, he stopped hesitating after that. A cloud of white paint molecules came her way. She ducked and ran around the corner, almost crashing into Mica, who was working on the side of the shuttle.

"Ah, no. Don't get me involved in this," she said, backing away with her hands up.

Since Alisa was being chased relentlessly, she couldn't pause to say anything. She raced toward the ramp of the *Nomad*, hoping Leonidas wouldn't spray-paint her cargo hold in his effort to continue painting her. In her haste, she tripped over the edge of the ramp and fell forward. She would have smacked down chest and face first, but Leonidas sprinted a few steps and caught her before she struck down.

He swooped her up in both arms, and she wasn't sure whether she was rescued or imprisoned.

"My savior and my tormentor in one," she remarked, noting his still-narrowed eyes. And the smudge of paint on his cheek.

He opened his mouth to reply, but someone at the top of the ramp cleared his throat.

"I thought I should come to select my preferred specimens personally," Tiang said.

Alisa started to comment, but stopped, gaping when she saw Jelena standing next to him.

"Uhm," Jelena said and held up a large stencil of a basket of fruit, one of several she had dragged to the ramp. "Yumi said I should bring these out to you."

Leonidas set Alisa on her boots, her boots that were spattered with white paint.

"Yes," Alisa said, "those will be perfect for after the base layer dries." She wiped at moisture on her cheek, and her hand came away white. "In all locations."

"Can I, uhm…" Jelena frowned doubtfully at Leonidas.

"Do you want to help?" Alisa waved her paint can in invitation.

"I was practicing my telekinesis in the kitchen, and some boxes fell over. That was really Jiziri's fault, but Tommy said, maybe I would be better at painting." She continued to send wary glances toward Leonidas and did not come down the ramp.

"I, too, have been forbidden to help in the kitchen," Leonidas said. "Due to overly efficient knife skills."

He sounded stern rather than conciliatory, and it took Alisa a moment to realize he was trying to make an overture toward Jelena.

"Yes, you two are practically the same." Alisa smiled. "Shall we all finish the white together?"

Tiang cleared his throat again.

"You can have my can," Leonidas told Jelena, holding it aloft. "I believe I have another duty. A very temporary duty, I hope."

"There are hundreds of rats in the junkyard," Alisa said. "Since you're so fast and agile—" she wiped away more paint, "—I'm sure collecting a few won't take long."

"Six to eight," Tiang said brightly as he strolled down the ramp. "I prefer young healthy ones."

Jelena walked hesitantly down after him, eyeing the paint can in Leonidas's hand.

"Here," he said, turning to offer it to Alisa, probably realizing Jelena wouldn't be comfortable taking it from him.

Alisa stepped back and clasped her hands behind her back. Not sure if she was doing the right thing, she said, "She can get it from you if she wants it."

Leonidas grimaced.

"Smile," she whispered as Jelena came closer. "And look approachable."

"How do I do that?" he whispered back.

"Smile," she repeated.

He bared his teeth at Jelena.

"Suns' hells, not like that." Alisa slapped him on the arm. "You look like an Octavian Blood Bear luring a hunter back to his den."

A clunk sounded behind Leonidas. He and Alisa turned to look, but there was nothing there. Jelena darted forward, took the can from his grip, and jumped off the ramp and to safety.

Alisa snorted. With moves like that, they were sure to be fast friends by nightfall.

"Good tactic for bears too," Leonidas said and saluted Jelena.

"There's a nice plump rat in the corner," Tiang called.

Leonidas gave Alisa a dirty look and jogged off to join him.

Alisa's comm beeped.

"Captain?" Beck asked.

"Trouble in the kitchen?"

"No, I think most of the troublemakers have gone. Though Alejandro could be more useful. Right now, he's sampling everything he cuts."

Alisa was surprised Alejandro had joined in with the work at all.

"We just got a message from our employer," Beck said, "through the company site."

"And?"

"We now have a meeting location."

"Nearby, I assume?" Alisa asked. Since they were supposed to be ready in just over a day, the meeting couldn't be three planets away.

"A spot near Baku Moon. It's on the far side of Aldrin's orbit from here. Paint fast. That shuttle is going to have to lift off in a few hours to make it in time, and I've got to get all this food cooked along the way. I doubt the shuttle has the capability to do more than keep things hot."

"Sorry, I didn't think to ask my team to steal a vessel equipped with a full kitchen."

"I'm used to making do with the *Nomad*. But, Captain? I'll admit to you, I'm real nervous about this."

"We've been in crazier situations and bigger battles," she said. "Or are you worried about the ratings that the diners will give to your new catering company?"

"No, it's just that my last dealings with the mafia didn't go well. You think White Dragon will be here? Medric might have had time to rethink our last meeting and realize we were influencing him. And doesn't Henneberry know what you and Leonidas look like? How are you going to sneak past her?"

"I've already got costumes on board."

While dithering in dock, Alisa had ordered those, as well as a few new shirts and undergarments to replace the frayed, hole-riddled items in her cabinets. She had also ordered Jelena some clothes, so she wouldn't have to run around in that black robe indefinitely if she didn't want to. Unfortunately, Jelena seemed rather taken with it. Or maybe it was required for group tutoring sessions. At least she had worn the cats-in-space pajamas the night before.

"I haven't told Leonidas about his costume yet," she added. "He's still dealing with the last problem I made for him."

She watched as Leonidas raced past, his legs moving too fast to see. He darted behind a debris pile and came back grasping a rat long enough and squirmy enough to be a ferret. With giant fangs. He held it out to keep it from biting him.

"Excellent," Tiang said. "That's one. Seven more, please."

Leonidas gave Alisa another dirty look.

She grinned at him, lowered her comm unit, and made sure Jelena was several feet away, and then whispered, "I love you, Leonidas."

CHAPTER NINE

Alisa took them into the air, pausing a few times to pick at tenacious paint under her fingernails. Water soluble. Maybe if that water came via a pressure washer. Her only solace was that Leonidas had just as much paint clinging to him. Not to mention all the rat fur and a few bite marks that his hunt had left him with. Cyborgs were speedy and fast and strong, but junkyard rats weren't wimps, especially when their instincts told them they were being rounded up for lab experiments. Alisa hoped they didn't end up with angry telepathic rats that could hurl objects around with their minds.

The sensors showed the shuttle taking off behind her. Bravo Six was at the helm over there, working to further Alisa's schemes for no pay. She wished she could reward him with something. A replacement eyeball, perhaps.

The *Nomad* and the shuttle, now a perky white craft with steaming meals and baskets of vegetables painted on the sides, headed over the city and toward the part of the dome that held the exit—and the energy barrier that guarded it.

As Alisa flew over the buildings and closer to that barrier, she reached for the comm so she could get permission from air traffic control. It beeped first with an incoming message.

"*Star Nomad* and unidentified shuttle," a woman said, "you have not been cleared for exit."

"Can you clear us?" Alisa asked reasonably.

"Not at this time."

Alisa's stomach sank. Had Solstice changed her mind about letting them leave? Because she'd read between the lines that Alisa and her team intended to do something at that meeting. As far as she knew, Solstice had never commed Leonidas to tell him the location. All of their information thus far had come from their chef contact on Henneberry's ship, the one who presumably believed Beck was running a legitimate company, a fearless legitimate company that had no trouble providing meals for all of the mafia heads at once.

"What time would be better?" Alisa asked. "I'll record it on my calendar. Oh, look. I have an opening in two minutes."

The air traffic controller closed the channel without responding.

Alisa sighed and turned them to fly along the inside of the dome. The city was thirty miles wide, so they could take a few laps before seeing all the sights, but Alisa wasn't interested in sightseeing now.

"Leonidas," she commed ship-wide, not sure if he had finished scraping off paint or not. "I may need you to chat convincingly with Solstice to get her to let us leave."

He did not answer, but a minute later, he padded into NavCom wearing nothing but a towel around his waist, his body still gleaming with the cleaning spray from the sanibox.

"Uh," Alisa said, letting herself ogle him for a moment, "I suppose that *is* the appropriate outfit for convincing chats with Solstice."

"Oh? Will she be impressed by the paint in my armpit hair?"

Alisa snorted. "How did it get under there?"

"My opponent was crafty." He gave her a long look that seemed to contain equal parts admiration and exasperation. She found it appealing and wished she were in a towel with him—or maybe less.

"You're lucky Jelena didn't team up with me. Just wait until next time." Alisa smiled, still pleased that Jelena had spent an hour painting with her, talking about what she was learning from her tutors. The curriculum sounded balanced, with the children studying traditional academics as well as Starseer mental skills. If Durant—or someone who was less of an asteroid kisser than Durant—had come to Alisa to explain Jelena's potential and what the studies would entail, she might have eventually been won over without the need for kidnapping and subterfuge. Of course, she had to remind herself that Durant wasn't likely the only imperial loyalist in the group—or the only one that thought Jelena might further his future. "I think once we get Thorian back and life can return to a semblance of normality, she may be willing to help me paint you."

"Enticing." Leonidas slid into the co-pilot's seat and poked through the comm messages to find Solstice's information.

"Yes, you are," she said with a wink, but he didn't acknowledge it. His speculative look had disappeared at the mention of Jelena.

It was just as well. No point in ogling and leering when they couldn't— or at least *shouldn't*—do anything now. Peals of laughter floated up from the direction of the mess hall. Jelena was still running around the ship with two of her age mates. Alisa hadn't had much luck with enforcing a bedtime yet, since she and the adults had been up late with their projects, and that led to some crabby mornings. She admitted to being a touch gun shy at disciplining Jelena right now, not wanting to be the mean mom after so long apart, but bedtimes were on the list of things that would, she promised herself, return to normal once they finally finished dealing with Tymoteusz.

"You've been letting Durant use the comm?" Leonidas asked.

"What? No. I mean, I haven't stopped anyone from sending messages from their cabins, but he doesn't have a cabin."

"Looks like this came out of Abelardus's cabin. Let me contact Solstice, and you can take a look."

"At someone's private communications?"

"I know that's a hobby of yours," he said dryly.

"You eavesdrop a couple of times…" Alisa trailed off since Solstice's face had come up on the monitor.

Leonidas leaned forward. "Solstice, we'd like to leave your dome. Is there a problem?"

"Colonel, love, is that a collarbone I see? You're getting me terribly excited."

"I told you," Alisa mouthed.

"We have an appointment that must be kept," Leonidas said.

"Whatever you're planning, don't do it. There are Alliance ships in orbit all over the place up here."

Up here? Had she already left for the meeting? Alisa tried to tell if she was on a ship instead of in her compound. She spotted a couple of blinking lights behind Solstice, but curtains and more art lined the wall, too, and she couldn't tell for certain.

"We're aware of the warship," Leonidas said.

"There are more coming this way."

Alisa frowned. Was that true? And if so, would it scare away the mafia heads? Would the meeting be postponed or moved?

"Further, I'm off to the very important meeting that you convinced me I should go to," Solstice said, smirking at him. "Presumably so you can seduce me in order to get information from me later."

"She knows I'm sitting right next to you when she says these things, doesn't she?" Alisa grumbled, irritated that the woman had no understanding of the word *taken*.

"I believe you were going to give me the location of that meeting," Leonidas said.

Alisa raised her eyebrows, wondering why he was asking when they already knew the location. She supposed it would be good to verify that Beck had been given the right spot. It was always possible that Henneberry's people had seen through their catering front and were setting a trap for them even now. Alisa gritted her teeth and took them for another lap around the dome.

"Colonel, love," Solstice said, this time with a patient, parental tone to her voice, "if you were to show up at that meeting, after I told Ms. Henneberry that you were dead, I don't believe my next visit with the woman would go well."

"I'm suspecting we may be locked in this dome for reasons that have nothing to do with her protecting us from the Alliance," Alisa muttered.

"Is that your secretary blathering in the background?" Solstice asked.

"My secretary?" Leonidas asked.

"Yes, the scruffy woman who follows you around and gets herself into trouble. I do hope she services you in some way."

Leonidas opened his mouth, perhaps to say she was the captain, but Solstice already knew that. She was just being obnoxious.

Alisa leaned in and smiled at Solstice. "Of *course* I'm servicing him. Mornings. Evenings. Nights. All night, usually. Are you familiar with cyborg stamina? It's *amazing*."

Leonidas touched her shoulder and gently pushed her back to her seat. Solstice looked a tad stunned, which should have mollified Alisa, but mostly, she felt silly for her childish outburst. That woman brought out the worst in her. She glanced at the hatchway and was relieved not to see Jelena or any of the other children lurking in the corridor.

"Open the forcefield, Solstice," Leonidas said, "or my captain with her creative, scheming mind will be left to find ways to open it on her own. Or perhaps we'll get one of our Starseers to manipulate the mind of the person sitting by the button."

Solstice frowned at him. "Promise me you won't show up at this meeting."

"Will you give me the location of Tymoteusz when you learn it?"

"If I learn it, yes."

"If I have his location, I'll consider staying away from the meeting then."

"You'll *consider* it. Colonel…"

"If you find yourself in any trouble because of my actions, we'll offer you sanctuary on this ship."

"What?" Alisa asked.

Solstice winced. "I've seen that ship. It's far more of a dungeon than a sanctuary."

"Nevertheless, we'll take you aboard. And I'll personally do my best to protect you."

Alisa managed not to make a disgusted noise, but she couldn't keep from curling her lip.

Solstice sighed dramatically and cut the comm.

Leonidas turned a palm upward. "I don't know what else I could have said. Manipulating people isn't my strength."

"You could have lied to her and told her we were going to the Waterfalls of Wagoo to experience the stimulations and pleasures of the famous ten-drilled taloor fish."

"Lying isn't in my nature. And I'm poor at it."

The comm flashed. "You've been cleared for departure, *Star Nomad*."

"Ah?" Alisa veered away from her circuit and zipped straight for the exit, checking to make sure Bravo Six was still behind her in the shuttle. A square of gray appeared ahead, the cloudy sky of Cleon Moon. She flew out, glancing at her sensors to make sure there weren't any ships waiting to pounce on them. There weren't, not down here anyway. Up in orbit was another matter. Alisa set a course that would take them up on the opposite side of the moon from the Alliance ships, hoping they wouldn't notice the *Nomad* slipping away.

As she flew, she noticed Leonidas sitting back in the co-pilot's seat, watching her.

"I know that was immature of me," she said, feeling judgment in his difficult-to-read gaze.

"Yes," he said agreeably, "but it has resulted in me thinking about what *servicing* may entail."

Heat rushed to Alisa's cheeks. "I would love to show you."

"But not now," he said.

"No, not now." She glanced at him. "But if you don't put on more than a towel, it may be hard to remember the reason *why* not now."

Leonidas started to get up, but paused, pointing to the comm. "Did you want to check Durant's message?"

Alisa hesitated. "He's still off the ship with Ostberg." And she had very deliberately not told him they were leaving. She'd thought about not telling Alejandro they were leaving, either, but he'd commed wanting directions to the junkyard, and had rejoined them before the painting was done. "Whatever messages he sent shouldn't matter now." Probably true, but she called up the information about the comm contact anyway. "It's a one-way video recording. Sent to…someone on the Vega Sisters. Butch."

"Butch?"

"That's all it says. Shut the hatch, will you? I like to eavesdrop in private."

He grunted, but complied and sat back down. She played the message.

"Butch," Durant said, "it's me. You're the only loyal imperial *chasadski* I know. I need you to forget about our past disagreements and get a message to Tymoteusz."

Alisa straightened in her seat. Maybe she should have been eavesdropping on Durant's messages from the beginning. Except she hadn't considered that Abelardus would let him use his cabin—or that Durant would sneak into his cabin to use the comm. Why would Durant have wanted to contact Tymoteusz? Didn't they want different things? Entirely different governments for the system?

"I know he has Thorian and that he didn't kill him outright." Durant took a deep breath. "For that I'm thankful. Putting aside the matters of an imperial legacy and birthright, antiquated and outdated notions if you ask me, the boy has great potential. I first met him two years ago, after he came into his powers, and I offered to tutor him then. His father, not surprisingly, had other matters on his mind at the time, and much of the boy's power is still locked away. Send this to him, will you, Butch?" Durant leaned forward, eyes imploring. "Listen to me, Lord Tymoteusz. Please. I know you see him as a threat, but he's so young. He could be controlled, fostered to grow up as we wish. I would rather work with you in this matter than against you. Imagine how much easier a time you would have ruling over the system with a legitimate heir to act as your figurehead. The common man knows nothing of the Staff of Lore, and most have forgotten Alcyone's significance in the shaping of our system. But they recognize Prince Thorian. Many would rally behind him. You, on the other hand, they will always see as an enemy. Do you not realize that? They fear the Starseers, and you having such a powerful weapon will only make them fear you more. Maybe you revel in that—I don't know. But the boy gives them someone else to focus on. You could be the shadowy figure behind the throne, barely noticed, barely acknowledged, but in control over all. I would work for you, of course, just as I've promised to work for the prince."

Durant flinched and glanced to the side, looking like someone afraid he was going to get caught. Alisa wagered he hadn't gotten permission from Abelardus to send that message.

"Please consider the wisdom of keeping the boy alive, Lord Tymoteusz," Durant said, facing the camera again. "He has value. That is all. I thank you for listening." He clasped his hands in front of him and performed a hurried bow before snapping the camera off.

"There's no return message," Leonidas said, scrolling through the comm history. "No way to know if Tymoteusz received it."

"If he did receive it, would he have paid attention? It sounds like he has his own plan for conquering the system and that Thorian doesn't play a role." She waved outward to indicate the ships that had to be coming in for the mafia meeting.

"Indeed. I wonder why he took him instead of killing him." As usual, Leonidas spoke bluntly, but his lips pressed together, showing his displeasure at the idea.

"I don't know, but we can't assume our time to find and retrieve him is infinite."

"No."

"I hope our plan succeeds, and that the meeting leads us to him."

"*Our* plan?" Leonidas arched his eyebrows.

"You were the one to let me know about the catering gig. And your willingness to go along with it has given you partial ownership in it."

"Is that how that works," he murmured.

"Wait until you see the costumes I got us. Yours will make you sexy."

He looked down at the towel fastened around his waist and the bare muscled thigh that was clearly visible. "I'm not sexy normally?"

"Oh, you're quite lovely, but a woman does enjoy seeing a man in formal wear. I just wish my own costume was that fetching. I did order some attractive new underwear for myself while I was shopping for costumes and clothes for Jelena. For practical purposes, of course. It's hard to thwart the plans of megalomaniacal despots when you have holes in your underwear."

"I imagine so."

"I also got a slinky nightie. In case you were curious."

"I suspect I am." His gaze strayed down her body, making her wish she had something slinky on now—and that she could take advantage of that closed hatch to let him fondle it. "What constitutes slinky, exactly? In clothing."

"You'll have to wait until I can show you."

"Waiting." His mouth twisted. "It's more frustrating than I realized it would be."

"For me too," she said quietly. Had she known their first night together would be their last, she would have made more of it—and refused to answer the door the next morning when Bravo Six and Mica had come calling. "I miss—"

The proximity alert bleated, and she cursed, whirling toward the sensors.

"I miss the days when Alliance warships were friends instead of enemies," she said. "Damn it."

"They're heading toward us?"

"Yes, we're just about out of the moon's gravitational field, but they've broken orbit to come see us."

"They're still after Tiang," Leonidas said. "And they won't be happy that their first attempt to get him failed."

"No." Alisa tapped the comm. "Abelardus, or any other Starseers that want to practice their mind control powers on Alliance pilots, please report to NavCom."

"Stanislav is the only one who's proven himself talented at that."

"I know. It's quite rude of him to be locked up on that warship, rather than here in NavCom where he could be of use."

A knock sounded at the hatch, and Abelardus's face appeared in the window. Even though Alisa hadn't locked it, he didn't come straight in. He was gaping at Leonidas's bare torso through the window.

"Abelardus is ogling you," Alisa told him.

"That's disturbing."

There's a difference between ogling and being horrified, Abelardus informed her silently. *Don't you have a dress code on this ship?*

"If I had a dress code, bathrobes certainly wouldn't be allowed," Alisa said, drawing a frown from Leonidas, who then glared back toward the window. He grew irked whenever Abelardus communicated telepathically with her. Rightfully so, she thought.

Abelardus opened the hatch, revealing not only himself, but Jelena standing there. Her head had been too low to be visible through the window. She smiled and started in, but faltered at the sight of Leonidas.

Er, Alisa would have shooed him out already if she'd realized her daughter would show up. He wasn't *indecent*, that thigh notwithstanding, but she was fairly certain eight-year-old girls weren't supposed to see full-grown men in towels.

Abelardus must have felt the same way because he dropped a hand over her eyes. "Jelena wants to help."

"Help?" Alisa asked blankly. She lifted a hand to wave for Leonidas to go change, but he was already on his feet.

"I'll put on my combat armor," he said, glancing toward the sensor display.

"At the least, put on some underwear," Abelardus grumbled. "There are children on this ship."

Leonidas skewered him with a dark look as they moved aside to let him pass, but he didn't pause for further banter.

"I interrupted him in the middle of armpit washing to comm Solstice," Alisa said. "It was important." She reminded herself that she was the captain and didn't need to justify her actions to anyone—so what if she kept a near-naked cyborg in NavCom with her?—but Jelena's arrival had her flustered.

"You said on the comm," Jelena said, pushing Abelardus's hand down, "that any Starseer who wanted to practice mind control could come to NavCom. I *love* practicing." She flounced in, heading for the co-pilot's seat. "So far, I'm best with animals, but I want to learn more. I want to be ready to get Thor back. Will we find him soon? Now that we're leaving the moon? How far away is he?"

Jelena started to slide into the seat, but Abelardus picked her up with both hands and nudged the fold-down sensor seat down. "Here, Jelena. Sit here instead of there. That seat isn't sanitary right now."

Alisa kicked him in the shin. "Knock it off."

Jelena seemed to have already gotten over her surprise at seeing a shirtless Leonidas, so Alisa didn't want to dwell on it.

"I'm merely trying to keep the children on the ship from being traumatized," Abelardus said. "You should thank me for being such a conscientious passenger." He eyed the co-pilot's seat for himself, then lifted the hem of his robe to wipe it down thoroughly before sitting.

Alisa rolled her eyes and looked back at Jelena. She was far too perky for a girl who should have been in bed an hour ago.

"There's a warship chasing us down," Alisa said, turning her focus on Abelardus. "Can you convince the pilot that he or she was mistaken and that we are, instead of a freighter, a particularly uninteresting piece of space debris?"

"I'll see what I can do, but as I've told you before, it's hard to fool multiple people, and helmsmen tend to have first officers and captains standing behind them."

"Fool the captain, then. I don't care, so long as they let us leave the moon's orbit without another fight."

"I don't know why you're so determined to let Tiang stay here. Especially now that he's brought vermin on board."

"It's not the first vermin we've had on board," she grumbled, thinking of Durant.

"Now, now, my brother is noble in his own eyes."

Alisa pointed at the sensor display. "The warship, if you please."

"What should I do?" Jelena asked brightly as Abelardus closed his eyes to concentrate.

"Uhm." Alisa couldn't imagine a child knowing enough about the minds of adults—or anyone—to successfully trick one into doing something, but she didn't know how it all worked. She assumed it would be better if Jelena didn't try to tinker with the same person as Abelardus. "You said animals are your specialty?"

Was her daughter experienced enough at this to *have* a specialty?

"I love animals. That's why I want a pony. And a dog. And kittens. Kittens aren't very big. Could we get some kittens?"

Alisa rubbed her face, quite certain Jelena didn't realize that they were in danger, even though the warship was now close enough to show up on the cameras, its hulking white body appearing on the view screen.

"Maybe a kitten," Alisa said, though she imagined that a cat living on the same ship as chickens might not work well. "But how do you use your powers on them?"

"I talk to them. Well, not really talk, because they don't have language like we do, but it's easier. You just think in pictures. I read that if you can think in smells that's even better for some animals. Like dogs. A dog's whole world is what it smells, did you know?"

"Are there any animals on that warship?" Alisa asked, thinking that giving Jelena something to look for might keep her busy. She didn't have time now for in-depth conversations on the lives of dogs.

"I can check."

"Good."

Jelena's face scrunched up, reminding Alisa of Ostberg. She hoped he was doing all right in his regen tank down there. She could have used his talents on this adventure.

While she waited to see if her Starseers could make magic, Alisa checked the sensors for other ships in the area. She didn't have any delusions that anyone would help her out here, especially not against a big Alliance warship, but maybe she could throw one of those tax collectors in Agosti's path.

The comm beeped, and she thought it might be the warship, but Bravo Six's face appeared on the monitor. She had almost forgotten that he was sailing along behind her, matching her speed in the shuttle.

"Lady Captain, are you aware of the Alliance warship approaching?" he asked.

"Very aware, Six. We're attempting to dissuade them from following. Or attacking."

"An excellent plan. Please inform Chef Beck that I've created a heating system for the containers of food he wishes to bring aboard the shuttle."

Alisa hadn't realized the android had been tasked with that job, but she said, "I will." Assuming the Alliance didn't blow the shuttle and the freighter out of the stars.

"The pilot officer has orders to snatch us with a grab beam," Abelardus murmured, his eyes still closed. "And a boarding team is being readied at their airlock hatch."

"Better than being blown out of the stars." Alisa pushed the engines for more speed, not that it would matter. The warship would catch them easily, and they were far enough away from the moon that there was nothing to hide behind. Even with her Starseer allies, could Leonidas and the rest of her people keep another team from storming the ship?

"I'm having a hard time influencing the pilot," Abelardus said. "I believe they may have taken something similar to Yumi's qui-gorn."

Alisa slumped in her seat. If the pilot had, she wagered that boarding team had too. As she knew from experience, that drug wouldn't keep a

Starseer from hurling the men into bulkheads—or dropping asteroids onto them—but it would surely thwart Abelardus's manipulation attempts.

"There's a dog," Jelena said cheerfully. "I think it's the captain's dog. It's in a really big cabin. And it's a big dog." She sounded delighted at this find. "Huge and furry and gray. Like a shaggy pony."

"Any chance you can convince that dog to run down to engineering and chew on some wires?" Alisa asked, more as a joke than as a serious request.

"Wires probably wouldn't taste good," Jelena said.

"Probably not. Maybe you could convince him there's a big, raw steak hidden somewhere in engineering, behind a lot of vital wires and components."

"I don't know what's vital."

Since Jelena wasn't objecting to the idea outright, Alisa commed engineering. "Mica, can you come share your brain with my daughter? The way you did with Ostberg the time you showed him where crucial parts of engineering were on an Alliance ship?" She caught Abelardus looking at her, and whispered, "Could this work?" She was well aware that Ostberg was five or six years older than Jelena and had presumably been training for much longer. Did Jelena truly know how to do anything useful at this age?

"There *are* Starseers who specialize in animal husbandry," Abelardus said, but his expression was skeptical.

"But?" Alisa asked, sensing a but.

"Your daughter is eight."

Jelena opened her eyes and glared at him. "I can do it. And I'm almost nine."

"Well, that changes everything," Abelardus said.

Jelena's glare deepened. Alisa remembered a report from her sister-in-law mentioning that Jelena had grasped the use of sarcasm at a young age. A precocious child. At least when it came to inappropriate humor.

"You're my daughter for sure," she murmured.

"What?" Jelena asked.

"Never mind." Alisa spotted Mica in the corridor in her pajamas and waved her into NavCom.

"This brain isn't available at your whim, you know," Mica said, though the words turned into a frown when she spotted the warship looming on the screen.

"Are you sure?" Alisa asked. "I thought that was in the employment contract. Engineer's brain: available at captain's whim."

"I didn't sign an employment contract."

"You didn't? You're sure? You probably shouldn't be getting paid then."

"I'd settle for not getting boarded." Mica made a rude gesture at the warship.

"What does that mean?" Jelena asked.

"Nothing," Alisa said. "Mica's going to share her brain with you. Can you see what she's thinking and then try to send it to the dog? Along with the promise of the steak?"

"But there's not a steak, is there? That will be mean, to fool him."

"Then promise him the excitement of a romp around the ship. Whatever works." Alisa grabbed the controls and steered them into some zigzags, hoping to make it harder for the grab beam operator to target them. The ship ought to be close enough to latch on any second.

"She's a tyrant, isn't she?" Mica asked, crouching beside Jelena.

"We're close enough now that I'm able to do some telekinesis," Abelardus said. "I'm making problems for the bridge crew to delay them."

"Like what?"

"The captain's pants just fell down."

"I'd like to say that your sense of humor is appalling," Alisa said, "but I fear you fit right in on this ship."

"I know I do."

"It's surprising that you object to nudity in NavCom."

"Just cyborg nudity. It's alarming due to its...magnitude."

"I'll let Leonidas know you've noticed his magnitude."

"It's hard to miss it, when he's—"

The warship's grab beam shot out, trying to engulf the *Nomad*, and Alisa threw them to the side in a roll. The freighter shuddered as the beam brushed it, but it did not catch hold. Not this time.

"The dog is loose," Jelena said, clapping her hands. "He's so happy to go for a romp."

"Is he going to romp into engineering?" Alisa felt a twinge of hope, even though it was probably ridiculous to believe a dog could truly destroy some critical piece of equipment. Once again, she missed Ostberg and his aptitude for mechanical manipulation.

"We're working on it," Mica muttered. "You're lucky I know Alliance ships so well."

Alisa took the ship into a dive. There was another freighter approaching Cleon Moon, so she veered toward it, hoping she might befuddle the grab beam operator by hiding behind the other ship. Unfortunately, that freighter had weapons. She hoped she didn't befuddle the captain into attacking her.

"The communications officer on the warship is receiving a message," Abelardus said. "I've got her believing there's smoke coming from her panel, but she's stubbornly insisting on answering it anyway."

"Good," Alisa said, Cleon Moon's dingy gray surface appearing on the view screen again as she dove for that freighter. The warship pursued.

"The dog is in engineering," Jelena said. "His name is Brock. People are shouting at him a lot. Someone's trying to grab him. I hope they don't hurt him."

"I don't think anyone would dare hurt the captain's dog. Wires, Mica?"

"I'm thinking about them for anyone who is paying attention," Mica said, eyeing Jelena.

Jelena plopped a hand onto Mica's head.

"Interesting," Abelardus said. "The communication is from another Alliance ship. An admiral is ordering Agosti to stop what he's doing and come to a rendezvous point."

"I hope Agosti is listening then," Alisa said. The warship was still on their tail. She did a loop and came up on the opposite side of the freighter, then matched its speed and direction. The warship would have to do some dancing to target her with the grab beam now.

She glanced at the sensors, wondering if she had to worry about any of the other Alliance vessels. Had they, too, left orbit to pursue her?

The warship flew over the freighter, trying to get to the *Nomad*. Alisa flew under the freighter's belly.

The comm lit up. "Listen, you ugly little junk hauler," an irate man said, "if you don't get yourself and this warship off my ass, I'll pound you into a million pieces."

"You want to answer that?" Alisa asked Abelardus.

He snorted. "Right."

"Brock is chewing on things and having a grand time," Jelena announced. "He doesn't like the taste of the metal, but some of the wires aren't bad."

"Glad to hear they're palatable. Mica, can you tell *what* he's chewing on?"

"No, this is a one-way communication for me." Mica waved at Jelena's hand on her head.

An alarm beep came from the sensors. The freighter was arming its weapons.

Alisa sent the *Nomad* off in another direction. She had no doubt that it would fire at her, not the massive Alliance craft.

The warship started after her, but it didn't come fully around to chase her. Instead, it made a partial turn, and sailed toward a distant star. She suspected the communication the ship had received was the reason for the course change, but Jelena clapped her hands together, as if she'd won a great victory.

"Brock made a mess. Three men caught him and got a leash on him, but not before he tore things up."

"Good," Alisa said, pushing her engines to top speed to take them farther from the moon and the warship. Fortunately, the other freighter returned to its route without firing at the *Nomad*.

"The captain of the warship is taking guff from the admiral," Abelardus said.

"About his pants?"

"About his dog."

"Ah."

"It looks like they've agreed that they don't have time to deal with us right now. Apparently, something important has come up, and they're calling all their ships into the area."

Alisa grimaced. Something important? Was it possible that the Alliance had already figured out where Tymoteusz was? What if they got to Thorian before she did?

"I hope this doesn't interfere with the mafia meeting," Alisa said. "Seeing all those Alliance ships may make Henneberry want to move it."

"Why?" Abelardus asked. "Isn't her business completely legal? Just because she's consorting with the mafia elite…"

"I don't know, but I suppose she wouldn't move the meeting spot without telling the caterer."

"Let's hope," Mica said.

CHAPTER TEN

A few minutes after Mica left NavCom, Leonidas appeared in the hatchway, all of his armor on, save for his helmet.

"The warship is heading off in another direction," Alisa said, smiling at Abelardus and Jelena.

"You mean I put on all my gear for no reason?" Leonidas looked disappointed that there wouldn't be a battle.

"Oh, there was a reason." Abelardus curled a lip at him.

"So I can pummel obnoxious Starseers?"

Jelena's eyebrows flew up, and she sank away from him.

Leonidas winced, catching the movement and apparently realizing his mistake.

"Leonidas only pummels select Starseers," Alisa said, twisting in her seat to pat Jelena on the shoulder. "The ones who are obnoxious to him."

"I'm not obnoxious," Abelardus said. "I'm refreshingly blunt."

Alisa did not deign to comment on his refreshingness. She hit the comm. "Beck?"

"I'm not going to need my armor, am I, Captain?" Beck asked, sounding harried. "Because I'm busy whipping egg whites for the dessert here."

"Wouldn't your armor enhance your ability to whip, chop, slice, and dice?"

"Er, I suppose it might. I've never tried."

"You may want to consider it, because we're on track to reach the rendezvous point in eight hours. We'll have to move the food over to the shuttle before then, and either Bravo Six or I will pilot the *Nomad* to a safe, out-of-the-way spot to wait while the catering mission goes on." She didn't yet know where that safe spot would be with all the Alliance ships around, but if she flew the craft out into space, staying out of the freight lanes, it should avoid notice.

"Either you or Bravo Six?" Beck asked. "You're not coming along for this event you cooked up?"

"I haven't decided." Alisa hated the idea of not being involved, but... "That would mean leaving the *Nomad* and my—" she looked at Jelena, "—cargo for a while."

"I can take care myself," Jelena said, lifting her chin.

"And there's Lady Westfall to keep an eye on her," Abelardus pointed out.

Alisa smiled sadly, more because she suspected the words were true. She hadn't expected to find such an independent little girl when she caught up with Jelena. Alisa supposed she'd had to learn that these last six months. Aside from her Starseer tutors, people she couldn't have been sure she could trust, she wouldn't have had anyone she could lean on. It shouldn't sting not to feel needed, and she told herself that as she nodded firmly.

"I'll definitely consider that. Get ready for either scenario, Beck. The rest of us should get some sleep." She waved to Leonidas, Abelardus, and most pointedly to Jelena. "Thank you for your help with the dog," she added quietly.

Jelena grinned. "Wait until you see what I'll do when we find that creep who kidnapped Thor."

"Sic dogs at him?"

"Maybe a whole pack, if I can find one."

"I know someone with a pack of chickens."

"That's a *flock*, Mom." Jelena rolled her eyes.

"Either way, they can be fierce."

Abelardus yawned and headed for the hatchway.

Leonidas lingered. "You said *us*, Alisa."

"Hm?" she asked.

"The rest of *us* should get some sleep. You have to be tired too."

"I am, and I will. After I make sure the Alliance isn't going to change its mind and come after us."

"You could set up an alert that you would hear in your cabin. I could *carry* you there if that would help."

"I'd rather you carried Jelena to *her* cabin. She has a hard time remembering where her bed is located when the lights dim for the night cycle."

Jelena's eyes grew round.

"I don't need to be carried," she blurted, and darted out of NavCom, sucking everything in to squeeze past Leonidas.

Alisa sighed sadly. "I suppose I could use you as a threat if she doesn't eat her vegetables. Eat your broccoli, or the big bad cyborg will get you… But I'd really rather she wasn't afraid of you."

"I'm sure that'll come with time. You were afraid of me at first, too, as I recall."

"I most certainly was not." To avoid meeting his eyes as she said that blatant lie, Alisa programmed a route for the autopilot on the control panel. She could feel his skeptical gaze on the back of her head. "Not *often*, anyway. Only when I pushed your buttons."

He stepped into the room and touched the side of her head. "From pushing my buttons to servicing them in only a few months. A decided improvement."

Alisa snorted. "You don't even know what servicing is yet."

"No, but I have ideas." His gentle touch turned into a massage of her scalp.

"Do you?" She leaned her head back into his hand, forgetting all about those controls she had been programming. Hopefully, they weren't on course to fly into Aldrin.

"I look forward to finding out if my ideas match yours." His voice came out husky, and he cleared his throat. "I should go before…before."

"Yeah," she said, letting her head loll back even further until she could look up at him. The way he gazed back into her eyes made her body heat, her muscles changing from relaxed to excited as he continued to rub her scalp. Little prickles of sensation ran up and down her nerves. "Maybe it's a good thing that you're still in your armor. Not much can happen with such a sturdy barrier between us."

"It can come off in seconds."

"Really? I haven't gotten out of mine in less than two minutes, and that usually involves tripping and falling onto my bunk."

Leonidas blinked slowly, his eyes intense as he gazed down her whole body. "I am now picturing that."

"Is it sexy?"

"Very much so."

"Does it lead to servicing?"

A wolfish grin spread across his face, but then he looked away, took a breath, and stepped back. "I better go."

"Leonidas…?"

He stopped with his back to her, his hand on the hatch jamb.

Alisa bit her lip. She didn't *want* him to go. But she also didn't want to be the horrible mother who was boinking a man her daughter was afraid of.

"I've been thinking of seeing Alejandro," he said, his words barely audible since he wasn't facing her.

"To check up on your…situation?"

He looked over his shoulder grimly. "To see if he's got a drug that would calm my libido. Or eliminate it. Until it's convenient to have a libido again."

"Is it as bad as it was those first couple of days?"

"A little less intense and demanding now, but it's still—" He cleared his throat. "As I said, I'm uncomfortable being around your telepathic daughter because I'm constantly thinking about *you*."

"Constantly?"

"Nearly. Sometimes, I take a break to think about food."

"Food is important."

"But then you sashay by me, and brush some curvy part up against my arm, and everything stands to attention."

"Leonidas, I do *not* sashay."

"Then why do I keep noticing your hips?"

"Because they're amazing. But look, I'm not trying to provoke you or flirt with you. You're just big, and it's hard to get past you in a corridor without touching something. I didn't know your arm was so sensitive."

Leonidas clunked his head against the hatch jamb. "I know you're not. It's not your fault."

Except, in a way, it was. She had insisted on his surgery, and now that it had worked, she couldn't be with him.

"I thought a drug might help," he said, "though I hate to turn to such things, since I either metabolize them too quickly to be of much use or they do odd things to my system."

"What if we see Yumi instead of Alejandro?" Alisa finished programming the autopilot, made sure there wasn't trouble nearby, and stood up. "She might have something more natural. And then Alejandro wouldn't insist on giving you a checkup."

"We? You're coming with me?"

She patted him on the back. "Couples should select their drugs together."

"Now?" He looked toward the dim corridor. "You think she'll be up?"

"We just had a run-in with an Alliance ship. I imagine everyone is still up." She gave him a shove, though she might as well have been shoving a wall. "Better to get it taken care of *before* we go on a critical mission where you don't want to be distracted by sashaying hips."

"I *knew* you sashayed."

"Not intentionally."

Leonidas ducked into the corridor and turned at the intersection toward Yumi's cabin. He knocked lightly at the hatch.

"Yes?" came a muffled call from inside. Yumi did not sound overly groggy.

"It's Leonidas."

"Come in."

He opened the hatch. Yumi and Young-hee were both inside, lying in identical corpse-like poses on mats on the deck. The lights were dimmed, and their eyes had an odd glassiness to them.

"Are we interrupting something?" Alisa asked, suspecting that their drug dealer might be sampling her own wares.

"We're moving toward wholeness through one of my breathing practices," Yumi said. "Would you care to join us?"

"Not at this time."

"There's mandala drawing in the next session," Young-hee said.

"Exciting," Alisa said.

Leonidas leaned back, looking like he was rethinking his decision to come here for help.

Yumi rolled into a sitting position. "What can I do for you, Captain? Leonidas?" She looked back and forth between them, her eyes closing to thoughtful slits.

"We're looking for something to…relax a person," Alisa said, resting a hand on Leonidas's shoulder. She almost withdrew it, thinking of his comment about casual touches arousing him, but he was still wearing his armor. She doubted he even felt the touch.

Yumi smiled widely. "I knew it was only a matter of time before you took me up on my offer." She scrambled to her feet and climbed onto her bunk to poke into the tin-filled cabinets above it. She grabbed one painted purple with a squat orange mushroom on the top. "Here we go." She hopped off and handed the tin to Leonidas. "Bliss. Over a hundred doses in here. Scientifically proven to increase the likelihood of relaxation, meditative thoughts, and intense orgasms that last far longer than typical."

Leonidas stared down at the container in his hand. Young-hee also stared at it, and then at him, and then at Alisa. A flush of heat warmed Alisa's cheeks, even though she hardly considered herself uncomfortable when discussing such matters. Leonidas shot Young-hee a wary look. *He probably wasn't enthused about discussing his sex life—or drugs to enhance his sex life—in front of her.*

"There's been a misunderstanding," Alisa said.

"You may want to remove your armor first," Yumi advised. "I believe it would impede relaxation and the ability to free your heart and your soul." She grinned. "And other things."

"This isn't what I had in mind," Leonidas said, giving Alisa a we-should-have-gone-to-Alejandro look. He stepped back, as if he would flee the scene, but Alisa rested a restraining hand on his forearm.

"Yumi," Alisa said. "While we appreciate your willingness to share this drug, we actually came looking for something that would lower a man's interest in sex. Temporarily, of course. Until we've figured out how to work our new family dynamics." She looked at Leonidas, who appeared mortified at having this conversation so openly. "Though I wonder if the qui-gorn would help, too, to keep Jelena from being able to read your thoughts. Or would she find it suspicious that she couldn't read you as well as others?"

"I would prefer not to have the thoughts at all," Leonidas said, his face turning glum. "Until such time as it would be appropriate to act upon them. For now, they just interfere with my efficiency."

"That must be why the empire didn't want horny cyborgs. Poor efficiency." Alisa meant it as a joke, but he didn't smile.

"I see," Yumi said. "I do have compounds capable of lowering a man's libido. There's one made from mussafras root that's a favorite of wives on Targos Moon. If their husbands were bothering them when they weren't in the mood, they would mix mussafras powder into their tea or wine. Or if their husband's eyes strayed, they would use the powder to make sure they were incapable of following their eyes with other organs. One moment please."

Alisa frowned at the idea that this was some kind of punishment for Leonidas. She wanted him to enjoy life, not be miserable. And she wanted to have sex with him and love him, not push him away. Sighing, she leaned her forehead against his shoulder while Yumi returned to her cupboard to rummage.

"If you ever just want time alone together," Young-hee said, "I would be happy to babysit. To keep Jelena suitably distracted."

"Thank you," Alisa said, not wanting to explain that it wasn't just that she wanted to be able to have sex with Leonidas without Jelena knowing. She didn't feel she *could* until Jelena had accepted him, if not as a surrogate father—surely that would take a long time—but as her mother's friend and partner. She didn't want to sneak around behind her daughter's back for her own pleasure. Even if it would be for Leonidas's pleasure too.

"How is sex handled in Starseer families?" Yumi asked, opening a different cabinet door to poke around. "If the children develop telepathy by the age of eight or nine, then you must have to deal with them knowing what's going on behind the parents' closed bedroom door. Are the parents open with it?"

"Starseer parents would be able to shield their thoughts from their children, so a closed door usually suffices," Young-hee said, "and the children are used to their parents being intimate from a young age, generally. There's less privacy overall in a household with people with extrasensory awareness. But it can be awkward, certainly, in a situation such as this, where a new mate replaces an old, a biological parent perhaps."

"Any advice?" Alisa asked. She wasn't sure if Young-hee's father had been a part of her life or if there had been other suitors along the way.

"My mother had a discussion with us girls. And then played the music loud in the bedroom."

Leonidas grunted.

Yumi hopped down from the bunk, this time with a purple tin with a brown root painted on the top. It was very similar to the first tin.

"Labeling those and listing the dosage and side effects might be more helpful than painting them," Alisa pointed out as she handed the tin to Leonidas.

"I would usually do that if I was making a little bag for someone," Yumi said, "but I understand cyborgs have fast metabolisms. You better just take the tin. Use what you need and bring the rest back whenever your situation has changed."

"Any side effects?" Leonidas eyed both tins warily.

"The mussafras may put you in touch with your feminine side."

His lip curled.

Alisa linked her arm with his. "Finally, I'll have a chance of getting needlepoint art for my wall."

"The masculine and feminine should be represented in each soul, regardless of sex," Yumi said. "I don't believe you'll experience anything untoward."

"So long as he doesn't become attracted to Beck instead," Alisa said.

"Well, I've told you what to do if his eyes stray." Yumi smirked.

"Here." Leonidas handed her the first tin.

Yumi stepped back, lifting her hands. "Keep it. Perhaps a time will come in the not too distant future where you wish to experiment." Yumi gave Alisa a pointed look, and Alisa wondered if she somehow knew that her and Leonidas's first—and sadly only—night together hadn't been as star-shattering as she had hoped, since he'd been so careful, so afraid he would hurt her.

Leonidas muttered a thanks and headed toward his cabin. Alisa stifled a yawn, thinking she should get some sleep, too, but with so many ships out there, she figured she should sleep in the pilot's seat.

"Goodnight, Leonidas," she said softly, pausing at the intersection. She groped for a way to say something more, to thank him for understanding her need to keep him at arm's length, but words eluded her.

He paused at his hatch to give her a long look over his shoulder, his gaze raking her entire form, his eyes hungry but with a hint of anguish there was well. "Goodnight," he said, and ducked into his cabin, closing the hatch firmly behind him.

Feeling lonely, Alisa headed to NavCom.

CHAPTER ELEVEN

Alisa slid her hands over the control panel in the imperial shuttle's cockpit, appreciating how easy it was to see the craft's stats on the floating holodisplays. The view screen stretched across the entire space, wrapping around Alisa and making it feel like a window looking out onto the stars, letting her see more than one hundred and eighty degrees around her. The shuttle had been built ten years earlier, but compared to everything she had flown for the Alliance—and since—the craft felt sleek and new. Too bad she was only using it to deliver food and her catering team, rather than flying it into battle. Or maybe not. The torpedo bays were empty, the blazer banks depleted. The shuttle would work well for obstacle courses and dodging enemy fire, but it was in no position to attack.

"Is black practical for a caterer?" Leonidas asked, walking up the aisle to take the other seat in the cockpit. He hadn't yet put on the grayish-blond wig and contoured nose, jaw, and cheek prosthetics that would change the look of his hair and face, but he was wearing the formal waiter's uniform she had ordered for him complete with button-down shirt, bowtie, and lapel jacket. He, however, managed to look like a bodyguard even in the servants' clothing. "What if Beck dusts me with flour? I thought cooks were supposed to wear white."

"I hate to demote you when you've imagined yourself in that lofty position, but you'll be carrying hor d'oeuvres on trays, not cooking anything."

Beck had finished all the preparation on the *Nomad*, so he shouldn't be in need of Leonidas's meager chef's skills. He'd found trays with lids somewhere—possibly back in the junkyard—and they had transferred everything over to this shuttle for the ride to the meeting spot. He, Abelardus, Yumi, and Young-hee were back there now, alternating between stirring things to keep them from solidifying and changing into serving costumes of their own. Alisa was surprised that Yumi and Young-hee had wanted to come, especially since Yumi's mafia ex-employer might be at this meeting, but maybe that was the very reason she'd wanted to come, to confront him and convince him to leave her alone. If so, Alisa hoped she would wait until after her team had planted the tracking device and filed back onto the shuttle.

Mica was back on the *Nomad* with the chickens, children, Alejandro and Tiang, and the rest of the Starseers, and had muttered something about engineers not being babysitters. Bravo Six had proven himself capable of piloting the freighter and was manning the controls in NavCom. He would get the ship out of trouble if trouble came looking. Or so Alisa hoped. She had second-guessed herself several times, wondering if she should stay aboard and let Beck and Leonidas lead this mission, but the entire thing had been her idea, and she felt she should be there to direct if things went wrong. Somehow, she couldn't imagine it going smoothly.

"Carrying food trays?" Leonidas asked. "Is that all?"

"You may get to carry drinks too."

"Hm. And what will *you* be doing during this scheme?"

Beck had been relieved that Alisa was coming along to take the onus of command off him. Leonidas hadn't seemed quite as enthused, but he had not objected. Alisa didn't know if that was because she'd finally gotten him to accept that she would throw herself into the chaos if at all possible or if he just didn't feel comfortable commanding a catering mission.

"I'll also be carrying trays," Alisa said. "I figure the waiters will make the best spies. We can mingle with the guests, and at some point, I'll find an opportunity to sneak away and place the tracking device." She patted her jacket, the feminine version of the one Leonidas was wearing, where she had the tracker snugged in a pocket. It was small, slender, and had a tacky substance on the back, so she could stick it under a table or shelf. Months ago, the Alliance had used something similar to track the *Nomad* to the Starseer temple on Arkadius.

Leonidas draped one of his meaty arms over the back of his seat and gazed thoughtfully at her. He seemed relaxed, and there was nothing intense or salacious about his gaze, as there sometimes had been lately, and she realized he might have taken some of Yumi's drug. She had noticed the hungry looks he'd sometimes given her in the last week or so, but hadn't realized how much of a charge there had been about him, the air almost crackling with electricity. This was old Leonidas, the one who was indifferent to sex. It was for the best, at least for now, but she missed the other looks, the ones that made her feel desirable and alive.

"Are you armed?" Leonidas asked.

"With my wits, yes."

His eyes closed to slits.

"What kind of waiter would wander around with an armory?" Alisa asked.

Leonidas opened his jacket, revealing his destroyer nestled in an inside holster.

"What if we're searched?"

"I'll growl ferociously at them to discourage that."

Alisa expected to have to walk through a security checkpoint to get aboard Henneberry's vessel and imagined alarms sounding at Leonidas's hardware. She wondered what else he had secreted inside his costume.

"As it is, we may have trouble if they ask to see our identifications," she said.

"We're a legitimate catering company with several ten-star reviews, Captain," Beck called up from the back. "And we'll be carrying trays of delectable food. I bet they'll just wave us toward the banquet hall."

"Unless they've been doing research and figured out our legitimate company has only been around for three days."

"We went out of our way to make it appear that we've been around longer," Yumi said brightly. "When would you like your drugs?"

"Not until right before we go on board," Alisa said. "And this time, you can tell us how much of a dose to take."

Leonidas's eyebrows rose.

"Just in case some of Tymoteusz's people are at the meeting," Alisa said. "I'm assuming this is preliminary, and that they won't be here, but if they are, I don't want them reading our thoughts as soon as we walk on."

She hoped that having a couple of Starseers on her infiltration team would give *her* the advantage instead.

"I see." Leonidas shifted his jacket back into place, hiding the big gun. "Can you see my bulge?"

"Uh, you're not supposed to ask a lady that."

His brow furrowed, but then he seemed to grasp the innuendo. "Not ever?"

"At least not in public places."

No, not ever, Abelardus said into her mind. *Nobody wants to hear about his bulge.*

Alisa checked the sensors as an excuse to ignore him. "We're coming up to the meeting coordinates, and there's a bunch of ships waiting at them. Lots of yachts, with one big one in the middle. And when I say big, I mean gargantuan. That thing rivals an Alliance warship. I have a feeling that's where we're going to be directed to go."

It seemed strange to see all these ships out here, loitering in empty space. Aldrin and Baku Moon were still on the sensors, but there was nothing out this far, not so much as an asteroid tumbling past.

"I wonder how big the crew is," Leonidas said, eyeing the big yacht. "Is it surprising that, on a ship that large, she wouldn't have had enough people to handle the meal preparation in-house?" He scratched his jaw. Wondering if they were flying into a trap?

But who would want to bother to trap them? The Alliance wanted the *Nomad*, yes, and the empire might want Alisa's team, too, if it believed they had information on Thorian's whereabouts, but what would some entrepreneurs and mafia families care about her people? That Henneberry woman had been interested in having Alisa executed, but now that she thought that had been taken care of...

Alisa frowned as it occurred to her that Solstice might have lied about that. What if she'd told Henneberry that she and Leonidas had escaped? And were looking for her?

"This is more than meal preparation," Beck said from the back. "This is an event. It requires an exquisite dining experience."

"Is it hard to prepare exquisite meals when your portable grill is the main cooking source for everything?" Young-hee asked.

"Absolutely not. My grill is amazing, and my sauces make everything divine."

"Is it just me, or has he grown more pompous about his food since I came on board?" Abelardus asked.

"He's gotten a couple of big deals since then," Alisa said. "His pompousness is deserved."

"Thank you, Captain," Beck said. "I think."

A comm button flashed, and another holodisplay popped up, this one displaying a woman's face. Her dark hair was pulled back in a bun, and she wore a blue uniform of sorts. It wasn't Alliance or imperial. Something Henneberry had concocted for her staff?

"Personal Touch Catering Company Shuttle," she said, "This is the *Starry Elegance*. We look forward to having you aboard. Please fly your shuttle into our port bay for docking."

"Yes, ma'am," Alisa said, without offering her name. She'd made one up for this, but was hoping Beck was right and that he wouldn't be asked to present identification for his individual staff members, that the baskets of veggies painted on the side of the shuttle would convince people of their legitimacy.

"We're clearing you for landing now."

"Thank you."

Alisa closed the comm. "A bay instead of an airlock."

"We won't be able to fly away of our own accord if things turn bad," Leonidas said.

"Abelardus may be able to convince whoever's in charge of the doors to open them," Alisa said, "but I agree, attaching via an airlock would have made me feel freer."

"I wonder if they have a grab beam."

"On a civilian yacht? That seems like an unlikely accessory."

"They have weapons." Leonidas pointed to e-cannon ports visible all over the hull of the ship, then tapped a few spots that might have represented blazers. "They could have other combat accessories."

"I had no idea civilian yachts needed to be so militarily equipped."

"They may be recent upgrades. The system is more dangerous these days."

Alisa tightened her jaw and resisted the temptation to get into their old argument. Besides, she couldn't deny that there had been more lawlessness in the system since the empire had fallen.

"Looks like eighteen ships here in total," Alisa said, counting on the sensors as they flew closer. The larger ones were floating near the Henneberry yacht—they must have sent shuttles over to its bays—while a few medium-sized craft were hooked up via airlock tubes. Those vessels too large for the bays and without shuttles of their own, Alisa assumed. "Henneberry must have gotten a lot of the mafia families interested in her establishing-an-all-new-government scheme."

"One friendly to corporate and mafia interests, no doubt," Leonidas grumbled.

"Even less appealing than having the Alliance in charge, eh?"

His grunt wasn't exactly one of agreement. "I'm surprised you didn't tell the Alliance about this party. I'd think your government would relish the opportunity to take out a bunch of rebels at once."

"It crossed my mind, but every time I've called the Alliance in to deal with our mutual enemies, it hasn't gone well for us. Besides, I don't see Tymoteusz's ship here. Unless he's arriving fashionably late, we need to hope that Henneberry will lead us to his location. If the Alliance were to come in with cannons blasting, that wouldn't likely happen." And they wouldn't find Thorian. She had promised her daughter that they'd get him back, so she had to put that above all other concerns. Besides, stopping revolutionaries wasn't her job.

"True."

Alisa flew the shuttle around an oval-shaped merchant vessel attached to the yacht, and the port bay entrance came into view. There weren't doors, but a forcefield, and she watched the sensors as she put them into a good position to fly inside. The energy field disappeared.

Feeling a twinge of nervousness, she sailed into a cavernous bay, one where a dozen other shuttles were parked, magnetically sealed to the deck. Most were clearly civilian models, a couple with paint jobs that made them stick out—Beck cleared his throat uneasily when they flew over a green shuttle with white dragons cavorting on the hull. Two, however, were imperial military shuttles, or had been once. One had been painted a garish gold and silver. The other was black, with nothing changed except for the name. Instead of the usual numerals and letters nomenclature the military had used, the white letters now read: *The King's Darter.*

"Which one of these arrogant blowhards thinks of himself as a king?" Alisa asked, choosing a landing spot well away from the imperial shuttles. She didn't need anyone noticing that their catering craft was of a similar make.

"Which one doesn't?" Beck asked.

"Well, presumably not Solstice," Yumi said. "Were you able to tell which ship was hers?"

"No, she never offered me a tour of her flagship when we were there," Alisa said, glancing at Leonidas. "How about you?"

"She offered. I did not accept."

"She probably only wanted you to tour her bedroom."

Jealousy, Alisa? Abelardus asked silently. *So unseemly.*

I'm not jealous. I'm petty. There's a difference.

Is the latter less unseemly?

Probably not.

"Do I get to make snide comments someday when a pretty man wants you to tour his bedroom?" Leonidas asked.

"I don't think you're capable of snide comments, you being rather noble and honorable and such, but that would absolutely be within your right."

"Excellent. I shall prepare them."

"Now we just need to find a pretty man to incense you into using them."

Leonidas looked over his shoulder to where Abelardus was sneaking samples out of one of Beck's covered trays. "Hm."

Alisa might have pointed out that Abelardus never would have lured her to his bedroom, but she was too busy setting the shuttle down in an empty spot hemmed in by two other craft.

"Better put your new face on, Leonidas," Beck said. "It won't take them long to pressurize the hangar bay and come looking for their victuals."

Leonidas rose to his feet and touched Alisa's shoulder. "You, I hope, have a face kit too. You're just as notorious as I am, these days."

"Flattering."

"Did you just say victuals?" Abelardus asked Beck. "Are we back in the Old West on Old Earth?"

"Well, I wouldn't be surprised if we ended up in a shootout in the shuttle bay corral."

"There will be no shootouts," Alisa said, turning off the engines. A soft *kerthunk* came from underneath the shuttle, as the magnetized docking station came on. "This will go smoothly with no trouble." Perhaps if she told herself that, it would be more likely to happen.

"No need for the cyborg to show anyone his bulge?" Abelardus asked.

"No need whatsoever."

"That's a relief."

Alisa unfastened her harness and trotted into the small lav where she had stashed her costume. The imperial shuttle had once been used for combat missions and was full of seats for burly infantry soldiers—perhaps even burly cyborg soldiers. There weren't a lot of amenities, such as mirrors in the lav. She had to wave Yumi in to help with her prosthetics, since one-handedly using the reverse camera image on her netdisc proved difficult.

"How do I look?" she asked when Yumi backed away.

"Pretty."

"Pretty? That's not important. Do I look innocent and wholesome? Not like someone scheming up trouble?"

"I don't think any amount of makeup could create that look for you," Abelardus said, stepping out of another lav. With his long braids of hair, there wasn't much to be done to disguise them—he hadn't been willing to entertain the notion of a head shaving—but he had pulled them back in a bun, and he had traded his black robe for blue snagor-hide trousers and a similar top and jacket to the one Leonidas wore.

Alisa waved at the trousers. "The waiter's bottoms didn't fit?"

"They were too tight in pivotal areas. Your cyborg isn't the only one with magnitude, you know."

"Ew," Beck said. "Don't let him talk during the mission, Captain. He'll only get us in trouble."

"I don't know. He's handsome. I thought he could flirt with Ms. Henneberry and keep her and her bodyguards distracted while Leonidas and I snoop and find a place to stick the tracker."

"Henneberry?" Abelardus asked. "Is she young and nubile?"

"Nubile?" Beck asked. "Now who's using words that went out of style before the colony ships left Old Earth?"

"She invented CargoExpress," Alisa said, "and I'm fairly certain they delivered my diapers when I was a baby, so I'll let you guess as to her age and nubileness."

Abelardus curled a lip.

Young-hee, who was already in her outfit—cook's whites, the same as Beck—slapped him in the chest. "Don't dismiss a woman just because she's older than you."

"What if she's a *lot* older than me?"

"She'll probably be honored by your attention. Unless handsome young men often flirt with her, in the hopes of getting some of her money out of her. You don't want her money, do you?"

"If I wanted money, I could go to a casino and get it, the same as you. Why are you interrogating me, Young-hee?"

"Because you deserve it," Alisa said.

"Is that true?" Abelardus looked around the gathering.

Young-hee, Yumi, Beck, and Alisa nodded at him.

Leonidas also nodded as he stepped out of one of the lavs, his gray-blond wig and prosthetics in place. The pale hair made him look older, as had been her intent when choosing it. She figured an older cyborg wouldn't be so intimidating and might even make people less likely to realize what he was. The prosthetics made his face softer too. Less lean and fierce. Alisa would have known him anywhere by his blue eyes, but she didn't think someone who knew him less well—or spent less time gazing into his eyes—would recognize him. Good.

"I believe we're ready," she said, looking around at her people.

Beck had a full prosthetic mask on, changing his every feature—he must not have wanted to take chances with the White Dragon people. Abelardus and Young-hee hadn't donned prosthetics, since Solstice had never seen them, and Alisa doubted the other mafia people had any familiarity with the Starseers either. Yumi wore a black uniform identical to the one Alisa had, and she had face alterations of her own accord, rounding her chin and changing her snub nose into a more prominent straight one.

A knock sounded at the rear hatch.

Alisa took a breath. "Time to find out how tough their security is."

And whether her team was walking into a trap.

CHAPTER TWELVE

Leonidas walked at Alisa's side as she pushed a wheeled serving cart down the ramp and onto the shuttle bay deck. He carried a stack of covered trays that rose to his chin. Hopefully, security would be too interested in his load to give him a good look and notice that those arms and shoulders were a touch big and meaty for a normal human being. People might believe that a cyborg had retired from the imperial army and become a bounty hunter, pirate, or security professional, but a caterer? That might be hard to buy.

Yumi, Young-hee, and Abelardus came behind them, Abelardus also with an armload of trays, while the women carried hand tractors, hovering the rest of the serving dishes along after the group. Mica had complained vociferously about having her precious tools taken, and she'd made Alisa promise to return them. Or buy fancy new ones if they were lost.

Beck led the way, his hands empty, a chef's hat on his head, the logo for their fake company on his chest, and an arrogant tilt to his chin. Naturally, the chef and owner of the business wouldn't carry his own food. He would greet and hobnob with the important people. And security.

A couple of those people—armed men in blue uniforms—waited at the bottom of the ramp. Alisa reminded herself to keep her mouth shut, that Beck was in charge here. She was a simple waitress who would serve drinks and food. And sneak away from her employer at the first opportunity.

"You're wearing your scheming expression," Leonidas murmured.

"Not my you're-sexy-when-you're-scheming expression?" Alisa smoothed her face. So much for the prosthetics making her look innocent.

"My awareness of sexiness is somewhat blunted by Yumi's drug."

"I suppose that's for the best," she said, though she still felt guilty that he was taking a drug because of her—and her daughter. Jelena wasn't along on this mission. He wouldn't have needed to do it here.

"This way, sir," one of the security guards said after conferring with Beck for a moment.

Alisa exhaled a long, relieved breath. Neither of the men had asked for identification.

Whistling cheerfully, Beck followed them. Alisa pushed her cart along the flight deck, wincing at a wheel that rattled. They were supposed to be a high-end catering company, not one that had rescued rusty equipment from a junkyard.

"Trouble," Leonidas murmured before Beck and the guards reached the door.

It was made from clear Glastica, and Alisa could make out a couple more people in uniforms waiting on the other side, but she wasn't sure yet what Leonidas meant, other than that the two men were large, their heads nearly brushing the ceiling. A much smaller, dark-skinned woman in white waited behind them, dwarfed by their size.

As the group drew closer, Alisa started to get an inkling of what Leonidas meant. Those guards weren't just tall. They were huge. Broad-shouldered with tree-trunk arms and legs. Their uniforms must have been custom tailored.

"Cyborgs?" Alisa whispered.

"I recognize them," Leonidas murmured back so quietly she barely heard him. There was a hardness in his voice, not the warmth of someone spotting old comrades.

Reminded that other cyborgs would share his enhanced hearing, all she did was give him a quick, bleak look and touch her nose, hoping to imply that his costume should save him from being recognized. Assuming he didn't talk. If they had been in his unit, wouldn't they recognize their commander's voice? They probably hadn't spent as much time as Alisa gazing into Leonidas's blue eyes, but between his size and his voice, anyone familiar with him would be sure to recognize him.

"You better play the role of a mute cyborg caterer," Alisa breathed.

The door opened, and Leonidas did not respond.

Alisa should have found the cyborgs intimidating, especially since one had a scar from eye to lip that made him look like a villain out of a horror vid, but after squinting suspiciously at Beck, both men waved their noses toward the trays floating or being carried into the wide, marble-tiled corridor outside of the bay. Now familiar with cyborg nasal enhancements and cyborg appetites, she could easily picture them scheming ways to get samples for themselves. Neither man was very old, mid-twenties perhaps, so they couldn't have been more than corporals or maybe young sergeants when the war had ended. She hoped that would make them polite to Leonidas if they *did* figure out who he was, but the hardness that had been in his voice when he pointed them out made her uneasy.

"Chef Brier?" the woman said to Beck.

"Yes, ma'am. Chef Lunquist, right?" Beck lifted his hand in a salute that looked comical in conjunction with the white cap on his head. "We've been conversing about the menu via texts."

"Yes, we have. I haven't heard of you before, Chef." Lunquist was a diminutive woman, even without the seven-foot-tall bookends, but she launched a formidable glare.

"Oh? I grew up around here. Are you from the Aldrin Moons?"

"No, but I've heard of most of the important chefs from around the empire and beyond."

"The empire isn't beyond much of anything anymore," Beck said, and shrugged. "If it helps, I haven't heard of you either."

Judging by the cool squint Lunquist gave him, that didn't help.

Alisa noticed the cyborgs had stopped looking at—and sniffing—the food trays. Now, they were eyeing Leonidas.

Alisa shifted uneasily. Already, this wasn't going as smoothly as she had hoped.

"I'll let my food put me in your memory, Chef," Beck said, waving over his shoulder at Alisa and the others. "If you'll show me where I can set up?"

Lunquist looked at the cyborgs. "You going to search them?"

Search? Shit. Alisa pointedly did not look at Leonidas—or his bulge.

"Maybe this one," Scar said, walking forward to take a closer look at Leonidas, or maybe so he could frown down at him from an intimidating height.

Since Leonidas was six and a half feet tall, Alisa never thought of him as small, and the mutant extra six inches these two carried still didn't make him look tiny, but for once, he wasn't the biggest man in the room.

"Who are you?" Scar poked Leonidas in the shoulder.

"That's Clive," Alisa said. So much for hoping nobody would notice Leonidas was a cyborg...So far, he hadn't reacted. He was staring straight ahead, as if he were an android. "He's not a big talker," she added.

She wouldn't go so far as to claim he was mute, but maybe she could imply it and they wouldn't demand answers.

"Words are hard, huh?" Scar's buddy said, a brown-skinned man who apparently subscribed to the same fashion magazine as Beck, because he, too, had his hair dyed, though his was white instead of blond. Alisa dubbed him Whitey because it did not sound intimidating.

"Nice suit," Scar told Leonidas, poking him in the shoulder again. "You a waiter?" He sniggered, as if a cyborg waiter was the most hilarious thing.

"Jobs were hard to come by after the war," Alisa said. "I used to be a pilot. Now I carry trays. So, what?"

"Nobody's talking to you, Lips," Scar said.

Alisa glared at him, wishing Leonidas *could* reveal his identity. She wagered these asteroid kissers would wet themselves if they found out he had been their C.O.

She looked over her shoulder at Abelardus. *You listening to my mind, by chance?*

I'm always attentive to your needs.

Can you convince these brutes to leave Leonidas alone?

Absolutely not. This is lovely.

Abelardus. If they search him, they'll find his destroyer. And they'll want to see all of our idents.

"Can't you talk, mech?" Scar prodded Leonidas again. Those were not gentle nudges. Leonidas visibly braced himself to keep from being shoved backward.

"What's the problem here?" Beck asked, puffing out his chest, though at six feet, he was dwarfed by the towering cyborgs. "Ms. Henneberry won't be happy if you buffoons spill her guests' food."

"Buffoons?" Scar's arm whipped out too fast to follow.

Alisa was aware of Leonidas stepping forward, but he could not do anything with his arms full of food, and there was nowhere to set it down. Beck tried to dodge the cyborg, but he was too slow. Scar grabbed him by his jacket, hoisted him into the air, and jammed him against the bulkhead.

"*Jason,*" Chef Lunquist hissed.

Jason. What an inappropriate name for such a thug. Alisa was on the verge of rolling her cart over his foot and spilling soup on his trousers when he dropped Beck.

"You're not anyone fancy," Scar said. "Don't think you can order me around or insult us."

Beck sniffed and smoothed his white coat.

"Either search them or don't," Lunquist said. "We don't have a lot of time to set up, and I want to get them started."

"Just a minute," Scar said. "I'm suspicious about this one. He's a cyborg, and he doesn't talk."

"Better than a cyborg that talks too much," Alisa said.

You're about to get yourself jammed up against the bulkhead too, Abelardus informed her as Scar pinned her with a glare.

Alisa decided to keep her mouth shut, mostly because she had a feeling Leonidas would drop those trays and react—ferociously—if Scar did that to her. Instead, she smiled at Lunquist, assuming she was nominally in charge here.

"We're eager to get set up too. Can you show us to the banquet hall, or whatever the equivalent is on this ship?"

"Yes, this way." Lunquist waved for them to follow and turned down the corridor.

Alisa started to feel relieved, but the cyborgs only let Beck pass before positioning themselves to block Leonidas's way. What was wrong with these idiots? Did nobody on the fancy yacht bake them cookies?

"We want to know who your porter is before you go in," Scar said, glancing at Alisa instead of Beck, who had paused a few steps beyond them.

Had he picked up that she was in charge? And if so, would that mean trouble?

"Clive?" Beck asked. "We already gave you his name. You want his résumé too?"

"Maybe they think he's cute," Abelardus said, "and they want to ask him on a date."

Scar turned his humorless glower onto Abelardus and took a step toward him. But Leonidas shifted slightly, and the thug bumped into his shoulder, pulling Scar's attention back to him.

Alisa wasn't sure that was a good idea. Abelardus ought to be able to protect himself with some coercion or telepathic attack. Scar didn't seem like he had the mental fortitude to resist a Starseer's mind games.

Please, Abelardus said silently, *he doesn't have the mental fortitude to resist the mind games of a rock.*

"Were you in the military, mech?" Scar asked, leaning close enough that Leonidas would feel his breath on his cheek. "I don't recognize you, but you *are* old."

Only someone who knew Leonidas well would catch the flash of indignation in his eyes. Other than that, he did not react. He was too wise to risk the mission over some personal slight. He tried to take a step forward, but Scar shifted to block him again.

"Answer me, or you're not getting in, old man."

"He's suspicious, isn't he?" Whitey asked.

"There aren't that many cyborgs around, and I've never seen one acting as a servant." Scar sneered. "No veteran would choose such a menial job."

"As opposed to being the security thugs for some rich old woman?" Alisa muttered. "*So* important. I'm sure the entire system would fall into the suns if you weren't here servicing Henneberry's needs."

She expected the comment about servicing to go over their heads, as innuendos had for Leonidas before his surgery, but Scar clearly knew he was being insulted. His face reddened, and he lunged for her, almost knocking Leonidas's trays out of his arms.

Alisa jumped back, bumping her shoulder against the bulkhead. She would have been too slow, but Leonidas managed to rearrange his load so that he could grab Scar, catching his wrist with one hand.

"Civilian model," he said, as Scar whirled toward him with fury in his eyes.

"What?" Scar demanded.

"Me. Not all cyborgs were soldiers." He was lowering his voice, making it gruff to disguise it.

"Civilian. You got all the surgeries just so you could carry dishes?" The sneer returned, derision in Scar's eyes. He jerked his hand away, and Leonidas let him go. "That mean you've never killed anyone, mech?"

"Only those who harass my employers." Leonidas held his gaze, his own eyes utterly cold, utterly deadly, the prosthetics not softening his face, his intent, as much as Alisa had intended for them to. She was glad he never looked at her like that.

"I bet," Scar grumbled. He considered Leonidas for another long moment, then opened his mouth. But no words came out. His forehead scrunched up, and several seconds passed.

Alisa noticed Young-hee looking at him intently.

Alisa caught Abelardus's gaze. *Is she doing something?*

Alas, yes. She didn't find this encounter as entertaining as I did.

She's wise and mature for her years.

I just wanted to see your cyborg flattened to the deck with soup all over his face, Abelardus said.

You are not wise and mature for your years.

Your words are a dagger to my heart, Captain.

Scar shook his head, mumbled something under his breath, and stepped aside so Leonidas could pass. "I'll be watching you, mech. I don't trust you."

Without a word, Leonidas continued forward, his trays in his hands. Alisa walked at his side, and they caught up to Beck and Lunquist. Young-hee, Yumi, and Abelardus came behind with their own loads. Unfortunately, the cyborgs walked right behind them. Alisa had hoped their duty was to guard the flight deck and that they would stay there, but her luck wasn't that good today. At least they hadn't asked to see her team's identifications.

Cyborgs seem to handle security issues with pissing contests, Abelardus commented silently. None of them spoke aloud, not when they were hemmed in by the enemy.

Those two aren't wise and mature for their years either, Alisa thought.

They were the kinds of thugs who had driven terror into her people during the war, far more like what she expected from cyborg soldiers. She'd met a couple of younger ones who'd seemed like reasonable people—at least when they had known who Leonidas was—but suspected Leonidas was an exception rather than the rule. Maybe he had also been an asshole when he'd been twenty-five.

Such unflattering thoughts for you to have of your devoted lover.

Is there a reason you're in my head right now? Alisa asked. They were winding through spacious marble-tiled corridors, the threat subsided, at least for the moment.

So I can leap to eagerly obey your commands should the need to arise.

I'm so fortunate to have an eager crew.

You are.

Their walk ended in a vast hall as large as the shuttle bay, but far less practical. The space rose several stories, with massive chandeliers floating near the ceilings, each one containing thousands of crystals. Velvety curtains framed huge rectangular portholes that looked out upon the stars. Golden banners curled up tall marble columns with dragons and other mythological figures carved into the stone. The tile floors gleamed, not a speck of dust on them or anywhere else.

Here and there, plush sets of furniture invited guests to sit, and many people were taking advantage of them. Perhaps a hundred people already occupied the space, many in opulent clothing, some sporting eccentric fashions. Some wore suits made from rich materials. Others wore simpler suits and carried stun guns openly at their hips as they scrutinized the hall. Several people like that turned to watch the catering team walk in. Bodyguards. Probably at least one for each mafia representative or business tycoon in attendance.

Lunquist led Alisa's group to long stone tables set up in the back of the hall, lacy tablecloths only partially hiding their stout legs. They were not the types of tables that could be folded up and easily stored away when not in use. It would probably take a couple of androids—or cyborg thugs—to move one.

"Set up there," Lunquist said. "Buffet style is fine. A lot of the guests here are people of—" she sniffed, "—simple tastes."

Ah, was she not enthused by her employer's decision to include the mafia families in her scheme?

"We will expect you to carry drinks and hor d'oeuvres around on trays." Lunquist waved at Alisa, Leonidas, and Yumi, those in waitstaff attire. "I'll have a couple of my people come down to help you. We don't use androids or robots for serving here. Ms. Henneberry prefers the human touch. That said, don't even think about spilling something on a guest."

The two cyborgs, who were still lurking nearby, stood right behind Leonidas. Whitey jostled him in the back, as if to encourage spilling. Leonidas ignored him.

They're really drawn to him, Alisa thought.

Yes, I have a theory, Abelardus replied in her head.

What? she asked warily, certain it would be more puerile than enlightening.

They've got those enhanced senses, right? Maybe they're like dogs.

I'd happily compare those two to dogs, except that seems unfair to dogs across the system.

Ever see how fixed dogs act around an intact male?

Uh, not really. There hadn't been many packs of hounds roving the *Nomad* when she had been growing up.

They harass him, and fights are common. Probably because they can smell that he's got something they don't.

Alisa snorted, skeptical at the hypothesis. She had a feeling these two were just assholes through and through and would bully anyone they perceived as weaker than they were. Which would be most people in the system.

"We have a sommelier too," Lunquist said, finishing her spiel. "He'll come down with wines appropriate for the occasion."

"That's a relief," Beck muttered after she left. "The *Nomad's* wine cellar was a touch sparse."

"Sh," Alisa murmured, tilting her head toward the cyborgs. Mentioning the name of their ship where those two could overhear was not a good idea.

Beck wiggled his fingers in acknowledgment, then waved to the table. "Let's get set up. Looks like a lot of the guests are already here. This shindig might be starting soon."

Alisa unloaded her cart while the others did the same with their trays. Leonidas looked relieved to have his hands free again. Even if he was doing a good job at ignoring the ribbing, he did flex his shoulders and eye each of the cyborgs.

"Plates, did you not bring plates?" a man with an effeminate voice said, striding up to them and tsking mightily as he maneuvered a hand tractor. Cases of wine floated behind him. "Syria, bring trays, plates, napkins, everything we need for our guests. Oh dear, this is lackluster. I was expecting much more thoroughness. Will there be enough food for all?" He pressed long, slender fingers to his cheek as he surveyed Alisa's team and the food being spread along the tables.

Beck led the man aside, and they talked in low voices.

A couple more servers came out with the requested items, and they filled wine glasses, working with impressive efficiency. Alisa soon found herself with dozens of glasses of a sparkling white wine balanced on a tray in her hands. She needed to slip away as soon as possible to find an out-of-the-way spot to place the tracker, but she would take a couple of laps around the hall first, see if she heard any useful information. It crossed her mind to simply place the tracker under one of the heavy stone tables, since they didn't likely get moved often, but if Henneberry's people grew suspicious of her catering team later on, they might search all the spots they had been. Besides, she was sure there would be cameras monitoring this hall. Slipping off to a remote lavatory and sticking the tracker behind the toilet seemed like a better bet.

Young-hee moved out into the room with Alisa, also carrying a tray full of wine glasses, even though she wore a cook's uniform. Alisa didn't object, since she could more effectively spy on people with her mental talents.

They passed numerous bodyguards, either lurking outside of groups of chatting men and women, or leaning against the walls and watching everything. They never accepted wine glasses. A lot of the guests didn't accept the alcohol either. Some of them were laid back, talking and chatting easily, but at least two-thirds of the people in the hall looked warily at their colleagues as they spoke, their hands never straying far from holsters hidden by jackets. A few arguments broke out. These people were rivals, if not outright enemies, and Alisa began to realize the magnitude of what Henneberry was planning. Getting a bunch of mafia families to work together would be a challenge, to say the least.

"Captain?" Young-hee whispered, drifting closer, half the drinks on her tray gone.

"Alisa," Alisa corrected, not wanting anyone to overhear her being addressed as anything other than a waitperson.

"That man in the dark blue suit over there…Do you see him?"

Alisa followed her gaze, picking out the middle-aged fellow with an affable presence who did a lot of hand waving as he chatted. He was among a group of men who laughed easily, seemingly enthralled by whatever story he was telling. Despite the blue-suited man's civilian attire, he had short hair, appeared lean and fit, and, with another outfit and a cooler demeanor, could have easily passed for one of the bodyguards.

"Yes," Alisa murmured.

"I think he's a spy."

"Oh? For whom?" She assumed Young-hee could read his thoughts and was basing her assumptions on that.

"I don't know. I can't see what he's thinking, as I can with the rest of the guests. He may have taken qui-gorn."

"Why would he have done that to come here?" Alisa hadn't seen anyone in black robes yet. As much as she wished Tymoteusz were here, his ship hadn't been out there, so she didn't expect him. Presumably, this was a preliminary meeting, and those who proved interested after hearing Henneberry talk might be invited to actually meet the *chasadski*.

"Like us, perhaps he wasn't positive Tymoteusz wouldn't be here," Young-hee said.

"Is a drug the only thing that could be keeping you from reading his thoughts?"

"He could have Starseer training himself. I can't tell my own kind just by looking at them."

"Are your people allowed to go out in public without a robe?" Alisa couldn't imagine the affable man with a staff and robe. Starseers all seemed stuffier and more self-important than this fellow.

Young-hee raised an eyebrow, but if she was reading Alisa's thoughts, all she said was, "On occasion," and plucked at the hem of her costume.

Someone else in the group started talking, and Blue Suit took a sip from a wine glass. A very small sip. Like a man pretending to drink without imbibing enough to impair his senses. He looked across the room, past groups of people, and his gaze locked onto Alisa. It wasn't a cold gaze, but it did seem to be a *knowing* gaze. And that made her uneasy.

A woman walked past, and Alisa offered her tray. "Something to drink, ma'am?"

She positioned herself so that the woman, when she paused, stood between her and Blue Suit. By the time the guest selected her drink and moved away, the man had turned his attention back to his group and was chatting again. Still, Alisa remained unsettled by the way his gaze had landed directly on her and stuck. He couldn't have recognized her through her costume, could he? If he was a Starseer, it might be easy to see past physical appearances.

"Young-hee," Alisa murmured, heading back to the tables, ostensibly to refill her tray. "I believe I'll leave the spying to you and Abelardus. Please feel free to root through people's minds to gather information. In the meantime, I'm going to try to sneak away and place the tracker."

If she didn't get that done, and if her group got caught, then this whole scheme would have been for nothing.

"Seems like a good idea," Young-hee said, peering over her shoulder and frowning at the blue-suited man.

CHAPTER THIRTEEN

As Alisa approached the table to refill her tray, in the hope that she might meander into the corridors with it and nobody would find that unusual, Scar's obnoxious voice reached her ears. Beck was talking with the sommelier, Yumi was stirring the various dishes to keep them fresh, and Leonidas was standing at the end of the tables, his arms folded over his chest. He looked far more like a bodyguard than a server. Scar hadn't left his side, and the other big brute lurked nearby, too, though he was at least pretending to watch the hall and the guests.

"So tell me, civvie cyborg," Scar said as Alisa reached the table, "how many roasted turkeys do your implants allow you to carry at once? Is that how your usefulness is rated?"

Alisa gritted her teeth as she placed glasses on her tray. She wished Leonidas could flatten the brute, but she didn't truly know if he could do that. He'd beaten a younger cyborg before, but he had also admitted to her that the younger soldiers tended to have more recent and more advanced implants, along with the usual perks of youth. It certainly seemed unlikely that he would be able to handle two of them in a fight.

And they couldn't fight. Not here. She couldn't even imagine what would be done to the members of her "catering company" if cyborgs started flying all over the hall, smashing into tables and hurling food onto guests. Even if her team made it back to the shuttle bay, they wouldn't be able to leave without a yacht crew member hitting a button somewhere to lower the force-field. If she'd had Ostberg along, he might have had the mechanical aptitude to manipulate computers from a distance, but she didn't think Abelardus or Young-hee had that gift. She doubted any of them had any idea about the layout of this fancy yacht or where the shuttle bay controls were located.

"Nah, not turkeys," Whitey said. "Perunish hens. Bet his implants were considered a success if he could carry a hundred Perunish hens in one arm, maybe juggling them while he was at it."

"Yeah, juggling," Scar said. "Do you use your implants to perform for your customers, mech?"

Leonidas met Alisa's eyes. She expected a pained or aggrieved expression, but instead, he flickered his gaze toward a corridor behind the tables.

Had he heard about something going on back there that she might want to look into? Or maybe he thought the corridor would be a good place to place the tracker? She had seen guests filtering into the banquet hall from that direction and didn't know if she agreed. The servants had come out of a different passage, one that might have all manner of storage rooms and closets—maybe she could put the tracker in the wine cellar—but she would have to walk past the cyborgs to access that corridor. She didn't particularly want to draw their attention. Even if they were pestering Leonidas endlessly, it was better that they be focused on him than on performing actual security duties.

Abruptly, she realized that might be why he thought this would be a good time for her to explore. She looked at the corridor he had indicated and met his eyes. He nodded almost imperceptibly.

"I can carry one hundred hens, fifty turkeys, *and* throw obnoxious people out of the kitchen at the same time," Leonidas said, turning toward the cyborgs.

"Is that right?"

They puffed out their chests, and one cracked his knuckles, as if they thought they were about to get the fight they clearly wanted. Alisa hoped that was not the case, but she took advantage of their distraction, sliding the full tray into her arms and stepping away from the table. She tried to catch Young-hee's eye, thinking it would be smart to take her and her Starseer senses along to warn her about trouble coming, but some smarmy old man had made his way to the table and was trying to charm her. Abelardus was on the far side of the banquet hall, delivering small skewers of grilled fowl, and looked like he was mentally eavesdropping on people.

One of them was Solstice, who stood in an elegant beaded dress with a swooping neckline, two android bodyguards standing nearby. She glanced toward the catering table a couple of times, a worried expression in her eyes. She had probably picked out Leonidas, and maybe Alisa, even with the costumes. At least she didn't look like she wanted to rat them out.

"Alisa?" Yumi murmured, coming over to stir a chafing dish next to her.

"Grab a tray," Alisa said. "Let's go for a walk."

Yumi might not have Starseer senses, but she could stand outside a door and warn Alisa if someone was coming.

Yumi nodded and hurried to place drinks on an empty tray.

Murmurs arose across the hall, and the cyborgs stopped harassing Leonidas. Ms. Henneberry had appeared, striding across the marble floor in a dress that swept the tiles. Two men almost as burly as the cyborgs followed her, clearly acting as bodyguards. Maybe they even *were* cyborgs. Had she hired half of the ex-imperial battalion?

"Better go now," Yumi murmured. "Everyone will be listening to her speech."

"Right." Alisa glanced toward Leonidas to make sure his buddies weren't paying her any attention. They weren't. Even though they had paused to watch their boss's entrance, they were sticking to him like magnets.

I'll try to keep an eye out for you, Young-hee's voice sounded softly in Alisa's mind.

Good. Thank you.

Taking her drink-laden tray, Alisa headed for the corridor Leonidas had indicated. A man and woman with linked arms walked out of it as she approached. She lifted the tray, glad for an excuse to be heading this way.

"Wine, sir? Ma'am?"

Without acknowledging her, they plucked drinks from the tray and continued into the banquet hall. Alisa smiled slightly. In this case, it was good to be invisible.

She headed up the corridor with Yumi strolling behind her. It proved as wide, spacious, and marbled as the other passages, with sculptures of famous figures on pedestals here and there. Alisa almost laughed when she spotted Alcyone with the Staff of Lore. Maybe Henneberry had yearned for that artifact long before it reappeared in the system.

"Do you know what's back here?" Yumi asked as they walked.

"No idea."

"Are we picking a spot at random then?"

"Any place that looks like it wouldn't be searched often, preferably a room not likely to have a camera in it." Alisa still had a lav in mind but would settle for a closet.

Unfortunately, all the carved wooden doors looked like they led to state-rooms for important people rather than to broom closets. The corridor the servants had been using might have been a better bet.

Up ahead, two women came out of a room, one finishing adjusting her dress. As Alisa came forward and offered them drinks, she glimpsed a sink inside. It was a public lav. Not as remote as she would have preferred, but maybe it would do.

The two women took drinks and headed toward the banquet hall, where Alisa could hear Henneberry's voice now, an amplification system helping it to carry. She couldn't make out all the words, but it sounded like a welcome and the opening remarks of a speech. Claps followed whatever she said first.

Alisa waited for the women to reach the hall before reaching for the lavatory door. But someone burst out of another door farther up the corridor, and she paused.

A man with his shirt tails dangling out and lipstick on his collar mumbled something about being late and shoved past Alisa and Yumi to enter the lav first.

Not wanting to be caught lurking around the facilities—who knew if the servants were even allowed to use this one?—Alisa headed farther up the corridor.

"Young-hee says there's a linen closet that way, past that intersection and then after that turn up there," Yumi whispered.

"That could work."

Alisa didn't want to look too determined as she strode farther and farther from where she was supposed to be working, but walked quickly anyway. The sooner they planted the tracker, the sooner they could return and calmly serve drinks until the event was over.

She peered left and right at the intersection, hoping it would be empty. It was, but a sign on a pair of closed doors at one end made her pause. *Bridge Access*, it read.

Alisa had wanted out of the way, but if this was the route to the bridge, it wouldn't be nearly as remote as she had hoped.

I doubt the bridge crew leaves to check linen closets often, Young-hee spoke into her mind. *Keep going. The bridge is up three floors—that's just the doors to the private elevator leading there. There are only a few people up there, and they're chatting with each other and monitoring the other ships. They're wary, worried that one or more mafia families might try to take advantage of this get together to rid the system of rivals.*

Thanks, Alisa thought, glad for the extra intel.

She continued through the intersection and up the main corridor, turned the corner, and almost ran into a man coming out of his cabin.

Yumi sucked in a startled breath, bumping into her shoulder. The gray-haired man looked more like one of the guests than the crew, so Alisa hoped he wouldn't think anything of them wandering around.

"Wine, sir?" she offered.

The man blinked bleary eyes, peering at her and then at Yumi, his gaze snagging on Yumi, though he appeared more puzzled than suspicious. Yumi offered her tray without saying anything, though her eyes darted from side to side, like she was thinking of fleeing.

"Wine?" the man asked, still sounding puzzled. "Yes, wine. That should wash things down, eh?" He thumped Alisa on the shoulder. "The old witch started talking yet?"

"Uh, I believe so, sir."

"Hm. Better make an appearance." He grabbed a glass of wine and walked toward the corner, his gait uneven.

"Looks like he's already been drinking," Alisa murmured.

"Drugging. That was the man I told you about. The one whose children I tutored."

"The secret mafia prince? He didn't seem too intimidating."

"Not when he's high, no. But if he's here, and any of his enemies are here, you can expect trouble." Yumi waved toward a bulkhead, or perhaps toward the ships surrounding the yacht.

"Enemies? Other mafia clans?"

"Yes. He's conniving. I could see him using this as—"

The man came back around the corner and frowned toward them. Yumi flinched. Had he heard her voice and recognized it? He wore that puzzled expression again as he walked toward Yumi.

"You remind me of someone," he said.

Yumi shook her head. And here Alisa had been worried that it would be Leonidas's voice that would get them in trouble.

"She grew up in Southern Sarki," Alisa said. "One of the remote tribal villages. She doesn't speak Standard."

"Huh. Well, she doesn't have to speak." He grabbed a second wine glass, then gestured toward the door he had originally exited from. "Come see me later, eh? I'll make sure you have a good time. Tell her, will you?" he asked Alisa.

"Of course," she said, careful to keep the distaste off her face.

"Excellent." He checked out her chest. "You can come too."

"I'm so honored."

He winked and ambled out of sight again.

"He's less of an ass when he's sober," Yumi said, after peering around the corner and making sure he was truly gone this time. "He can be quite genteel."

"As he's swiving servants. I can imagine."

Yumi sighed. "He fooled me for a long time. And his children adore him, think he's a wonderful father."

Alisa had a hard time imagining that, but it didn't matter right now. She had a mission.

She headed for a door as carved and elegant as the others but positioned close enough to another door that it looked to be a lav or closet instead of a cabin. Like the others, it had an old-fashioned doorknob to match the real wood. It opened easily, no lock.

Yumi lingered near the corner, reaching into her jacket for something. She pulled out a pen and looked around.

"Yumi?" Alisa whispered. "Come watch my back, will you?"

Yumi came over to join her, but her eyes were narrowed thoughtfully. Alisa walked into the most elegant linen closet she had ever seen. It was well lit, with marble shelves of towels and sheets neatly stacked and rising well over her head. A cadre of cleaning robots rested on the floor in the back. She had been hoping for a dark, dingy, and rarely visited closet, but the meticulousness of the place made her think it was visited—and inspected—often.

"Let me know if anyone comes," she whispered to Yumi, then set her tray on a stack of towels, the glasses clinking together, and dug the tracker out of her jacket.

Maybe if she tucked it under a shelf in the back...

"I will." Yumi leaned in and grabbed a card off a stack, the fronts monogrammed with H's. The bottom was blank, probably for leaving some note about cleaning services. Yumi stepped back into the corridor with it.

Alisa knelt down next to the robots, noticing one with a big dent. It was in the back corner and dustier than the others. A broken one, perhaps. On a whim, she picked it up and stuck the tracker to its low profile belly. The amount of dust and lint stuck to the bottom made her hope the robot cleaner had been back here for years and wouldn't be taken in for maintenance anytime soon. She flicked a switch to activate the tracking device and hustled out of the closet with her tray.

She caught Yumi finishing penning a message on the back of the card.

"Nobody's coming," she informed Alisa.

"Thanks," Alisa said dryly.

Alisa closed the door and strode for the corner. The sooner she got away from this spot, the better. She wasn't surprised when Yumi lingered behind again, pausing at the door of the room her mafia prince had exited. The door wasn't locked, and she disappeared inside.

Alisa sighed and waited, peeking around the corner to make sure the way remained clear.

"Sorry," Yumi whispered, rejoining her.

"Was that a note telling him you wouldn't be able to accept his invitation?"

"More that he would be unwise to harass one Yumi Moon, due to her powerful new friends."

Alisa raised her eyebrows.

"I told him I was surrounded by Starseers and cyborgs," Yumi said.

"I'll give you Starseers, but is it possible to be surrounded by one cyborg?"

"Leonidas is a large man." Yumi stretched her arms out wide.

"This is true." Alisa had been surrounded by him before, certainly. "Ready to get back to him?"

Yumi nodded.

They crept around the corner, trays in hand, and made it to the intersection without seeing anyone. Alisa thought they might make it back without anything bad happening. Then the bridge access doors opened, and a man with a familiar face and a familiar cocky amble walked out. Commander Tomich.

"What the—" Alisa blurted, so surprised that she couldn't clamp her mouth shut in time. Worse, she was so busy gaping at him, that she bumped against the corner of the intersection. Her tray only clipped it, but that was enough to cause glasses to clink and wobble. "Shit."

She reached for two teetering on the edge, but they tumbled over the side before she caught them. They hit the marble floor and shattered, spraying her leg with wine. It was all she could do to steady the tray before the rest of the glasses pitched to the deck.

Tomich slowed down, but kept walking toward them as he stared at Alisa. He wore the same blue uniform as the security people did, but there were silver embroidered rings around the cuffs of his sleeves, and he wore a cap with more silver embroidery on the bill.

Yumi set her tray down on the floor and pulled a towel from the belt of her uniform.

Alisa was too busy staring at Tomich to bend down to help. What in all three suns' hells was he *doing* here? And had he recognized—

"I don't know the face," Tomich said, after a glance over his shoulder, "but I know that voice." He jogged forward and gripped Alisa's shoulder. He looked up and down the main corridor before whispering, "What are you *doing* here, Marchenko?"

"I was just wondering the same thing about you." Alisa plucked at his embroidered sleeve. "Are you *working* here? What happened to—"

"Sh," he whispered, glancing toward the ceilings. "Cameras. Let's hit the lav."

Two floor-cleaning robots zipped down the corridor from the direction of the linen closet. Not the out-of-commission one, fortunately. Yumi scurried back as they flung themselves atop the water and glass, making crunching and slurping sounds.

"Yumi," Alisa whispered. "Can you take my tray back? I'll meet you back in the hall in a minute."

"Yes, of course." Yumi looked daunted at the task of balancing both trays, especially after seeing Alisa crash, but she did her best and tottered down the corridor.

Barely waiting for Yumi to move out of the way, Tomich grabbed Alisa's arm and dragged her to the lav the lipstick-besmudged man had gone into a few minutes earlier. She opened her mouth to warn him that it might be occupied, but Tomich shoved the door open and pulled her inside before she could speak. It was empty.

"No cameras in here?" she asked, still staring at Tomich, her brain not able to puzzle out how he had come to be here, or *why* he was here.

"No. What are you doing here, Marchenko?"

"What are *you* doing here? I'm a notorious criminal these days, aren't I? Accused of kidnapping and colluding with the empire, and the suns know what else? Shouldn't I be tangled up with the mafia?"

He snorted. "You tell me. You're not still trying to catch up with that staff, are you?"

"I don't give a damn about the staff. I'm after...Tymoteusz."

"*Why?* He's not the one with your daughter, is he?"

"He's the one with..." Alisa realized she would set herself up for further accusations of colluding with the empire if she admitted she was after the prince. "Someone," she finished lamely. "Someone I promised to get back."

Tomich opened his mouth, no doubt to question her on Someone's identity, but she rushed on, hoping to distract him. And she wanted answers of her own, damn it.

"I think Henneberry will lead me to Tymoteusz," Alisa said. "Tomich, what are you doing here? In that uniform?"

"Spying, what do you think?"

"You're not a spy. Unless they sent you to intelligence school in the last year."

"All right, I'm the pilot for the spy. But my chain of command set it all up so I could believably get a job here. That's why I was seemingly publicly embarrassed, locked away, then kicked out of the military."

She stared at him. She hadn't heard that last addendum.

"It was to make it plausible that I'd be searching for a civilian gig. And Henneberry was happy to get me."

"You're here because of the meeting?" she asked. "Not the staff?"

"Well, we want the staff, too, of course, but this—" he waved a hand to take in the yacht, "—has been in the works for months, and our intel people caught a whiff of it a while ago. We can't let these thugs even contemplate taking over the system. Business moguls and mafia brutes. It would be even worse than the damned empire." He pushed a hand through his hair, seemingly forgetting that he had a cap on, for he knocked it off, cursed, and had to pick it up.

"Your spy," Alisa said slowly, "is it the man in the blue suit?"

"You *knew?*" Tomich cursed. "I'll tell him he's not being nearly as circumspect as he thought. He's supposed to be one of the entrepreneurs Henneberry invited. The *real* man is locked up on Arkadius for tax evasion. He's in a costume and designed to look like him. How did you know?"

"My spies are better than yours."

He gave her an aggrieved expression, and she almost laughed despite the uncertainty of this predicament. It was good to one-up him.

"You brought some of those damned Starseers along, didn't you?" he asked. "That's cheating."

This time, she *did* laugh. She supposed that answered her question about whether the blue-suited man was a Starseer. He must simply have taken some of that drug.

"Look, maybe we can work together," Alisa said. "I've just placed a—"

Voices sounded outside the door, *right* outside.

"That's the captain," Tomich whispered, pressing a finger to his lips.

The door opened.

Before Alisa could start to think of an excuse for why she would be in the lav with the pilot, Tomich pressed her against the wall, grabbed her ass, and kissed her. Vigorously. She was too stunned to do anything more than stand there, though she eventually realized she should look like a participant and not a victim. She put her hands on his waist and rubbed him through his clothes, while hoping that he didn't knock off her fake nose with his enthusiastic kissing.

A throat cleared as the door opened fully.

"Commander Tomich," a white-haired man with a gravelly voice said, his tone extremely dry. "Your reputation is for screwing admirals, not serving wenches."

Wenches? Alisa wanted to comment on that, but figured she had better keep her mouth shut. She did *not* want to be brought to Henneberry's attention.

Tomich, feigning that he was surprised to see his captain there, pulled back and faced the door. "That's true, sir," he said, plastering that insouciant grin of his across his face, "but she has a nice ass. I couldn't resist." He grinned at her, too, though there was a glare wrapped up in it, and she had a feeling he was blaming her for putting him in a suspicious position.

Well, the hells with him. He'd been the one to drag her in here.

The captain stuck his head far enough into the lav to look at Alisa's butt. She didn't know whether to sigh or feel embarrassment. There were people standing in the corridor behind the captain. A couple more blue-clad officers, and—her gut twisted—Leonidas. Holding a tray of hor d'oeuvres. What was he doing out there with those crewmen? And had he seen that ridiculous kiss?

"It is nice," the captain agreed, "but I expect you to keep your ass-squeezing to after hours, and certainly not during Ms. Henneberry's big event."

"Yes, sir. Sorry, sir. I didn't figure you'd need me right now."

"What I need is the lav." The captain jerked his thumb toward the corridor.

Tomich slunk out, though he appeared more amused by all of this than chastised. He frowned at Leonidas, but walked past him without comment. The two officers who had been looking into the lav continued down the corridor once the captain walked inside. Alisa scooted out, and the door thudded shut behind her. She and Leonidas stood alone in the corridor.

He gave her the blandest look she'd ever seen and held out his tray. "Amuse-bouche?"

"Amuse what?"

"Beck said that's the proper term for his snacks. They amuse your mouth."

"Ah." Not wanting to be there when the captain finished in the lav, Alisa headed toward the main hall. Maybe Leonidas hadn't seen the kiss or heard the conversation about asses. She watched him out of the corner of her eye, finding that unlikely.

He looked over his shoulder in the direction that Tomich had gone. "Is this the time for snide comments regarding pretty men and bedrooms?"

"I think it would be appropriate." She wrapped an arm around his waist as they walked. "But Tomich isn't that pretty. And he's not as good of a kisser as he thinks."

"Can I punch him if he tries to use you again to improve upon his skills?"

"Absolutely. What are you doing up here? Where'd your playmates go?"

"I heard the voices of the officers and came to check on you. Young-hee is entertaining the cyborgs."

"Those two are major assholes," she said, lowering her voice as they approached the end of the corridor. Henneberry was still talking out there, but if Leonidas had heard the officers from out by the food tables, the cyborgs might hear their conversation now. "Who are they?"

"A private and a corporal." He slowed to a stop before they reached the hall. "They enlisted late in the war, less than two years before the end. They were both in jail and given the option of joining and having the surgeries as an alternative to a long sentence. Sometimes, the discipline of the military straightens people out; sometimes, it doesn't. For them, it wasn't long before their files came across my desk in a matter that required punishment. They both would have been booted out, or sent back to jail, if we hadn't been so in need of personnel." His mouth twisted with bitterness. "I recognize them because they were on Tandari Base, fighting alongside the men who died defending the emperor. As far as I knew, *they* were dead. The only reason I made it out was because the emperor ordered me to take Thorian and escape. If those two are alive, it's because they found a way to flee, a way to abandon Markus." His eyes burned with indignation. "For them to show up here, with cushy jobs on some luxury boat…" He ground his teeth.

She squeezed his waist. "Maybe they'll irk Tymoteusz, and he'll use the staff to shake all their implants out through their noses."

"Would it be immature to hope for that?" Leonidas shifted his tray to one hand and wrapped an arm around her.

"I'm certainly going to."

His eyes glinted. "That didn't answer my question."

She turned her consoling arm squeeze into a slap on the butt, then reluctantly let him go. Henneberry's voice had stopped, so maybe her speech was wrapping up.

"We better get back in there before Young-hee gets into trouble with those two," she said.

"Agreed."

A crash sounded, dozens of glasses breaking. Alisa and Leonidas rushed out of the corridor in time to see a man hurtling across the room to land on one of the stone tables, sending trays of food flying. It was Beck.

CHAPTER FOURTEEN

Alisa ran toward the tables as the trays struck the floor, red and white sauces spattering the stone tiles and the nearby wall. Sauce struck guests standing nearby, too, though they'd started scattering as soon as Beck landed on his back. He groaned now, lifting his head and looking in the direction from which he'd come. Leonidas charged that way, placing himself between Beck and the table and a group of men that were fighting, exchanging punches.

Alisa's first thought was that they were White Dragon people who remembered Beck and the trouble they'd had with him. But none of the men chased after him. They were too busy attacking each other. A portly fellow with a drooping mustache was flung so hard that he skidded across the floor, landing at the feet of another table. Alisa rushed to Beck's side, helping him to his feet.

"What's happening?" she asked. "What did you do?"

Other groups of people were backing away from the fight, but a few men ran toward it instead. Someone drew a blazer pistol.

"Me?" Beck asked, trying to wipe red sauce off his white jacket. "Nothing. I was just offering someone wine." He waved to a tray and dozens of broken glasses on the floor near the group, even as someone ran through the area and slipped on the spilled wine.

The two cyborgs appeared, charging in to stop the fight. Whitey grabbed the blazer pistol before it could be fired, then crumpled it between his hands and threw it at the owner's feet. Scar stepped between two men throwing punches, gripped each of them by the shirtfronts, and hoisted them into the air. Someone else darted away from the group, reaching into his jacket. The man made the mistake of running into Leonidas's orbit. Leonidas grabbed him, yanking a bullet-firing revolver from his holster, and lifted him into the air. The man's legs kept pumping, as if he might run away while he dangled a foot above the ground.

With the hulking cyborgs in the mix, the fight soon quieted. But by now, the hundreds of people occupying the hall were looking toward the group.

"Put him down," Alisa whispered to Leonidas. The other two cyborgs might have picked him out for what he was, but he didn't need to demonstrate his strength so everyone would know.

Leonidas lowered his captive to the floor, but pulled the man's arms behind his back to restrain him so he couldn't run.

"Well," Henneberry said from the far side of the hall—she'd been giving her speech from a stage in front of the large portholes. "I guess that means the Carvers and the Clariday family are not open to working together for the collective attainment of power beyond anything any of us have known."

That drew a few wary chuckles.

Henneberry's voice was dry, but a hint of exasperation touched it too. She stepped down from her stage and strode toward the fight. The cyborgs had separated the troublemakers, so she must have deemed it safe. Alisa drew back behind the table, ostensibly to clean up the fallen trays, but mostly to stay out of the woman's sight. She wished Leonidas would let his captive go and do the same. The man in his grip, however, was straining and trying to get away from him, his face red, and his fingers flexing as he glared at a white-haired man still in the group.

Henneberry stopped and addressed Scar. "Take them to their shuttles, and see to it that they leave."

"Yes, ma'am."

That's the tip of the iceberg, Abelardus spoke into Alisa's mind.

She spotted him halfway across the hall, holding an empty tray under his arm and talking to a trio of women.

What is? That fight?

The tensions in here are high in case you didn't notice. Henneberry is lucky that didn't devolve into a full-fledged war with everybody picking sides and leaping into the fray. She's starting to regret that she came to these people with her plan.

Who else would join her in a scheme to try and take over the system? Alisa asked.

Exactly her reasoning for gathering the mafia families. But if these people could work together cohesively, they could have taken over the system centuries ago.

After Scar and Whitey shuffled out of the hall, leading the troublemakers, some by their collars, Henneberry approached Leonidas. He'd released his captive to the care of the others, but he hadn't moved into hiding behind the table, as Alisa wished. He was standing out there like a guardian, glaring at anyone who looked like trouble.

"It's odd how many cyborgs I'm running into lately," Henneberry said, peering fearlessly up at his face.

"Ma'am," he said, ducking his head and making his voice gruff.

"How many were left alive in the Cyborg Corps at the end of the war?" She squinted at him, and Alisa groaned to herself, certain suspicion lurked in her eyes.

"Couldn't say, ma'am."

"Clive," Alisa called, waving from behind the table. "Will you come help me clean up this mess?"

Beck walked out and sidled in between Henneberry and Leonidas. "Ma'am, do you want us to continue serving?"

Her gaze shifted from Leonidas to Beck. "Just clean up the mess and keep the drinks flowing."

Yes, that was just what this shindig needed. More alcohol.

Henneberry called out to several people in the crowd and waved for them to follow her. The selected parties headed off to join her near the corridor Alisa had been up before. Bodyguards peeled away from the walls to trail behind. Yumi's mafia prince was among the group. So was the blue-suited man, and he gave Leonidas a curious look as he crossed the hall. Henneberry was also looking at Leonidas again, her eyes narrowed with suspicion. Her gaze did not shift until her group had fully gathered, and she led them up the corridor.

Those are the ones that are important, powerful, and also willing to work together, Abelardus informed Alisa. *That would be a good meeting to spy on.*

Can you do it from a distance? I don't think we're going to be invited in. Alisa didn't want to ask if Henneberry's group needed drink service, not when her team had already garnered suspicious looks.

Four cleaning robots whirred out of the corridor and headed over to the sauce-spattered floor. Alisa backed away before one could run over her foot in its determination to fulfill its mission.

Yumi and Young-hee returned to the tables and helped Alisa clean up what the robots couldn't handle. A few more people came by for drinks and snacks, but after Henneberry left, the guests started dispersing.

Chef Lunquist approached the table. "You can pack up and head out now. Leave some of the grilled fish, eggplant, and brittle. Those were Ms. Henneberry's favorites, and she'd like leftovers." Lunquist sniffed, as if the idea of some old leftovers was beneath her.

"Of course, Chef," Beck said.

"Our security people are busy so you can see yourselves out."

Beck waited for her to leave before telling Alisa, "Best news we've had. Our departure should be painless. Did you get the thing done?"

Alisa nodded, though she worried things wouldn't be as painless as he thought. That long look Henneberry had given Leonidas as she walked out lingered in her mind. Was it possible she'd figured out who he was?

They packed the food quickly, Abelardus not returning until they were almost ready to go. He waved and smiled at the three young women he'd been entertaining. They tittered and waved back. Alisa rolled her eyes. She couldn't imagine that they were important people within their own rights. Someone's daughters, perhaps.

Young-hee scowled at him as he joined them. "You'd have more luck securing a relationship with a woman if you weren't openly flirting with others."

He blinked at her. "I'm not seeking to secure a relationship with a woman. The captain hasn't seen fit to toss her cyborg aside and embrace me with open arms."

"That's because she's wise," Young-hee muttered, stacking trays firmly enough that they clanged.

"And because cyborgs are too big to toss aside," Alisa murmured, watching Young-hee's irritated expression and Abelardus's oblivious one.

For people who could read minds, the Starseers weren't as all-knowing as one might expect.

"Is there anything you want to search before leaving?" Leonidas asked Alisa quietly as the group made the final preparations. He nodded toward the banquet hall, where only a handful of groups remained. "This might be the easiest time to explore without being questioned."

Alisa hesitated. She didn't want to explore the massive yacht, but she was tempted to try and find a way to eavesdrop on that meeting. But she'd already planted the tracking device, and lingering and poking around would only be suspicious. If they were caught, Henneberry's people might look more deeply into their identifications—and what they had been doing here in addition to delivering food. Besides, stopping this mafia alliance wasn't her job. The Alliance was here keeping an eye on things. All she needed was to be led to Thorian, so she could keep her word to her daughter. And to Leonidas.

"No," she said. "Let's go."

Leaving the cleaning robots whirring along the floor behind the tables, Alisa and the others carried their trays toward the shuttle bay. Despite her words to Leonidas, she was tempted to explore some of the side passages along the way. But to what end? They would only find trouble, she was certain.

Leonidas was leading the way, and he slowed down as they neared the Glastica door to the bay.

"Problem?" Alisa murmured, peering around his shoulder.

She glimpsed blue uniforms through the clear doors. A lot of them.

"Someone waiting for us?" she added.

"Many someones," Leonidas said. "They're armed."

He looked toward Young-hee.

"Give me a moment," she whispered, resting her palm on the bulkhead and closing her eyes.

"Sorry, you're out of moments," a voice said from behind them.

Leonidas must have heard Scar approach, because he'd already put his back to the wall and was looking in that direction. Scar and Whitey stood at the last intersection the group had passed, each carrying big blazer rifles. They were blocking the passage, making sure the only way Alisa's team could go was into the shuttle bay.

"Explain yourselves," Alisa said, but she feared she already knew what had happened. Someone watching the cameras had noticed her sneaking into that linen closet and had gone in and found the tracking device.

"You didn't think it odd that you people, nobody caterers with nobody credentials, were picked for this party?" Scar asked, smirking.

"Uh." Beck lifted a finger. "I am *not* a nobody in the culinary world."

Scar grunted. "You're a puny little zero. All of you are. You didn't get worried when so many important people were discussing their plans for galactic domination in front of you?"

Alisa stared at him. She hadn't been discovered, after all? They were in trouble simply because they had taken the job? No wonder no one else had wanted it...

She noticed Leonidas signaling to Abelardus and decided to keep the cyborgs talking if she could.

"Technically, they're only trying to dominate the system," Alisa said. "Unless CargoExpress has faster-than-light technology it hasn't unveiled yet."

"Wouldn't be surprised if that was next," Scar said. "Imagine how quickly your packages would arrive. But you, sadly, won't live to see that day." He took a step forward, pointing his blazer in Leonidas's direction. "Where do you think you're going, pretend-mech? You're an embarrassment to everyone who's made the sacrifice to serve."

I'm going to make a barrier to stop them, Abelardus spoke into Alisa's mind, *and Leonidas is going to run out and deal with the security men in the bay. You, Younghee, Yumi, and Beck are to run to the shuttle and get inside. Just stay out of the way, and don't get hit.*

"What sacrifice?" Alisa propped her fists on her hips, hoping to keep Scar's attention on her. She didn't like the idea of Leonidas flinging himself into a battle with dozens of armed men when he wasn't wearing his armor, but she couldn't argue the plan with him without alerting the cyborgs. Out of the corner of her eye, she could see Leonidas heading for the door and Abelardus moving up toward her. "I heard you two were plucked out of jail to be cannon fodder for the empire," she added, keeping the cyborgs' gazes on her.

She couldn't imagine it mattered now if Leonidas's cover was blown, and she was rewarded with an exchange of startled looks between the two cyborgs.

"Now," Leonidas whispered, and charged the door, flinging it open. He disappeared into the bay, and gunfire opened up, blazers squealing and bullets cracking.

The cyborgs fired, crimson beams streaking toward Alisa and Abelardus, and her heart leaped into her throat. Instincts drove her to dive to the floor, trying to dodge the blazer bolts. But they bounced off an invisible barrier halfway between Abelardus and the cyborgs.

"If you're done inspecting the deck for dirt, you could get to the shuttle," Abelardus told her, glancing down.

Alisa scowled, but didn't reply. They had to hurry. It sounded like an entire battalion of men out there firing at Leonidas. She jumped up and caught up with Beck, Yumi, and Young-hee just inside the door. She wanted to burst out and hurry to get to the shuttle, so Leonidas wouldn't have to draw fire for long, but Beck was blocking the way.

"Go," she urged. "We're supposed to run to the shuttle."

An orange blazer beam slammed into the Glastica, and Beck jumped back. A crater appeared in the door, smoke wafting upward.

"Just waiting for an opening," Beck said.

"Sorry," Alisa said. "I see that."

She couldn't see Leonidas from the corridor, and it made her crazy with worry. Her shoulder blades also itched, because she could hear the cyborgs behind her, firing relentlessly at Abelardus's barrier. They had advanced and were shooting point blank. She didn't know how much energy his barrier could absorb before it faltered.

My shield and I can go all night long, Captain, he drawled into her mind.

The concentration on his face and the sweat already dripping down his temple belied the statement.

"He's got them following him around those shuttles over there," Beck said. "We better risk it. If they get him…"

"They're not going to get him," Alisa said firmly. It seemed like a good time for optimism.

"Now," Beck whispered, and pushed open the door. He used his body to protect them from the bay—a few men in blue were visible, but they were on the far side and focused on something in the corner.

Alisa gulped as she eased out—they didn't have Leonidas cornered, did they?

The boom of a destroyer sounded. Leonidas's secreted weapon. Now, Alisa wished she'd dared to sneak weapons in under her jacket too.

She led the way along the wall. Young-hee and Yumi, both with wide eyes, stuck so close to her that they nearly tripped her a couple of times. The squeal of blazer fire echoed throughout the bay, and more than one bolt ricocheted off the wall above or ahead of them. Alisa jumped when one blast struck close, leaving a sizzling crater in the bulkhead. She was all-too-aware that she wasn't wearing her combat armor. Neither was Leonidas.

They ran along the body of a large black shuttle, using it for cover, then slowed to a crawl and checked the way before darting out from behind it. As Alisa ran across the open stretch, several other craft came into view out in the bay. Blue-uniformed men lay here and there, groaning on the deck, some flat on their backs and some curled against the bases of shuttles. Most seemed to be moving, so Leonidas must not be trying to kill anyone.

Alisa faltered when she spotted Leonidas racing away from a group of men. One aimed right at his back and fired. Leonidas anticipated it some-how, throwing himself forward into a roll. He somersaulted across the deck, red beams of energy sizzling through the air above him. He careened around the front of a shuttle while still rolling, sprang to his feet, and leaped up to the rooftop of the craft. He ran along the top, back the way he had come, firing down upon the startled men who hadn't seen him jump. They scattered, fleeing for cover.

Leonidas leaped from one shuttle to another and disappeared from Alisa's sight.

The thug-brothers left the corridor, Abelardus informed her as she continued along the wall, trying to reach their shuttle. *They're going to find another way in.*

Alisa grimaced. They had already passed one door, a metal one rather than a Glastica one. She had no idea if it led to a corridor or a closet, but she could see another clear one not far from where their shuttle waited.

I'll try to watch for them, Abelardus added.

Beck raced out of an alley between two shuttles, startling Alisa as he appeared a few feet away. "Almost there," he panted. "Follow me."

They reached the front of their white shuttle with meals painted on the side, and Alisa allowed herself to feel hope. But not much hope. They still had to get the forcefield down and figure out how to fly away past more than a dozen enemy ships. The troop transport shuttle had minimal shielding and no weapons.

Beck raced down the long side of the craft, using it for cover, then poked his head around the corner where the back ramp was still down. He jerked back. Blazer fire slammed into the deck a foot from him.

Alisa stopped a few feet behind him, and Yumi and Young-hee came up behind her.

"Young-hee," Alisa whispered, "can you distract whoever is—"

Two security men leaped off the ramp. Weaponless, Beck couldn't fire back. Instead of running—as if there was anywhere to run—he sprang at them. One got a shot off before he reached them, and a cry of pain escaped Beck's lips.

"No," Alisa shouted, a surge of protectiveness rushing through her.

She leaped forward and launched a side kick at the man who'd shot Beck before he realized she was there. Her boot caught his hand, and the blazer pistol flew away, striking the bulkhead.

Beck slammed into the second man, taking him down, despite his injury. Alisa lashed out at the other guard again, kicking twice more before setting her foot down. He managed to block the blows and back away, but she lunged after him. His shoulder clipped the corner of the shuttle, giving her a second to catch up. He was six inches taller than she, but in her anger, she didn't care. She barreled into him, throwing palm strikes at his sternum. He reached for her as she connected with a solid blow and felt bone crunch under the heel of her hand. His fingers brushed her shoulder, but he gasped and bent over in pain without gripping her. She curled her hand into a fist and slammed an uppercut into his chin. Pain burst from her knuckles, but his head whipped back, and she pressed the advantage. She slammed her knee into his groin and followed up the attack with two more palm strikes, one to the chest and another to the jaw. He fell to the deck, curling in on himself.

A dark shadow dropped down in front of her, and she lifted her fists, prepared to fight again. But it was only Leonidas. He nodded once at her and gathered Beck in his arms. His opponent was moaning on the deck in front of him, but Beck gripped his abdomen, blood staining his white jacket. Holding him, Leonidas sprang onto the ramp and rushed into the shuttle to set him down.

Young-hee and Yumi passed Alisa to run up after him. She started to follow, but paused, spotting Abelardus racing toward her, blood streaming from a gouge in his temple.

Go, go, he urged. *The cyborgs are coming.*

Alisa ran up the ramp with her neck craned over her shoulder. Scar and Whitey were charging toward them from that other doorway she'd noticed. She pumped her legs, knowing she had to get inside and hit the button to close the hatch, or they would be in all manner of trouble.

Leonidas jumped past her as she made it across the threshold.

"Stay inside," she barked, lunging for the hatch controls.

Abelardus raced up the ramp. In the cluster of people at the narrow entrance, he tripped over Beck and went down. Leonidas strode out onto the ramp, hands in fists as he faced the closing cyborgs.

Alisa hit the button. "Get back," she told him.

He sprang back as the ramp was sucked into the base of the shuttle. He landed on the threshold in a fighting crouch. The hatch started to close, but the two cyborgs were too close. They jumped into the air, Scar trying to bowl through Leonidas. But Leonidas was a wall, and he shoved the cyborg back. Scar fell to the deck, but Whitey had made it to the threshold, and he caught the hatch as it came down, trying to close atop him. He held it up with his raw power, even managing to kick at Leonidas with one leg.

That kick was so fast that Alisa could barely register the movement of the boot, but Leonidas caught it in midair and lunged close. He grabbed the cyborg and tore him away from the threshold and the hatch that was still trying to close. Instead of shoving him out, as Alisa would have wished, he slammed the younger man against the bulkhead inside. The hatch shut, keeping Scar out but keeping Whitey in.

"Pilot," Leonidas barked at Alisa, even as he rammed his foe against the bulkhead again, as if to shake the fight out of him. His eyes burned into the taller cyborg, and for the first time, the man hesitated. "You fled the empire to join a greedy rich woman trying to take over the system?" Leonidas growled.

"I—"

"Was the emperor even dead before you abandoned your platoon?" he demanded. "How many men did you leave behind to die?"

Alisa wanted to stay and watch—she so rarely saw Leonidas genuinely angry—but he was right. They needed to get out of here.

As she flung herself into the pilot's seat, a bang came from the hatch. Scar. She wagered he had the strength to tear it open.

She fired up the engine, glad the shuttle had been designed to be ready quickly, and took them into the air. Another clang came from outside. More thumps came from within as the cyborg got over being startled by Leonidas's ferocity and fought back.

Abelardus flung himself into the seat next to Alisa. "Working on getting that leech off the damned door," he said, eyes focused in intense concentration.

"Good." Alisa glanced back as she flew them over the other shuttles in the bay. With the forcefield up, blocking access to space, all she could do was go in circles. "Young-hee? Any chance you can find the button that lowers that forcefield?"

Young-hee limped toward a seat on wobbly legs, her hand to her waist, Yumi helping her. Only then did Alisa realize she had also been shot. No wonder she hadn't been able to do much. Beck was on the deck on hands and knees, crawling toward one of the seats—or maybe just trying to get away from the fight in the back. Leonidas and the younger cyborg were locked in a wrestling match, pausing only long enough to throw punches or head butt each other. Metal groaned as a fist struck the hull.

"They'll destroy the ship from within," Alisa muttered, turning her attention back to the view screen. As she flew over the shuttles, skimming past the forcefield, Scar came into view, grabbing a couple of blue-uniformed men on the deck and racing for a doorway.

"I convinced him that we knew a way to lower the forcefield, and that the bay would depressurize in a second," Abelardus said.

"I wish that were true." Alisa's words were drowned out by more thumps from the rear, followed by a gasp of pain. She couldn't tell if it was Leonidas or the enemy cyborg.

Alisa thumped the side of her fist on the control panel. They had to do something. Sooner or later, Scar would figure out that they didn't have a way to lower anything, and he would return with reinforcements. And rocket launchers.

"Young-hee?" Alisa asked. "Can you do anything?"

"I'm sorry, but I don't know much about ships," Young-hee said in a pained voice. "And I'm having a hard time concentrating now."

Abelardus looked at her and blinked a few times. "Young-hee, you were shot?"

"Nice of you to notice," she murmured.

"Is there anything I can do?" He left his seat and knelt beside hers, laying a hand on her arm. "Do you know how to do a meditative trance to minimize your awareness of your pain?"

"Of course, but this hardly seems like an appropriate time to drift off," Young-hee said. She sounded irritated—or maybe just uncomfortable, but she didn't pull away from him. Indeed, she slumped against him.

"Better than being in pain," Abelardus said, his brow pinched as he considered her with concern.

"Abelardus?" Alisa asked. "If she can't help, I'm going to need you."

"Yes, of course," he said, though he didn't leave Young-hee's side as he looked toward the view screen. "I'll try to get one of these lumps to think about the controls and let me know where they are." He flicked a finger at the uniformed security men that Leonidas had knocked to the deck. Many of them were limping or crawling toward the exits. Scar must have shouted a warning for them to get out. Good. If, by some chance, Alisa figured out how to lower the forcefield, she didn't want to kill people by venting them into space.

She looked at the comm panel, wishing she had a code for Tomich's personal comm unit. Not that he'd necessarily be able to answer it on the bridge, even if he had it with him. He wouldn't be able to give up his cover, not even for her.

But an idea popped into her mind. Maybe…

She opened the comm and hit reply on the message that had come in earlier, first letting them into the yacht. "Greetings, *Starry Elegance*. This is the crazy captain of the catering shuttle. We don't really want to die down here, but we're desperate. We might do something alarming if you don't let us go."

Unfortunately, the person who replied wasn't Tomich.

"Surrender your shuttle," a woman said coolly. "You can't escape."

Was that comm officer on the bridge with Tomich? Alisa hoped so.

"Oh, are you sure about that? You might want to lower the forcefield and let us out. I've activated the self-destruct on my shuttle, and when it blows in three minutes, I figure it'll take out the lower third or so of your fancy yacht."

"You're bluffing," a new speaker said. It sounded like the man who had checked out her ass and gone into the lav.

"No, Captain, I'm not. You've got my back against the wall. You people called us in to work for you, all along intending to kill us."

"What is she talking about?" the captain muttered to someone.

Alisa almost rolled her eyes. Maybe he had no idea. Maybe Henneberry or even someone as lowly as Chef Lunquist had been the one to set this all up.

"Also, one of your cyborg traitors is trying to kill *my* cyborg in here," she said, raising her voice to be heard over a screech of metal and a thud that came from the back. A chair that had previously been bolted to the deck smashed against the hull. "You've made us desperate. I'm not getting captured. I'll do anything to escape. Two minutes. Say, you don't have anything important down here on this side of the ship, do you? Engineering? Fuel tanks? Your boss's styling salon?"

"Just let her go," a voice in the background said. Tomich. Good, he was going to help her. "It'll be easier to blow up that shuttle once it's clear of the ship than it will be to bring it down in the shuttle bay. Your people will just make a mess in there."

Blow it up? Maybe Tomich wasn't going to be as much help as she'd hoped.

The captain cursed. Alisa had no idea if that represented agreement or disagreement. She also didn't know if the captain realized she was the same person he'd seen in the lav. If he did, he might be suspicious of Tomich's motives.

A beep came from the control panel.

"The shuttle bay is depressurizing," Abelardus said. "Yes. They're going to let us go."

Alisa nodded, but did not get her hopes up too much. That forcefield wasn't down yet. She kept flying in circles, her fingers poised to take them out if it lowered for even a second.

On the deck below them, the last of the security men made it to one of the Glastica doors, turning sideways to lunge through as it automatically shut, red lights flashing around the frame.

A thud and a crash sounded, and Beck cried out. "Damn it. Keep your fight in the back."

He escaped the thrashing cyborgs and clawed himself off the deck, past Abelardus, who was still in the aisle at Young-hee's side, and into an empty seat, slumping against the hull. The bloodstain on his white jacket had grown, and his face was pale and pinched with pain.

"We're almost out of here, Tommy," Alisa said, hoping her smile was reassuring.

"Hells, you're calling me by my first name? I must look like I'm going to die for sure."

"Nah, I just thought you needed some coddling. Once we get back, Alejandro will fix up your wound in no time."

"Coddling? Maybe cuddling." Beck closed his eyes and let his head thud back against the hull.

"When Abelardus is done cuddling Young-hee, I could probably get him to cuddle you."

"Your bedside manner is alarming, Captain."

Abelardus raised his eyebrows but did not otherwise object to the idea that he was "cuddling" Young-hee. She had closed her eyes and was leaning fully against him. They were both ignoring the battle in the back. Alisa didn't know if she should order Abelardus to help, or if he would only get in the way.

"Open the hatch," came a growl from the back.

"Leonidas?" Alisa asked.

He had gained the advantage and straddled the younger cyborg. His jacket had been torn off, and his wig and most of his prosthetics had also disappeared in the fight. A deep gouge ran down the side of his biceps, and blood dripped down his arm and onto his foe. The other man looked just as bad. He stared up at Leonidas, eyes puffy, and blood running from the side of his mouth.

"You heard me. We're not taking this coward with us."

"Colonel...?" The voice of the cyborg suddenly sounded young, fearful. Full of dread.

"The bay is depressurizing," Alisa said. "The forcefield could open in as few as twenty seconds," she added, glancing at the sensor display. "There's still some air but—"

"Then he better run fast."

Abelardus was the one to wave his hand and activate the button that opened the hatch. "Hold your breath."

The hatch opened partway, and Leonidas hoisted the cyborg to his feet.

"Colonel, I didn't realize..." the man started, his voice full of apology.

Leonidas shoved him through the partially open hatch, then hit the button back there to close it. It snapped shut, and the internal circulation fans buzzed on, filling the cabin with oxygen.

Though injured, the cyborg landed on his feet. He sprinted around two shuttles and made it to the Glastica door. It didn't open for him.

"Forcefield's coming down," Abelardus said.

The cyborg drew back his arm and punched the door. It cracked with the first blow, and he hammered it two more times, enough to get his fist through.

Red lights flashed within the bay, and the forcefield disappeared. The cyborg's legs flew up, as the lingering atmosphere was blown out. Somehow, he managed to find the leverage to tear that door open and pull himself into the corridor. He tried to push it back shut, but with that fist-sized hole in the

Glastica, it would need repairs. Alisa couldn't hear it, but she could imagine a wailing from within the yacht, announcing the breach.

"Get out of here," Leonidas said. "They're going to close the forcefield as soon as they realize they have a breach."

"Already on it," Alisa said, guiding the shuttle out. The red lights stopped flashing, and she feared the field would be raised any second, so she gunned it, probably leaving scorch marks on the deck. Oh, well. Something else for Henneberry's people to repair. They deserved the hassle for trying to kill her team.

The shuttle zipped away from the shuttle bay, the blackness of space wrapping around them. Alisa wished she could relax, but there were mafia ships all over the place around the yacht. All it would take was one of them firing at her shuttle to disable it. Or, as Tomich had suggested, the yacht itself might fire at her as soon as they were clear of its hull.

"Making best possible speed," Alisa whispered, choosing a route that would take them between two freighters that didn't look as intimidating as some of the other mafia ships.

She'd no sooner set her course than a hulking black ship bristling with weapons started into motion.

"Uh-oh," she said.

The sensor panel flashed an alarm, as that ship powered up weapons. Two other mafia ships turned in the shuttle's direction, and several more detached from the yacht's airlocks.

"Young-hee," Abelardus said, touching her jaw. "Since you won't go into a trance right now, will you help me work on this?"

Young-hee, still gripping her wounded side, looked daunted by the idea, but she took a deep breath and nodded. "I'll do my best."

"Just follow my lead," Abelardus said with gentleness in his voice that Alisa hadn't heard before.

She hoped he was planning something miraculous. She watched the sensors and the holodisplay showing the positions of all the ships in relation to her shuttle, and threw a few zigzags into their escape flight, hoping to make a tougher target if—when—someone fired at them.

Before they reached the freighters she'd meant to fly between, the first e-cannon blast came. The sensors lit up in warning, and she banked hard.

She should have been too late, but the blast skimmed starboard of their previous position. It would have missed even if she hadn't dodged. It wouldn't have missed by much, but it would have missed.

"That's the yacht," she mused, continuing evasive maneuvers as she kept heading toward the freighters. If she could put one of them between her and the yacht, it would have a harder time hitting her.

Another e-cannon fired. Alisa dove hard enough that the shuttle's artificial gravity had trouble compensating. Beck groaned. She didn't know if it was from queasiness or his wound.

Outside, the e-cannon blast zipped past, a fiery orange streak that trailed through the space they had occupied.

"We're going to have a hard time dodging them forever if they give chase," Alisa said. Thus far, the yacht had not moved. She hoped they were busy dealing with the chaos she had left behind.

"Just keep doing what you're doing," Leonidas said quietly from the back. He was sitting on the deck, his back to the hull, a hand on his abdomen, his arm bleeding freely.

Alisa worried about how much damage he had taken, and Beck and Young-hee were injured too. She *had* to get her team away. They needed Alejandro's attentions sooner rather than later.

"Yumi," Alisa said, flying under the belly of the freighter that hadn't moved yet. "I'm promoting you from science officer to nurse." She was the only one who wasn't wounded or concentrating on Starseers things. "Can you find some bandages for our injured?"

Yumi was gripping the armrests of her seat with white-knuckled hands as she stared at all the ships on the display, including those giving chase. But she jerked out a nod and started hunting for first-aid supplies.

"Feel free to drug them if that'll make them feel better," Alisa said.

A third e-cannon blast came from the yacht, this one missing well wide. Alisa dodged, pretending she was worried about those attacks, but she'd already figured out that whoever was at the weapons controls over there wasn't trying to hit her. She assumed it was Tomich. Unless she and her ass had left more of impression on the captain than she thought.

Unfortunately, Tomich couldn't do anything about the mafia ships. Even though she hadn't done anything to them, that black one and three others were arrowing after her. They all had more speed than the shuttle. This craft was more maneuverable than the *Nomad*, but that was all it had going for it.

"The black ship is firing," she said, diving again, wondering how she would get away. The mafia ships were being conservative now, with so many of their brethren in the area, but once Alisa took the shuttle into open space, it would be an easy target.

"But not at us," she said, dumbfounded as the blazer bolts she'd thought were heading for the shuttle instead clipped the wing of another mafia ship.

An accident? Intentional?

Before she could decide, the ship fired back. *Several* ships fired. And not all at the big, black craft. It raised its shields and turned, no longer following the shuttle but facing the vessels firing at it. Soon, at least seven of the mafia ships were flinging attacks at each other.

A broadcast message lit up the comm panel, and Alisa turned it on, even though she doubted it was for her.

"Cease fire, cease fire." That was the captain of Henneberry's yacht. "This is a peaceful meeting, as promised when we contacted you. If you continue shooting at each other, we *will* step in and put an end to the fighting."

Alisa glanced at Abelardus. "Is that you two?"

"Riling up the mafia bridge crews?" Abelardus opened a single eyelid and smiled slyly at Young-hee. "Perhaps."

She managed a return smile for him—at some point, she'd laid her hand atop his hand, which still rested on her arm.

"They're natural enemies," Young-hee told Alisa. "It's not taking much to stir them into combat mode."

"But we'll be out of range before long," Abelardus added. "We won't be able to continue to influence them then. Fly fast, Captain."

"Working on it." Alisa stopped the evasive maneuvers and set a course straight back toward Aldrin. She could veer off to rendezvous with the *Nomad* once she was sure there wouldn't be pursuit.

"Nice job," Abelardus murmured quietly to Young-hee.

She nodded at him. "Thanks, you too."

Beck sucked in a pained breath when Yumi cut away his shirt to apply bandages to his bullet wound.

"You doing all right, Beck?" Alisa asked, alternating between watching the ships on the sensors and making sure her people weren't dying.

"Been better."

Leonidas was slumped in the back, his eyes open, but he didn't look like he had the energy to move forward and take one of the seats. Maybe the deck seemed more comfortable.

"I appreciate you taking that bullet for us, Tommy," Alisa said. "Thank you. I guess we should all bring weapons with us next time we cater."

Leonidas cleared his throat and gave her an expectant look. Yes, he had taken *more* than a bullet for them. He'd taken a *cyborg*—and dodged fire from all those security men.

"I was going to thank you next," Alisa said. "Beck looked more pitiful, so I did him first."

"More pitiful? Are you sure?" Leonidas looked down at his arm and grimaced. That gash he'd received had cut through flesh and muscle, all the way to his implant, a glimpse of the grayish material visible through the blood. He seemed to realize that and shifted his arm so it wouldn't be visible to her.

She smiled gently at him. As if she didn't know about his exotic insides by now.

"Thank you for protecting us, Leonidas," she said softly.

"You're welcome."

A beep came from the control panel. Alisa groaned and turned back to it. Had one of the mafia ships decided to chase them?

"It's that Alliance warship again," Abelardus said. "The one with your favorite admiral."

He was right. And it was flying straight toward their shuttle.

Alisa would have preferred dealing with the mafia, but she tried to smile for her beleaguered team. "Isn't this fortuitous? If they capture us, we can rescue Stanislav while we're there."

"Uh," Beck said, "who will rescue us?"

CHAPTER FIFTEEN

The grab beam enveloped the shuttle with a flash of blue and a jolt.

"That didn't take long," Alisa said glumly.

She had changed course several times to try to evade the warship, and she'd thought about fleeing back to the mafia ships, but she knew Henneberry and her buddies wouldn't hesitate to kill her. She hoped that the Alliance, still wanting to get Tiang back, would keep her alive, at least long enough to question her.

She leaned back from the controls, letting go. There was little point in fighting now. The beam held them immobile.

A forcefield lowered on the side of the warship, and the shuttle was inevitably drawn toward a large bay, this one stark, white, and utilitarian. Military.

"Rude of them to capture and delay us when we've got people in need of medical treatment," Beck said.

"I agree," Alisa said. "I'll try to get them to send a doctor in to fix you up while they're interrogating me."

"That's thoughtful of you, Captain."

"Interrogation," Abelardus said. "I can't wait."

Alisa thought about asking him to try to find the person operating the grab beam and tinker with his mind, but with nothing but open space for hours around them, Alisa couldn't imagine that it would matter. Even if she managed to escape the warship once, it would have plenty of time to catch up to the shuttle again. Besides, if she was taken aboard, maybe there was a chance that she could escape, find Stanislav, and free him.

Too bad her most powerful ally was lying on the deck in the back with his eyes closed.

I resent that, Abelardus spoke into her mind. *I'm just as powerful an ally as he is. Did your cyborg cause twelve mafia ships to start firing at each other? I don't think so.*

I only saw seven firing.

You were counting?

So I could shoot down your hyperbole later, yes, of course. Alisa managed a quick smile at him, though her gaze was soon drawn back to the hangar bay opening as the shuttle was pulled closer and closer to it.

I think their grab-beam operator is drugged, Abelardus said. *As is the bridge crew. I'm not able to get a read on their thoughts.*

They must be getting wise to the proliferation of Starseers in the system these days.

More likely, they're scared pissless that Stanislav will wake up in his cell. And be cranky.

That might be true. If Agosti had received a full report on how Stanislav had thwarted his boarding team back on Sepiron Station, he would know to be wary of his powers.

The shuttle entered the bay and floated down onto the deck between two rows of bombers and strikers. Even though she was in a perilous situation, Alisa found herself gazing wistfully at them. She missed the days of flying for the Alliance, of being a faithful, trusted, and unquestioned member of the organization.

A thunk sounded, and an alert flashed on the control panel as the shuttle was locked down. The forcefield rose again behind them. Alisa turned off the engines. They weren't going to get a chance to fly anywhere, not anytime soon.

"Do we have a plan?" Beck asked.

"Yeah," Alisa said, "you sit there and let Yumi fondle your shoulder while I go chat with Admiral Agosti."

"I'm not opposed to feminine fondling, even though she stabbed me with an injector, so I can't feel it much right now. But I don't think you should go out there without some tough men to guard you."

"Abelardus can come with me."

Beck's head lolled to the side so he could look at Abelardus. "He doesn't look very tough when his hair is twisted up in that girly bun."

Abelardus pulled his braids down so they hung around his shoulders. "Better?"

"Maybe Leonidas is strong enough to go with you," Beck suggested.

Abelardus glared at him.

"No," Alisa said, looking at the view screen. A door had opened, and two squads of combat-armor-wearing soldiers were marching out. "You and Leonidas will stay here. Yumi and Young-hee too. Yumi, if you get a chance, Leonidas looks like he could use some bandages."

"He's my next stop."

Alisa stood up and hit the button to open the hatch, doubting anything could be gained by making the soldiers cut their way into the shuttle. Two men without combat armor came into the hangar, following the squads of soldiers. One was the dour-faced Admiral Agosti, which did nothing to reassure Alisa, but the second wore stately whites and grays, with a cape that nearly brushed the deck behind him. The dark-skinned man walked with a slight hitch to his step, as if he wore a knee brace under his elegant trousers. Admiral—now *Senator*—Hawk.

Alisa didn't know how much reassurance to take from his presence, but he'd at least worked with her team and fought alongside Leonidas back in that volcano on Arkadius. Maybe he would be more reasonable than Agosti.

She picked her way past Yumi and walked down the aisle of seats toward the open rear hatch. At some point in the last thirty seconds, Leonidas had gone from horizontal to vertical. He stood with his jacket sliced in several spots, blood still dripping from his wounds, but he clenched his destroyer in one hand, and his jaw was set in a fiercely determined visage.

With concern and love tightening her throat, Alisa peeled the last few shreds of his prosthetics off his face. She grimaced at the bruises starting to darken his skin and the swelling of a split lip. That fight had been rougher than she had realized.

"Why don't you wait here for nurse-in-training Yumi?" she suggested. "Or *there*," she added, pointing at the deck. "In a supine position. With pillows and a mug of hot cocoa."

"I don't think this shuttle came equipped with pillows or cocoa."

"Probably not. It *was* an imperial troop shuttle, after all. I'm sure the empire would have hated the idea of its troops luxuriating with comforts."

"Very much so."

Leonidas must have heard the soldiers approaching outside because he turned from her, stepping up to the threshold of the hatch and facing outward. The ramp had not deployed. Maybe it had been broken—or ripped off—when the cyborgs had been trying to get in.

As Leonidas glowered down at the armored soldiers who came into view, pointing their rifles at his chest, Alisa stepped up to his side. She tried to ease in front of him, hoping the men would be less likely to shoot an unarmed woman, but his arm came up to her waist, anchoring her to the deck. It seemed he would accept her at his side, but he wouldn't let her be a shield. Not that she was surprised.

"Afternoon, gentlemen," Alisa said to the glassy faceplates of the soldiers—from her angle above them, she couldn't see any of their eyes. "It's fortunate you came by. There's this epic mafia meeting going on over that way." She waved in what might have been the direction she'd come from. "You should probably check it out. I understand they're planning to overthrow the government. *Our* government." She pointed at them, then touched her chest. She was still a loyal Alliance citizen, yes, sir. And she would appreciate it if they treated her like one.

The men—there had to be at least twenty of them—stared at them without answering, their rifles pointing unwaveringly at Leonidas's chest.

"But if you insist on spending time with me and my team," Alisa went on, smiling and trying not to feel daunted, "several of my people were injured while confronting those would-be usurpers. If you could call a medic or two down here, that would be extremely useful."

"What kind of fool confronts multiple mafia ships in a shuttle without weapons?" a familiar voice asked.

Senator Hawk stepped around the back corner of the shuttle and looked up at Alisa, his eyebrows raised.

"Sir," Admiral Agosti whispered, easing into view and grabbing his arm. "You shouldn't get so close. She's got her pet cyborg with her."

"I'd say from past experience that she's more dangerous than he is."

"Really," Leonidas said, managing to sound indignant despite his injuries.

"I'm sure he's referring to my wild unpredictability rather than my martial talents," Alisa said.

"Indeed," Hawk said. "If you'll be so good as to drop your weapons and come down here, I'm sure it would set these soldiers' minds at ease." He extended a hand toward the armored men. "Then we can relax and have a nice chat. One where you let me know where my soon-to-be father-in-law is."

"Probably turning my ship into a quarantine zone."

Hawk's eyes narrowed slightly. He was being amiable enough, but she doubted he would hesitate to use force against them if pushed.

"Better put down the destroyer," she told Leonidas.

His eyes also narrowed. She thought he would prove mulish and refuse, but he flipped the weapon's safety on, held his arm straight out, and dropped it. It clattered to the deck.

"Anything else?" Hawk asked, eyeing his belt.

"No," Leonidas said.

Hawk looked at Alisa.

"I don't have anything," she said. "We've been posing as caterers. We didn't so much confront the mafia people as we got ourselves invited to their shindig. But as it turns out, you can board the ship of a rich business-woman easily enough. It's leaving that's a problem."

"Come down." Hawk pointed at the deck. Maybe he didn't want to have their chat where he had to crane his neck to look up at them.

"We will," Alisa said, "but can you please send a medic? I wasn't joking. I have a man with a bullet in his gut, an injured woman, and Leonidas could use…" She looked him up and down, not sure where to start the list.

"Hot cocoa," he murmured.

Hawk's eyebrows rose.

"It's been a rough day," Alisa said.

Sensing that they would soon lose their patience—they no doubt wanted to search the shuttle and make sure nobody with weapons lurked inside—she put her hand on the hatchway to hop down. Leonidas landed before she did. A couple of the armored men twitched, their rifles shifting toward the destroyer on the deck. Alisa didn't know what they thought would happen if he lunged for it. They were all protected by their armor. Of course, technically, Agosti and Hawk were close enough that Leonidas might have lunged for *them*. She doubted he would make a hostage of Hawk after they had worked together. Agosti might be a different story. He had, after all, rudely ordered an attack on the station while Leonidas had been undergoing his surgery.

"Search the shuttle," Agosti ordered as soon as Leonidas and Alisa stepped away from the entrance. He glanced at Hawk, who nodded slightly. "Take the injured men to sickbay. Under guard."

Alisa took some comfort from the fact that Hawk appeared to be in charge. It seemed strange, since he had only a small amount of gray in his wiry black hair, whereas Agosti must have been fifteen to twenty years his senior, but Agosti hadn't been a war hero and wasn't now a government representative. Indeed, Alisa found Hawk more intimidating in civilian clothes that seemed stately and fitting for a man in office than she had when he'd been an officer in combat armor.

"There's someone here you may want to see," Hawk said, nodding toward the door, then walking in that direction.

Several of the soldiers hurried to follow him, their boots ringing on the metal deck. Agosti stayed behind, waving for one squad to hop up into the shuttle. Though Alisa wanted to follow Hawk—there was only one person on this ship he could mean—she glanced back, worried her people wouldn't be treated well.

I'll make sure they don't get too handsy, Abelardus informed her silently. *Go see your dad.*

Thank you.

Alisa started after Hawk, but two of the soldiers blocked the way, insisting on searching her and Leonidas before letting them go. Her pat-down was cursory. They were much more thorough with Leonidas and kept a rifle on him while they searched. He wore a stony expression, and his jaw seemed to be permanently clenched. She rested a hand on his bare forearm. He looked down at it, then gave her a look she couldn't decipher.

"You could go to sickbay with the others," she said. "I think I'll be all right with Hawk."

"*Senator* Hawk," the soldier searching Leonidas growled.

"I'll go with you," Leonidas said, ignoring the man. "Left to your own devices, you might say something lippy and get yourself locked into the cell next to Stanislav."

"How would your being along stop that?" She squeezed his arm.

He looked down at her hand again, and she was about to ask if something was wrong—did he mind the familiarity in front of the enemy?—but the soldiers stepped back and waved for them to head to the door where Hawk waited. Alisa did not attempt to hold his hand or touch him while they walked, but he looked rough enough that it was hard for her not to offer support of some kind.

She expected Hawk to lead them through the winding corridors of the ship and to the brig, but found herself gaping at a black Starseer robe as soon as they walked into the room with the controls for the shuttle bay. It was a grimy robe with more than a few tears in it, but the person wearing it looked well, his short beard and hair trimmed, and his eyes far more alert than Alisa had expected.

Hawk extended a hand toward him and started to say something, but Alisa rushed forward and hugged Stanislav.

He made a startled noise, but soon returned the hug.

"I wasn't expecting this," he murmured quietly.

"Well, you were killed, or so I thought, before I got a chance to decide if I liked you or not." Aware of the soldiers looking on, Alisa backed up. She lifted her hand quickly to brush moisture from her eyes, the tears surprising her.

"Hm, I shouldn't have allowed that to happen." Stanislav smiled slightly.

"No, you shouldn't have. I ordered you to follow us, and you got this stupid idea in your head about staying behind to sacrifice yourself."

"Stupid? I thought it was noble."

"I mistake those two often," Leonidas said, "in her eyes."

"The eyes of family are the most important ones," Stanislav said.

Alisa noticed he wasn't cuffed or restrained in any way. He didn't have his staff, but that hardly made him weaponless, especially considering he did not appear to be drugged.

"They're letting you roam about freely?" Alisa asked, glancing at Hawk. He was standing back but watching, as were four of the armored men. "When I saw a vid of you—when Agosti tried to bribe me—" this time, her glance at Hawk was a darker one, "—you were unconscious in a brig cell."

"Yes, the admiral kept me there for quite a while. I remember little of it, since napping was enforced."

"With drugs," Alisa said.

"With drugs," he agreed. "But when Senator Hawk arrived, he had me woken so he could make a deal with me."

"Deal? What deal?" She looked at Hawk again, though she didn't know why she bothered. He wasn't responding to any of her looks. He simply stood with his shoulder against the bulkhead, his arms folded over his chest, waiting and watching. Thinking he might gather some juicy intel?

"I've agreed to help the Alliance defeat Tymoteusz," Stanislav said.

"Weren't you going to do that anyway?"

"Not if I was locked in a cell and drugged out of my mind," he said dryly. "I've also agreed to help them take the staff from the *chasadski*."

Alisa squinted at him. She could believe that he would want the staff out of Terrible Tym's hands, but did he truly want the Alliance to have that weapon?

"Well, we have very similar plans." Alisa didn't mention Thorian, since she doubted Hawk or anyone in the Alliance particularly wanted him to come out of this alive. "You should come back to the freighter with us, and we'll chase Tymoteusz down together. Maybe we'll even come up with a plan that can defeat him before getting in a squabble with him this time."

"We *have* a plan," Hawk said.

"Really? Because so far, your people have let him saunter past under their noses without even reacting. And for that matter, so has the empire. He's taken over their people and used them against us."

"We've acquired a sufficient supply of qui-gorn that such things won't happen to us when we confront him. I cannot speak to what the empire has come up with to battle him, but we weren't planning on inviting them to the showdown when we locate and confront Tymoteusz."

"They have a habit of inviting themselves."

"So I've noticed." Hawk frowned, not at her but at Leonidas. He was standing back while Alisa had her reunion, saying nothing.

"He's not telling them anything," Alisa snapped.

"So you think."

"So I *know*. You think I don't monitor the comm channels on my own ship? You can ask him. I've eavesdropped on him *plenty* of times."

"She does eavesdrop often," Leonidas agreed blandly.

Great, the first words he'd spoken in front of the soldiers, and they were to agree that she was shifty. Even if she had set herself up for that, she gave him a dirty look.

"Don't forget to arrange for my cocoa while you're negotiating," he told her, unaffected by her look.

"This isn't a negotiation," Hawk said.

"So, no cocoa?"

Hawk frowned at him.

"Leonidas didn't used to make jokes at inappropriate times," Alisa informed him, "but I've rubbed my tendencies all over him, and he's picked some up."

"I hope he enjoyed all that rubbing," Hawk murmured.

Leonidas's tight smile had a devilish aspect. He seemed to be in a better mood. Alisa wondered if Stanislav was speaking to him telepathically. Maybe reassuring him that he would keep the soldiers from pestering their team unduly? Did Stanislav have that kind of sway now that he'd cut his deal?

"All right," Alisa said to Stanislav, "you've agreed to help them defeat Tymmy. That's good. Since we're going the same way, we can help too. And you can ride along with us."

"That would be acceptable to me," Stanislav was quick to agree.

"Absolutely not," Hawk said. "She's not going to get her rickety freighter involved in a space battle. That's ridiculous. *He* can come if he wants to help—" Hawk pointed at Leonidas, "—but not her."

"Space battle?" Alisa asked, ignoring the jab at the *Nomad*. "*That's* your big plan for dealing with Tymoteusz? A space battle?"

"We're bringing a fleet."

"A fleet he'll have shooting at each other before you get into weapons range with him."

"I already told you that we have a drug that can counteract attempts at mind manipulation," Hawk said.

"Fine. Let's say that's effective. What about the staff? I had the delightful experience of being on an asteroid base that he shook into pebbles remotely with the thing. He could quake your ships into pieces. Your big weapons and shields wouldn't mean anything against that power."

"He can't wave his hand—or staff—and destroy a fleet all at once. We have enough ships that he won't be able to handle them all. He's in a simple transport ship. All we need is to get a few rounds off, and it'll be obliterated. I don't care how powerful he is; he will die in the vacuum of space, the same as anyone else."

Alisa opened her mouth to object—how did he *know* that Tymoteusz couldn't wave the staff and destroy a fleet all at once?—but he continued over her.

"I agree that he may be able to seriously damage our ships and kill many of our people before we take him down," Hawk said. "That's why we have someone who can go in first and keep him busy while we approach and attack." He nodded to Stanislav.

Stanislav did not appear particularly gleeful at the role he'd been given, but he did nod back.

"You're not going to sacrifice yourself again, are you?" Alisa asked, alarmed and distressed. She'd just gotten him *back*. "Didn't he kick your ass in your last confrontation with him?"

"It wasn't quite that bad," Stanislav murmured.

"Leonidas carried you out of that field."

Hawk's lips thinned. That probably wasn't the intel he'd hoped to gain. "You're his brother, right? Aren't you of similar levels of talent?"

"You mean, am I as powerful as he is?" Stanislav's mouth twisted. "In addition to having his power amplified by the staff, he spent thirty years studying the *chasadski* ways—the *dark* ways. I spent two years in that camp after events left me...disillusioned with the system and humanity as a whole—" he turned a sad smile on Alisa, "—then, finding the whole practice distasteful, went off to be a hermit. I made some tools, kept some bees, and bred goats. I wasn't testing myself against other Starseers in battle and trying to learn more about the dark arts, because I didn't care about them. I minded my own business. Of course, my parents had died by then, and I foolishly did not know that I had family out there besides Tym."

"Goats?" Alisa asked.

"Did I not mention them before?"

"You didn't. Were there any horses? Jelena has expressed an interest in horses."

Hawk lowered his face into his hand, looking like a man whose amazing plan had just been shredded apart by a five-year-old. Or, in this case, a fifty-five-year-old, goat-raising hermit.

Stanislav held her gaze. "You found her."

Hadn't he poked into her mind yet to see that? She supposed they had been discussing other matters.

"We did," she said.

"Senator Hawk," Stanislav said. "I would like to see my granddaughter before we head off to confront Tymoteusz."

Hawk lowered his hand. "Where is she?"

Alisa had expected him to refuse outright. "On my ship. Back near Aldrin." Even though she didn't think the Alliance—or at least Senator Hawk—wanted to fly over and pulverize the *Nomad* right now, she kept the specific location to herself. She didn't trust anyone fully these days, except for her own crew.

Hawk shook his head. "We can't take the time to backtrack. Henneberry's yacht, and the mafia ships she seems to have selected for her new coalition, have already taken off. Our operative over there says they're heading out into the middle of nowhere, not back toward Aldrin."

"I'm sure Operative *Tomich* can update you on their final location when they arrive."

Hawk stared at her. "How do you always know as much as we do about what's going on?"

"I'm sly and crafty."

Leonidas, good man that he was, did not bring up her eavesdropping tendencies again.

"I thought you didn't care about the staff," Hawk said. "I thought you just wanted to get your daughter back, which it sounds like you've accomplished."

"I *don't* care about the staff." Alisa sensed that he didn't believe her, but she didn't know how to change that. "And all I *did* want was to get my daughter back. But Tymoteusz stole one of her schoolmates, and I found myself promising that I would help get him back."

Leonidas stirred behind her, and even though she wasn't looking at him, she could feel his gaze suddenly boring into the back of her head. No, he wouldn't want her bringing up Thorian to the Alliance.

"One of her *schoolmates?*" Hawk asked. "What would a megalomaniacal future dictator want with—oh. Prince Thorian."

"They were studying under the same tutors," Alisa said.

Hawk frowned. "Our intelligence said—" He looked toward the doorway into the shuttle bay, perhaps searching for Agosti, but all the men had disappeared, Alisa's crew included. They must have gone out another door and, she hoped, straight to sickbay. "We assumed he was dead. Tymoteusz was reputed to want him dead."

Alisa was surprised how much the Alliance knew, considering they hadn't been in the middle of things, the way her ship had been. But they hadn't known Thorian was alive. And she'd just informed them of that.

She closed her eyes. Stupid, Alisa. Stupid. She and Leonidas could have retrieved Thorian and sent him off with the Starseers to be educated someplace where he wouldn't be harassed by people who wanted him dead or who wanted to use him. Or hells, he could have even stayed on the *Nomad*, where he and Jelena could have played with Zizblocks. And if Stanislav returned to them, maybe he could have tutored them.

But, no. She'd opened her mouth. And Hawk had gotten the free intel he'd hoped for.

She couldn't look at Leonidas, but she apologized silently to him. Later, she would apologize aloud. She hoped this wouldn't end in a way that left her apologizing for the rest of her life.

"Well," Hawk said, "we'll try to get him out alive if there's any chance, but if we have the opportunity to blow Tymoteusz's ship out of space, we have to take it."

Alisa swallowed, again feeling Leonidas's gaze upon her.

"Let us come along," she found herself offering. "You do your fearsome fleet plan, but Stanislav can ride with us, and then he'll distract Tym while we find a way to board his ship. We'll get Thorian and the staff, which the Alliance can have for—"

"Nobody's *boarding* the ship," Hawk said. "We're blowing it up from as far away as possible. If the staff survives the explosion, we'll pick it out of the wreckage later."

"But there are innocent—"

"The prince was raised from birth to be a player on a field of strife and politics. He's known his fate from his earliest days. He'll understand."

"Why he's being blown up? How lovely for him."

Hawk shook his head, his eyes saying that he wasn't discussing this matter further. "You're not going along. Whatever scheme you've been hatching, it ends here."

Alisa clenched her jaw, but did not argue further. Let him think what he wanted. She wasn't done hatching schemes.

Stanislav smiled faintly.

"If I let you go," Hawk said, speaking slowly as if he was analyzing whether or not this was a good idea even as the words came out, "will you agree to lead one of our shuttles back to your ship to pick up Admiral Tiang?"

"Tiang doesn't want to go. I've been trying to get rid of him for weeks."

Hawk's brow wrinkled.

"He's locked in his cabin, doing some strange medical research. He made Leonidas catch him rats in a junkyard on Cleon Moon."

Hawk looked at Leonidas, who nodded once. Odd that Leonidas's word seemed to mean more to Hawk than hers. Or maybe not. They'd bonded together while fighting the Starseers.

"Well," Hawk said, "Admiral Tiang has a commission in the Alliance fleet, which means showing up to work every day. His leave is long over, his daughter is worried about him, and Headquarters wants his butt back in a medical research facility on one of their ships. I have to insist that he leave your ship." He looked Alisa in the eyes. "I could make the release of your team and your shuttle contingent on our ability to retrieve him. But I would prefer you simply did the right thing and led us to your ship so we could get him. Whether it was your intent or not, you are harboring an officer who is, at the least, AWOL, and may be in more trouble than that."

Alisa wanted to tell him to go kiss an asteroid and to find Tiang on his own, but the regret in Hawk's eyes as he spoke that last derailed her. He probably didn't *want* to bring his future father-in-law back for possible punishment, but even senators couldn't do whatever they wanted. He must feel he had no choice.

Alisa looked at Leonidas, wondering what he thought. The main reason she'd wanted to keep Tiang was because whatever he was working on might be useful against Tymoteusz, but Hawk was standing here forbidding her and her "rickety" freighter to get involved in that battle. Not that she intended to obey him—after all, she'd planted that tracking device for a reason. But was it worth incurring further animosity from the Alliance by extending Tiang's refuge?

"Whatever he's working on," Leonidas said, "your military probably has a better chance of deploying it and putting it to use than we do."

She sensed that he had more on his mind, more that he wouldn't say in front of Hawk. She would have to wait to ask him later.

"If you'll let my team go," Alisa said, "we'll lead one of your shuttles back so you can retrieve Admiral Tiang. Stanislav—"

"Stays with us," Hawk said firmly. "That's the deal."

Stanislav smiled sadly and did not deny it.

"Then I reluctantly accept it," Alisa said. "My team would like to leave as soon as possible."

That tracking device wouldn't have infinite range. If Henneberry was even now heading off in one direction, and the *Nomad* was back in the opposite direction, Alisa already risked losing her prey. If the shuttle were capable of flying interplanetary distances, she might have simply taken off in that. No, that wasn't possible, she realized. Mica had the other half of the tracking equipment back on the *Nomad*.

"Good," Hawk said. "I will arrange it."

He waved his fingers toward a couple of the soldiers and moved over to talk to them.

I would have liked to meet your daughter, Stanislav spoke into her mind, *but I made this deal before I knew you had her.*

It's fine, Alisa thought. *You can see her after you shove that staff into your brother's exhaust port. Painfully.*

I hope I'll survive to have that opportunity.

You better survive. Jelena needs a teacher, and I don't trust this Westfall lady.

You wish me to teach her? Do you trust me?

I'm working on it. Besides, you're a relative. I figure you won't charge much for tutoring. Payment in cookies, perhaps.

Stanislav snorted.

Alisa noticed that Leonidas had moved closer to her, and she turned to lean against his uninjured shoulder. Since he was wounded, she ought to be offering *him* support, but she felt drained, physically and emotionally. On the one hand, she was delighted to have been reunited with Stanislav, but on the other, it wasn't much of a reunion. He was about to be taken off on a mission that sounded suicidal to face a man who was more powerful than he. Tymoteusz might have stopped short of killing Stanislav before, due to their kinship, but would he stop again? Especially when Stanislav would be showing up with a fleet of soldiers? Even if Stanislav and the Alliance managed to pull out a victory, it didn't sound like anyone intended to get Thorian out before blowing up the *chasadski* ship. She had promised Jelena she would get her friend back. How could she go back to the *Nomad* and say that wouldn't happen now?

Leonidas must have sensed her angst because he wrapped his arm around her and pulled her into his chest. She appreciated the gesture, but she felt too guilty to derive comfort from it. She'd also promised *him* that they would get Thorian back.

She blinked away tears before they could fully form and took a deep breath. No, she wasn't giving up yet. As she'd told herself, they could track Henneberry to the meeting spot and arrive not much later than the Alliance fleet. Maybe Tymoteusz would be late in joining up with his new mafia allies, and Alisa would have time to get the *Nomad* to the party. And then, while the battle was engaged, somehow she and Leonidas could take a team in to retrieve Thorian. True, that sounded utterly suicidal, considering ships would be firing at the *chasadski* ship while she was attempting this infiltration. But maybe she could think of something. Depending on where Henneberry and her allies were going to meet Tymoteusz, she might have days to plan.

"Are you taking solace in my arms?" Leonidas asked. "Or scheming?"

"What makes you think I'm scheming?" Alisa tilted her head back to meet his eyes.

"You're standing very still. Usually you hug me back, and your hands roam a bit when you're taking solace."

"Well, my father is a few feet away. I wasn't sure how boldly my hands should roam." She smiled over at Stanislav, but he merely shook his head and wiggled his fingers in a continue gesture. He also turned away to give them some privacy.

"I enjoy it when they roam," Leonidas murmured softly.

"Oh? Are you able to enjoy it now?" She looked back at him and noticed he was watching her through his eyelashes. "Drugs worn off?" she whispered.

"Possibly. My head is clearer."

Implying that he had experienced some side effects from Yumi's concoction? Alisa once again lamented that he felt the need to take them.

"Other things are more noticeable too," he said, sliding his hand down her back to rest on her butt. "And I have this urge to stamp out your memories of spending time in lavatories with other men."

"Oh?" She smiled. "How would this stamping be done?"

"If we were alone, I'd show you."

She thought about pointing out that they could spend time together on the shuttle on the way back, but since she had to pilot it and the only private spots were the compact lavatories in the back, that wouldn't be the ideal place for coming together. Especially since those lavatories weren't particularly soundproof, as far as she'd noticed.

Hawk came back into the room and lifted an eyebrow at Leonidas's hand placement. "Is this how the rubbing off of tendencies is accomplished?"

"Sometimes," Alisa said.

Leonidas released her, and she stepped back.

"One of Agosti's surgeons is removing your man's bullet and patching up the woman," Hawk said. "I'm having a shuttle prepared for Admiral Tiang. It will pick him up and take him to a transfer station on Sherran Moon so he can get a ride home. It will fly back with you when your people are ready to go." His gaze hardened slightly, as if to warn her that he knew her reputation as a pilot who could escape from unwanted pursuit and wouldn't appreciate it if she tried to do so this time.

Alisa sighed. Unfortunately, she had no such plans, not with time pressing. She would have to hand Tiang off and immediately head after the tracking signal with the *Nomad*.

"Can it take non-combatants to the moon too?" Leonidas asked, then looked at Alisa. "The children. And the Starseers who haven't shown any aptitude for battle."

"Not *all* of the children," Alisa said, having no intention of letting Jelena go again. But she conceded the point about the rest of the crew. Yumi might wish to stay behind too. This wasn't her battle.

"You don't think she should be taken somewhere safe?" Leonidas asked.

"With whom? Westfall? So she can disappear before we can come back to get her? I don't trust that woman, and I'm not risking losing Jelena again." She could understand his concerns, and maybe he was even right, but the idea of having to spend a year looking for Jelena again…It made her clench her fists and want to pummel Starseers.

"As you wish," was all Leonidas said.

Alisa scowled, but did not say more. Hawk was probably already wondering why the *Nomad* needed to send its passengers somewhere "safe."

"Do you want to get fixed up too?" Hawk asked, pointing at Leonidas. "You've been bleeding on Agosti's deck."

Leonidas shook his head and started to speak, but Alisa interrupted him.

"Yes, he does."

Leonidas arched his eyebrows.

"I know you adore it when Alejandro seals you up, but we have to wait for the bullet removal anyway, right? You should get patched up here in case we run into trouble before we reunite with him. It makes sense for you to be at your fittest."

He doesn't want to leave your side, Stanislav informed her silently, a smile tugging at his lips.

She wondered if he felt pleased that he had been instrumental in getting them *all* the way together.

Alisa patted Leonidas's chest. "We'll come with you," she said, pointing to Stanislav.

Hawk did not object. "This way," he said, and headed into a corridor.

Alisa and Leonidas followed him, Leonidas wrapping an arm around her waist again as they walked.

He was hoping to find some privacy while he wasn't leaving your side, Stanislav thought, trailing after Alisa and Leonidas.

All right. I don't need you translating his thoughts for me. I get enough of that from Abelardus.

Ah, quite right. I shall give you both your privacy.

Besides, she didn't need a translator. She knew perfectly well what it meant when a man's hand kept finding its way down to cup her butt. It occurred to her that if she sent Jelena away with Westfall in the shuttle, she and Leonidas could have some private time as the ship tracked down Henneberry. There wouldn't be any need to have him drugged. But it seemed such a selfish thought. Of course, keeping Jelena aboard when the ship would be flying into danger seemed selfish too. It was too bad Perun was so far away; she might have arranged commercial transport for Jelena back to her sister-in-law in the capital, and then picked her up after Tymoteusz, the staff, and Thorian had been dealt with, but it was over a week to Perun from the Aldrin moons. That was a long time for an eight-year-old to be sent off alone. And would the Starseers even *allow* Alisa to take Jelena from them? They were all so insistent that she needed tutors.

Alisa sighed as they followed Hawk into a lift, wishing she knew the right thing to do.

CHAPTER SIXTEEN

The comm flashed in the shuttle's cockpit.

Alisa yawned and answered the familiar signal. "Marchenko here. Is that you, Mica?"

Behind her, Beck, Young-hee, and Leonidas were sleeping, stretched across seats or on the deck. Abelardus was playing a game on someone's netdisc, and Yumi dozed in the co-pilot's seat. The blocky shape of the *Star Nomad* coasted through space on the view screen.

"Who else would it be?" came Mica's voice over the comm. "Hardly anyone else on here knows how to work this dilapidated control panel."

"Well, I assumed Bravo Six was still flying."

"I'm here, Lady Captain," came Six's deadpan voice.

"He's flying," Mica said, "but he called me up here to ask if we should be alarmed by the fact that you've picked up a stalker."

"The Alliance shuttle snuggled up to my butt is here to pick up Tiang," Alisa said.

"Good."

"I see you're going to miss him."

"I've got him quarantined in sickbay. It's the only place with self-contained air and filtration."

Alisa frowned at the comm panel. "And that's necessary, because…?"

"One of his rats got loose. I found it having a seizure on the deck in the middle of the corridor. It died while I was knocking on his cabin to tell him to take care of it."

A tendril of worry wormed its way through Alisa's gut. "He's created a virus or bacteria or something? And it's out? Are the *children* in danger?"

Don't forget to be concerned about the rest of us too, Abelardus spoke into her mind.

You're not even on the ship. She waved dismissively over her shoulder.

I'm about to be. And so are you. I'm sure if you have the genes, you could be affected, whether you've ever manifested powers or not.

I know, but that doesn't matter. Alisa hadn't been on the ship for the last twenty-four hours. She was far more worried about Jelena. And yes, the other children. She had promised those Starseers a safe haven.

"Tiang says no," Mica said, "but I think he's naive. And when he talks about what exactly he's doing, it goes over my head. Alejandro also isn't certain about what Tiang has made. He's the one who suggested locking him in sickbay with some rat bars and a bucket to piss in. The Starseers have barricaded themselves in the rec room of their own accord. There's not a separate filtration system in there, so I'm not sure what they hope to accomplish, but I haven't minded the quiet. I was a little tempted to lock the hatch to make sure they stayed in there."

"Lovely. I'll let the Alliance soldiers know that they might want to wear their combat armor or decon suits to pick up their wayward admiral."

Mica snorted. "We working with them now?"

"Not...exactly." Alisa thought of Stanislav, the way he'd waved good-bye through the door when Alisa had piloted the shuttle out into space. He'd said little of his fears, but she got the sense that he didn't expect to live to see her again. Or to see Jelena ever. That upset her and angered her too. He had already tried to sacrifice himself once. He didn't need to do it again. She would come up with something. "They're taking Tiang back to his people, and that's it. His leave ended, and he's been AWOL for a while."

"Understood."

"Since the *Nomad* only has one airlock, we'll dock this shuttle first, transfer everyone in, and then have Bravo Six come pilot it out alongside us again. The soldiers can come in after that."

"Nice of you to accommodate them."

"I didn't have much choice," Alisa said.

"I bet. Good to have you home, Captain." Mica sounded sincere.

Alisa could imagine how it must have been to deal with Tiang and a bunch of scared Starseers. It would make wrangling Yumi's chickens seem easy in comparison.

As she relayed the information to the Alliance shuttle, Leonidas roused himself from the deck and came to stand behind her, running his gaze over the holodisplays and checking the status of everything. She wouldn't have minded having him stroke her hair, but he merely clasped his hands behind his back, the image of the professional soldier. Probably preparing himself for the idea that Jelena would be in there, perhaps poking into his thoughts soon. Alisa lamented that she hadn't found a private moment for a tryst with him. He would take some more of Yumi's drugs when they got inside and forget the desire for private moments.

We'll figure it out, she thought silently toward him, though her brain hurt from how many things she had to figure out. At least, there wasn't any trouble as she guided the shuttle in to dock with the *Nomad*. The Alliance pilot also accepted that he would have to wait his turn. She'd thought he might object, but his little shuttle had shields and weapons, so he probably wasn't too worried about losing the *Nomad* and his objective now that she'd led them to the ship.

Alisa almost tripped when she walked into the cargo hold. The chickens were in their coop, and they squawked uproariously when Yumi appeared. But that wasn't what startled her. Near the coop, half under the walkway and against the hull, something was being constructed. Something that looked suspiciously like a cross between a tank and a pond.

"Mica," Alisa yelled as the rest of her crew filed off the shuttle. "What is this...*this* in my cargo hold?"

How had Mica found time to build anything while worrying about viruses and quarantines?

"It's going to be the pond," a delighted voice said from the walkway. Jelena skipped down the steps, faltered slightly when she noticed Leonidas, but hugged Alisa anyway.

Leonidas made a wide berth around them and headed straight into the ship. To drug himself? Alisa felt frustrated anew, but she was also pleased to see Jelena and to receive the hug. She returned it before remembering…

"What are you doing roaming the ship, little girl? I thought all the Starseers had barricaded themselves in the rec room."

Jelena offered her sly smile. "*Almost* all of them."

Alisa snorted, though she couldn't help but feel concerned. If Tiang had unleashed some virus that affected those with Starseer blood, she would prefer Jelena be locked in a closet somewhere.

"I needed something to build," Mica said, stepping out onto the walkway. "When I was banging at things with a hammer, it made it harder for people to complain to me. Not impossible, unfortunately, due to that pesky Starseer telepathy."

"Now we can get ducks and geese," Jelena said brightly.

Abelardus and Young-hee, perhaps not interested in the fowl outcome, headed up the stairs together.

"I didn't know you were eager for those, Jelena," Alisa said, feeling like she was losing a battle she hadn't even signed up to participate in.

"I've been feeding the chickens while Yumi was gone."

"I'm sure they appreciate that," Yumi said, gazing fondly at the tank. "Thank you."

"It's good practice," Jelena said. "For when I get my horse friend."

"Uh, I thought we discussed that, how we would go riding on Upsilon Seven, but not actually have horses on the ship."

"Oh sure, Mom. I know, but I'll think of any horse I ride as my horse friend because I'll talk to her in her mind, and we'll be real close."

Bravo Six jogged along the walkway and down the stairs. He headed for the airlock and the shuttle, but Jelena ran over toward him.

"Watch this, Mom. Arm, please, Bravo Six."

The android slowed and glanced at Alisa. "May I pause for approximately thirty seconds, Lady Captain?"

"Uh, sure," Alisa said, having no idea what they had in mind. She doubted the Alliance soldiers were in a hurry to get over here now that they knew they might be entering a quarantine zone.

Six stuck his arm out straight from his shoulder. Jelena jumped up and grabbed it with both hands, swung her legs up, tucked them in, and did a somersault to land on her feet again.

"His arm doesn't move at all," Jelena said, grinning. "It's like a bar at the playground."

She did another somersault to demonstrate while Bravo Six stood patiently with his arm out.

"Ah, very acrobatic, Jelena," Alisa said, "but Six has some flying to do now."

"All right."

Six retracted his arm, bowed slightly to Jelena, and strode into the airlock. Alisa looked wistfully in the direction Leonidas had gone, wishing Jelena would approach him at some point. She felt certain that he would volunteer an arm as sturdy as a metal bar for gymnastics purposes.

Alisa walked over and hit the controls to cycle the airlock. She watched as the tube withdrew, and the catering shuttle flew out of sight. The Alliance shuttle zipped in without hesitation, extending a tube of its own.

"I suppose someone should go up and warn Tiang that he needs to go back to his people," Alisa said.

"*What?*" came a distressed cry from the direction of sickbay.

"I believe Abelardus or Leonidas informed him," Mica said.

"Ah." Alisa hit the button to let the soldiers in once they finished their docking procedure, then headed for the walkway. Jelena had wandered over to join Yumi in feeding the chickens. "Jelena, come with me, please."

Alisa did not want her down here when soldiers she didn't know came aboard the ship, and also did not want her here when the soldiers dragged Tiang and his equipment through the cargo hold. She could easily envision some vial dropping and breaking, the contents oozing out and exposing Jelena to whatever he'd made.

Jelena hesitated.

"I'll wait until you come back to feed the rest of them," Yumi offered.

"All right."

Jelena skipped over and jogged up the stairs with Alisa. She missed the days when she'd had that much energy. Wasn't it close to the night cycle on the *Nomad*? She ought to make sure Jelena had eaten and send her to bed while these transfers of people happened.

"But I need to be here when you go to meet the *chasadski*," Tiang was saying when Alisa approached sickbay.

Leonidas was the one who had delivered the message and was standing in front of the hatchway. Jelena dropped back, walking behind Alisa and eyeing him dubiously.

"Is it safe?" Alisa whispered to Leonidas while pointing at Jelena.

"He assures me that there's nothing deadly out," Leonidas said, looking coolly into sickbay, presumably at Tiang.

Still in the corridor, Alisa couldn't see him yet.

"There was *never* anything deadly," came Tiang's voice. "Who started this rumor?"

"The dead rat Mica found," Alisa said.

"There are things that will kill rats that won't kill humans. Besides, that one was the first. I didn't know how much of the compound to deliver."

"Compound for what?" Alisa asked, easing forward. She peered into sickbay and wasn't that reassured by what she saw. Chemistry apparatuses were set up all over the counter, and Tiang wore that biohazard suit again.

"Technically, it's a retrovirus that I purchased from a research laboratory back on Caravan Circle Station, but I've altered it significantly and embedded nanobots to produce EMPs," Tiang said. "These will cause seizures, but no permanent damage. There may be some temporary brain trauma that will debilitate a man, perhaps knocking him unconscious, but the goal is to deny the Starseers access to their mental powers. A seizure will most certainly result in that."

"Go to bed, Jelena," Alisa said, waving for her to continue past Leonidas as she experienced terrifying thoughts of seizures and mutated viruses infecting her daughter. How much testing had Tiang done? Did he *know* there wouldn't be permanent damage? Did he have any idea how his concoction might affect children?

"But—"

"No buts," Alisa said. "Just do what I say for now. I'll come check on you later."

Jelena's face grew sulky, and she glanced back, as if she might dart off into the cargo hold to hide, but the sound of boots clanging on the deck came from that direction. She slunk past Leonidas, who backed up so she could pass, and hurried away.

"Admiral," Alisa said. "Please pack up everything you've been working on. Senator Hawk personally sent these men to collect you."

Tiang blinked his watery eyes. "Hawk?"

"Yes, your soon-to-be son-in-law. He's been worried about you, and your leave is up, so the military is worried about you too."

"My leave is up? So soon?" Tiang sounded genuinely surprised.

Alisa wagered he had no idea how many days had passed since he boarded the *Nomad*.

"Do you have anything we might use that's ready now?" Leonidas asked quietly as the clangs of boots grew louder. "Against Tymoteusz?"

"I have a prototype," Tiang offered.

"Will you leave it?" Leonidas looked at Alisa, then nodded toward the walkway where the first soldiers had appeared at the top of the stairs. He ducked through the hatchway into sickbay.

Alisa headed toward the men, lifting her hands to delay them in case Leonidas needed a few minutes with Tiang. She cringed at the idea of keeping some kind of weapon on her ship that might hurt Jelena, but she *had* been the one who had originally been hoping for an advantage that would work against the *chasadski*.

"A moment, please," she said, planting herself in the path of a burly sergeant who looked like he knocked things out of his path for a living. "We're having Admiral Tiang get his belongings, but Senator Hawk said you'd also be able to take some of our other passengers to safety. Is that right?"

The sergeant glanced behind him at a lieutenant. The officer stepped forward.

"Yes, he gave that order. We have room for up to twenty. We're going to Sherran Moon, no extra stops."

"That sounds fine." Alisa dug out her comm unit. "Abelardus, are you around?"

"Always around."

"Let Westfall and the others know their ride is here, will you?"

"They already know," Abelardus said.

The sergeant and the lieutenant eyed each other uneasily, and Alisa wondered if they knew their passengers would be Starseers.

"Is Jelena going with them?" Abelardus asked.

Alisa hesitated. She had wrestled with this question—multiple times—on the flight back to the *Nomad*, and she still doubted her final decision. She took a big breath and said, "No. She stays here."

"Ah," was all Abelardus said, then closed the comm.

The soldiers shuffled their feet, and a young man behind the officer fingered a rifle.

"Admiral?" Alisa called over her shoulder without giving any ground. "Are you ready for the soldiers? Do you want help carrying things?" She faced the lieutenant again. "He's been doing some medical experiments, and there could be dangers in moving his belongings."

"You're not delaying us for some reason, are you, Captain?" the lieutenant asked.

"Only for a moment to make sure you don't rush into sickbay, knock something over, and infect my ship with a disease."

"We're not gorillas, Captain," the lieutenant said.

"Only Max," someone in the back said with a snicker.

There were six soldiers lined up on the walkway now. Alisa suspected Hawk hadn't trusted her fully and had informed his men that they were to take Tiang by force if necessary.

Leonidas stepped out of sickbay, and the soldiers murmured, trading more uneasy glances. He wasn't wearing his fearsome red armor, but it didn't seem to matter. They knew who and what he was.

But Leonidas had some kind of spray pump and tank in his arms, and all he did was nod at Alisa and back away from the group.

"Don't put that in your cabin if you're still having nightmares," she murmured, hoping he'd hear her words and that the soldiers wouldn't. She didn't want that tank anywhere that it could be damaged.

He looked back over his shoulder, seemingly in acknowledgment, then disappeared into the mess hall. She trusted that he would find a safe place for it.

"Excuse us, Captain," the sergeant said, lifting a hand.

He did not touch her, but it was clear that he would if she didn't step out of the way. Alisa found herself reluctant to let Tiang go—he was an odd man, but he had helped Leonidas and had been far less of a burden on her ship than many of her other passengers—but she pressed her back to the bulkhead so the soldiers could pass.

The lieutenant and the sergeant entered sickbay, where Tiang said, "That goes. And that. No, that's Alejandro's. Get that trunk though."

As the litany continued on and more soldiers went in to pick up cargo, Alisa went from thinking the six-man squad was overkill to wondering if they had brought enough people. Four soldiers walked out with their arms full before Tiang came out with the lieutenant.

"Goodbye, Captain," Tiang said, stopping in front of her. "I did not realize how much time had passed. It's been a lovely stay."

Lovely? That was not the word Alisa would have used to describe the weeks since she had met Tiang.

"I'm glad you enjoyed your research time," she said.

"I do hope you'll be able to bring the staff to me for further research. I am most saddened that we did not reacquire it before my leave was up."

Aware of the lieutenant narrowing his eyes at this suggestion, Alisa said, "I'm afraid the staff is out of my hands now. Senator Hawk has made it clear that his people will handle its retrieval."

"Ah, Hawk is a good boy. And so is the colonel." Tiang looked toward the mess hall. "I forgot to say goodbye to him. I do hope that he'll reconsider joining the Alliance one day."

Alisa thought that unlikely, but she did not say so.

"You two are, of course, invited to my daughter's wedding," Tiang added.

Alisa doubted Suyin would appreciate seeing either her or Leonidas at her wedding, but she kept that thought to herself too.

"As is Beck. Beck is most passionately invited." Tiang's eyes widened with a new thought. "Maybe he could cater it!"

"Uh, I'll pass that suggestion on to him, but we may be temporarily retired from the catering business. Since the last people who hired him tried to kill his entire team afterward."

Tiang scratched his jaw. "I don't think that's allowed on Arkadius."

The sergeant cleared his throat and tilted his head toward the cargo hold and his ship. Three of the research Starseers originally from Sepiron Station walked past them, their meager belongings in bags over their shoulders. The soldiers eyed their staffs and shuffled aside to make room.

"I guess you better get going, Admiral," Alisa said.

"Hm, yes. I truly had no idea that my leave was already up. How did that happen?"

"Time flies when you're inventing brain-damaging nerve agents."

"Indeed."

Alisa stepped forward to hug Tiang and kiss him on the cheek, hoping that he had decontaminated himself thoroughly before leaving sickbay. He returned the hug and surprised her by holding it.

"Keep me apprised of Leonidas's penis status," he said. "I should be most curious as to whether he's able to produce offspring. You'll be encouraged to know that the sperm samples I tested were fertile and showed motility."

"I, uh, yes. I'll be sure to send you a message."

"Excellent." Tiang released her and trundled off after the soldiers.

The lieutenant must have caught that last comment because he gaped back and forth from Tiang to Alisa.

"We've decided he's not like other admirals," she offered.

"Er, no." That was all the lieutenant said before heading after Tiang, still looking slightly stunned.

Two more Starseers and three children walked past. Alisa followed the group. Someone would have to man the airlock controls and seal up once they had all their passengers boarded.

She had made it down the stairs and halfway across the cargo hold when a shriek echoed from the upper deck of the ship. Alisa stiffened in terror. Jelena.

She raced for the stairs. What was going on? Had Tiang's contagion gotten out? Had one of the Starseers been hurt? Killed? Was someone trying to hurt *Jelena*?

Alisa pounded down the walkway and burst into the mess hall, almost crashing into the back of a black robe. Abelardus. She tried to shove him aside, but he caught her and held a finger to his lips.

She's all right, he said silently.

"What in the hells is going on?" Alisa demanded, stepping past him until she could see up the corridor in the direction of NavCom, the direction Jelena's scream had come from. Two more black-robed figures stood near the intersection, partially blocking her view, but thanks to Leonidas's height, she could see his head over them. He stood in the middle of the intersection.

"You can't make me go," came Jelena's fierce cry. Was she behind him?

"Step aside, Colonel," one of the Starseers said—Lady Westfall.

"She doesn't want to go with you," Leonidas said.

"She's eight. It doesn't matter what she wants. It's about what's best for her."

"I'm not *going*," Jelena shrieked, reminding Alisa of some of the passionate tantrums she'd had when she was younger.

Even though she now realized that her daughter wasn't in pain or danger, Alisa took a step, her instincts telling her to stop this.

But Abelardus kept hold of her arm. *I promise you she's not going to pick a fight with your cyborg*, he thought dryly.

Alisa didn't know why that mattered. Jelena needed her mother now, and Westfall needed to know that Alisa had already decided that her daughter would stay with her.

"I'm going to get Thor," Jelena added. "He needs my help. I *can* help! Like with the dog!"

"Step aside, Colonel," Westfall said again, her voice harder. "That shuttle won't wait for us indefinitely. We're not letting the captain take a child into a battle zone."

"Alisa wants her daughter to stay with her," Leonidas said.

Westfall snorted. "She doesn't know what's best for a Starseer child. Or any child, it sounds like."

Alisa clenched a fist. That woman was about to get a punch in the back of the head.

"You're not taking her," Leonidas said, speaking slowly. His voice like ice.

"You think you can stop us?" the man next to Westfall asked.

"Yes."

"We can knock you aside with our minds," Westfall said.

"I can break your skull with my fist. Ask Abelardus. He's never gotten the best of me."

Abelardus sighed softly, but he didn't call out to correct him.

Nobody in the corridor moved, but tension thickened the air. Alisa shook her arm free from Abelardus, walked closer, and peered past the Starseers, finally spotting Jelena. She crouched in the corridor behind Leonidas, using him as a shield. He stood with his legs spread, his chest puffed out, making an impressive shield.

"Jelena is staying," Alisa said.

Westfall jumped. Apparently, she had been so intent on Leonidas that her super Starseer senses hadn't told her that someone had come up behind her. Alisa propped her fists on her hips and glared at her when she turned around.

"And I can't tell you how much I *don't* appreciate you trying to take her off my ship without talking with me about it."

"You just got here," Westfall blurted, looking guilty. Had that woman truly intended to take Jelena without asking? To sneak her away before Alisa realized what was happening?

"I've been here longer than the shuttle you want to skulk away on has. You could have spoken to me."

"We're not *skulking*. You think I don't know what's happening? What that crazy doctor has been working on? What you plan to do with this clunky freighter? Heading into a war zone to fight a bunch of fools who want to take over the entire system is ludicrous. You almost got killed on that asteroid base. Surely, you of all people should realize how foolish it is to go after him."

"Somebody has to," Leonidas said.

"Not *children*."

"That's why I want you to take the others," Alisa said. "But Jelena isn't yours to make decisions for."

"She should be," Westfall said. "You're being selfish and not doing what's best for her."

"I highly doubt *you're* what's best for her."

"She needs a teacher."

"She'll have my *father*." Alisa realized her fists were clenched so hard that they hurt, but she couldn't unclench them. "As soon as he's done with Tymoteusz, he'll be back. He'll teach her."

Westfall opened and closed her mouth a few times. Alisa thought she read the words, "done with Tymoteusz," on her soundless lips. She definitely read the disbelief on the woman's face. Was she so sure Stanislav couldn't defeat Tymoteusz?

Alisa stepped to the side and pointed toward the cargo hold. "Get the rest of your people and your students, and get off my ship."

Westfall looked back at Jelena, as if contemplating taking her by force. Jelena had eased out from behind Leonidas to watch the argument, but she darted back quickly, disappearing behind his muscled bulk. Leonidas did not move, and his face was as cold as ever, his eyes stony as he stared at the Starseers.

"*Go*," Alisa said.

"Very well. Don't blame me when—"

"Are you *still* here?" Alisa demanded. "Leonidas, will you please escort our passengers to their shuttle?"

"Yes," he said promptly and strode forward.

Westfall lifted a hand, as if to throw some mental attack at him.

He blurred into motion and, between one eye blink and the next, had his hand around the back of Westfall's neck and his destroyer pressed against the second Starseer's spine.

"Walk," he said in an icy voice that matched his eyes. "Or I will carry you."

"We're leaving, everyone," the man called, then sprinted for the walkway, bumping Abelardus in the shoulder and almost knocking him over as he ran.

Westfall glowered, and Alisa thought she might test Leonidas further, but she started walking of her own accord. Leonidas let go of her. He hadn't gripped her hard—there were no marks—but Alisa hoped the woman knew how easy it would have been for him to kill her.

Westfall paused in front of Alisa to say, "Do not think you or your daughter will be welcome among our people again, especially if you have some pariah teach her."

Leonidas growled from behind her, and she flinched and scurried off.

After she was gone, Jelena wiped her eyes and approached Alisa and Leonidas. She looked at him warily again, as if she hadn't just been hiding behind him. She concentrated for a second and did the trick where she made a noise sound behind Alisa and Leonidas. Even though Leonidas was wise to it this time—his eyebrow twitch gave that away—he obliged by turning to look. Jelena ran forward, hugged him, then sprinted away. A hatch soon clanged from the direction of her cabin.

Leonidas blinked. "Huh."

"You're welcome," Abelardus said.

"For what?" Alisa asked. "Not interfering?"

"For not letting *you* interfere." He winked and headed off to his own cabin.

Alisa let out a soft, "Huh," of her own as she considered how he had deliberately stopped her. Because he'd seen this as a chance for Jelena to come to appreciate Leonidas? If so, she was impressed by his perceptiveness.

Leonidas still looked faintly stunned by that hug. Alisa stepped forward and gave him a hug of her own.

"Thank you."

As his arms came around her, a rumble of pleasure emanated from his chest. Alisa wanted to drag him off to some hidden nook on the ship—if Mica wasn't in engineering, perhaps it would do—and push him up against a wall and have her way with him, but she had to be responsible and go check on Jelena. Still, she couldn't keep from sliding her hand up his back and kissing him on the side of the neck. One day, she promised herself. One day, he would be hers again.

He seemed to be thinking similar thoughts, because when she backed away, his eyes smoldered as they held hers.

"Goodnight, Leonidas," she quietly.

"Goodnight, Alisa," he said, his voice a touch raspy.

She forced herself to walk away, even though she did not want to.

CHAPTER SEVENTEEN

Alisa popped into NavCom before going to check on Jelena. With the immediate crisis averted, Alisa thought her daughter would be all right for a few minutes, and she wanted to check on the status of the tracker. Had Mica been able to locate the signal and link up with the device?

"There you are," Mica said, when Alisa stepped into NavCom. "I thought you didn't want to delay."

"I don't. There were Starseers blocking the passage."

"And screaming girls. I heard." Not sounding particularly bothered by either, Mica moved from the pilot's seat to the co-pilot's seat and tapped the holodisplay on her netdisc to life. A compact box of wires sat next to it, plugged into the comm panel. "They're already at the edge of our range." She pointed to a couple of blips on the display. "That's them. We're here. This is where they were when I first started tracking them about six hours ago if you want to take the points and plot their current course."

"Will do." Alisa sat down and reached for the navigation controls and also commed the Alliance shuttle. "Are you boys about ready to depart?"

"You in a hurry to go somewhere *Star Nomad?*" came the reply.

"Got some cargo to pick up and a life to get back on track."

The soldier grunted. "We'll leave shortly."

Alisa closed the channel.

"Cargo?" Mica asked. "Like a prince and a staff?"

"We've been forbidden from showing up at Tymoteusz's ship."

"Oh, and I'm sure you have plans to obey whoever gave that order." Mica waved at the blips on the display.

Alisa eyed those blips, worried that Henneberry's ship would fly out of range while they dallied here. She opened the comm to their catering shuttle, wondering what they should do with it now that the gig was over. Leaving it here in empty space would be wasteful. Ideally, she should return it to whomever Leonidas had purloined it from, even if it had been originally stolen from the empire. But she didn't want to send Bravo Six away with it when he might be a valuable resource against the *chasadski*. With no mind to control, he might have a better chance of sneaking up on them and deploying Tiang's weapon than any of them. She had expected the research Starseer who had originally owned him to request that he be loaded onto the shuttle with the rest of their people. But he hadn't said a word yet. Of course, after dealing with Leonidas, the Starseers might not have many words for Alisa, at least not ones they would say to her face.

"Six?" Alisa said. "Take a look at the fuel in that shuttle, will you? How much farther do you think it can travel?"

"That will depend on the number of course adjustments I must make, Lady Captain. There's fuel enough to power up to full speed, and if the shuttle can coast, it could theoretically travel across the system. I have no need for life support, so mid-flight power requirements are minimal."

"Ah, good point."

"What is our destination? I can plot a course now."

"We're not sure, but I'll send over our tracking data so you can make a guess. Be prepared to leave shortly."

"Yes, Lady Captain."

"And Bravo Six?"

"Yes?"

"I'm glad you're still with us."

Six paused, his logic circuits perhaps looking for an appropriate response. "This service is satisfying to me, also, but I do hope for a chance to resume research eventually."

"If we survive this, I'll make sure that happens," Alisa said. "I bet Tiang wouldn't mind a medical research assistant."

"Interesting."

"Assuming he doesn't get court-martialed," Mica said.

Alisa closed the comm. "I don't think that's likely. But I'm sure there will be ramifications for his AWOL status. I just hope he gave us something that will be useful." She finished plugging a course into navigation. "As soon as the Alliance leaves and disappears from the sensors, we're taking off."

"To seek cargo out in the middle of nowhere?"

"We've found cargo there before," she said, thinking of the staff.

The Alliance shuttle commed them.

"We're detaching from your airlock now," the soldier said. "Let me say what a total pleasure it is having all of these Starseers on board. Thank you so much for sharing your refugees with us."

"I sense sarcasm in your tone. Are they already harassing you?"

"Three of them are talking into my head. Is that normal?"

"For them it is. *Nomad*, out." Alisa made a shooing motion at the blip on the sensor display that represented the Alliance shuttle, willing it to pull away quickly and zip toward Aldrin's moons.

She didn't wait until the shuttle was out of sensor range before kicking her thrusters to life. She doubted Henneberry and however many mafia ships were going along with her to meet Tymoteusz would be traveling at top speed, but it didn't take much speed to outpace the *Nomad*. With the passing of each minute, Alisa worried that they would fall out of range of the tracking device.

"Let's hope they don't think it's odd that you're going to look for a cargo in the same direction that their fleet of Alliance ships is heading," Mica said.

"I'm hoping that pilot isn't paying attention to us at all with those Starseers staring at the back of his head and chatting him up. Think how you would have felt a few months ago, before we'd met any of them, if a bunch of black-robed figures had descended on our ship. It was rough enough getting used to Abelardus."

Really, Abelardus thought into her mind.

Shouldn't you be getting some rest? The *Nomad's* night cycle had started, the corridors automatically dimming. *I'm not sure how far we'll travel before Henneberry leads us to Tymoteusz, but being well rested would probably be a good idea.*

You sound so motherly when you say things like that.

Alisa needed to find Jelena and say motherly things to her. She watched as the Alliance shuttle, heading in a different direction, grew distant on the sensor display.

I thought you should know, Abelardus said, *that Young-hee has stayed to help. As have Nyarai and Aaron, some of the Starseers originally from the Arkadius temple. They've been wanting a chance to strike against Tymoteusz and get that staff out of his hands.*

Good. Tell them thank you.

Should I tell me thank you too?

Sure. Feel free to deliver that message to yourself.

"Do you mind watching NavCom for a while?" Alisa asked when the shuttle disappeared from sensors. "I just need to be notified if Henneberry changes her course, so I can come up and make an adjustment."

Mica frowned. "Believe it or not, I have work to do. I wasn't planning to spend the night in NavCom."

"If you're referring to that unauthorized construction project in the cargo hold, you most certainly do *not* have work to do. Unless it's to disassemble it."

"Beck authorized its construction before he left."

"Beck doesn't have the power to authorize anything more than the purchasing of brownie-making supplies."

"You're sure? He seemed quite positive that adding a pond was within his realm."

"I won't be gone that long," Alisa said, standing. "I'll come back to relieve you, and you can go work. Or sleep."

"Just leaving for a quickie with your cyborg?"

"Sadly, no. There haven't been any quickies—or longies—since Jelena returned."

"She doesn't approve of your sex life?"

"Not when that sex life doesn't revolve around her father." Alisa grimaced, not wanting to explain the details. "I need to go check on her."

"Fine, go. But don't leave me for too long or I might start contemplating things I could build up here in NavCom. Yumi once mentioned that parakeets are cheerful. Maybe I could hang a cage next to the stuffed spider there."

"You're a mean woman, Mica." Alisa walked through the hatchway.

"Yes, I am."

Alisa checked Jelena's cabin first and frowned when she found it empty. She wasn't off skulking around the ship in the dark, was she? Or visiting the chickens? Deeming the latter likely, Alisa turned toward the cargo hold, but she noticed that her cabin's hatch was ajar with faint light coming from it. She opened it and peeked inside.

Jelena lay curled in a ball on the bunk. The wall lamp was on low, showing her face. Her tears had dried, but she didn't look happy.

"Everything all right?" Alisa asked, stepping inside and closing the hatch.

"They're all gone," Jelena mumbled, her voice barely audible.

"Your teachers? I thought you didn't want to go with them."

"I don't. I want to help find Thor. I meant the other kids. There's nobody left to talk to or play with. It's…"

"Lonely?" Alisa suggested, coming over to sit on the edge of the bunk. "You can talk to me, you know. I've missed having you do that. I get lonely too."

Jelena seemed to contemplate that. Puzzled by the idea of adults getting lonely?

"Do you miss Dad?" she asked quietly.

"I do." Remembering that her daughter would sense far more than she said, Alisa felt the need to explain further, lest her simple response seem dishonest. "I especially miss him when I'm alone and there's nothing to distract me. I've been so busy these last few months, looking for you and getting all caught up in this Staff of Lore craziness, that there hasn't been much quiet time for having thoughts of what used to be."

She frowned, not sure if that would make sense to a child.

"I miss him now," Jelena said. "And I missed him a lot when I was staying with Aunt Sylvia. After Durant came…and we were running, and then my life was getting super weird…sometimes, I forgot to miss him too."

"I think it's natural for the living to continue to live when people have passed, and life does get busy sometimes, and you forget to mourn, but maybe we can make some special times together where we can do that, remember how your dad was and remember why we miss him." She smiled, trying not to feel awkward as she spoke of such things. Jonah would have been much better at explaining death and the appropriate way to deal with it. Inconsiderate of him to be gone now instead of here, having this discussion with Jelena.

"How?" Jelena sounded interested.

"Well, I could try to find some candles, and we could have a little service, the way the Xerikesh describes, or we could just take turns talking about what we liked about him and what we miss." She didn't know if there was anything as poetical as a candle anywhere on the ship. Alejandro might have a couple in whatever box he kept his prayer beads, but she didn't want to ask him for favors. If they wanted to mourn by an open flame, she might have to borrow Beck's portable grill.

Jelena giggled softly.

"What?" Alisa asked.

"A grill? You can't get religious by the fire of a grill."

"No?" She ruffled Jelena's hair. "I don't think the Xerikesh mentions grills one way or another."

"You're silly."

"Yes, I am. All right, we'll just share what we miss about Dad, then. Sound good?"

Jelena nodded and shifted positions, giving up the pillow and coming over to lay her head in Alisa's lap. Alisa blinked away tears and stroked her hair. She'd thought she had missed watching cartoons and making candies with her daughter, but she had missed this even more. Being needed. Being the person that another person relied upon.

"I'll go first," she said when she trusted her voice. "I miss the way your dad always knew how to handle situations and never lost his temper. He was much more even-keeled than I am. He knew better than to get cranky and spout off to his bosses and colleagues." Many of whom had been imperial loyalists...Yes, he'd been far better at navigating treacherous waters than she. Now, aware of his secret Starseer abilities, Alisa wondered how much of that had been a defense mechanism. He'd dared not make trouble, lest that secret come out and endanger his family. Still, even at home, where it wouldn't have mattered, he'd always been slow to anger and quick to smile.

"I miss how he gave me rides and swung me through the air in the living room," Jelena said. "And remember when we went to the swimming pool, and he tossed me up in the air so I could do flips?"

"I do remember that."

It crossed Alisa's mind that Leonidas would be excellent at tossing children and catching them, but she pushed the thought aside as soon as it arose. This wasn't the time to try to bring him into their little family. She couldn't push that. It would have to happen with time. She could at least be pleased by that tiny bit of progress tonight, that Jelena had recognized him as someone it was safe to hide behind.

"I miss the way your dad was good at listening," Alisa said. "A lot of people aren't, but he always seemed to remember what I said, even if he was reading or watching one of his documentaries at the time. And I heard from his students that he was good at remembering little details they'd shared with him too."

"I miss that he would have gotten me a horse," Jelena said.

"What?" Alisa laughed. "We lived in a flat in a high-rise in the middle of the city. I'm quite positive he never promised you a horse."

"He did. While you were gone. He said we'd go out to Grandma's farm once the war ended and it was safe to travel again, and he said I could ride the horses there."

"I'm not sure that's quite the same as giving you a horse."

"I just want to ride one a little. And talk to it."

"We'll do that, like I said. As soon as…" Alisa didn't quite know what to call this upcoming confrontation with Tymoteusz.

"As soon as the war is over?" Jelena asked quietly.

Alisa winced, sad that her daughter saw their current situation as little different from what it had been like living in Perun Central that last couple of years. Did she believe that her world would change once again and that people would die and that there wouldn't be a horse trip?

"As soon as we get Thorian," Alisa said firmly. "Which we are going to do."

Blessings of the Suns Trinity, she had never been much for praying, but she closed her eyes and begged any deity that might be listening to allow her to get that boy and take her daughter horseback riding. Jelena made a contented noise.

"You haven't told me much about him," Alisa said.

"Thor?" Jelena yawned. "We used to play together because most of the others were all older or acted like we didn't know anything. And I *didn't* know anything. I didn't know anything about Starseers or how to be one. Aunt Sylvia didn't teach me anything. She wasn't one. It's not her fault. She didn't know. But Thor showed me some stuff and helped me get caught up, and we used to sneak away together sometimes and explore these tunnels that were around one of our schools."

Alisa listened in mild horror, realizing those must have been the tunnels under Cleon Moon. The kids were lucky they hadn't been eaten by dinosaurs.

"He cried sometimes," Jelena said. "I punched Travis when he saw it and laughed. Then I got in trouble for hitting one of the other kids. But I didn't tell them why I did it. Thor didn't want people to know he'd cried. But he was sad a lot. *Both* of his parents died. We were kind of the same."

Alisa smiled at the idea of her daughter being "kind of the same" as the prince and heir to the empire, but she supposed kids didn't worry about titles and governments. And with the empire gone, what was Thorian anyway? Just a ten-year-old boy in need of a family.

"I miss him," Jelena murmured, yawning again. "And I miss Dad."

"I know." Alisa continued stroking her hair, suspecting she would doze off soon.

Jelena turned her head to look up. "What should I call your…him?" She waved toward the wall in the direction of Leonidas's cabin.

"Your him?" Alisa teased, because teasing was easier than broaching this difficult subject. "Is that the way those Starseers taught you to speak?"

"There aren't rules on how to speak when you're telepathing."

"Ah." Telepathing? Was that a word? Maybe it was one of those fancy Starseer symbols she'd seen etched on their old ruins.

"Tommy told me to call him Tommy, but it's weird saying grownups' names. Remember how Grandpa used to make me call him *sir*?" Jelena made a face.

"He wanted me to call him sir too." Alisa smirked. "I'm sure Leonidas wouldn't mind if you called him Leonidas." He would likely be tickled if Jelena spoke to him at all. Alisa didn't think that had happened yet.

"Lady Westfall calls—called—him Colonel." Jelena's face scrunched up. "Did you fight together in the war? But he's a cyborg. Aren't they…"

"He was an officer in the imperial army, yes."

"So you were enemies?"

"Technically, but we never met when I was serving the Alliance." For that, Alisa was grateful. She still shuddered at memories of cyborgs in red combat armor invading her ship and mowing down her fellow soldiers. And friends. "The war is over now. People are just people. He's agreed to work for me."

Jelena's confusion faded, and she offered her sly smile. "That was stellar when you told him to make Lady Westfall leave, and he did. And she ran away."

"Yes, he's a good ally to have." Alisa did not say more, afraid the conversation might touch upon the kiss Jelena had seen her share with Leonidas in sickbay. She didn't want to talk about that now. They would get Thorian, slip away from whatever battle remained, and go ride horses together. She imagined Leonidas on a horse and smirked again.

"He would need a *giant* horse," Jelena said, apparently monitoring her thoughts. She turned her head, resting her cheek in Alisa's lap again.

"Maybe two."

"*Mom*, you can't ride two horses."

"If anyone could, he could."

"I just want one," Jelena murmured, her voice sounding groggy again. "To pet and to talk to. To be friends with."

"We'll see what we can do."

CHAPTER EIGHTEEN

Alisa stood up, stretched, and grimaced when her spine cracked. She had been sitting in NavCom for two days, watching Mica's tracking program, constantly worrying that the blip that represented Henneberry's ship would move out of range and disappear. She also worried that the *Nomad* would stumble across some Alliance ships, zooming past to join Hawk and Agosti's fleet. If any of them saw her freighter, they might report it to their superiors.

Alejandro walked into NavCom in his gray robe, his three-suns pendant dangling from his neck and what looked like a copy of the Xerikesh tucked under his arm. He gazed thoughtfully at the holodisplay featuring the blips.

"Have you been praying that we'll catch up to Tymoteusz and the staff?" Alisa asked, feeling she should say something, even if he would have preferred it if she didn't.

He had been avoiding her path, or she'd just been too busy to notice him, so they hadn't butted heads too often of late.

"I have been praying that Thorian is still alive," Alejandro said. "I fear… that much time has passed, and that Tymoteusz may have decided the boy doesn't have a role in this new government he's concocting."

"Perhaps not." Alisa remembered Durant's message and wondered if his plea had ever made its way to Tymoteusz's ears. "Would you lament his loss because he's a nice boy who deserves to live or because your empire doesn't have a figurehead left without him?"

Alejandro's lips thinned as he glared at her. "*Both*. He's a smart boy. He could become a good leader on his own one day. And with the Starseer power, he could deal with many who opposed him or attempted to manipulate him. But he needs time to finish his studies and mature."

He needs time to be a *boy*, Alisa thought. "Yes," was all she murmured aloud.

"Any guesses as to where they're heading?" Alejandro nodded toward the blips.

"Currently? Toward the middle of nowhere—no planets or moons or stations align with our current heading. But Henneberry has changed course a few times, so it's hard to predict her final destination. She may suspect she's being followed. The tracker hasn't been deactivated, so that's good at least. She probably doesn't suspect *we're* following her."

"She probably wouldn't worry about us even if she knew."

"Good. Then we'll surprise her with our amazing competence."

"I know *I'd* be surprised," Alejandro muttered and walked out, his hand wrapped around his pendant.

"Ass," Alisa muttered.

She grudgingly admitted he wasn't wrong to be skeptical. What had her ship and passengers managed to do against Tymoteusz in previous meetings? Absolutely nothing.

Realizing she hadn't gotten the details yet on the tank Tiang had left them, Alisa checked on the blips a final time, tapped a couple of instructions for the autopilot, and stood up. She needed to find out what Tiang had told Leonidas. Would it be possible to deliver that retrovirus using what they had? Could she count on having a secret weapon useful against *chasadski*?

Alisa tapped the stuffed spider dangling over the co-pilot's seat on the way out, suspecting she would need any luck she could get in the days ahead. First, she checked Leonidas's cabin, but he did not answer. She headed to the mess hall. Beck had served a dinner of cumin-rubbed snagor skewers a while ago, but perhaps Leonidas had returned for a second helping of dessert.

When Alisa entered the mess hall, the lights were on, and the scent of vanilla and cinnamon hung in the air. Beck was washing dishes while his portable grill sat on the table, the lid down with something presumably baking inside. She started to ask if he'd seen Leonidas, but Beck turned, a finger to his lips, and pointed under the table.

Alisa squatted to peer between the benches. Jelena was curled on her side with a blanket wrapped around her, and three chickens at her back, nesting in the folds. Eyes closed, she seemed to be sleeping. So did the chickens. Alisa had never heard of chickens sleeping with humans. Even Ostberg, who they'd followed around the ship, hadn't slept with them, insofar as she knew. Alisa didn't know whether to be concerned or proud that her daughter had developed an affinity for animals. Or was that affinity *from* animals?

"She helped me mix up the bread pudding," Beck whispered, pointing toward the closed grill, the source of the vanilla and cinnamon scents. "She asked if I'd bring her a piece if she went to bed. I said she'd probably be sleeping before it was done and cooled, and that I wouldn't want to wake her up. Figured she could have some in the morning."

"And?"

"She wasn't willing to wait." Beck lifted his eyebrows. "It seems impatience runs in the family."

"I don't know what you're talking about. I'm not impatient. I'm quick and decisive."

"Due to impatience."

Alisa stuck her tongue out at him. As long as she was being impatient, she might as well be immature too.

"She brought a blanket out and camped there, so she'll wake up when the bread pudding is done," Beck said, turning back to the dishes.

"And the chickens?" Alisa spotted chicken droppings on the deck near the corridor and frowned. There was a reason she preferred them to stay in their coop. Too bad she hadn't thought to steal one of those floor-cleaning robots from Henneberry's ship. Normally, she wouldn't entertain theft, but it seemed a fitting way to reward a person who thought the service workers were expendable.

"They'd been wandering around, and I guess she didn't order them back to their coop."

"Hm." Alisa straightened up. She thought about carrying Jelena to her cabin and putting her in her bunk, but the chickens would probably start squawking and wake her—and everyone else who had gone to bed. "Have you seen Leonidas?"

Beck pointed his thumb toward the cargo hold. "He headed that way with his hover pads a while ago. Said he wanted to get some extra training in before we meet up with the *chasadski*. But from the way he was sniffing at my grill, I think he might have been looking for a reason to stay up until the pudding is done too."

"It wouldn't surprise me." Alisa waved to him and headed toward the cargo hold.

Sickbay was dark, so Alejandro must have decided on praying from his bunk instead of his workspace. The entire ship seemed quiet with so many of their passengers departed. Alisa hadn't truly appreciated having all those Starseers around, but the children hadn't bothered her, and she missed the noise of them playing, footsteps thundering on the deck as they raced everywhere. Why would one walk when one could run?

For the first time in...a while, she wondered what it would be like to have more children. She'd been lonely from time to time as an only child growing up on the *Nomad* with just her mother. She remembered wishing that she had some siblings. Did Jelena ever wish that? Back in their flat on Perun, there had been schoolmates for her to play with, but it was much quieter out here in deep space, and adults were now her only options for companionship. Of course, even if Alisa had more children, Jelena would be at least nine when the first was born. She probably wouldn't consider a baby that much fun to "play with." Instead, she'd find herself pressed into babysitting duties as she grew older. Still, Alisa couldn't help but wonder what it would be like to have more children running around the ship. And to be around Jelena more than she had been these last four years.

The lights were dimmed for the night in the cargo hold, and Alisa did not hear anything as she approached, certainly not the *thump, thump, thump* of Leonidas's boots and fists connecting with those pads. She stepped out onto the walkway, reminded that Leonidas and his enhanced eyes could see perfectly well in the dim lighting.

A few clucks came from the coop, but the chickens down there seemed as torpid as the ones under the table.

"Leonidas?" she called softly when she reached the stairs.

There wasn't any light coming from engineering either. Mica must have finished her projects for the night and gone to sleep. Alisa wished she could forget about Tymoteusz and the staff and change course, head off to restart her life. Pick up a contract, haul some freight, go horseback riding with her daughter on a stopover.

But her promise to find Thorian bound her to this course.

"Down here, Alisa," came Leonidas's voice from somewhere under the walkway. He sounded oddly mellow, not at all like a man who had been exerting himself.

"Half lighting," Alisa ordered and started down the steps. Leonidas might be able to see in the dark, but *she* did not have that ability.

The light rose to a twilight level. Not so much, she hoped, that the chickens would wake up and start demanding food. Alisa paused at the bottom of the stairs, surprised to find Leonidas lying on his back under the walkway with his hands pillowing the back of his head. He gazed upward, like someone lounging in a grassy meadow to stargaze. But all he could be looking at was the ceiling, or perhaps the two hover pads floating in the air above him, as if he had paused their program.

"Is your exercise equipment malfunctioning?" Alisa asked.

"No." He lowered his chin to his chest, watching her through his lashes.

"Are *you* malfunctioning?"

He snorted softly. "Perhaps."

She left the stairs and joined him under the walkway, sitting down with her back to the bulkhead. "What does that mean?"

"I took the wrong powder."

"What?" Her first thought was of Beck's bread pudding recipe, that perhaps some powdered substance had been involved, but then she remembered the tins Yumi had given him.

"I was talking to Abelardus, who was pestering me and following me to my cabin. I wasn't paying enough attention when I grabbed the tin. They look similar, you know. It wasn't until the powder hit my tongue and tasted different that I realized my mistake."

"Well, at least you didn't have a tin of poison sitting on your desk." Alisa eyed his stretched-out form. He *did* appear relaxed. Maybe that wasn't a bad thing. She couldn't help but remember some of the other effects that drug was supposed to have on those who used it, and her cheeks warmed at the thought of the amazing orgasms Yumi had promised.

"I could have spit it out," Leonidas said. "As soon as I tasted it, I knew."

"And you didn't?"

"I almost did. But...I was curious." His head lolled to the side, and he met her eyes in the dim lighting.

Alisa wished they *were* in a meadow with stars stretching above them. "About relaxation?"

"Among other things."

"You sound mellow. How do you feel?" She resisted the urge to look toward his crotch, then blushed further, feeling silly that such a thought had come to mind. But she couldn't help but wonder about the drug and what it did. Could one truly be relaxed and aroused at the same time? She supposed so, though Leonidas had seemed tense whenever he'd been aroused around her in the past, worried about hurting her and worried about who knew what else.

"Well, I didn't punch Abelardus on my way out of my cabin," Leonidas said, "and that had been on my mind on the way in."

"What was he bugging you about?"

"Just saying that we needed to come up with a plan for battling Tymoteusz because I proved so inept last time."

"As if he was *ept*."

"I think we need to see what we're dealing with and where, and figure out whether the Alliance will be playing a role before spending a lot of time making plans."

"Probably true. I admit that I came down here to ask you about something similar. I hope it won't put you in the mood to punch me."

"I doubt it." He smiled a lazy smile. He looked more like a man on the verge of falling asleep, rather than one contemplating arousal and orgasms. "What's your question?"

"I was wondering about the tank Tiang gave you."

"It's safe. I locked it up, and I've got Mica making some canisters to store weaponized doses."

Alisa shivered at the term weaponized, even if that was exactly what they needed. The fact that her genes and Jelena's genes were similar to Tymoteusz's made her all too aware that this stuff would affect her.

"I know what it's supposed to do, sort of, but do you think it'll work?" she asked. "Can it truly help us?"

Leonidas pushed himself into a sitting position and scooted back to lean against the bulkhead, his shoulder touching hers. "Possibly," he said. "If we get close enough to use it. From what Tiang explained to me—and there wasn't time for a thorough explanation—his retrovirus is able to temporarily disable the immune system, so the invasion won't be detected, and then amp up brain activity to cause seizures. He also said the bug is designed to cling to a Starseer barrier, if not burrow right through to get inside. If it clings, it'll get through as soon as the person drops it."

She listened to him as he spoke, concerned about the ramifications—what happened if the concoction was sprayed on one of their Starseer allies? Or in Jelena's or Thor's presence?—but she was also growing aware of the warmth of his shoulder against hers, the way his heat seeped through the fabric of his T-shirt and into her body. His forearms were bare, the shadows from the walkway bars playing across the corded muscles.

"So," she said, reminding herself that she hadn't come down here to admire his physique, "you'd have to be very close to use this weapon, right? To make contact with your target?"

"You smell good," Leonidas said, turning his head toward her again.

"What? I mean, I'm glad. I walked through Beck's kitchen, so I probably smell like vanilla."

"Faintly," he agreed, and shifted toward her, his nose coming to touch her hair, his lips brushing her ear as he inhaled.

Her senses sprang to life, and her awareness of him shot from medium to off the charts.

"Sorry," he murmured, drawing back and looking upward, perhaps thinking of the ship and the crew—and Jelena. "Mellowness isn't the only thing I'm feeling. Once you came down, ah, never mind. Yes, the way he has it designed, it would be a short-range weapon, but the canisters I mentioned—I think I can modify that grenade launcher I got at Solstice's to throw them fifty, a hundred meters, at least. The canisters would disperse their contents on impact."

"Impact?" Alisa mouthed, struggling to follow his words now that her thoughts had shifted from the practical to the libidinous. She wasn't supposed to be the one who was extra horny after twenty years of abstinence, but she couldn't help but think that Jelena was sleeping, and that even if she woke up, her focus would likely be on desserts. And she was way up there. Alisa and Leonidas were down here and could move into engineering and close the hatch. They would be unlikely to be interrupted until morning.

"We could shoot at him from afar," Leonidas said, "but obviously, we'd still have to be on his ship."

"Yes." This time, Alisa shifted toward him, lifting her hand to rest on his chest, to feel the swell of his firm muscle beneath her palm. The thin material of the T-shirt did not hide much. What would he do if she kissed him? Feeling she should make a pretense at continuing this conversation, one she had come down here to start, she managed to pull her thoughts together enough to say, "But boarding his ship was going to be a necessity anyway. To get Thorian."

"Yes," he murmured.

His chin dropped to his chest, and he looked at her hand. She could feel his heartbeat beneath her fingers, the rise and fall of his breaths. She stroked his chest and looked him up and down, trying to gauge if he was less tense than the previous times they had been close enough to touch. Parts of him were—other parts were plenty tense. Unlike with his combat armor, his gym clothes did not hide a lot.

Seeing that he was having thoughts just as libidinous as hers sent a surge of heat through her, and she shifted sideways, putting her leg atop his, thoughts of climbing fully into his lap coming to mind.

Leonidas licked his lips. "We should...not. Right?"

It wasn't a very firm *not*, and when she didn't answer right away, his arm slipped around her waist, pulling her across him, astraddle his lap, just as she had imagined. She sucked in a breath, feeling him against her. His other hand came up to the back of her head, fingers pushing into her hair, nails scraping at her scalp, sending delicious shivers through her body.

"Probably not," Alisa whispered, her gaze snagging on his lips, the desire to kiss him flaring within her, along with the desire to fully mold herself to him, to feel the hard contours of his body against hers. She almost said that Jelena would never know, but if she poked around in either of their thoughts tomorrow, wouldn't she? Unless they could avoid thinking about this, avoid thinking about the way Leonidas's fingers slid under her shirt and meandered across the bare skin of her back, sending fire along her nerves. "But you must have expected...what were you thinking when you didn't spit out the powder?"

She pushed his shirt up, letting her own fingers roam across warm, bare flesh.

"It crossed my mind..." He cleared his throat—his voice had gone hoarse. "I promised myself I wouldn't go to you, wouldn't bother you."

"But you hoped I would come to you?"

He snorted. "I've hoped that every night I haven't been on the drug. Most mornings too." He managed a lopsided smile, his hands continuing to stroke her under her shirt, his thumb slipping beneath her bra to follow the curve of her breast.

"It would have been sad if I hadn't come then."

"Very sad. I would have had to entertain myself down here."

"My cargo hold isn't the stuff of sexual fantasies, at least not as far as I've noticed."

"Well, those are brand new hover pads I'd intended to work out with."

"New hover pads get you excited?"

"A little." His hand shifted around to cup her more fully. "But not as much as you."

"My womanly ego is mollified now that I know I'm more exciting than gym equipment."

"A little." His smile turned into a wolfish grin. "We could drug ourselves tomorrow," he offered. "Might as well sample Yumi's entire pharmacological cornucopia."

"I suppose that would be a possibility." Alisa still had some of that qui-gorn. They could mask their thoughts. She felt bad about the idea of using something like that, of keeping things from her daughter, but was it wrong for her to have a private sex life? With someone she loved and who loved her back? Especially when they were going into what might be impossible odds, and there was no guarantee that either of them would live through this battle?

"I want you, Alisa," Leonidas said, shifting under her thighs, as if to make sure there was no doubt of that statement. "But I don't want to do anything to harm your relationship with your daughter."

"I know you don't. And I love you for that."

As she rubbed his chest, fingers growing bold with the need to touch all of him, she leaned closer and kissed him on the mouth, sensing that he wouldn't be the one to initiate an encounter, even though he clearly desired it. This was her decision, her mistake to make, if it was one. As soon as their lips touched, she knew it wasn't, or that if it was, she would rather deal with the consequences later and have him now.

Leonidas did not hesitate to kiss her back. For the first time, he did not seem tense or worried that he might apply too much pressure. And he didn't. Not that she had expected an overly aggressive cyborg tongue to send her flying, but *he* always seemed worried. He melded into her, awakening her entire body, making her ache with the need to be with him tonight. Forever.

When she pulled back to make a suggestion, she was panting. "Engineering?" she managed to get out, though all she wanted was to return to kissing—and more.

"What?" he asked, stroking her cheek with his hand, his thumb tracing the contours of her face, her lips.

"We can shut the hatch, and nobody will hear us over the thrum of the engines unless we're...very noisy."

For a moment, he kept touching her face, as if it were formed from some priceless metal instead of mundane skin and bone, and she almost asked him his thoughts. He wasn't having doubts, was he? If so, perhaps another kiss would change his mind...

She shifted in his lap, intentionally rubbing against him, and leaned toward his lips again. He growled like a panther and returned the kiss. Had he ever done that before? It sent a shiver down her spine.

As he kissed her, he shifted his weight, wrapping his hands around her butt. Not letting go, he rose to his feet, keeping her pressed against him, and she gasped, throwing her arms around his shoulders.

"I wouldn't drop you," he murmured against her lips, sounding dryly amused as he walked toward engineering.

"No," she said, wrapping her legs around him. "I know you wouldn't, but a girl likes to hang on."

"Hang on all you like," he said, a hint of that growl in his voice again.

"I will." She gripped his shoulders, running her hands over his hard muscles as she kissed him. She probably should have stopped so he could see where he was going, but this new closeness, their bodies locked together with no secrets between them, made it hard for her to contemplate stopping.

Even without the ability to see through her head, he strode confidently past the hatch, pausing only to tug it shut with his foot. Inside, the lights were dimmed, but dozens of indicators spread their red, blue, and green glows into the machine-filled room. Alisa could just make out the strong features of Leonidas's face, the way his hair was tousled—maybe she had done that with her hands. Grinning, she lowered her lips to the side of his neck, kissing and nibbling. She shifted her weight, flexing her legs around him, deciding their clothes were problematic.

He groaned, her name slipping out.

"You're thinking of the clothing problem too?" she murmured against his skin, teasing him even as she enjoyed his warm taste. She nipped at the tendons in his neck, then lifted her mouth to his ear, rubbing her face in his hair as she nibbled here and there.

His grip tightened, and he pulled her harder against him, his breaths coming more quickly in her ear. Maybe she should have been afraid of those powerful arms wrapped around her, that he would unintentionally hurt her, but she wasn't. She trusted him, even if he didn't trust himself.

"If you want me," she whispered into his ear, "take me."

He did not hesitate. He pushed her against the bulkhead, as she'd imagined so many times, and she gasped as her shirt came off far more quickly than it had gone on. His hands explored her body, sending tingles of heat through her wherever they touched, as he found her lips for a long, demanding kiss. She kissed him back while shoving at his shirt, wanting it off. He yanked it over his head, and somehow, the rest of the clothing followed, even though Alisa refused to fully let go of her grip on him.

The cool metal of the bulkhead at her back contrasted with the heat of his body, and she reveled in being pinned there as he stroked her. She gripped the back of his head, whispering something inarticulate. She wasn't even sure what. Just that she wanted him. Forever. He was hers, and she was keeping him. One way or another, they would both get through this, and they would spend the rest of their lives together. She vowed it as they came together, his touch an exquisite mingling of bold and gentle. This time, if he paused or held back, it was only to let the fire within her build, to tease her—she saw that in the pleased gleam in his eyes—to draw out her pleasure. And to enhance his. When he threw back his head, the tendons in his neck leaping out against his flesh, she knew he enjoyed his release with an intensity he must not have felt for a very long time. Seeing the raw ecstasy on his face brought her to her own climax, the satisfaction of experiencing his pleasure even better than her own.

When they finally stopped moving together, sweat dripped down their bare bodies, and his hands cupped her butt again, holding her against the wall, holding her against him. And by all the gods in the universe, she liked them there. She liked *him* there, not a hint of air between them.

"You don't know how long I've wanted you to ram me up against a wall and have your way with me," she said, grinning.

He dropped his face to her neck, nuzzling her but also catching his breath. She grew smug in knowing that, with all his enhancements and extra stamina, he had run out of breath having sex with her.

"I'm glad," he finally murmured, kissing her neck. "I was feeling guilty about not stopping to look for that cot I know Mica keeps in here."

Alisa lifted her hand to the side of his face, stroking him, tracing his ear, loving him. "She'd give us a hard time if we sweated all over her cot."

"But the bulkhead and the deck are allowed?" He lifted his head, his eyes warm as they held hers.

"We probably shouldn't mention those either."

CHAPTER NINETEEN

Alisa woke in her cabin, curled on her side on her bunk, her blanket tugged up around her shoulders. A grin spread across her face as she remembered the night before, though she didn't remember leaving engineering. Leonidas must have carried her up here after she dozed off. Either that, or she had dreamed everything. But she was naked under the blanket, and she didn't usually shuck all her clothes in dreams. In the dim lighting, she could see them folded on the desk chair. Folding was something else she didn't do in dreams. Or while awake.

A soft knock sounded at the hatch, and her grin returned. Was this to be their ritual? He wouldn't sleep with her after they had sex, but he would pad over barefoot and bare chested in the morning to slip into bed with her for cuddling? Or perhaps activities more vigorous than cuddling?

"Come in," she called softly, her grin broadening.

As the hatch opened, the brighter light from the corridor slashing into the cabin, a thought occurred to her. What if it wasn't Leonidas? What if it was Jelena, wanting to know if she could have Beck's bread pudding for breakfast? Would Alisa be able to hide her thoughts of the night before? She had some of that drug around, but there wasn't time to dig it out.

Fortunately, the tousled black hair and broad shoulders that leaned into view did not belong to anyone short or related to her.

Leonidas slipped inside, closing the hatch behind him. He was fully dressed, which was lamentable, but he probably hadn't wanted to risk running into Jelena while half nude. Alisa hated the idea of them sneaking around to avoid her daughter, but she couldn't regret last night. Especially when it had been so…wonderful.

The idea of crediting Yumi's drug made her want to sneer, but Leonidas had *definitely* been relaxed. He hadn't hesitated, and if he had worried at all about hurting her, he hadn't shown it this time. It had been as though being together was the most natural thing in the universe.

She couldn't wipe her silly grin away as he walked over and sat on the edge of the bed. She was sure he had no trouble seeing it because he smiled back, his own smile almost shy.

"I didn't know if I should come over," Leonidas said. "But you've seemed sad in the past at the notion of waking up alone. And I was already up and heard you wake up."

He'd *heard* her wake up? She hadn't even made any noise. A rustle of a blanket, maybe.

"I do hate waking up alone," she said, lifting a hand and sliding it along his forearm. She gripped him, pulled herself into a sitting position, and wrapped him in a hug. "I hope you enjoyed yourself last night."

"I enjoyed myself *immensely*," he said, sliding an arm around her waist. "I hope you did too. You seemed…more vocal this time."

She blushed, remembering crying out more than once as he'd pinned her against the bulkhead. She was relieved they had thought to close the hatch to engineering—and hoped that nobody else on the ship had cyborg hearing.

"Because you were wonderful," she said, kissing his neck. "I couldn't contain myself."

He made a noise, sort of a pleased smug grunt. But his tone was dry when he said, "All it took was Yumi's drug."

"I think it just made you relax and stop worrying."

"Oh, I'll agree to that. I do think…now that I know you can survive my more vigorous…vigors…that I don't have to be quite so careful, and I'll be able to…"

"Push me up against a bulkhead and have your way with me more often?" She pulled back slightly so he could see the silly grin that she couldn't contain. She wanted him to know how much she had enjoyed his *vigors*.

"Perhaps so. It didn't take much force for me to, uhm, *thoroughly* enjoy myself. Especially when you were so enthusiastic. That made it…" A silly grin to match hers was sprawling across his face. "Well, it wasn't so awkward this time, was it?"

"I should say not. We should do it again and see if we can replicate it." She leaned in and kissed him, fully willing to replicate it again right there, but after a few enjoyable moments, he leaned back and stroked the side of her head.

"Jelena and Beck are playing games in the rec room. I'm not sure how long that will entertain them. Her. Beck is feeding her that cake he made last night. He claims it's a balanced breakfast because it has bread and bananas in it."

"And a pound of sugar." Alisa caught his hand and clasped it between hers. "We should probably not do this again until…for a while, but no matter what happens, I don't regret last night, all right?"

"I don't either," he said. "You were *much* more entertaining than my hover pads."

"It's a gift."

The comm beeped. "You awake, Captain?" Mica asked.

"Of course," Alisa said, glancing at the clock. "It's two hours into the day cycle. Why wouldn't I be awake?" She flushed, not having realized she had snoozed that late.

"Because you and your cyborg were doing untoward things in my engineering room last night."

Leonidas's eyebrows rose.

"How did she know?" Alisa mouthed. Despite thinking about it, they hadn't stopped to hunt for Mica's cot.

"You think I can't tell when my engine room smells like cyborg sweat and sex in the morning?" Mica asked. "One of you better be down there with a sponge and disinfectant later to clean up the deck and bulkheads and whatever else you were pressing your bare sweaty butts against."

Alisa rubbed her hand over her face. She had been worried about being heard. Who knew her engineer had some kind of mutant nostrils?

"As important as that is," Mica said, "it's not the reason I commed."

"Is something wrong?" Alisa asked, relieved to change the topic.

241

"You might want to come take a look at what's on the forward cameras."

Alisa groaned. "Be right there." She closed the comm. "I guess cuddling will have to wait for another time."

"Cuddling wasn't what I had in mind," he said dryly.

"Haven't taken any of Yumi's drugs this morning, eh?"

"That, and you're sitting there naked with your blanket down around your waist." He wiggled his eyebrows as he eyed her bare chest.

"Ah, I was too busy being mortified to be aware of my nudity."

"I wasn't." He looked like he wouldn't mind ogling her some more, but instead, he kissed her and stood up. "I'll meet you in NavCom."

Apparently, he wouldn't have trouble looking Mica in the eyes after that conversation. Maybe he'd even have that pleased smug look.

Alisa grabbed her clothes, promising herself a sanibox visit later. So long as they weren't heading into the maw of a dragon. Or an armada of mafia ships.

As she turned at the intersection, she heard the sound of Beck saying something and Jelena laughing. Well, he had promised he was good with kids. Having a knack for baking sweets couldn't hurt. Alisa was glad there were adults around that Jelena felt comfortable with—she just hoped that one day she would include Leonidas on her list.

"What interesting things are happening?" Alisa asked, stepping into NavCom.

Mica was sitting in the co-pilot's seat. Leonidas stood with his back to the bulkhead, his arms folded over his chest, as he looked at the view screen. At least they weren't discussing engine room sanitation.

Neither dragons nor mafia ships were on the screen. Some kind of beacon or warning buoy floated in space ahead of them. It wasn't until Mica gave her a significant look that the ramifications sank in. Oh. She shouldn't be surprised. She'd known which way their most recent course change had turned them.

"You didn't mention that we were heading back into our favorite zone of space," Mica said, her tone ensuring everyone knew that she wasn't pleased.

"What's the matter? You didn't want to get irradiated again?"

"Sure, you can make jokes. You have mutant genes and probably won't die going back in there." Mica frowned at Leonidas. "I hope you enjoyed your sex. It may be the last sex you ever have."

"Isn't it early in the morning for such pessimism?" Alisa asked.

"Only for people who slept two hours into the day cycle. I've been up for hours. I've had plenty of time to work up a good head of pessimism."

Alisa sighed as the *Nomad* sailed past the warning buoy. Mica flicked on the comm to receive the message it was transmitting. Since Alisa had heard it before, the last time they'd come out to this quarantined space and eventually found Alcyone Station, she didn't need to hear it again. The warning to stay away—or else—had not changed. She'd half expected the Alliance to blow up the station after they finished researching it or to find some way to close that dimensional rift, but maybe the majority of their forces had been sent to chase after the staff.

"We're not going all the way back in there, are we?" Mica asked. "We don't have special radiation shielding any more than we did last time, and just because you've purchased some combat armor doesn't mean the rest of us have anything."

Alisa pulled down the seat at the sensor station and checked to see if any ships were around. Maybe Tymoteusz had chosen the quarantined area as an ideal meeting spot, figuring the space would be devoid of random travelers.

"The mafia ships won't likely have anything for dealing with excessive radiation either," Leonidas said.

"Unless they were warned in advanced to bring suits," Mica said.

Alisa eyed the sensor readout. The warning buoy and Bravo Six's shuttle were the only things within range. No sign of the Alliance. No sign of Tymoteusz. "Are we still the same distance away from Henneberry's ship?" she asked, turning toward the holodisplay showing the tracking blips.

"About," Mica said. "They've slowed down, which is the only reason we've been able to stay in range."

"No way to guess *why* they slowed down?"

"Maybe they're meeting someone who also travels slowly. Or who isn't at the designated spot yet."

Alisa tapped the comm. "Bravo Six, how are you doing over there?"

"I have few projects to occupy my cerebral processor, Lady Captain," came the android's monotone voice. "Do you require assistance with anything?"

"In about ten minutes, I'd like you to comm Alejandro and offer him assistance on refining his drug treatment for radiation poisoning. He'll fill you in on the details."

"Yes, Lady Captain. I listened to the warning of the buoy, but it said very little of use. I will monitor outside radiation as we continue into the off-limits area."

"Thank you." Alisa closed the comm. "I like that he doesn't argue with me. He just cheerfully goes where I ask him to go."

"Because he's *immune* to radiation," Mica said. "And probably doesn't care if he dies anyway. I care. I'm fond of living. I find it very exciting. You two should too." She scowled back and forth from Alisa to Leonidas.

He merely gazed back, his arms still over his chest, his expression thoughtful.

"Mica?" Alisa asked. "Will you go down to sickbay and tell Alejandro the news? So he's ready when Bravo Six comms him?"

"You can't tell him yourself?"

"I could, but then you'd still be in here. I'd like a private moment with Leonidas."

"Round Two?" Mica grumbled something else inaudible, then strode out.

"Do you want me to shut the hatch?" Leonidas asked.

"No. I just…" Alisa sighed and switched from the sensor station seat to the pilot's seat. She waved for him to take the co-pilot's seat.

"What's wrong?" he asked quietly, sliding in behind her instead of next to her. He tapped a few controls at the sensor station, but he also rested a hand on her shoulder.

"I'm afraid I was wrong to keep Jelena with us, especially if we're going into…" She waved toward the route ahead. "Just because she, and apparently I, have some resistance to radiation hardly makes us immune. At her age…who knows what exposure might do?"

He squeezed her shoulder but did not answer.

She looked back. He was frowning at the display.

"Something just came into our range," he said quietly.

"Mafia? Alliance?"

"Too small for either. And it doesn't look to be moving."

"Some hapless ship that ran into the mafia and got picked on for target practice?"

"It's possible. It's not far off our path, so I can get more data as we continue flying closer."

He tapped a few more buttons, and Alisa faced forward again. She could increase their speed slightly, but they were already close to their maximum. And she wasn't sure if that ship was anything she truly wanted to get close to.

"I understand why you didn't want to let her go again," Leonidas said quietly.

"Jelena?"

"Yes. You're right. There was no way this wasn't going to be dangerous, but she wouldn't have necessarily been safe going away with Westfall either."

Alisa wasn't sure about that, but she didn't argue against him. She didn't want to argue in favor of her being a selfish fool who was risking her daughter's life because she hadn't been willing to lose her again.

Leonidas lowered his hand. "It's the *chasadski* ship."

Alisa swiveled in her chair. "What?"

"The same ship Tymoteusz was flying in on Arkadius and that we encountered on Caravan Station and again in the asteroid belt."

Alisa stared at the representation of the ship on the sensor display. "It's alone there? Not moving?"

"It's not moving. Its aloneness will be determined as we get closer."

She bit her lip. Right. There could be more ships out there, just outside of range. This could be the big meeting spot. "No, it can't be," she muttered with realization.

"Hm?"

Alisa pointed at the tracking display. "Henneberry's yacht is well past that ship, farther into the quarantine zone. If they were meeting there, she would have stopped."

"True."

"So, what's going on?"

A few long minutes passed before Leonidas answered.

"I'm not reading any engine power. No power at all, in fact," he said.

"Were they damaged? Fired upon?" Alisa doubted there was any point in hoping the Alliance had already been there and blasted Tymoteusz to bits. She shouldn't hope that anyway, because if they had, Thorian could have been blasted to bits too.

"We're still too far out to get a precise reading, but it's possible."

More long minutes passed, and eventually, Alisa could catch the ship on one of the cameras with maximum zoom.

"I don't see any damage," Leonidas said, sounding puzzled. He was still frowning at the sensor display.

Alisa put the ship on the view screen. "I don't either."

"Do you need any help, Captain?" Yumi asked, peering into NavCom. Her eyes widened when she spotted the *chasadski* ship on the screen.

"Leonidas is handling the sensors, but if you want to take a look, you can arm wrestle him for the chair."

Yumi looked at one of Leonidas's brawny arms. "Can I drug him first?"

"I would."

"In certain circumstances, he's willing to drug himself," Leonidas murmured, sliding Alisa a sidelong look.

"We liked the relaxation one, Yumi," Alisa said, feeling she should acknowledge that they finally took her up on one of her copious offers. She doubted Yumi would ask for details—or mock them for leaving cyborg sweat in engineering. Alisa was still suspicious about the source of Mica's knowledge of their night together. If she had walked down and peeked inside, Leonidas would have heard it. Probably. He *had* been distracted. She bit back a smirk and told herself to focus on the current problem. So what if Mica had secret cameras in engineering or something of that ilk?

"That's wonderful," Yumi said. "Both of you?" She wriggled her eyebrows at Alisa.

"One was enough."

"You'll have to try it yourself next time."

"I don't want to risk getting addicted to some powder, no matter how tantalizing it might be." Alisa tapped the edge of the control panel with a fingernail, tempted to veer toward the *chasadski* ship for a closer look. But Henneberry's yacht was still heading off to wherever it was going, and she did not want to lose it.

"Current studies show that addiction has more to do with the mental health and feeling of social belonging of the individual, rather than an inherent irresistibleness of a substance. I believe that with your daughter here and the camaraderie from your crew, you should feel that you have an important place in the lives of many and that what you do matters. If you have doubts, or are not experiencing contentment in your position as captain, perhaps we could do some meditation exercises together. I could guide you in—"

"Let her win, please, Leonidas," Alisa interrupted.

"What?" he asked.

"The arm wrestling contest. Let her win and take over the sensor station so she has something to do besides analyzing me."

Leonidas slid out of the fold-down seat without the contest, bowing Yumi into it. He touched the back of Alisa's head as Yumi took the position.

"What you do *does* matter," he said quietly. "And you *are* important."

"I don't remember asking, but thank you. I'm still not taking the drug." She swatted him as he sat in the co-pilot's seat.

"You didn't seem to need it." His eyes crinkled. He seemed far more relaxed today than usual, almost like the night before, and she thought about asking him if he'd taken another dose, but he didn't have that overly mellow tone to his voice that he'd had the night before. Maybe he simply felt better because they'd had sex, he'd let himself go, and no overly eager pelvic thrusts had sent her sailing across the engineering room in a disastrous crash.

"There are no signs of life aboard," Yumi said.

Alisa broke the gaze she'd been sharing with Leonidas, wiped the goofy grin off her face, and returned her attention to the view screen. They were passing the other ship now, but the camera had shifted to track it, and she could see that the running lights were out. It seemed dead in space.

"No power, no residual heat from the engine department," Yumi said.

"Any dead people hugging radioactive artifacts inside?" Alisa shuddered, remembering their run-in with that pilgrim ship. She hadn't even boarded, only seeing the mad, nearly dead woman through Leonidas's helmet camera, but the way she had raved and taken her own life still chilled her.

"Impossible to tell, since they wouldn't show up on the sensors," Yumi said.

"No, I suppose not."

"I'm not, however, reading abnormally high radiation."

Alisa snorted. "We didn't last time either. Because the *Nomad's* sensors are about as precise as a wrecking ball. Or one of Mica's explosives."

"I haven't noticed you objecting to using her homemade explosives," Leonidas said.

"No, because I don't require precision. Knocking down an entire wall to kill a scorpion works, after all."

"Sometimes."

Leonidas waved at the ship as it receded from their camera. "We're not stopping to explore?"

"I don't want to risk losing Henneberry. Besides, I highly doubt Tymoteusz did something as stupid as getting himself and his crew irradiated." Her gut clenched at the idea of Thorian dead on that ship, either from some mishap with the radiation from the station or just by Tymoteusz's hand.

He's not dead, Jelena spoke into Alisa's mind, startling her.

She was used to Abelardus butting in, but Jelena had only spoken to her telepathically a few times. She didn't seem to pry into Alisa's mind constantly the way Abelardus did. Only when they were close together and talking did some of her comments prove that she knew what Alisa was thinking.

Leonidas turned to look through the hatchway, and Alisa did the same, suspecting Jelena was close. She stood in the corridor, only one eye visible as she peered inside.

How do you know? Alisa asked silently, glad Jelena hadn't come up earlier when she had been staring dreamily at Leonidas.

He's my friend. I'd know if he died.

Even from a great distance? If he's not on that ship, he can't be anywhere close. There aren't any other ships on our sensors.

"I'd know," Jelena said firmly.

Yumi glanced back at her. Leonidas did not seem surprised by what was, to him, a random statement. He must have gotten used to silent Starseer conversations going on around him.

"They could have had engine problems and called on Henneberry to pick them up when she came through," Leonidas said.

"If they're all together now," Alisa said, "presumably with all of their mafia buddies, then why are they still flying deeper into the quarantine zone? Isn't the middle of nowhere as good a place as any for a meeting?"

"I don't know. If Henneberry continues on her present course—" Leonidas waved at the tracking display, "—then where will she end up?"

Alisa started to answer that their route would eventually take them out of the system and into the empty blackness beyond, but she first checked to see if Henneberry's course had changed at all since the last time she had checked it and programmed the autopilot. It had. Only slightly, but slightly turned into a great deal when compounded over millions of miles.

"Damn it," she muttered, slumping back in her chair.

Leonidas glanced at Jelena, then looked at Alisa.

"I've heard Mom swear before," she informed him, or perhaps she was speaking to the room in general.

Alisa barely registered the comment. She was too busy feeling numb from what her new calculations told her.

"Their current course will take them to Alcyone Station," she said.

CHAPTER TWENTY

"Nothing yet?" Alisa asked.

"No, Captain," Yumi said from the seat behind her.

Hours had gone by since they passed the dead *chasadski* ship, and they had not come across any other vessels yet, but the blip on the tracking display had slowed to a stop. Alisa believed that stop had been made near Alcyone Station. It and the rift were too far away for the *Nomad's* sensors to pick up yet, but the location was in the ship's navigational maps from last time.

"I was hoping to see sign of the Alliance fleet before ambling up on Henneberry's ship," Alisa said. "Especially since she's likely out there with all of her closest mafia friends. I wonder if Solstice went with her." She would have looked at Leonidas, but he had wandered out of NavCom to hit his hover pads and get some lunch. Maybe she should call him back to see if he would try comming her. Did he know how to contact her ship specifically?

"It does seem like it would be unwise of us to fly into the spider web without the spider being suitably distracted," Yumi said.

Are we there yet? Abelardus asked into her mind.

Alisa had wondered where he was. She hadn't seen him, and he hadn't made any snide comments into her mind all day about her night with Leonidas.

That's because I was having wonderful and glorious sex of my own, he informed her.

By yourself?

Of course not. Not this time, anyway.

She snorted, drawing a glance from Yumi.

"Starseers," Alisa said.

"Ah." Yumi's face grew wistful for a moment, that I-wish-I-could-do-Starseer-things look crossing her face, but she turned back to the sensors.

Young-hee? Alisa guessed, though it wasn't any of her business. Still, captains should know what was going on aboard their own ships, right?

She finally saw into my heart and realized how magnificent it is, Abelardus said.

I bet you apologized to her for being an ass, finally noticed that she's a quiet beauty, and told her that you'd been a fool not to appreciate her before.

Abelardus hesitated. *It wasn't in that order.*

Congratulations. Alisa didn't know if he deserved Young-hee, but if he was in a relationship with her, he ought to spend less time butting into her thoughts.

You're as magnanimous as you are selfless, Captain. Don't worry—I'll always have time for you. Now, are we there yet? Young-hee and I have been discussing strategies for sneaking the staff away from Tymoteusz.

You can come up to NavCom and see what we're dealing with yourself.

That's not necessary.

Leonidas isn't here.

I'll be right up.

Less than a minute later, Abelardus ambled into NavCom and flopped down, flinging an arm over the backrest and one of his sandaled feet onto the control panel. Maybe Alisa shouldn't have mentioned Leonidas's absence.

"We're on the way to Alcyone Station?" he asked.

"Or a position not far from it." Alisa pointed to the blip of the now-stationary Henneberry ship.

"Are you sure that's her ship and that she didn't find your tracking device and throw it out a porthole?"

Alisa blinked. "No, but I imagine she would have destroyed it instead of throwing it into a garbage chute. Probably with much stomping of her boots."

Abelardus scratched his jaw. "What could they want with Alcyone Station?"

"Maybe Terrible Tym has realized that he'll be hunted to the ends of the system as long as he has the staff, so he's decided to return it to Alcyone's tomb to get rid of it."

"That's wishful thinking. He probably just thought this would be a snazzy meeting place. He could be setting up a podium right now, where he can have the appearing and disappearing station as his backdrop. Its perky radioactive glow will make him look special."

"Hm." Alisa supposed there could be something to that. Maybe Tymoteusz planned to do something mad like walking the halls of the station without radiation protection, just to prove that he was blessed by the suns and the obvious choice to rule the system. If that was his plan, Alisa hoped the radiation aged him a hundred years and wilted his balls into raisins.

Thinking of your uncle's balls may be the sign of a sick mind, Abelardus told her.

Before Alisa could reply, Yumi said, "We're going to soon reach a point where an important decision must be made."

"Whether or not we should get any closer?" Alisa asked.

"The Alliance ships, Henneberry's yacht, and some of the mafia ships are all likely to have superior sensor range to this freighter."

"Meaning they'll see us long before we see them." Alisa sighed. "I know. I've considered that. I was hoping that before we reached that point, we would find sign that the Alliance was in the vicinity, perhaps challenging Henneberry and her cohorts right now."

Her plan had always been to slip in while the Alliance was keeping Tymoteusz and the others busy.

Maybe the Alliance found out where the meeting was being held, Abelardus said silently, *and they didn't want their balls wilted.*

They've been here before. In radiation suits.

The ideal attire for fighting battles.

The comm beeped. Alisa half-expected some hail from Henneberry's ship, but it was the internal system.

"Marchenko," she answered.

"Why is that android comming me and sharing his plans for radiation treatment?" Alejandro asked.

"I asked him to."

"Yes, why?"

"Because we're heading back to Alcyone Station again. Or close to it."

Alejandro paused before answering. "You've confirmed on the sensors that the ships are there? Or that's where the tracking device is leading us?"

"We're not within sensor range yet, but the tracking device stopped moving. We're debating on how close we should get."

"Not close at all—we've all had enough extra radiation from our previous visit to last a lifetime."

"I thought you wanted the staff and Thorian," Alisa said.

"What makes you think they're there?" Alejandro snorted derisively. "That woman may have found your tracking device, put it on a shuttle or unmanned robot ship, and sent us all on a fool's errand. She could be meeting Tymoteusz on the far side of the system right now."

Alisa wanted to snap at how ridiculous that was, but she ended up frozen with her mouth half open. Technically, that *could* have happened. She had assumed Henneberry's people would destroy the tracker if they discovered it, but Henneberry had money to waste. She *could* have sacrificed a shuttle to get rid of her pursuers, to make sure they were far, far away when she met Tymoteusz. If she'd found the device, she might have even believed that some Alliance spy had planted it and that they were the ones following her. If she had, that would be even more of a reason to waste a shuttle for such a mission. She might believe she was diverting an entire fleet.

"There's no way you can tell from this far away, is there?" she asked Abelardus.

"Not me, no."

Alisa wiped her hand slowly down her face, suddenly finding Alejandro's scenario disturbingly possible. "We'll get close enough to check. Prepare your radiation drug, and listen to Bravo Six if he has any good advice."

Alejandro swore, then muttered something about Alliance wenches before cutting the comm.

"We're not on a pointless sightseeing trip, are we, Yumi?" Alisa asked, hoping for confirmation that it was unlikely.

"Unknown, Captain. Has the ship we've been tracking changed course since we left the Aldrin area?"

"Yes, a few times."

Yumi's "hm" did not sound encouraging.

"I assumed they were hoping to avoid the usual kind of pursuit."

"Hm," Yumi murmured again.

Alisa sighed. "I'll get us close enough to find out. And stretch those sensors as wide as they'll go. If there's another ship out there, I'd like to see it before it sees us."

"What you'd like and what's possible given the age of this ship may not be compatible. Might I recommend some upgrades to the sensor array the next time we're in a spaceport?"

"If we survive the next twenty-four hours, you can recommend anything you want."

"Excellent."

"While we're getting sensor upgrades, don't forget better towels for the lav," Abelardus said.

"Yes, I'll put them on the list." Alisa shooed him out of NavCom and tapped the control panel to fly them closer to the tracking device.

Yumi's third "hm" came about a half hour later.

"A ship?" Alisa spun in her chair. The *chasadski* ship had long since disappeared from the cameras, and nothing except empty space and the occasional rock had floated past on the view screen.

"Something just came into sensor range. Something large."

"A warship?"

"I don't believe so. It has a different shape."

Alisa leaned over her backrest for a better view. "But it's a ship, right? You're not reading the station, are you?"

The blips on the monitor were not that illuminating, but the data scrolling past gave estimates of size and power being emitted.

"No, it's a large ship," Yumi said. "Larger than a warship. You may want to halt us, as we may already be visible to their sensors. I'm reading an energy signature."

Alisa tapped at the controls, reversing thrusters to bring the *Nomad* to a halt. Whatever was waiting for them, it wasn't an Alliance ship, not unless they'd brought some kind of mobile weapons platform with them.

"No other ships around?" Alisa glanced at the tracking display, thinking to compare the location of the blip to the location of the ship they sensed, but for the first time in days, the blip had disappeared. She frowned and swiped at the holo controls hovering over the netdisc. "What happened there? We were catching up with them because they were stationary. They couldn't have flown out of range."

"Maybe the tracking device flew into the rift," Yumi said dryly.

"You're joking, I hope. That place sounded like it would be a worse place for a meeting than the corona of a sun."

"It certainly would have a very high amount of radiation, but yes, I was joking. I think it's more likely that the tracking device was destroyed. Or, if the ship carrying it has been in close proximity to the station, the radiation might be interfering with the signal. The sensors show that the large ship is very close to the spot where the rift and the station were showing up before, and I'm reading residual radiation in that area, but no sign of either being present in our dimension right now."

"Present in our dimension. That sounds so odd. You think the station is still cycling in and out of our space?"

"The residual radiation suggests that. If you give me more time and get me closer, I could probably make an estimate as to when the station will appear again."

"I'm not sure we want to get closer to this large ship you've found." Alisa frowned, trying to guess who might be out there. Henneberry's yacht had been sizable, as had the private vessels of some of the mafia families, but none of them had been larger than an Alliance warship.

"It could be a mining ship," Yumi said after studying the sensor display a while longer. "I'm reminded of the length and width of the vessel that Malik and his pirates had taken over."

"Who would bring a mining ship out here? There wouldn't be any point in tearing that station apart for the pieces, would there? It's centuries old, and if the artifacts that came out of there could kill people within days, I imagine the rest of the pieces of the station could too."

"That does seem likely," Yumi said. "And as I recall, there weren't any precious metals in the station composition. I did a scan when we first visited."

"Maybe this is someone exploring, hoping to stumble across riches." Alisa slumped back in her seat, trying to stave off the feeling of defeat creeping over her. This wasn't Henneberry, and it wasn't Tymoteusz. If Henneberry had somehow placed the tracking device on that mining ship, and Alisa had been following *it* all along…Alejandro could be right. They could be days and days from whatever meeting spot those people had chosen. They would never find Thorian now.

"Mom, Mom!" came Jelena's voice from the corridor.

Alisa tried to fix a smile on her face and turned as she scrambled into NavCom. "Yes? I'm here."

Jelena rushed up beside her, gripping the edge of the control panel and looking at the view screen even though nothing but stars was visible there now.

"I sense him," she blurted. "We're close."

"Who? Thorian?" Alisa couldn't imagine her daughter trying to sense anyone else out there, but how could that be? Unless he was on that mining ship, but how could that make sense?

"Yes, he's alive, like I said. And he's out there ahead of us." Jelena pursed her lips. "But he's afraid…I think. We're too far for me to talk to him, but I think…I can feel that he's hurt and afraid. And trapped. Somewhere small and dark."

"Can you tell if Tymoteusz is there too?" Alisa frowned back at the sensor display. Could Tymoteusz have moved his people over to the mining ship for some reason? And abandoned his smaller vessel?

Jelena bit the side of her lip. "I don't know. I don't want to look for him. He's scary."

"That he is." Alisa decided to wait for later to tell her that the crazy old man was her great-uncle.

"More ships just came onto the sensors," Yumi said.

"The Alliance fleet?" Alisa asked hopefully. Now would be a good time for Senator Hawk and Stanislav to swoop in and distract the *chasadski*.

"I don't think so. Those look like civilian ships."

"Henneberry's people?" Alisa asked.

Maybe they had been following her the whole time, after all.

"It seems possible. Yes, these look familiar. So far, there's the yacht and a couple of personnel transports. There could be many more ships just out of our sensor range." Yumi frowned over at Alisa. "Captain?"

"Yes?" Alisa asked, doubting she wanted to hear what came next.

"One just veered away from the main group and is heading toward us."

CHAPTER TWENTY-ONE

"Leonidas and Beck," Alisa said over the comm. "We have a problem coming our way. You may want to get armored and fierce."

Jelena, still standing between the pilot's and co-pilot's seats, nodded solemnly. "I'm ready to be fierce. For Thorian."

Alisa gripped her shoulder. "I'd prefer it if you hid in your cabin under your bunk."

"It's hard to be fierce while cowering under the furniture," came Leonidas's voice from behind them. Already clad in his crimson armor, he ducked into NavCom, his helmet tucked under his arm. "Just ask Alejandro," he added.

He wore a weapon Alisa hadn't seen before on a band across his torso, and he also carried a rifle in one hand. Jelena shifted closer to Alisa and gripped her arm.

"He's the same man who kept Westfall from taking you away," Alisa pointed out.

"But he's wearing that...*that*." Jelena pointed at Leonidas's armored chest. "Like the bad people on Andromeda Android. The empire always has soldiers in black and red armor."

"I keep telling you to paint that suit pink, Leonidas," Alisa said, keeping her tone light, though she kept glancing at the view screen. That ship had come into camera range, a civilian transport, as Yumi had mentioned, but one that had weapons mounted on every surface. Its artillery options made the *Nomad's* two e-cannons seem like toys in comparison.

"I thought you said stickers would be sufficient to take away the menace," Leonidas said. He hadn't come any further into NavCom than the hatchway and gave Jelena one of his solemn nods even though she looked nervous. "But you did tell me to get armored and fierce."

"Yes, you were amazingly prompt," Alisa said. "I take it you were already dressed."

"I anticipated trouble."

"Because you heard we were getting close? Or just because I'm piloting?"

"Indeed," he said, eyes crinkling at the corners.

Jelena relaxed some at this banter and loosened her grip on Alisa's arm.

Alisa commed the shuttle—Bravo Six was faithfully following along behind the *Nomad*. "Six? You see that we have trouble coming?"

"According to my sensor readouts, this sector appears to be full of nothing but trouble, Lady Captain," the android said, almost sounding dry. Or maybe she was reading emotion into his monotone voice.

"An accurate assessment. There aren't any weapons on that shuttle, so if we get into trouble, do your best to stay out of the way, all right?"

"Understood, but since this ship is largely superfluous, might I propose that in the case of an emergency, it could be used for ramming purposes?"

"That doesn't sound healthy for the pilot," Alisa said.

"Correct. But it's possible that the shuttle might have enough mass, especially at sufficient velocity, that it could severely damage an enemy vessel, especially if its shields were down."

"Listen, Six. *You* aren't superfluous. Do you understand? You're not sacrificing yourself out here."

"I am merely an android, Lady Captain."

"You're an asset, and we don't want to lose you, so just fly wide of any battles, understood?"

"As you command, Lady Captain."

Alisa closed the comm with a grimace. She didn't need a noble knight of an android that wanted to get himself killed out here. She hadn't even gotten his eyeball fixed yet. He wasn't going to sacrifice himself on her watch.

"I don't suppose there's any chance Thorian is on that ship?" Alisa asked, pointing toward the vessel coming toward them. The others were too far to pick up on camera as of yet.

Jelena shook her head. "He's on the ship with the scary Starseer, the one who stole him at the station."

"Tymoteusz?" Leonidas asked.

Jelena shrugged. Right. They hadn't yet been formally introduced.

"Then there's little point in getting in a fight with this ship, is there?" Alisa raised their shields and powered up the thrusters again. She flew straight toward the mining ship. The armed transport would intercept them easily, so she flexed her fingers, preparing for some fancy maneuvering.

"No point," Leonidas agreed. "That's one of the ships that was at the meeting."

"One of Henneberry's allies then," Alisa said. "It probably got sent over to deal with us."

Leonidas lifted his chin. "It can *try*."

Jelena smiled slightly, perhaps in approval.

"A few more ships are coming into range," Yumi said. "They're behind the area where the rift will appear."

"Still no Alliance ships?" Alisa asked.

"No."

Where *were* they? Hadn't Tomich been sending the directions to his people? Or was it possible that his cover had been blown, and Henneberry had realized he was a spy? If so, the Alliance might not have any idea where this meeting was being held.

"The transport will be in weapons range soon," Yumi said quietly.

"I'm going to do my best to avoid getting shot," Alisa said, "but we may want to see if we can distract them with a few e-cannon blasts of our own."

"I'll handle it." Leonidas stepped forward slowly, looking like he didn't want to startle Jelena. There wasn't much room for him to squeeze in with her in the aisle.

Jelena leaned closer to Alisa to make room. Alisa thought about swooping her into her lap, but she was about to need all of her concentration for flying. Besides, Jelena had grown too tall for sitting in her lap, at least when she needed to see.

"Go stand back there, please," Alisa said, pointing to the hatchway. "Or you can go to your cabin if you're scared."

"I'm not scared," Jelena said firmly. "I'm going to help. To get Thorian."

"We have to get past this ship before we can get to the one with him on it."

"Do you think he's on this ship?" Yumi asked Jelena, pointing to the big blip on the sensor display.

With the question distracting her, Jelena didn't seem to mind Leonidas squeezing past. She went behind Alisa to peer over Yumi's shoulder as Leonidas took the co-pilot's seat and activated the weapons controls.

"Yes," Jelena said. "That's where all the bad Starseers are and..." Her face screwed up in concentration.

"Did you want me to be fierce too?" Abelardus asked, walking into NavCom. He wore his black robe, as usual, and had his staff in hand, his long braids tied back.

"Definitely," Alisa said. "And see if you can fiddle with the mind of whoever is at the weapons station on this closest ship, please."

"Fiddling away." Abelardus leaned against the bulkhead and closed his eyes.

"There's a lot of people on there," Jelena said.

"On the mining ship?" Yumi asked.

"Yes, that one."

"How many is a lot? More than a handful of *chasadski*?"

"How many is a handful?" Jelena asked.

"Ten? Twelve?"

"I think there's a hundred people there. Maybe more."

"Did he take over the ship without bothering to ask the miners to move out?" Alisa asked, dipping the nose of the *Nomad* as the transport's forward cannons flared. Twin blasts of white streaked through space, almost glancing off the *Nomad's* shields. She threw them into a roll even as she zigzagged to make a harder target. "I need more fiddling than that, Abelardus."

"Sorry," Abelardus said. "I think I was—"

"Their shields dropped," Leonidas said. "Firing."

Thrums echoed through the ship as the *Nomad's* e-cannons fired. The blasts of energy hammered into the side of the transport. Leonidas fired again, but fiery orange flared around the hull, the attack deflected.

"They've got their shields back up," Yumi said.

"Someone else took over the position," Abelardus said. "I made the one lower shields, but they've got backup people."

"Fiddle more," Alisa said, sweeping the *Nomad* up as the transport turned to give chase. The pursuer's side was charred where those blasts had gotten through, but it didn't look like the e-cannons had done serious damage to the heavily armored ship.

"Working on it," Abelardus said.

Even as Alisa did her best to evade their pursuer, she kept them heading toward the mining ship. She tapped the camera controls, thinking it might be close enough to see now. Yes, there it was in the distance. As Yumi had said, it was huge, a hulking rectangular vessel, a mile long and a half a mile wide, with all manner of retractable tools for cutting and digging and gathering mounted on the hull. Alisa spotted weapons, too, additions to the original ship's makeup.

"I don't mean to question you, Captain," Yumi said, as blazer fire streaked past to their port side, "but you're flying toward that ship like it's a beacon of safety, and, ah—"

"There are no beacons of safety out here," Alisa said. "I know. But that's where Thorian is."

"And the staff," Abelardus said.

Alisa chopped her hand in the air. As if she cared about that staff.

"The only way we're going to get Thorian is by boarding that ship," Alisa said, banking as their pursuer fired again. This time, she wasn't fast enough, and one of the blazer bolts smashed into their rear shields.

Leonidas fired twice. "I've hit them square on several times. Their shields should be worse off than ours."

Unfortunately, there wasn't any way to tell that, not on the instruments.

"They are," Abelardus said. "The captain is communicating with Henneberry. Two more ships were just dispatched to help."

"Wonderful," Alisa muttered, turning them toward the mining ship again.

"When you say we need to board the ship," Yumi said slowly, "do you mean forcibly? Because I've had time to thoroughly scan that craft. It's been reinforced and is far more dangerous than a typical mining ship."

"I guessed that," Alisa said, "when I saw the weapons mounted all over it like cactus thorns. We're not going to be able to force our way anywhere. We're going to have to be captured."

Even though Leonidas was busy firing, he gave her a long look. What, he hadn't assumed that was what she had in mind?

"They may simply destroy us," he said.

"How silly would that be when we have a proposal to offer?" Alisa waved over her shoulder. "Yumi, do you have enough of that drug to fuzz the minds of everyone on our ship?"

"I'll see what I have on hand, Captain," Yumi said, rising from her seat, "but it's not a guarantee. Also, a powerful Starseer may be able to see through the, ah, *fuzz*."

"I'll take my chances," Alisa said, banking hard to evade another round of fire. "Leonidas, have you not fiercely made our pursuer dead yet?"

"Working on it." He fired again. "Their shielding is—"

"Abelardus, get those shields down." Alisa hit the comm. "Young-hee, can you come help Abelardus? He needs a co-fiddler."

"I do not," Abelardus said stiffly.

"I want those shields down. Permanently." Alisa glanced at the sensors and grimaced, both at the armada of ships waiting near the rift and at the two quickly cutting the distance between them and the *Nomad*. "Why couldn't my mother have gotten a *fast* freighter? A nice smuggling ship, perhaps."

"Shields are down," Leonidas said, firing.

"You're welcome," Abelardus said.

"Disable that ship, please," Alisa said.

Young-hee appeared in the hatchway, slid inside, and stood next to Abelardus. Without opening his eyes, he wrapped an arm around her and pulled her against him. She did not object, though she wore an extremely worried frown as she eyed the mining ship on the view screen.

Leonidas fired again, thrums going through the ship and the lights flickering as the e-cannons drew power. His blasts struck the transport ship head on despite the crazy spins and gyrations Alisa was putting the *Nomad* through.

A blast of orange and yellow appeared on the camera, and a beep came from the proximity alarm. Only when shrapnel pinged off the shields did Alisa realize the ship had been more than disabled. As the light of the explosion disappeared, she gaped at the wreck that remained, the entire front half blown up.

"Is it dead?" Jelena whispered.

It. As if there hadn't been people aboard.

Alisa swallowed and bit back the accusation that formed on her tongue, that she had wanted it disabled, not destroyed. Yes, these people were out here trying to overthrow the government—her government—and that made them criminals, if their mafia connections hadn't already accomplished that, but it was hard to condemn them without knowing them. She and the Alliance had once been considered criminals too. To the empire. More practically, she had just declared war on a lot of powerful ships, and she had absolutely no backup out here.

"Here's the drug," Yumi said, trotting into the room.

"Right here." Alisa held out her hand. If she wasn't able to convince Tymoteusz to capture her ship—while keeping them alive—then they needed to be ready to run fast and pray hard. It might be far too late for that. Henneberry might have let them go before they had blown up one of her allies, but now?

Alisa licked the bitter powder that Yumi poured into her hand, swallowing more of a dose than she had the last time she had used it. She hoped there weren't any side effects that would affect her ability to think. Or that would kill her.

Scowling at the taste, she reached for the comm controls, but she paused. "How long does it need to kick in?"

"Not long," Yumi said, passing doses to Leonidas, Young-hee, and Abelardus. "Give it five minutes."

"We don't have five minutes," Alisa said, glancing at the sensor display. The two new ships would be in firing range in a minute. Already, they were veering apart, moving to surround her.

"Do I give any to Jelena?" Yumi asked.

Jelena wrinkled her nose dubiously at the powder. Alisa hesitated. Jelena wouldn't know her plan, most likely, but if she was determined to get Thorian back, that would be in conflict with what Alisa was going to tell Tymoteusz.

"Remember the way he controlled the soldiers on the asteroid base," Leonidas warned.

"I haven't forgotten." Alisa nodded toward Yumi. "Give it to her. And everyone else on the ship too."

"I don't want any," Jelena said, shying away from Yumi's extended hand.

"You have to, sweetie." Alisa smiled and patted her shoulder as she changed course, doing her best to continue toward the mining ship while evading the mafia vessels' attempts at surrounding her. "It'll help us get Thorian. Tymoteusz is too powerful for us to face without trickery. But if he knows we're tricking him it won't work."

Jelena curled her lip and made no move to take any of the powder. She might have sensed how distasteful Alisa found the stuff. Understandable that she wouldn't want to try it, but there wasn't time for bargaining and wheedling right now. She opened her mouth to use her stern mom-voice, but Leonidas spoke first.

"If you lick some of that powder," he said, "I'll put stickers on my armor."

Alisa snorted, not expecting that to work—Jelena had been dubious throughout that conversation, after all. Leonidas didn't look like he expected the offer to influence her either. He gave Alisa an I-tried shrug.

"What *kind* of stickers?" Jelena asked.

"Andromeda Android?" Leonidas suggested, even though Alisa was positive he hadn't seen the cartoon before. He had been paying attention though. Good man.

"*Kittens*," Jelena said.

"What?" he asked.

"Only kittens could make you less scary. *Lots* of kittens."

Judging by the horrified expression on Leonidas's face, he knew he had made a mistake. But he nodded and extended a gauntleted hand. "It's a deal."

Jelena hesitated, but licked the powder straight out of Yumi's hand.

Alisa smacked her forehead. Yumi looked bemused but did not flinch away.

Jelena grasped Leonidas's hand. "Deal."

"Good," Alisa said, bumping Jelena's shoulder with her hand. "You can start shopping for stickers for him as soon as we rescue Thorian."

"On the way to ride horses," Jelena said.

"Seems like a reasonable time." The closest ship fired at the *Nomad*, and Alisa put both hands on the controls again, launching into evasive moves. "Yumi, drugs for everyone else, please."

"On my way."

Alisa programmed the comm to raise the mining ship. The two ships trying to gang up on her might be civilian ships rather than military vessels, but as with the last one, their hulls appeared reinforced, and numerous weapons had been installed since they left the factory.

Blazer fire pelted the back of the *Nomad's* shields.

The comm flashed, letting her know of an interior message coming through as the ship tried to contact the mining vessel.

"Not now, Mica," Alisa said, certain her engineer wanted to know what she had gotten them into.

The exterior channel opened. The mining ship.

Alisa took a deep breath, wondering if Tymoteusz would answer or if it would be one of his minions. Or one of the miners or whoever else was on that ship.

"What are you doing here, woman?" a male voice asked, sending a shiver through Alisa. Tymoteusz. "I let you live before. *Twice.* Why do you continue to follow me? To attempt to interfere with my plans?"

"I thought it was time for a family chat, Uncle," she said, hoping vainly that the familial connection would mean something. She wasn't sure she believed he had intentionally spared her in that asteroid collapse—she would have been crushed into a pancake if not for her armor—but he definitely had back on Arkadius.

"Is that so," he said, sarcasm dripping from the words.

"With Stanislav dead, you're my only choice," she said, praying to the sun trinity that he couldn't read her thoughts.

"Stan isn't dead, woman." The sarcasm had shifted to derision.

Hells, had it been foolish to think he wouldn't know? After all, Jelena had been certain Thorian was still alive. True, that might only be wishful thinking on her part, but it could also indicate that Starseers could bond and sense each other across impossible distances.

"He has to be," Alisa said, putting a puzzled note in her voice. "We left him behind on Sepiron Station, fighting the Alliance. I saw the station blow up. He made time so we could escape. He sacrificed himself, because he wanted me to be able to get my daughter. Your grandniece."

She looked at Jelena, hating to bring her up, but she couldn't think of anything else that might appeal to the man. This scheme filled her with sheer terror, however, and her heart was slamming against her ribcage as if she were running a marathon instead of talking. Talking and flying. The mafia ships weren't leaving her alone for this conversation, and she kept doing her best to evade them, as the bristling form of the mining ship grew larger and larger on the view screen.

"If he's not dead," Alisa said, "that's good, but he might as well be for my purposes, because the Alliance will have him locked up somewhere."

"A *zhadski* is not easily locked up."

It took her a second to remember that word, to remember that the *chasadski* did not call themselves pariahs—the Starseers did. Abelardus had defined *zhadski* as prophets and disciples of the gods. Their term for themselves.

"What are your *purposes*, woman?" Tymoteusz asked.

"*Alisa*," she said firmly. "Though I'm glad my sex hasn't escaped you."

Leonidas lifted his eyebrows. Right, she should be more polite to her uncle, especially since she wanted him to get these thugs off her butt and save her life.

"I should think my purposes would be obvious," Alisa said.

Judging by the blank looks she was getting from everyone in NavCom, there wasn't much obviousness going on.

"My daughter has Starseer genes and the ability to use mental powers, as I'm sure you're aware." Alisa specifically remembered Tymoteusz acknowledging that when they had first met. Of course, he had denigrated her for not having the same abilities. "She's bright and displaying great ability." She had no idea if Jelena's abilities were great or average, but thought Tymoteusz would be more enticed by superior talents. "Since I don't have any power, I can't teach her, and I'm not about to let some arrogant fools that would kidnap her for their own gain become her instructors."

Jelena's forehead furrowed. "Does she mean Lady Westfall?" she whispered to Young-hee.

Alisa held a finger to her lips, wondering if she should ask Young-hee to take Jelena to the rec room.

"Since Stanislav is either dead or incapacitated, I naturally thought of you," Alisa continued.

Tymoteusz did not answer, and she looked at the comm to make sure the channel was still open. Another blazer bolt streaked toward the *Nomad*, biting into the shields. Alisa glared at their pursuers and manipulated the controls, taking the freighter through another series of dips and dives. She shouldn't be trying to scheme and talk while she had to evade enemies.

Leonidas fired, and one of their cannon blasts slammed into the nose of the closest pursuer. Unfortunately, the ship's shields absorbed the energy.

A tickle arose in Alisa's mind, making every hair on her body stand on end. There was nothing friendly about the touch—it felt like some avenging spirit wanted to possess her.

Praying the drug had kicked in, she did her best to think about nothing more than evading their enemies. If Tymoteusz or one of his people was trying to read her mind, she had to make it as difficult as possible.

"It *was* unacceptable for them to kidnap your daughter," he finally said.

"The mining ship is moving," Yumi said. "It's turning toward us."

Alisa did not say anything, aware that Tymoteusz would hear through the open comm.

"The *ashari* have never understood the true potential of our minds. If they had, they would not be cowering and hiding from the empire and now the Alliance. They would study all of their powers. They would know that it won't take many of us to rule the entire system."

Alisa shivered, hearing a hint of madness in his voice.

"Jelena needs a teacher," Alisa said, "and it's my job as a mother to find the best person available."

"I am the best," Tymoteusz said agreeably. "Even without the staff."

That sensation of a rake scraping across her brain matter came again, and Alisa swallowed. Through the link, she sensed him testing her. Did he think she had come for the staff? *No, Tymoteusz,* she thought. *I don't give a damn about that stupid artifact.* She did not know if he would hear her, but just in case, she forced herself not to add on that she would love to see it destroyed so nobody could use it for ill.

"The mafia ships have stopped firing," Leonidas whispered.

"He ordered them to stop," Abelardus said, his eyes closed.

On the view screen, the mining ship continued to grow larger. Soon its lumpy, tool-filled hull would be all they could see.

"You will come to me," Tymoteusz said. "I will meet the girl and assess her."

The words filled Alisa with dread—and she spotted Jelena gripping the back of Leonidas's seat and sinking down, as if to hide from the ship filling the screen—but she forced herself to say, "Good. That's all I ask."

The mining ship turned slightly, and an opening in its hull came into view, the giant orifice leading into an enormous hangar bay.

A flash of blue came from the view screen, and the *Nomad* jolted hard enough to throw Alisa against the control panel.

"What was that?" Young-hee asked.

"Grab beam," Leonidas said.

Alisa verified that, then powered down the engines. "He has us now."

She glanced at the sensors. The beam hadn't caught Bravo Six's shuttle. Alisa remembered his words about ramming enemies, and she hoped he didn't get any ideas. But even as she watched, a couple of mafia ships veered after the shuttle.

Alisa groaned and hit the comm. "Six, don't let yourself get blown up. Fly out of here. There's nothing you can do to help. Do you read me?"

"I will endeavor not to be blown up, Lady Captain."

"Thank you."

As the mafia ships closed on him and opened fire, she sank back in her seat in defeat. Was there any chance he could survive? That she would ever talk to him again? She still owed him an eyeball.

Alisa stared as the *Nomad* was drawn toward that hangar bay, reminding herself that this was what she had wanted. They hadn't been destroyed. They were being taken aboard, and this would be their chance to find Thorian...if they could get away from the *chasadski* and their minions.

"This is a bad idea," Abelardus muttered, also watching the screen.

Alisa wasn't sure she could disagree. She looked at Jelena's round eyes. What had she gotten them into?

CHAPTER TWENTY-TWO

In her cabin, Alisa stared at the faceplate of her helmet, gripped with indecision. And there wasn't time for indecision. The *Nomad* had been pulled into the giant mining ship's hangar and was being lowered to the deck even now. As soon as the bay pressurized, men with weapons or *chasadski* with staffs—or both—would storm out. She doubted Tymoteusz would have any trouble forcing the *Nomad's* hatch open and striding onto the ship, if he wished to do so. She had no idea if she had truly piqued his interest, or if he had brought her aboard for ulterior motives.

"Alisa?" Leonidas leaned into her cabin and frowned at the helmet in her hands. "You're not dressed."

"I wasn't sure if I should put this on or not." Alisa waved at the open armor case, the rest of the pieces still resting in their molds.

"Of course you should put it on." He looked at her as if she were crazy. "And then you should accessorize it with rifles."

"More than one?"

"It suits me." Leonidas stepped all the way into the cabin and hefted his own blazer rifle—a second one was strapped to his torso, and he also wore that other weapon, the launcher he and Mica must have made for the canisters hooked onto his belt. There were also grenades hooked there, and a pouch looked to hold a few more options.

"That's fine for you, I think. He'll assume my security officer would be armed. But if I walk out, talking about how I want to establish family relations and have him teach my daughter, wouldn't he find it suspicious if I was encased in armor and wielding weapons?"

"He's suspicious anyway. Trust me." Leonidas reached in and pulled the chest piece out. "He'll think it's odd that he couldn't read our thoughts."

Alisa hesitated.

"You *will* put your armor on," he said. "Or I'll put it on for you. All the pieces might not face in the right direction if I do it."

Even though she didn't like being told what to do, she understood and appreciated his interest in keeping her safe. She set the helmet aside for last and accepted the chest piece.

"Most men try to *un*dress women," she said as she donned the armor. "Not the other way around."

"I haven't had a lot of practice either way."

"We'll have to amend that when we're finished here."

"Absolutely."

"Leonidas?" Beck called from down the corridor. "Where did you put the grenade launcher?"

"The same place I always put it," Leonidas called back.

"If something isn't stored in the kitchen, I don't pay much attention."

"I'll meet you in the cargo hold," Leonidas told Alisa, kissed her on the cheek, and jogged out. "Don't forget a rifle," he called back.

Alisa felt the clank of the *Nomad* settling onto the deck and hurried to don the rest of her armor. She would need to check on Jelena on the way to the hold, make sure she stayed with Yumi or Young-hee. Or Mica. *If* Mica stayed aboard. Alisa hadn't decided yet if she would ask her to come along. She usually had some tricks in her tool bag that could come in handy. Alisa tugged at her braid more than needed as she pulled it back into a bun so she could put on the helmet. She was irritated that she had gotten herself into such a helpless situation. This hadn't been the plan at all. Where in all the suns' hells was Hawk with Stanislav and the Alliance fleet?

"Captain," Mica said over the comm. "We have a problem."

"We have a lot of problems. You'll have to be more specific." Alisa snapped her last piece of armor on, save for the helmet.

"Come down to engineering. I'll show you."

"Be right there." As Alisa stepped into the corridor, the lighting flashed several times, then went out. The emergency lighting embedded

END GAME

in the deck came on. "Beginning to get a hint of what that problem might be," she muttered.

She peeked into Jelena's cabin. It was empty. At the intersection, she looked toward NavCom, where she had last seen Jelena, but both she and Yumi had left. The view screen lay dark, only the dim red emergency lights glowing up there too.

"Jelena?" Alisa called as she jogged through the mess hall and past sickbay.

She almost ran into Abelardus, who stood on the walkway with Young-hee, both in their black robes and both carrying their staffs. Yumi was with them, doling out small travel packets of her drugs. Abelardus had refused to take the qui-gorn powder before, claiming that he could keep other Starseers out of his mind without trouble, but he accepted one of the little packets now. Maybe that represented maturity on his part—or Young-hee's wise influence.

I just know that your mad uncle can overpower me, Abelardus spoke into her mind.

So, you haven't matured at all?

Not in the least. He grinned at her.

Young-hee slapped him in the chest. Alisa wasn't sure if she had heard the mental exchange or just figured Abelardus deserved it.

"I am *too* going," came Jelena's voice from the hold below.

Uh-oh.

Alisa pushed past the others and ran down the steps. In the dim emergency lighting, she could see her eight-year-old daughter standing in her Starseer robe in front of Beck and the controls to the cargo hatch. Her fists were on her hips as she stared defiantly up at him. Alisa would have been proud of her for standing her ground if she actually *wanted* Jelena to stand her ground right now.

"Jelena..." she started, walking toward her and mentally bracing herself for a fight. "You need to—"

"Mom, you said we're going to meet an uncle, right?" Jelena asked, spinning around. "I know it's a trick, but he's going to think it's funny if I'm not there, right? And then when we're out there, we'll sneak away and find Thor."

273

"We will hope to get the opportunity to sneak away and find Thor, but it's too dangerous for you to go out there. We can't trust your great-uncle. He wants to take over the entire system."

"I don't care about that. I just want to find Thor. He's on board. I can tell, but he's in pain. He's scared, and hurt, and I'm not able to talk to him." Jelena swallowed—there was a hint of hysteria in her voice. "I have to find him. I think they did something to him."

"I'll find him," Leonidas said, striding out of engineering.

Jelena frowned at him, but looked back at Alisa, her eyes imploring. "You'll need me to lead you to him." She glanced at Leonidas again. "Both of you."

"Actually, I can sense him," Abelardus said from the walkway, raising his staff. He jogged down to join them.

Jelena only scowled, not pleased with his contribution.

Alisa gripped her shoulder. "Stay here with Yumi. If anyone can get Thorian, Leonidas can."

Jelena crossed her arms over her chest. "You need me."

"I can't risk you in this, sweetie."

"The uncle is going to expect to see me."

"I don't care what he expects. He's not anyone we can trust. He's—"

"Mom, you're not listening to me," Jelena said, her voice rising, a tantrum building. Alisa grimaced. It had been a while since she had seen a full-on meltdown, but she hadn't forgotten what they looked like when coming—or how much better Jonah had always been at deescalating them than Alisa. "I have to come," Jelena yelled, tears brimming in her eyes. "He needs me. I can tell. I'm his friend. Nobody else is his friend. You don't even know him. He—"

"I said I'll get him," Leonidas said. His voice wasn't loud, but it cut through Jelena's yells. It was the tone of a commander of troops, someone who didn't take crap from anyone, not even little girls. "When you're ten years older, have a rifle and a set of combat armor, *then* you can go out amongst the enemy. But not now." He pointed toward the walkway. "Stay with Yumi."

Jelena's face screwed up in a mulish expression. Alisa was tempted to throw her over her shoulder and lock her in a cabin.

"I'll bring him back," Leonidas said, his voice quieter this time. Earnest.

"You better." Jelena stalked away with her hands fisted at her sides, but she did go up the stairs in the direction he had indicated.

Yumi put an arm around her shoulders and led her into the ship's interior.

"Thank you," Alisa told Leonidas. She hadn't been sure that would work or that it was the right tactic, but did remember that Jelena had always been less likely to have a tantrum at school or with people she didn't know as well. She saved her stubbornness for home.

Leonidas nodded once.

"Captain," Mica said, sticking her head out of engineering. "Did you want to look at this problem today or wait until we're completely out of power?"

"What?" Alisa took a step in that direction, but a clang sounded outside.

"Better hurry," Leonidas said. "They're entering the bay."

"Be nice if we could turn on the camera display," Beck said, tapping the controls that would normally do that. The monitor remained dark.

Alisa jogged toward engineering, glancing at the walkway to make sure Jelena hadn't evaded her babysitter. She didn't need her escape artist of a daughter finding her way out of the ship while they were here.

Curses, grunts, and bangs met Alisa as she entered engineering.

"There's a problem, you say?" she asked, picking out Mica in the dim lighting. A lantern rested in the middle of the room, its light gleaming off no less than six panels that had been dumped on the deck.

"I've said that at least three times," Mica said, her voice muffled, her head stuck into a bulkhead, conduits visible inside. "Nice of you to finally check in."

Since there wasn't time for sniping, Alisa simply strode over and looked over Mica's shoulder. "What's going on?"

"Something is draining our power."

"Something? A leak?"

"Nothing leaks on a boat I maintain," Mica growled. "The source is outside the ship. Some kind of beam. I thought it was the grab beam at first, holding us in place in their hangar bay, but it's got to be more than that. Grab beams don't drain power." A clang punctuated her words.

Alisa eyed the dark light fixtures. "Will it drain *all* our power?" They already knew they would have to disable the grab beam somehow before they could leave. But this hadn't been in the script.

"I don't know. I didn't get a memo about it from Terrible Tym." Mica leaned back and slapped at a panel. It beeped and displayed a gauge. "We're down forty percent already. I cut off non-essential systems to conserve power, but if we don't figure out what the cause is and how to stop it, we're not going to be able to fly out of here."

"You're going to need to fix it then, because flying out of here is part of the plan."

"There's a plan?" Mica sent her a scathing look. "Who are you trying to fool?"

"Just get it fixed." Alisa slapped her on the shoulder. "I have confidence in you."

"I have confidence that your stupid antics are finally going to get us all killed."

"There's that pessimistic streak that I adore in you."

"I'll do what I can from in here to try and break the bond, but you're probably going to have to find whatever's draining us and turn it off. Preferably before we go to zero power."

"How much do we need to take off?"

"More than zero."

"Your precision is admirable."

"What would be admirable is you and your hulking security officer going out there to stop it." Mica waved in dismissal.

Alisa added the task to her already daunting to-do list and left engineering.

I am here, Tymoteusz spoke into her mind. *I await you and your daughter.*

From the way he emphasized the latter, Alisa suspected he was far more interested in meeting Jelena than her. That wasn't going to happen. All she replied with was, *On my way.*

"Gravity and air are in place outside, Captain," Beck said, reading the one instrument still working in the hold.

Alisa nodded, heading toward him, Leonidas, and Abelardus. Young-hee remained on the walkway, so Alisa assumed she wasn't coming along to storm the castle. That was fine—she wasn't exactly a battle-hardened veteran.

"Young-hee," Alisa said, "Mica would love it if you helped her figure out what's draining the ship's power."

"Yes, Captain. I'll do my best."

As Alisa lifted a hand to signal Beck to open the hatch, Alejandro strode out onto the walkway and gripped the railing.

"Captain?" he said.

"You're grabbing your medical kit and want to come with us?" Alisa asked.

He frowned. "I came to warn you that I was reading excessive radiation against the hull of the ship before my instruments went out. We're in close proximity to Alcyone Station and that rift."

"I'm aware of that. Do you have a drug or a recommendation?"

"I can treat you when you get back once I measure your radiation levels. I *recommend* that we leave the area."

"That's not an option right now. Besides, we need Thorian, right?"

"As quickly as possible, yes. The mining ship may have a reinforced hull that will offer more protection than your freighter alone, but we shouldn't linger."

"I wasn't going to linger." Alisa waved for Beck to hit the button as she looked at Leonidas. "Were you thinking of lingering?"

"No."

"Nobody here is going to linger, Doc. Promise."

A faint hiss sounded as the hatch unsealed, followed by a clank as the ramp lowered. Alisa imagined it landing on Tymoteusz's head and smashing him.

"Wishful thinking," she murmured.

Leonidas pointed to her helmet. He and Beck both had theirs on.

"I'm going to try chatting with him first," she said as the bright interior of the hangar came into view, along with several rows of armed men and women. They had glazed eyes and blank expressions, and even though they looked toward Alisa, they were not focused on her. Their weapons, however, were.

"You can do that with your helmet on." Leonidas stepped onto the ramp first, positioning himself to protect Alisa.

He also blocked her view. She paused to jam her helmet on before following him out—maybe he was right.

As she snapped the fasteners, Leonidas growled deep in his throat. It sounded like pain as much as aggression. He tried to lift the canister launcher he carried, but instead, he dropped to one knee, the weapon flattening to the ramp under his hand.

A few steps behind him, Abelardus bent forward, his staff clattering to the deck as he grabbed his throat with both hands.

Alisa rushed forward, immediately spotting Tymoteusz at the back of the hangar, just inside the door. He carried the Staff of Lore, the orb on the tip glowing cheerfully. The rows of men and women in front of him weren't Starseers, as far as Alisa could tell. They wore patched and grease-stained clothing with tool belts instead of weapons belts. Some of the blazer pistols and rifles they pointed toward Alisa's team looked like they came from a past century. They didn't wear headbands, like the people Tymoteusz had controlled in the Arkadius Temple, but they certainly seemed to be under his command.

"Stop, Tymoteusz," Alisa said, stepping forward and putting a hand on Leonidas's shoulder. So much for the drugs keeping the *chasadski* from using mind techniques on them. "We came to talk. We came in peace."

"Unlikely." Tymoteusz sneered, shifting the staff slightly. Leonidas hissed, one gauntleted fist dropping to the ramp, the pain in his body evident even through his armor. "Where is the girl?"

"She's here. Are you interested in teaching her, then?"

"Perhaps. I had not thought to, but I have no children of my own."

"Shocking," Alisa muttered.

"Perhaps another descendant of my father's loins would be a worthy heir to my knowledge," Tymoteusz said, not seeming to hear her. His eyes were focused on the ceiling, or maybe not focused at all. "She could be taught to carry on after I'm gone, to be my voice, to rule when the time comes."

"To rule what? A mining ship? All I want is for her to be educated by someone who—"

"What you want is irrelevant," Tymoteusz snapped. "You are a useless grub."

"Somehow, it's less offensive when Ostberg calls me that. Are you teaching Thorian to be an heir to your knowledge too?"

Tymoteusz's lip curled. "That boy is dangerous and would never be loyal to me. As soon as my putative *allies* have finished doing what they want with him, I will kill him with my own hands."

Alisa did not like the sound of that. She also didn't care for the reminder that there was a fleet of mafia ships waiting out there too. Even if Mica could return power to the *Nomad* and they could disable the grab beam and escape, they would be target practice for all those ships.

"The canister," Leonidas whispered, his voice so quiet and strained that Alisa barely understood. Of course. Tiang's drug. Tymoteusz had to be nearly fifty meters away, but this might be their best chance to shoot one of the canisters at him. Unfortunately, Leonidas did not look like he could move.

Beck must have heard the order, too, because he started down the ramp toward the launcher. But Tymoteusz wrinkled his nose, and some invisible force struck Beck. His boots left the ramp as he was hurled back into the cargo hold.

Alisa bent and snatched up the launcher. She fully expected a force to fling her backward, too, and moved as fast as she could, whirling toward Tymoteusz as her finger found the trigger. She barely took the time to aim before firing. A twang sounded as the canister launched, but the expected attack came an instant later.

It slammed into Alisa like a train. Wind whistled past her helmet, and before she knew what was going on, she crashed into the stairs in the cargo hold. Metal screeched as it bent, her armor warping the framework. Thankfully, she did not feel much of the impact inside of her suit, but the blow still knocked the breath out of her.

Aware of Leonidas on his knees on the ramp, nearly helpless, she forced herself to her feet. As she ran back across the hold, Tymoteusz spoke into her mind again.

Your belief in Stan's death was premature. His words were dry, no hint of fear or concern in them.

She doubted the canister had exploded anywhere close to him, but she hoped it had and that he hadn't realized the ramifications yet.

As soon as she reached the ramp, blazer fire streaked toward her from a dozen directions. Several bolts splashed off her armor, and she thanked Leonidas's insistence that she put her helmet on. She popped up her arm blazers and returned fire, shooting over the miners' heads, hoping to scare them rather than kill them. They were pawns, not enemies. Tymoteusz was the one she wanted to shoot.

But he had disappeared. And she saw no sign of the canister she had launched.

The miners, still firing, surged toward the ramp as one.

"Back," Leonidas barked, recovering enough to return fire. He growled again, as if he were trying to marshal himself, and pushed himself to his feet. "Get back inside, Alisa," he warned as the first men started up.

They were more like zombies than thinking human beings, but that didn't keep him from rushing down to meet them. Unlike Alisa, he did not hesitate to fire to kill.

Wincing, she backed up the ramp to the hatchway so she could take cover inside. Her armor wouldn't protect her indefinitely, not when fifty people were shooting at them.

Abelardus had recovered his staff, and he leaned out from the other side of the hatchway. He raised it, and several of the lead miners flew backward, slamming into those behind them. The men and women faltered but did not stop trying to move forward.

Leonidas ripped the blazer rifle out of one man's hands and used it like a club. He swung it back and forth, hitting the miners hard enough to send them flying. Alisa winced again, but breaking their bones was better than killing them.

"Captain?" Beck stood behind Leonidas on the ramp, firing into the crowd, looking like he was aiming for kneecaps and shins rather than vital targets. "Orders?"

"We have to get past them and into the ship if we're going to find Thorian."

"Understood. But I'd rather feed workers than shoot them."

"Me too, Beck. Me too."

Alisa also shot at non-vital targets, though she had no idea if Tymoteusz would help these people to medical facilities if they were bleeding on his deck.

The miners focused on Leonidas, clearly seeing him as the greatest threat. As Alisa fired, feeling like a coward for hiding in the ship and cherry picking them, she glanced at Abelardus. He'd thrown a few more waves of power to knock miners over, but the stubborn people kept getting up. Alisa feared that killing them or knocking them unconscious would be the only way to stop them.

"Any chance you can break the mind control he's got over them?" Alisa asked.

"I've been trying," Abelardus said, "but that's a *chasadski* power. Honorable Starseers don't try to turn other people into automatons."

Alisa grimaced at the idea of Tymoteusz teaching Jelena such powers. By the suns, what had she been thinking in delivering her to his ship? Did she truly believe they could find Thorian and escape?

"I do have some good news," Abelardus said.

"What's that?"

Before he could answer, one of the miners screamed and raced in from the side, evading Leonidas who was still knocking men left and right at the base of the ramp. This miner clenched something in his hand. A grenade? No, Alisa realized with a start. The canister. Somehow Tymoteusz had kept it from breaking open, but it was designed to unleash its contents upon impact, so if that miner threw it in the *Nomad*...with Jelena inside...

Alisa saw Beck turning toward the man, but she fired first. Her blazer bolt slammed into the miner's chest.

Pain flashed through those vacant eyes, and he halted before leaping onto the ramp. He started to topple backward, and Alisa sprang after him. As he fell, she snatched the canister out of his hand, terrified her armored fingers would apply too much pressure and break it.

She tried to hold it like a hollow egg, even as she flinched away from the man silently dying at her feet. She hated Tymoteusz for controlling all these people, throwing them to their deaths. Why had he even taken this ship? What had been wrong with the ship he abandoned?

"They're done fighting," Leonidas said from behind her. "They're not all dead."

"Good," Alisa said, her voice sounding hollow in her ears. She stepped away from the man she had killed, the canister still in her hand. She held it out toward Leonidas, who was walking back up the ramp to pick up his launcher. "Don't want to waste these."

"No," he said, accepting it.

"Do we know what the dispersal radius is?" Alisa hoped it wouldn't prove that she hadn't needed to kill the man, but she couldn't have taken the risk, not with Jelena in the ship. Not when she had no idea how Tiang's drug would work on children. He'd only tested it on rats. Who knew what it might do to a young human body?

"A hundred meters at least. Mica and I added a dispersal element to help it spread. It's hard to say how far it would go in a ship's corridors, but—" He lifted an armored shoulder. He understood.

"Young-hee and Mica," Alisa called into the dark ship. "Grab Alejandro and the two remaining Starseers and come tie these people up. Mica, you can look for the source of the power draw while you're out here. Leonidas, Beck, Abelardus, and I are going to find Thorian." And hopefully avoid Tymoteusz and any more loyal miner minions he'd created.

"Tie what up?" came Mica's distant call from engineering. "Busy here."

"We'll handle it," Young-hee said from the dark recesses, then called over her shoulder, "Alejandro. Get your medkit, please. And some rope if you have it."

"Alisa," Leonidas said. He had gone back down the ramp, several meters past it, and was looking toward the ceiling of the hangar. "Mica will want to see this."

"Mica didn't sound that interested in sightseeing," Alisa said as she ran out to join him, picking a path amid the fallen. Some of the miners were conscious, gripping abdomens or broken bones, but none of them made any noise despite the pain in their eyes. It was eerie and disturbing. "I'm not that interested in it either," she grumbled.

She wanted to find Thorian and leave.

"What if I give you that good news I mentioned?" Abelardus asked, following her down the ramp.

"I could use good news." Alisa glanced toward the door where Tymoteusz had been standing earlier, making sure there weren't any more threats charging in. It was closed.

Leonidas faced away from it, and when Alisa turned to look where he was looking, she almost wished she hadn't. Crackling blue tendrils of energy extended from a hole in the ceiling to the hull of the *Nomad*.

"That our power drain?" Alisa asked.

"Must be. I haven't seen anything like it before though."

Leonidas lifted one of his rifles and fired a quick burst at the hole. It disappeared inside with a quick flash of whitish-blue. Nothing noticeable happened to the energy strands reaching out to the *Nomad*. He fired again, this time a sustained shot. The flash was a flare this time, lasting as long as his shot lasted. Again, it didn't do any perceivable damage. If anything, the chain of energy seemed to grow brighter.

Leonidas sighed. "I think I'm feeding it what it likes."

"Let Mica figure it out. We have a prince to find."

"Do you want to leave her out here with only Young-hee and Alejandro? Tymoteusz could send more people anytime."

Yumi was there, too, babysitting Jelena, but she wasn't a fighter. And Jelena…she should have legions of troops protecting her, not a couple of noncombatant Starseers and an engineer.

"Beck, will you stay here?" Alisa asked, figuring they needed Abelardus to lead them to Thorian.

Beck and Abelardus had joined them and were also staring at the crackling energy.

"Yes, Captain. I'll help get these people tied up and keep an eye on the ship—everyone *in* the ship." Beck gave her a firm nod.

"Thank you." Alisa pointed toward the door. "Come on, you two. If he's distracted, or thinks we've been killed, this is our chance."

"He *is* distracted," Abelardus said. "That's my news. Stanislav is here."

Alisa nodded, remembering Tymoteusz's words. She'd guessed as much but hadn't had time to process it. "Is the Alliance fleet with him?"

"It is."

"Any chance they're on their way in to attack?" Alisa hadn't felt anything striking the mining ship yet, but with its hulking, reinforced hull, it might take a lot before attacks were noticeable. She assumed it had some shields too.

"They are, but the mafia ships have all gone to intercept. We're moving too, but not toward the battle. I can't read the thoughts of any of the *chasadski* on the bridge. I know Tymoteusz is back up there, but I don't know what he's doing."

Leonidas veered toward some monitors on a bulkhead on the way to the door. Four of them displayed what appeared to be camera angles from around the exterior of the ship. This vessel was probably as old as the *Nomad* and did not have holo technology. Leonidas tapped a couple of buttons while Alisa headed for the door. She was more focused on getting Thorian than the battle outside. Even though she was pleased that the Alliance had *finally* shown up, she was well aware that her entire ship was inside the main enemy ship. If Hawk, or whoever was leading over there, decided to ignore the mafia ships and focus on this one...She had better hope that Tymoteusz could defend it—at least for now.

Alisa waved at the door sensor, but it didn't open.

"I need some cyborg strength over here," she said, even if she wondered if she might be able to force it open with her armor's extra power.

Since Leonidas and Abelardus were both over by the monitors, she decided to try, positioning herself as she had often seen Leonidas do. She planted her hands and pulled. Even though she could feel the armor lending more power to her shoulders, all that happened was that her hands slipped, and the door remained shut.

"A learned skill, clearly," she muttered. "Are you two coming?"

"You may want to see this," Abelardus said.

"If it's the Alliance coming to obliterate us, not really." Still, she ran over to join them.

"I thought these might be the controls to that energy ribbon," Leonidas said, waving at a panel, "but they're just monitors so the operator can see ships approaching. And this." He pointed at the far monitor.

A familiar sight was displayed on it, albeit one Alisa hadn't seen in a couple of months. Alcyone Station.

"The rift opened," she said, glancing toward the *Nomad*, wondering if that would increase the radiation they were being exposed to and if

Alejandro would say anything. But he and Young-hee and Beck were busy treating and tying people, and he didn't notice her. "Does it matter?"

"I don't know," Leonidas said, "but we're moving toward it for some reason."

She looked sharply at him. "What?"

He only shook his helmeted head.

"All the *chasadski* are up there on the bridge," Abelardus said again. "This might be a good time to attack them, especially if they're planning something..." He looked at the monitor. "Foolish."

"That crazy megalomaniac doesn't think it would be a good idea to visit another dimension, does he?" Alisa asked.

"I don't know," Leonidas said again.

CHAPTER TWENTY-THREE

The door screeched open under Leonidas's assault.

"You'll have to show me how to do that," Alisa said.

"When there's more time, gladly," he said, striding into the corridor, his rifle at the ready, the canister launcher slung over his shoulder.

"Which way to Thorian?" Alisa asked Abelardus as they stepped into the corridor after him.

"That way." Abelardus pointed to the left.

Leonidas was already heading to the right. "We have to go to the bridge," he said without slowing. "And stop them from driving this ship into the rift."

Abelardus shrugged and started after him, but Alisa caught his arm.

"We're getting Thorian before worrying about Tymoteusz and that damned staff," she said firmly.

"I am only worried about Tymoteusz's power to destroy," Abelardus said, moving to stand beside Alisa. "The staff is…less important now."

"Glad to hear it," Alisa said. "We'll let the Alliance deal with Tymoteusz— we need to get Thorian and get out of here before they unleash everything on this ship."

"If all the *chasadski* are on the bridge, one canister may be enough to stop their threat permanently," Leonidas said. "Your Alliance will lose far fewer people and ships if we take them out."

Alisa doubted he cared whether the Alliance lost ships or not. He seemed to have some personal vendetta he wanted to carry out.

"Leonidas," Alisa said, "be realistic. All Tym needed to do was look at you to drop you to your hands and knees back there."

"I wasn't as prepared as I should have been. I won't make that mistake again."

"You're going without us, aren't you?" Abelardus asked, as if he already knew the answer.

Leonidas paused at a corner, checked around it, then turned to look at Alisa. "You and Abelardus get Thorian. If Abelardus is right and all the *chasa-dski* are on the bridge, you should be able to handle whatever trouble you encounter along the way. I'll come find you as soon as I deal with the others."

"*Leonidas*," Alisa said, frustrated. "You can't *deal* with them. They'll only kill you."

"Then I'll make sure they're distracted as they do it. You get Thorian, get in contact with the Alliance, and get your ship out of here."

"We're not going anywhere without you. You promised my daughter that *you* would get Thorian." Alisa glared at Leonidas, then glared at Abelardus, even though she wasn't sure why she included him. It would be nice if he backed her up in this.

All he did was lift his hands and glance down the corridor as if to point out they didn't have time for this. And he was right.

"Leonidas," Alisa said, "I *order* you to come with us."

He hadn't left the corner yet, but he looked down the intersection she couldn't see, as if it called to him.

"Are you or aren't you my security officer?" she asked. "And did you or did you not make a promise to a little girl?" Her voice cracked on the last word, and she growled at herself, annoyed that her emotions were flaring up now.

"I did," Leonidas said. He clenched his fist, but then he ran back toward them. "All right. Let's go. Hurry. Abelardus, lead."

"Naturally." Abelardus took off at a run, his robe flapping about his legs.

Alisa flung her arms around Leonidas for a quick hug, even though they were both running, and it was awkward. He patted her back once, then hurried ahead of her.

Alisa had to sprint to keep up with the men, and she was glad for the assistance her armor gave her. They raced through long gray corridors, conduits and pipes visible on the bulkheads of the old ship, panels occasionally missing. Even as she tore after the men, she wondered if there might be some sabotage they could do to the vessel. After they found Thorian, she would contact Mica and ask. She would much rather face some engineers than the *chasadski*. Maybe Leonidas thought he could do something against them, but she doubted him. Only in this one thing.

They charged around a corner, almost crashing into two miners. Before the men could bring their weapons to bear, Leonidas flung them down the corridor. They hit bulkheads hard enough that when they fell, they did not get up.

Once again, Alisa grimaced at the way they were hurting innocent people, but she foolishly hadn't thought to bring her stun gun. There was nothing to be done now.

"You know where you're going?" Leonidas demanded as they took another turn.

"Not exactly," Abelardus said.

"What?" The word came out as a snarl.

"I know where he is. Getting to him is another matter. Also, I'm trying not to take us near where there are many people." Abelardus looked over his shoulder at Alisa, his face grim. No, he wouldn't want to kill helpless people either. "He's not being held all that far from here, and we're on the right level, but I don't have a map of this place. I'm having trouble running and concentrating at the same—"

"Get me close," Leonidas said, "and I'll tear down the bulkheads."

Alisa eyed the one nearest them. These bulkheads looked sturdy, even by cyborg standards.

"Just give me a second." Abelardus stopped, breathing deeply as he pressed his hand to a bulkhead and closed his eyes.

The deck shivered under Alisa's feet. She, too, braced her gauntleted hand on the wall, fearing the jolts might get worse. It felt like someone was finally firing on the mining ship. Or maybe someone had been firing for a while, and the shields had just now dropped.

Leonidas paced, his fist clenched.

"I know you'd like to get the staff and rid the universe of those *chasadski*," Alisa said, "but if we can get Thorian and get out of here, the Alliance will—"

"It's not about the staff," Leonidas said. "That ass said he plans to kill Thorian. With his own hands."

Leonidas lunged to the side, slamming his fist into the bulkhead. Alisa jumped as it went through. He yanked his fist out, leaving a hole.

"But he's still alive now," she said. "And we're going to get him."

"I want that man dead. For what he wants to do and what he's already done these last few weeks." Leonidas ground his jaw back and forth.

Alisa wondered if Tymoteusz had spoken to him telepathically when he'd been hurting him. Had he taunted Leonidas about Thorian? Was that why Leonidas was so enraged now?

A distant bang sounded, and the deck shuddered again.

Alisa wished for Starseer senses so she could tell what was going on out there. But maybe it was better that she didn't know.

"Ready," Abelardus said, taking off at a run again. "I think I've got the way. This place is a maze."

Leonidas said nothing, but followed right on his heels. Alisa wanted to urge them to hurry, but knew they both were.

Mom? Jelena's voice sounded in Alisa's mind.

Alisa stumbled, but caught herself. *Jelena?*

She wouldn't have guessed her daughter had the range to talk to her from this far away. *Yes?*

I'm scared.

Alisa's heart lurched. *Did something happen back at the ship?*

Yumi said I had to stay inside, but they all went outside. They're trying to fix something, but some men with guns are trying to get at them. Tommy is shooting at them. I'm all alone in here. It's scary.

Stay put, sweetie. We'll be back soon. Alisa understood Jelena's fear, but would rather have her alone on the ship and scared than out in the hangar, especially if shooting was going on. *We're almost to Thorian,* she added, hoping that would give her daughter some solace.

"Damn it," Abelardus said.

"What now?" Leonidas lifted a hand, looking like he wanted to wring Abelardus's neck.

"He's twenty meters that way." Abelardus slapped a bulkhead. "If you want to damage something, damage that wall. I don't see where there's even a door to his room. Maybe he's in some bizarre oubliette and we're coming at this from the wrong floor."

Leonidas slammed his shoulder into the bulkhead, moving so quickly that Alisa thought he was dodging fire at first. But no, he was just determined. He dented the metal inward with his first two strikes, then ripped through to the interior with his third. He tore away panels with his armored hands, then kicked through to the other side. Alisa would have offered to help, but she only would have been in the way. He soon kicked a hole large enough for them to crawl through, his armored boot like a battering ram as it bashed away the bulkhead.

He was on what looked to be his last kick when his leg caught on something.

He blurted a startled oath, and his entire leg disappeared into the hole, as if someone was on the other side, pulling him. Alisa lunged to grab his arm, but everything happened too fast. Leonidas's entire body was yanked through the hole.

"Who the hells is in there?" she demanded of Abelardus.

"Nobody," he promised, squatting to peer inside at the same time Alisa did. "I checked. Nobody's in there."

They saw Leonidas's red armored form being pulled across a deck, but the only light came from their corridor, and he disappeared from sight again. Gripping her rifle, Alisa started to stick her leg through, but Abelardus pushed her back.

"I'll go."

Before she could argue, he dove through the hole, landing in a somersault on the other side and leaping to his feet with his staff. He raced into the darkness after Leonidas. Alisa had no idea what they were getting into, but she stepped through after them, ducking a broken wire that crackled with electricity.

The ship trembled all around her. Another attack.

Bangs and thumps came from the other side of the large room she entered. Tables lined one side and counters and cabinets the other. In the darkness ahead, something slammed into a wall—hard. She hoped that was Leonidas hurling his assailant around.

"Night vision," she commanded her armor—she'd almost forgotten that was an option.

The chamber came into view, harshly bright near the hole and a more sedate green further in. She spotted Leonidas in a grappling match with a woman—no, that had to be an android. A second one, also female and wearing a pale coat—a lab coat?—sprang at Abelardus. He pointed his staff at her, and air seemed to slam into her, pushing her back. But as soon as the android landed, she raced for him again.

Alisa raised her rifle, trying to line up a good shot, but with her own men fighting the androids, it was hard to find an opening. She had to be particularly careful around Abelardus, who didn't have armor to protect him from friendly fire.

Alisa tried to skirt her men, scooting along a counter full of tools and mechanical parts, so she could find a better shot. She had seen Leonidas handle androids often enough—and these white-clad females did not look like combat specialists—but Abelardus might have more trouble. He couldn't attack an android's mind. He had deflected his opponent twice now, but she moved with blinding speed, and if all he did was defend himself, he wouldn't be able to deactivate her—or keep her from calling for backup.

After the android tried a third time to get to Abelardus and failed, Alisa found the opening she wanted. She fired at the side of her head, careful to watch Abelardus in her peripheral vision, not wanting to risk hitting him if the android moved. And she did. As soon as Alisa's blazer beam bit into her head, she spun and raced toward her like a bullet. Even with the help of her armor's servos, Alisa didn't spring aside quickly enough. The android clipped her arm and shoulder, and they struck the counter together with a crash. Cabinet doors flung open, and tools and equipment spilled onto the deck.

Ignoring it all, Alisa threw a block up to avoid grasping fingers. She struck the android's arm away, then slammed her helmet into her opponent's face. Something crunched beneath the blow, but that didn't keep the android from shoving her backward. Alisa flung out a kick as she stumbled away, hoping to get lucky. The android was lunging after her, so the move paid off. She clipped her under the chin, knocking her head back. She found her balance and jumped in, kicking again. This time her armored heel slammed into the android's stomach, and she flew so far back that she struck the counter again.

Abelardus lunged in from the android's side, bringing his staff down on her shoulder. Electricity seemed to spring from his weapon, and it engulfed the android like a lightning strike. Alisa squinted as the brightness flared in her night-vision display, hurting her eyes. Still, she forced herself not to look away. She had managed to keep hold of her rifle, and she fired now, straight at their foe's chest. Abelardus must have been holding the android there somehow, because she stood and took it. He finished her with a strike from the staff, and she tumbled sideways, body jerky, hitting the counter again.

Something near Alisa's end tumbled off and rolled to her feet. She looked down, then dropped her rifle and screamed.

It was Thorian's head.

CHAPTER TWENTY-FOUR

"Alisa," Leonidas said, racing toward her.

Alisa clamped her hand to her faceplate, as if she could cover her mouth. Aware of her scream and that people might hear it, she cut it off. But she couldn't get past her shock and horror.

"What is it?" Leonidas gripped her shoulder. His dismantled android lay crumpled in the corner behind him.

She pointed down at the decapitated head. It had rolled onto its face, its short dark hair now turned toward them. But she knew what she had seen.

"Thorian," she croaked, but as she had more time to look at the head—she couldn't look away—she realized the neck seemed strange. It wasn't a bloody stump. It was…

Leonidas bent and picked it up, turning it over as if he were examining a piece of fruit for ripeness. "I saw the rest of the body over on the table while I was fighting." He waved toward the opposite side of the room as Abelardus walked over to join them.

"It's not real," Alisa said slowly, numbly. Her heart resumed beating in a normal, non-erratic manner as the realization sank in.

"No." Leonidas squeezed her shoulder, probably realizing why she had screamed. "But it's an exact replica."

Abelardus pushed some of his braids of hair back over his shoulder. "I don't get it. They're making an android Prince Thorian?"

"A very life-like one," Alisa said. "Maybe they thought they could pass an android off as the real thing? And use him to cement their right to lead? To remake the empire?"

"You don't think someone would notice when he never aged?"

"Maybe they were going to make new ones every year. Or maybe they didn't plan on needing him alive—or to *appear* alive—for that long." Alisa cringed at the idea of someone killing Thorian—of *Tymoteusz* killing Thorian. And that's what he had admitted he planned to do, wasn't it? Once the replica was built for Henneberry or whoever had come up with the plan, he could have gotten rid of the real boy.

Leonidas released her shoulder and squeezed the android head between his hands hard enough to crush it.

Alisa jumped. "What are you doing?"

"Destroying their plans." He dropped the dented head.

"Tymoteusz is definitely going to kill you the next time he sees you," Abelardus remarked.

"He can try."

Alisa spun slowly around the room—the laboratory. "So, where's the *real* Thorian? Abelardus, this isn't what led you in this direction, is it?" She pointed at the broken head.

"Not at all. I can't sense androids." Abelardus pointed toward the back bulkhead. "Thorian isn't far. A few meters behind there, I believe."

"Have you been able to contact him?" Alisa asked as Leonidas strode toward the bulkhead.

"I've tried," Abelardus said. "I can sense he's awake, but he hasn't responded. It's almost as if something is blocking our ability to communicate."

Leonidas punched a hole in the bulkhead.

"Nothing blocks *his* ability to communicate," Abelardus said.

"Not for long," Alisa agreed.

Another distant boom sounded, and the deck jerked.

Alisa commed Mica. "Any progress, Mica? Are we going to be able to leave once we show up with Thorian?"

She received a growl in response. Beck was the one to speak more articulately over the comm.

"She's trying a bunch of things with this energy device, Captain, but have you seen the monitors?"

"No. This lab doesn't include a viewing station."

"What was that?" Beck asked. "I couldn't hear you over whatever crashing is going on where you are. Are you in battle?"

"Leonidas is knocking down a wall."

"In a battle?"

"Just because it's in his way. Tell me what's on the monitors, Beck."

"The mining ship is launching hooks at the space station while the mafia ships keep the Alliance ships busy." Another boom sounded in the distance. "Mostly busy."

"Hooks?"

"I don't know what else to call them. They look like they're on some kind of energy chains. Mica thought we might even be supplying the energy for them. Unwillingly of course. The ship is hooking them to the station. Remember how we thought it was going to fly into the rift? It looks like maybe Terrible Tym wants to drag the station out of it so that it stays in our dimension."

"Where it will irradiate anyone who flies close to it indefinitely? What is that crazy man thinking?"

"He's *your* uncle. Shouldn't you know?"

"Why would I know?" Alisa asked.

"You've got the same genes. And you get your crazy moments too."

"Not the kind where I think it's a good idea to take over the system and turn people into mindless minions."

"Captain?" Mica broke in.

"How are my solutions coming, Mica?"

"We've got the grab beam disabled. I haven't been able to find a way to stop that energy sucker from depleting us yet, but I've planted explosives all around the ceiling where the tendrils are originating. I'm ready to blow it as soon as you get back."

"We'll hurry," Alisa said over the squeal of warping metal. Leonidas had pulled down a panel and made a hole through to the other side of the bulkhead.

Expecting more trouble in whatever room held Thorian, Alisa gripped her rifle and strode over.

"You better," Mica said. "We're down to thirty-five percent power. If we don't have at least fifteen percent left, we're not going to be able to take off."

"Understood."

Alisa closed the comm and stopped behind Leonidas. He was crouching in front of his hole, taking a long look inside before sticking his foot through this time.

"I can't hear anyone breathing," he whispered, and glanced at Abelardus.

"He's in there," Abelardus said, "and I don't sense any other people in the room, but there could be more androids."

"Going in." Leonidas sprang through the hole with his rifle at the ready.

"Wait," Abelardus whispered as Alisa started to follow. He squinted toward the ceiling. "Someone's coming. They're on the level above, but it might not take them long to get here. They may have figured out we've been mucking up their lab."

"All the more reason to hurry," Alisa said and stepped through the hole after Leonidas.

She almost bumped into him. They were in a small, tight room that felt more like a brig cell than someone's quarters. There was no lighting so she had to rely on her night vision again. The only furnishing or object of any kind in the square place was a waist-high box in one corner.

"Door up there." Leonidas pointed his rifle toward the ceiling.

Alisa swallowed. Whoever had said oubliette might have been correct.

"He's in there," Abelardus said, stepping into the room. He pointed at the box.

"You're sure?" Alisa asked. "That's not big enough to stand or lie down or anything. Is there even enough air? What kind of ass—"

In the tight space, Leonidas bumped her as he moved toward the box. He reached toward a dark control panel that seemed part of a locking mechanism.

"Wait," Abelardus blurted. "It's a Starseer tool. Or at least, that box has been imbued with power, like our staffs. That's probably why I can't communicate with him through it."

Leonidas reached for the box, regardless, looking like he wanted to tear that lid off and hurl it across the room—or the galaxy. But as soon as he touched it, a spark of green light flashed, and he staggered back, grabbing his hand.

"Booby trapped," he snarled.

A creak came from above, and light slashed into the dark room. Alisa whipped her rifle toward the trapdoor. It had opened a couple of inches, enough to reveal the black hem of a robe, but it hadn't yet opened all the way. She held her fire.

Abelardus pointed to Leonidas, then toward the trapdoor. "I'll work on that," he mouthed, heading for the box.

Alisa felt something probing her mind, that creepy-crawly feeling of fingernails scraping over her brain. Whoever was up there knew they were down here. Afraid to give them time to formulate a plan, she fired through the trapdoor opening.

She had a second to feel satisfied as her blazer beam sliced into the hem of that robe, hopefully cutting into someone's shin, before a huge weight seemed to push down onto her shoulders. It crushed her, driving her to her knees. Her mind flashed back to the asteroid base, to the tons and tons of rock coming down on her armor—on *her*.

It forced her down, flattening her to her stomach. She gasped for air, feeling like she couldn't get enough. Had the floors above come down on this one? She would be smothered all over again.

"No," she panted, trying to clear her mind, trying to push away the panic and reason with herself. The *chasadski* had to be doing something to her. Maybe they couldn't affect her mind through the drug, but that didn't mean they couldn't attack her body.

"Abelardus, get out of here," Leonidas yelled from somewhere nearby.

Was Leonidas still standing? If he could do it, so could Alisa.

She pressed her hands to the deck, pushing with all her strength to raise her body. Before she had gotten more than her head a few inches up, red armor flew past her, a boot nearly clipping her on the chin. Leonidas slammed into the bulkhead near where Abelardus was fiddling with the box.

"Get out of here, Abelardus," Leonidas growled again, his hands gripping one of his rifles. No, that was the canister launcher. He meant to unleash some of Tiang's concoction.

Alisa's armor would protect her, but Abelardus would be as vulnerable as the two *chasadski* who had just jumped down into the room beside her. She got her feet under her and flung herself at them, her arms outstretched, trying to hook both of them.

Energy crackled in the air. Another *chasadski* attack, she thought, but no. That was a fluidwrap. The crackling net flew around the *chasadski* and also caught Alisa, fine strands of energy grasping her armor with the stickiness of a spider web. Her arms were planted on the chests of her opponents, not because they were doing anything effective there but because all three of them were tangled in the strands now. Her foes seemed startled, and she did the only thing she could think of. She shoved off with her feet and drove them backward. She had the satisfaction of smashing their backs into a bulkhead before something slammed into the side of her helmet so hard it would have ripped her head off if she hadn't been armored.

Her head rang like a bell. Damn it, was there a third one in here? The fluidwrap made it hard to see anything.

Someone jabbed a knee into her stomach. She barely felt it through the armor, but another attack came from behind, striking her back so hard that it knocked her helmet into the face of one of the men tangled up with her. He cried out in pain. She would have felt satisfaction if she hadn't been in pain herself.

Then one of the men started thrashing, as if he had suddenly grown claustrophobic and knew he had to escape at any price. Again, the armor protected her from his flailing body, but the second man—or the one behind her—still had his sanity and was attacking.

A force tightened around her throat like a vice. This time, the armor did not protect her. It was as if a cyborg's strong hands were somehow inside of her neckpiece, cutting off her airway. She tried to gasp in air, but couldn't get a single oxygen molecule. And the force kept pressing tighter. Any second, cartilage and bone would crunch, and her windpipe would close forever.

"Leonidas," she tried to cry, wanting to tell him to shoot that canister, but nothing came out.

She kicked back with all her strength, hoping for luck, to connect with someone's chest. She clipped something, but the fluidwrap hampered her movements, and she couldn't tell if she struck friend or foe, human or bulkhead.

Abruptly, the force around her throat disappeared. She gasped in air, but struggled to recover. One of the men tangled up with her was still thrashing, and his wild movements tripped her, and she fell to the ground. All three of them fell, the two *chasadski* landing atop her. She managed to roll onto her back and shove the thrashing one off her, but there wasn't room to escape him completely. Finally, he stopped flailing. She realized the second one tangled in the net wasn't moving—and hadn't for a while.

The small room had grown quiet.

"Leonidas?" she rasped, her throat sore and tight after the attack.

She rotated her head as much as she could, but sharp stabs of pain came from her neck. The trapdoor was open above her, bright light coming through, and the two *chasadski* lay to either side of her. Several strands of the fluidwrap were plastered over her faceplate, and it wasn't until Leonidas's red helmet came into view above her that she spotted him.

"You weren't supposed to fling yourself at them at the same time as I threw the net," he said, cutting away the strands from her faceplate.

"I wasn't? You should have mentioned that during our pre-mission planning meeting." Talking hurt, and she cut her commentary short, reaching up for her neck. It needed a good massage, but sadly, she couldn't access it through her armor.

"There was a meeting?"

"Were you not invited? Clearly an oversight."

"Clearly." Leonidas hauled her to her feet, holding her in a hug for a long moment.

She gripped him back, looking around the small room as she did so. *Four* black-robed men crowded the floor around them, the two tangled in the netting and two others. No wonder she'd had trouble. Three weren't moving, but a fourth's arms and legs were twitching. A shattered canister lay next to him. Tiang's drug.

"Abelardus," Alisa blurted, stepping back. She looked toward the box, expecting to find him also twitching on the deck—or worse.

But he wasn't in the room. He must have climbed out before Leonidas fired the canister.

Concern for Thorian flooded her—he wouldn't have armor either—and she strode toward the box. Would it have protected him? Was it airtight? Or did it filter air?

Leonidas shot the twitching *chasadski* in the forehead, startling Alisa. She gaped at him as the man stopped moving, his eyes freezing over in death as they stared at the ceiling.

"They made their choice when they sided with Tymoteusz," he said, no remorse in his tone. "I'm not letting them live to continue to terrorize the system."

He strode to another one, his intent clear.

Alisa wanted to object to the cold-hearted murder, but was he wrong? These people had been with Tymoteusz at Arkadius, where that earthquake had killed thousands, if not tens of thousands. They had made their choice. Unless Tymoteusz had been controlling them somehow, they'd chosen to work with him to try to take over the system, and their intent hadn't been nearly as noble as the Alliance's when it had worked to overthrow the empire. Alisa winced when Leonidas fired again, but she didn't try to stop him.

She forced herself to look at the control panel on the box. An indicator flashed red. Had it been doing that before? She hoped that didn't mean a seal had been broken and that Thorian had been exposed to the drug.

Booms sounded in the distance, and when the deck shook this time, something crashed down in a nearby room or corridor. Alisa paid it no heed.

"This one's already dead," Leonidas said, standing over one of the men still tangled in the net. "Nose smashed and neck broken—that's what got him."

Alisa looked over, realizing he was talking about the one she had head-butted with her helmet. She was horrified to realize that her desperate attack had killed a man, that combat armor could make even flailing deadly. By the suns, maybe she would bury it in her case and shove it into storage when she returned to the *Nomad*. As a pilot, she had fired at ships and even blown some up in space, but killing up close was so personal. So disturbing. She was ready to retire from being a fighter.

"Fourth one is dead too," Leonidas said, now standing over one in the corner.

Alisa looked away. She didn't need to know how each of these men had died. Instead, she tried to focus on opening the box, but she could see Leonidas look over at her out of the corner of her eye.

"I didn't hit this one, and neither did you," he said.

"What?" she asked, her gaze pulled back to him. And the dead *chasadski*.

"I think the drug killed him."

Alisa licked her lips. "Tiang said it wouldn't kill anyone."

"Tiang only got to test it on rats."

"Shit." More horrified than ever, Alisa turned back to the box. "Thorian?" she whispered.

"Abelardus pushed the blue button with his mind," Leonidas said, walking toward her. "But the drug might not have dissipated yet. You should wait."

"He might be in there, already exposed."

Alisa pushed the button before she remembered that the box had shocked Leonidas. She was so worried about Thorian that she might have pushed it anyway.

A jolt of electricity ran up her arm, and some power flung her backward. She might have flown all the way to the bulkhead, but Leonidas caught her.

"That was stupid," she muttered to herself.

The lid of the box flung open. Abelardus rose up from inside it, and Alisa would have fallen over if Leonidas hadn't been holding her. She glanced at the trapdoor. She'd been certain he had gone that way.

"By all that's evil, it *stinks* in there," he growled. He reached down with both hands and pulled a slender, battered figure out of the box. Thorian.

He did not appear conscious. He wore the same black robe Alisa had last seen him in, but it was ripped and sodden, and his hair hung limply around his head.

"Get out of the room," Leonidas said, taking Thorian from his arms. "Don't breathe deeply until we're away from here."

Abelardus cursed before catching himself, then sprang from the box. He grabbed his staff from a corner where it had fallen, glanced at the dead men, but didn't say anything else until he'd leaped up, thrown his staff into the corridor above them, and pulled himself out of the dungeon. Alisa sprang after him, worried that more opponents might wait for them. But the corridor was empty.

The lights dimmed as Leonidas handed Thorian up to her, and an alarm started wailing.

"The hull has been breached," a computerized voice announced. "Containment procedures beginning. Power conservation measures activated."

"We need to get off this ship," Abelardus said—he'd scooted well down the corridor to wait for them and was eyeing the trapdoor warily.

Leonidas joined them on the deck and kicked the door shut.

"Can you keep carrying him?" he asked Alisa, hefting his rifle in one hand and the canister launcher in the other.

"I'm fairly certain I could carry *you* in this suit," she said, trying for a touch of humor, though her heart wasn't in it. How long had it been since Mica reported thirty-five percent power to the *Nomad*? Would the ship be able to take off even if they made it back before the Alliance blew this mining vessel into the nearest star?

"Something to try during our next training session," he said, clapping her on the shoulder.

He broke into a run, not waiting for Abelardus to lead this time. Alisa ran after him, cradling Thorian in her arms and trying not to jostle him. He was alive but far gaunter than he had been a few weeks ago—he looked like he hadn't been fed much since she had last seen him. If her asshole uncle had kept him locked in that box the whole time, she would strangle him with her own hands.

CHAPTER TWENTY-FIVE

Alarms continued to wail, and the lighting flashed red as Alisa, Abelardus, and Leonidas ran through the corridors. Alisa, still carrying Thorian, picked up speed when she spotted the familiar door that led to the hangar bay, warped and stuck two-thirds of the way open from Leonidas's forced exit. She hoped the ship would let them leave even if that door was broken and the bay wouldn't depressurize. If not, Mica would have yet another repair job to do.

"Leonidas?" Abelardus asked. He reached the door just before Alisa and looked back.

Leonidas had stopped in front of a big monitor embedded in the bulkhead. When Alisa had glanced at it earlier, she'd assumed it was a map or directory.

"You don't need to look at that," she said. "You're not staying here."

He didn't look at her. No, he seemed to be trying to memorize something.

An inkling of what he meant to do sank into her bones like a damp chill, and her shoulders slumped.

"Leonidas, we've got who we came for, and I know you don't care about that staff. Let the Alliance handle the rest of this."

"They're *not* handling it." Leonidas tapped a button, bringing up an exterior display of the mining vessel—of the battle. "They're outnumbered, and even if they manage to disable this ship, all Tymoteusz needs to do is take a shuttle over to one of his allies' ships. Several of those civilian craft are faster than your warships. We *can't* let him get out of here with that staff again."

Alisa's shoulders slumped further. Was it true? Were her people losing? Even with Stanislav's help?

"Abelardus?" Leonidas called, switching back to the map of the mining ship. "Are Tymoteusz and the rest of his people still on the bridge?"

"Most of them, yes," Abelardus said. "There may be a couple looking for us. There are *definitely* miners looking for us."

"But Tymoteusz is there."

"Yes."

"Good."

"Here," Alisa said, shifting Thorian's unconscious form so she could hand him to Abelardus. "Take him into the *Nomad*, and get everyone else in there too. Tell Mica she better be able to detonate those explosives remotely."

"Uh." Abelardus accepted Thorian, juggling him awkwardly to carry him over his shoulder while still holding his staff. "We can't leave without the pilot."

"You're a pilot."

"Your ship is a dilapidated wreck, and I've never flown it."

"If you and Mica can't point it in a straight line and get it out of a hangar, you're both fired."

"*Alisa*. Let *him* stay and be a martyr if he wants—" Abelardus jerked his head toward Leonidas, "—but don't you be foolish. This isn't your fight."

Someone finally noticed. "I'm not leaving him here to get himself killed."

"How will *you* being at his side stop that?"

"I may not be able to do anything against Tymoteusz, but if he—*we*—can somehow take him down, then there's no need for the battle to continue. The mafia could never take over the system without his help. I can comm the Alliance and tell them—they'll listen to me." Maybe. "They might even be so pleased that they'll pick us up and give us a ride back to the *Nomad*."

"You're delusional."

"I thought you were the one who wanted that staff."

"I did, but that was before I realized it wouldn't respond to me and before you made it clear we weren't going to have powerful Starseer babies who could grow up to use it."

Alisa smiled faintly. And here she'd thought that had been clear from the beginning.

She patted him on the shoulder. "Go. Take Thorian and get everyone to safety."

"Safety? Where in a million miles is that?" Abelardus muttered, but he did step into the hangar bay.

"We'll join you soon," Alisa called after him. "Tell Mica what I said. And tell Jelena—" Her throat tightened, and she struggled to get the words out. Not goodbye, damn it. She wasn't going to get herself killed. She was going along to make sure Leonidas didn't get *himself* killed. "Tell her I love her."

Abelardus waved his staff in acknowledgment, but from the way he shook his head, his long braids dancing on his back, he didn't agree with anything she was doing.

"What's new?" Alisa muttered and ran back toward Leonidas.

Her comm beeped before she reached him.

"Captain," Mica said. "We're down to twenty percent power. If we're to have any chance to take off and escape this ship, I need to get us in the air now."

"Get everyone inside and blow those explosives," Alisa said. "You're flying the ship out of here. Abelardus has more orders."

"Flying…What are you blathering about, Alisa? Where are you?"

"You heard me. Just do it. I'll get in touch as soon as I can." Alisa closed the comm.

Leonidas turned away from the map on the big monitor to face her.

"Where are we going?" she asked. "The bridge?"

"*I'm* going to the bridge, eventually, to make sure that bastard doesn't escape, and to make sure the Alliance doesn't get the staff. You're going to pilot the *Nomad* out of here."

"You're worried about the stupid staff? I thought this was about killing the evil bastard who locked Thorian in that box."

"It is." Leonidas pointed at the hangar door. "Go, Alisa. I'm not letting you come with me. This ship might get blown out of the sky any second."

"And *I'm* not letting you give me orders. I intend to make sure this ship *doesn't* get blown out of the sky, not with you on it, and also that you don't do something reckless and suicidal."

"Your daughter needs her mother."

"And she needs her cyborg too." She slapped him on the chest. "Even if she doesn't know it yet."

"Quit joking. I'm not arguing with you about—"

"We're wasting time," Alisa said, making herself stay calm and reasonable, though she could almost feel the heat of his temper radiating through his armor. "Whatever your plan is, let's go."

They were both still wearing their helmets and faceplates, but she had no trouble seeing the frustration and anger in his eyes. He gritted his teeth, looking very much like he was thinking about slinging her over his shoulder, throwing her in the *Nomad's* cargo hold, and locking the hatch behind her.

"You have a plan," Alisa said. "I can see it in your eyes. I'll watch your back while you do it, and I won't get in your way. Let's go."

He spun on his heel and stalked away. She jogged after him, trying not to feel stung that he clearly did not want her along. Maybe he was right in that her place was with the *Nomad*, with her daughter. But she'd seen how easily Tymoteusz could squash him in a confrontation. She was terrified that he would get himself killed, that he would let himself get killed if he knew that Alisa and the *Nomad* had already escaped and he was only fighting for his own life. Maybe she was foolish to think he'd be less reckless with his life if she was at his side, but she honestly believed she could help him. This needed a scheme, not just brute force. And scheming was what she did.

Leonidas took them into a lift that creaked when they entered. It was dark inside, only the indicators of the panel still lit, and Alisa doubted it would even work. But when he hit the button, the car started moving, albeit creakily. An explosion sounded in the distance, and the ship rocked and shuddered. Alisa prayed that Mica and the others could get the *Nomad* out of here. To lose her ship and her people—her daughter—under the assault of Alliance fire, after all she had fought for in the war... It was too horrible to contemplate.

"Down?" Alisa asked, noticing the doors opened on a lower deck. She'd glanced at that map and seen that the bridge was located on the top level, near the nose of the mile-long vessel. "We're not going to the bridge?"

"Not yet." Leonidas strode out without explaining further.

"Maybe you should tell me your plan, in case ten androids leap out from around a corner and incapacitate you. Then I can finish executing it on your behalf."

He did not answer. She scowled at the back of his helmet. Now he was just sulking.

They turned a corner and came face-to-face with a blast door that had been dropped into the middle of the corridor.

"Uh?" Alisa stared at it. "Is someone paying attention to us? And deliberately blocking our way?"

Leonidas checked a nearby wall panel, the rim of which flashed red. Someone had turned off the audible alarm, but emergency lighting continued to be the main source of illumination throughout the ship.

"There's a hull breach down there," he said, waving at the blast door. "The section has been sealed off, and there's no atmosphere on the other side."

"But we're going to visit it anyway?" Alisa eyed the massive door. It had dropped down from the ceiling, probably with the authority of a boulder. It looked thick and like it would be a lot harder to tear through than a regular door, even for a cyborg.

"We have to. I'm not walking onto the bridge without an advantage."

"An advantage other than me?" She smiled at him, even though she knew he wasn't in the mood. If they did end up dying, she didn't want things to end with him mad at her.

"Yes." There was no hint of humor in his voice, but he came to stand next to her in front of the door and touched her shoulder. "Is your oxygen tank full?"

"Yes, I always make sure it is before I store my armor." Which was good, because that had been the last thing on her mind when she'd been standing in her cabin, deciding if she should wear the stuff.

"Good. Watch my back." Leonidas slung the canister launcher across his torso and handed her one of his rifles.

"Gladly. You know it's a sexy back, right?"

"So I've been told." He squatted and ran his fingers along the crack between door and deck.

"Really? By whom? Not Solstice, I hope."

"I seem to remember Hawk mentioning it back when we were fighting at the temple." He wasn't able to force his gauntleted fingers into the crack, so he slammed his elbow against the base of the door instead, denting it heroically.

"You sure that wasn't your ass he was admiring?"

"It might have been."

"He seemed like an ass man."

After denting the door, the bottom lip curled up just enough for him to find purchase for his fingers. He assumed a wide, deep stance, and Alisa was about to admire all parts of his sexy backside as he lifted the door, but the sound of footsteps came from around the corner. He hesitated, looking back.

"Keep lifting," Alisa said, taking a step from the door and raising his rifle to the crook of her shoulder. "I'll handle it."

She hoped that was true. It sounded like a lot of footsteps. Fast ones too. Whoever was coming was running.

Leonidas inched the hulking door up, and a blast of wind swept past Alisa's armored legs, air racing into the vacuum on the other side. She thought he might shove the door high enough that they could both dive through, but their opponents ran around the corner first. Miners. They didn't hesitate to fire.

Alisa dared not hesitate, either, not when she and Leonidas had no cover. Their blazer bolts splashed off her armored chest. Hers slammed into their unarmored torsos. They keeled over backward, dying silently. When she fired at the men just behind the first row, her bolts once again bit in deep, but these miners did not fall. They kept running. She groaned, belatedly recognizing the silvery eyes of a pair of androids.

"Leonidas," she said. "Going to need help. Sorry." The door would have to wait.

Or so she thought. A hand wrapped around her calf, and she found herself pulled off her feet. She flew backward, dragged along the floor and under the door—Leonidas squatted under it, holding it up with his shoulder. He fired at the androids with one arm blazer even as he shoved her the rest of the way through.

Alisa jumped to her feet, only to have her feet leave the deck and her helmet crack against the ceiling. Oxygen wasn't the only thing missing from this section of the ship. Gravity was either gone or extremely minimal.

Grunting, she pushed herself back to the deck and ordered her boots to magnetize. Leonidas rolled past as the blast door slammed down again. Muted clangs and clanks came from the other side.

"Will they keep following?" Alisa asked as Leonidas found his feet.

"They might," he said, and she now heard him only over her helmet comm. "Those androids can do exactly what I did. Come on." He touched her shoulder again, indicating she should walk beside him instead of following.

She smiled, glad he seemed to have forgiven her for being stubborn. And probably wrong. "I promise you, their backs won't be as sexy when they do it."

"Good to know."

The corridor opened up into a much larger chamber, one full of conveyor belts for sorting. Pieces of ore and dirt floated around the area. Readings scrolled down the side of Alisa's liquid Glastica faceplate, warning her of the harsh conditions in the corridor and that she was now consuming air from her tank. Sometimes, the armor liked to state the obvious.

"There it is," Leonidas said, taking them around a large holding bin and into sight of a door along the bulkhead.

Environmental Control Center, a plaque read.

"I hope the vents will work," he said, punching a button to open the door. "I wasn't planning for airlessness when I thought of this."

"You probably should have run the idea by me. Or told me what the idea was at least." Alisa followed him into a room filled with clunky computers that looked to be a hundred years old. Alarms flashed. The space was as devoid of air as the rest of the section.

"I was afraid you would be so impressed by it that you'd insist on coming along to see it enacted."

"I'd say something sarcastic in response to that, but it tickles me to no end when you make jokes." The ship shuddered again, and a crack sounded in the distance. "Especially when our demise is imminent."

"This leads into the duct system for the entire ship," Leonidas said, heading to a hulking control unit in the corner.

"If you say so. Do you want me to watch the door while you work?"

"Yes." He already had his back to her and was pulling some of the canisters off his utility belt.

Was he going to flood the entire ship with that stuff? No, there wouldn't be enough. Maybe he thought he could program that clunky old equipment to send it straight up to the bridge. Would the ducts in the rest of this part of the ship be sealed and protected from the vacuum? She was glad he was the one trying to manipulate the system and not her.

Alisa returned to the door, leaning her helmet close and trying to hear the sound of androids coming before she remembered noise wouldn't travel out there right now.

The deck heaved—another round of fire bombarding the ship. How much more could this old garbage scow take? Was Tymoteusz still trying to yank out the station or had he given up on that?

Her helmet comm beeped. "Captain? You still alive?"

"Yes, Mica, and I can't tell you how reassuring it is that you sound like you don't expect me to be."

"I thought you should know we're about to blow the charges and try to leave."

"You haven't *done* that yet?" Alisa had figured the *Nomad* would be long gone by now.

"You didn't hear a huge explosion, did you?"

"I've heard a lot of explosions."

"Well, ours will be a big one. I wanted to warn you and make sure you weren't close. This could blow out the hull on this end of the ship."

"We're not close. Do it. Get my—get everyone out of there. Please. While you still can. And then comm Hawk and tell him not to shoot the *Nomad*. While you're at it, tell him not to shoot this ship for a few minutes too."

"I'm sure he'll be excited to obey my orders," Mica said and closed the comm.

Alisa tried to rub her face, but only clunked her faceplate. She growled, irrationally irritated with the armor that was currently keeping her alive.

"Ship all right?" Leonidas asked, joining her at the door. He still had the launcher, with a single canister loaded in it, but the ones that had hung on his belt were gone.

"It's still *here*," Alisa growled, not pleased. She'd thought the *Nomad* had already left. Would they have the power to leave when they tried? She hadn't thought to ask how the *Nomad* would be protected from that explosion. By raising shields? Did they even have power for shields?

"But leaving?" Leonidas asked, waving at the door sensor.

"It better be." Alisa wondered if she'd made the wrong decision. Did Leonidas truly need her help more than her crew did? More than Jelena did?

The door slid aside, and an android with a blazer pistol floated in the corridor right outside.

Alisa squawked in surprise and jerked her rifle up. Leonidas reacted more quickly, springing at the android. It fired into his faceplate, but he grabbed it by the arm and swung it toward the ore holding tank they'd passed on the way in.

It kept firing as it flew away. He pushed off the doorjamb after it, shouting, "Another one!" as he flew away.

Right after he disappeared from Alisa's sight, a hand clasped onto the doorjamb in front of her. She leaned out and fired into an android's face. These were the same two from the blast door. She hoped the miners hadn't also flung themselves out here, only to die in the vacuum.

The android took the hit without flinching. He pulled himself around the jamb, grasping for her helmet with his other hand. She slammed her palm into his face. He had a good grip on the doorjamb and didn't let go, but his head did jerk back. She stepped in, making sure her soles were securely anchored on the deck—that let her use more leverage than her floating opponent could apply—and launched another attack. A series of punches, this time.

Her blows landed, crunching his machine face, but the android knew no pain. He pulled himself closer despite her flurry of attacks. She tried to duck away, but he lashed out, clipping her helmet with a fist. The power flung her backward into the room. Her back struck hard against machinery, and she almost let go of her rifle. The android pushed away from the jamb and toward her, and she tightened her grip on the weapon. She fired, a sustained beam, trying to cut into the android's throat, to dismember him, the way Leonidas did when he fought these opponents.

But he reached her before she came close, hands grasping for her helmet again. She reversed the rifle and clubbed him. Since he was airborne at that moment, with nothing to grab onto, the android flew away from her, toward the ceiling.

As much as she would enjoy singlehandedly defeating an android one day, it would have to wait. She raced for the door while he was still trying to find a way to right himself. She almost smacked into a detached, floating arm as she ran into the corridor.

"Dismembering androids again, are you?" she asked.

Leonidas pointed his rifle through the doorway and fired at the one she had left inside. Alisa hit the button to close the door. He gave her a disgruntled look.

"You can come back and finish him later if the ship is still here," she said, firing her weapon at the control panel and—she hoped—destroying the locking mechanism.

Leonidas started to respond, but the entire corridor quaked, tossing them against each other.

"We better go," he said, helping her secure her boots back to the deck. "It won't take long for the aerosol to reach the bridge. Tiang never said how long the effects take to wear off, so if it works…"

"We want to be there when it's at its peak."

"Yes."

He looked toward the blast door, but must have figured that their enemies might be waiting on the other side. He turned and led Alisa in the opposite direction.

"Did you memorize the entire layout for the ship?" she asked him.

"Just the important parts."

She touched her hand to a bulkhead as they left the sorting area and grimaced at the trembles coursing through it. She could feel the deck vibrating, and occasionally shifting underfoot. How long would this place stay together? Had the *Nomad* been able to leave after that explosion? Or was her ship still stuck in the hangar? She hoped not—she was counting on a rescue if the mining vessel blew up, and she and Leonidas ended up floating in space.

They entered a corridor that ended at another blast door. Leonidas rested his hand on it for a moment, listening—or feeling—for vibrations that would suggest someone on the other side. Alisa dropped to one knee, so she could shoot under it as he lifted it. Once again, he dented it at the bottom, so he could find a grip for his fingers, then heaved upward.

The corridor was empty. They raced under the door and into a lift.

"This time, we go up," Leonidas said.

An indicator light flashed at the edge of Alisa's faceplate. The radiation detector. It was letting her know that the levels outside of her suit had grown dangerously high and that it would be wise to get away from the area. She would love to. Just one more task to finish…

Be careful, a voice spoke into Alisa's mind. It sounded far away and very weary, or maybe injured.

Stanislav?

You can…call me Dad…if you like.

I'll keep that in mind. Are you nearby? Are you fighting your brother?

Yes…and yes.

Good, Alisa thought. *Be careful.*

I see what you're trying to do, Stanislav told her. *I'll try to…keep him distracted…a few minutes more.*

Did that mean the only reason he hadn't personally annihilated Alisa and Leonidas was because Stanislav had been distracting Tymoteusz all along? At least since he'd run out of the hangar bay?

But hurry, Stanislav added. *He says he's…no longer going to…tolerate my disobedience because we're kin.*

Disobedience? Tell him he's a lunatic in a bathrobe, not a drill sergeant. Alisa stepped out of the lift after Leonidas. They were back in full gravity, and he took off at a run.

I'll keep that in mind, should I deem insults appropriate.

Insults are always appropriate. What's he trying to do with the station? Alisa suspected she should let Stanislav focus on his confrontation instead of peppering him with questions, but without being able to see what was going on outside, she had no idea how the battle was going.

Claim it as a base and holy shrine where people can come to worship him.

I'm so glad it's not something stupid.

Indeed.

I imagine his worshippers will enjoy being irradiated while they pray. Did the nut think he could decontaminate the place? After it had soaked up radiation for hundreds of years?

Stanislav did not answer. He was probably busy trying to deflect some assault from Tymoteusz.

Alisa did not know if he would hear, but she thought, *Thanks for the help. Dad.*

"Almost to the bridge," Leonidas said, passing doors to crew quarters and control rooms.

She thought he would sprint the rest of the way—she was barely able to keep up with him now—but they reached another one of those large monitors embedded in a bulkhead. It looked identical to the one he had used to look up the map of the ship. He turned toward it, tapping a few buttons to bring up a view of the ship's exterior.

Alisa hadn't been close enough to see much the last time he'd done that. Only now did she fully see the battle taking place outside. The hulking wheel-shaped form of Alcyone Station floated nearby—much *too* nearby. The mining ship had succeeded in pulling it out of the rift and had released whatever physical or energy chains it had used. She spotted a tiny shuttle lurking under the station's wheel—was that Bravo Six? She would have laughed if the battle hadn't quickly drawn her attention away. She was glad he'd found a place to hide—nobody else would likely get that close to the station, not with the radiation it was emitting. But what did an android care about radiation?

The eclectic assortment of mafia ships was lined up around the mining ship, protecting it. A couple of imperial warships were out among them. Who had invited *them*? Alisa's first hope was that they had come to join the Alliance, to keep these greedy corporate and mafia entities from gaining control of the system. But they weren't pointing their weapons at the mafia ships; they were pointing them farther away, toward the Alliance fleet, a fleet that wasn't as large as Alisa had hoped it would be. A great deal of wreckage littered the area around the Alliance vessels, signs of ships that had already been destroyed.

"You were right," she whispered, feeling numb as blazer beams and e-cannon blasts streaked across the starry battlefield. "The Alliance isn't winning."

There were small bombers and strikers, just as she had flown, harrying the mafia ships, with some getting through to pepper the mining ship, but they were outnumbered, thanks to those imperial ships. When had they decided to jump into bed with the mafia? Bastards.

"No," Leonidas agreed grimly. He left the display on and continued down the corridor, his stride determined.

Alisa knew she needed to follow him, but she lingered, hoping to catch sight of the *Nomad*. The freighter wasn't on the camera display. She hoped that meant Mica had flown the other way and that they were staying safe, staying out of the battle.

She took a step after Leonidas but halted when an Alliance warship exploded in a ball of fiery orange, so big and bright that it dwarfed the suns for a moment. She gaped, her gaze riveted. Stunned. It had been toward the back of the formation, and nobody had been attacking it. She would have seen the weapons blasts streaking toward it, and she hadn't.

"Tymoteusz?" she whispered. "And the staff?"

If he had waved his magical stick and done *that*…not only was that terrifying, but it meant that Leonidas's trick hadn't worked. Tymoteusz was awake and well on the bridge. Tiang's drug either had never reached him or he'd combatted it somehow.

"Leonidas," she said, but he had already disappeared around a bend.

She raced after him. She had to warn him before it was too late.

Alisa caught up with Leonidas in front of a pair of double doors. The doors to the bridge. Fortunately, he hadn't gone in yet. He seemed to be preparing himself, rifle in one hand, launcher with its one remaining canister in the other, and what looked like a grenade dangling from a pinkie finger.

"He's still alive and fighting," Alisa blurted, her breathing ragged after that last sprint. "Tymoteusz."

"I assumed," Leonidas said.

"I saw an Alliance warship blow up without any weapons striking it. It might have been the flagship. It was in the back. If Stanislav was on there, there's nobody left to oppose Tymoteusz." Or teach Jelena, she thought, emotion thickening her throat. She forced it down to deal with later. "And if Hawk and Agosti got killed…" If that happened, the entire fleet would fall back. What remained of it. How had that damned Henneberry woman gotten so many mafia people willing to go toe-to-toe with the military? Or was Tymoteusz somehow extending his control over them, the same way he had been with the miners? Who in all the hells could do so much? It was like fighting a god out of Old Earth mythology. Who could win against a god?

"I doubt we'll surprise him either," Leonidas said. He lowered his voice. "That's why I want you to take the helm while I run in there and do my best to kill him."

"Take the helm?" Alisa gaped at him.

"Stanislav told me what the rift cycle is now—the Alliance people have kept a ship out here to study it. It's shorter than it used to be. We have twenty minutes before it closes. I've been keeping track since he told me."

"And?" Alisa asked, not following him. She shifted from foot to foot, half expecting Tymoteusz to fling the doors open any second and blast them to death with that staff.

"I want you to fly this barge into the rift. With all the damage it's taken, I'm wagering that will be a one way trip." Leonidas smiled grimly behind his faceplate. "I don't care how powerful his staff is. There's not going to be anywhere over there to buy replacement parts."

Alisa felt her mouth drop open. "That'll be suicide for us. We'll be stuck over there too. Until we die horribly of radiation poisoning."

She wasn't telling him anything he didn't know. She could see it in his eyes. He'd intended all along for this to be a suicide mission. Maybe he'd hoped the drug would work and that flying the ship into the rift wouldn't be necessary, but he'd had this backup plan all along.

"I know," he said softly. "That's why I didn't want you to stay with me. But…I may not have been able to do it alone."

"You need a pilot."

"I need a pilot." Tears pricked at Alisa's eyes. She tried to dash them away but only banged her armored knuckles against her faceplate. "Damn it, Leonidas. This wasn't the plan."

"I know, but the last thing the system needs now is an ultra powerful dictator in charge."

He turned toward the doors, but she hugged him before he could hit the controls, careful not to knock his weapons or that grenade out of his hands.

He leaned his faceplate against hers. "I'm sorry," he whispered. "I love you."

"I love you too." She wanted to say more, that there had to be a better option if they could just take a minute to think, but the doors opened before either of them touched the controls.

Alisa glimpsed a black robe, but then Leonidas charged in, throwing his grenade, and there wasn't time for anything else.

CHAPTER TWENTY-SIX

The boom rattled the bridge, and smoke from Leonidas's grenade flooded the area before Alisa had a good look at how many opponents they faced. The golden glow of the orb atop the Staff of Lore gleamed, visible through the haze. She almost shouted that Tymoteusz was on that side of the bridge, but Leonidas was already springing in that direction, a fluidwrap ready to throw. Two *chasadski* turned toward him, raising their arms. Alisa sensed an attack directed at him, even if only the faintest brush of wind battered her armor. They weren't after her. They might not have even realized she was there.

She wanted to leap into the fray, firing at Tymoteusz, hoping to get through the shield he no doubt had around himself, but Leonidas had only asked her to do one thing, and she had to do it. It would take a few minutes to travel to the rift, and she could change course later if there was time. And if there wasn't…then the outcome of this fight on the bridge wouldn't matter.

Thuds and crashes sounded, but in the smoke, she couldn't tell if Leonidas was hurling *chasadski* about or if *chasadski* were hurling *him* about. Since nobody was attacking her yet—not with the big, armored cyborg flinging weapons and filling the bridge with smoke—she eased along the control stations, away from the fighting. She eyed the terminals lining the wall, trying to pick out the navigation controls in the dim, hazy lighting.

She sucked in a startled breath when her boot snagged on something. A fallen *chasadski*, his eyes open, but his arms and legs twitching, his torso jerking in spasms. So, the aerosol had made it up here. Some people had just been quick enough to react to get their defenses up. What had Tiang said about that? That his compound would cling to the particles of their shields and that they would be exposed whenever their barriers went down? She hoped so.

As she inched farther around the bridge, she got closer and closer to the glowing orb. It hadn't moved. Maybe Tymoteusz was locked in some mental battle across space with Stanislav and couldn't pay attention to what was happening around him.

Something flashed above her, and she lifted a hand, almost expecting someone with a weapon leaping down from above. But she found herself staring at the ceiling of the bridge, a clear dome ceiling, a window right out into space. Weapons fire streaked past, just missing the mining ship. Was that an actual porthole and not just a view screen? Something that could possibly be broken? With all the breaches across the ship, she already knew the shields were long down. What if all it took was a direct hit to the bridge to open a breach here? Would one of Leonidas's grenades work if she could set it up there somehow? Did he have any more?

"Alisa," Leonidas gasped from across the bridge, pain seeping into his voice. "Do it now."

"I will," she said.

She darted out into the center of the bridge. Navigation had to be in the middle, in one of the stations near the captain's chair. There.

As she lunged for the controls, she almost tripped over another downed *chasadski*, this one not moving at all, his eyes frozen open. She forced herself to look away. As Leonidas had said, these people all made their choices.

A flashing indicator on the panel warned her about the proximity to an energy anomaly. Since the rift wasn't visible to the naked eye, she appreciated that. It would show her where to steer this boat.

She batted away smoke, studying the layout of the controls as rapidly as she could. Normally, she would have needed a lot longer to familiarize herself with a strange helm, but this ship had been built in the same era as the *Nomad*. It shared many similar features, and her hands were soon darting across the panel. She hurried, doing her best to ignore the thuds and cracks from the side, from where Leonidas battled at least two *chasadski*, if not more.

"Course laid in," she muttered to herself. "And...go." She reached for the button that would kick the relic into motion, but a hand reached out of the smoke and latched onto her wrist.

She looked up. Tymoteusz stood on the other side of the control station, that staff glowing hungrily in his other hand. Sweat dripped down his face and from his chin, but he had the strength to sneer fully at her.

"We're not going anywhere," he said. "And now, you die."

Alisa tried to jerk her arm away, thinking he might be surprised by the power her armor gave her, but her great yank barely moved him. He did not let go of her wrist. She couldn't kick him or lash out effectively with the control station between them, but she launched a punch with her left hand. His eyebrow twitched, and her blow never landed. Her fist hung in the air between them, and she could neither push it forward nor pull it back.

A pounding started behind her eyes, some kind of freakish headache. It intensified quickly, and she felt like her brain would soon explode, bursting out of her ruptured skull. Tymoteusz stared at her, the sneer still there. Once again, she tried to yank her arm free. Once again, it did nothing. The pain increased until she was gasping, tears springing to her eyes. She couldn't kick him, so she kicked the console. Her boot broke through the casing, but it did nothing to stop his attack.

Dad, if you have anything left, Alisa thought, trying to project the thought out into the cosmos, *now would be a good time.*

She feared that having Tymoteusz standing in front of her, his attention on her fully, meant that Stanislav had already been defeated. The thumps and thuds of Leonidas's battle had grown quiet. Maybe there was no one left to help her.

Then Tymoteusz's sneer turned into a frown, and his lips parted, as if he might say something. His grip loosened on her wrist, and Alisa finally yanked her arm away. She lifted her blazer, hoping he was too distracted to defend himself. But before she could shoot, a red form blurred in from the side.

Leonidas crashed into Tymoteusz, taking him to the deck.

Alisa hammered the button to engage the engines. The mining ship groaned but rumbled into motion.

Leonidas flew upward so hard and so high that he hit that domed ceiling. Alas, not hard enough to break it. Tymoteusz grabbed the rim of the console to pull himself to his feet, but Leonidas landed right next to him and kicked out. Tymoteusz was hurled several meters, the staff flying from his hand.

Alisa activated her helmet comm as she worked her way around the consoles, hoping to get to the weapon. It lay on the deck between two stations.

"Mica?" she asked.

"Still here, Captain."

"You're clear of the ship?" Alisa asked.

"Hiding behind it, actually. Looks like you're going somewhere. That intentional?"

"For the moment. Look, I want you to find the dome on top of the mining ship and fire at it, preferably in a way that won't blow up the people standing right under it."

"That's asking a lot, both of my piloting skills and my aim."

"Do your best." Alisa scooted closer and reached for the staff as Leonidas flew past, some invisible force striking him.

"You really should be over here to perform this fancy maneuver yourself."

"I'll be there next time. Promise." Her fingers closed around the staff, but someone grabbed her armored calf.

She yelped in surprise, jerking her leg free as she whirled around. One of the fallen *chasadski* had risen to his knees. He reached for her again, this time stretching out his fingers, and she felt another attack starting on her brain. She lunged forward and kicked him in the shoulder. He'd been too busy attacking to raise his defenses, and she connected solidly. He skidded across the deck and crashed into a bulkhead.

Alisa snatched up the staff and sprinted for the doors. "Leonidas," she barked over her comm. "Get off the bridge. We've got an attack incoming."

Even as she spoke, a shadow fell across the bridge—the blocky form of the *Nomad* floating over the dome.

"Hurry," she yelled, pausing in the doorway.

But Leonidas and Tymoteusz were down on the deck, the *chasadski* atop him, his open hand gripping Leonidas's faceplate, as if he were an android with the power to crush it.

Alisa stepped back inside and fired at him. But Tymoteusz wasn't as distracted as the other *chasadski*. The attack bounced off an invisible barrier erected around him. Still, he paused just long enough to glare in her direction. It was enough, and Leonidas bucked him free, sending him into the air.

"Go," Leonidas said. "I'll keep him from getting away."

"I don't give a damn about him. I want *you* to get away."

"Fire incoming, Captain," Mica said over the comm.

Leonidas leaped up and took a step toward the doors, but Tymoteusz wasn't done. He rose behind Leonidas and flung his hands outward. Once again, Leonidas flew across the bridge, struck by a blast of wind that was strong enough to send Alisa stumbling into the corridor outside the bridge. Her back slammed against the bulkhead. She took a step back toward the bridge, but then remembered Mica's warning.

"Wait," she blurted on the comm. "Mica, give him a—"

White light flashed through the bridge as the attack came. An instant later, the thunderous boom sounded, ringing in Alisa's ears as she was hurled down the corridor again. Her shoulder hammered against the wall—or was that the ceiling?—and she dropped to the deck, skidding a dozen meters. Before she could leap to her feet, before she could run in and find Leonidas, a great wind whipped through the corridor. At first, she thought it was another *chasadski* attack, but as she was lifted into the air and sucked toward the bridge doors, she knew what had happened. The *Nomad's* blow had breached that huge domed porthole.

It was just what she had wanted, but sheer terror flooded her body as she was sucked through the doors, her helmet clunking hard on the jamb. She almost lost the staff, but she tightened her fist, determined that whatever happened, Tymoteusz would not get his hands on it again.

Her armored back smashed against the remains of the dome, its center now blown out, and then she bounced through the hole, away from the ship and into nothingness. She almost collided with a flailing *chasadski*, utter terror flashing in the man's eyes as the icy vacuum of space engulfed him.

Alisa toppled head over butt as she floated away from the ship, and she couldn't stop her ridiculous cartwheel. Ships were all around, everywhere she looked. And—her gut clenched—there was the station. And the rift would be right behind it. By all that was holy, what if, after all this, she ended up cartwheeling right into it?

The radiation indicator in her suit flashed an angry warning.

"Yeah, yeah, I know," she muttered at it, even as she craned her head, looking for Leonidas. Had he survived being right under that dome when it blew?

She spotted his red armor, lit up by the flashing of blazer fire all around. He, too, was tumbling away from the mining ship, but he wasn't flailing around like she was. He was limp in his armor. Unconscious? She swallowed. *Dead?*

"Captain?" Mica's voice crackled as it sounded in Alisa's helmet. "You alive in that suit?"

"I am," Alisa rasped. "Leonidas? Can you hear me?"

He didn't respond.

"Bravo Six is bringing the shuttle over to get you. He'll be better at the fine maneuvering it'll take to catch you two dolts."

"Save your terms of endearment for when we're safely aboard."

"You're both idiots," Mica growled, then swore. That vehemence was probably the biggest indication she would give that she was worried.

The space battle kept going in the background, blazer beams streaking between ships, as Alisa continued to tumble. Had anyone on those ships seen what had happened? Tymoteusz had to be out of it—he *had* to be dead. Surely, even he couldn't protect himself in space without a suit, could he?

The cylindrical white shuttle came into view, and Alisa laughed, albeit a touch hysterically, at the meals painted on the side. Her work. And Leonidas's. Jelena had done those strawberries.

Bravo Six swooped in to pick up Leonidas first. He still didn't seem to be moving, and Alisa cursed the rotation that had her in its grasp, because she couldn't watch every second of that pickup, couldn't watch for signs of life.

The *Nomad* lingered nearby. She wanted to tell Mica to fly it farther away, to get Jelena and everyone else away from all that radiation.

The shuttle flew toward her. All she wanted was to get out of space and back into atmosphere and gravity so she could yank her helmet off and wipe away the stupid tears tracking down her cheeks.

"The mining ship just flew into the rift," Mica said, her voice still crackling. "And disappeared."

"Can you tell if Tymoteusz went with it?" Alisa asked, doubt still nagging at her that, maybe somehow, he could have survived. That any second, the staff would be ripped from her hands and zipped over to him, wherever he was.

"A bunch of black-robed people got sucked out when we hit the bridge," Mica said. "I didn't stop to ask for their idents."

The shuttle filled Alisa's vision, blocking out everything else. She clunked against the hull and scrambled to turn and magnetize the soles of her boots and get one locked on. The staff made everything more cumbersome, and she had the wicked thought to simply point the thing at the rift and hurl it in. Too bad she couldn't see it with her naked eye. She didn't even know if it was still open. Had Leonidas's twenty minutes passed?

The outer hatch on the shuttle's airlock opened, and she pulled herself in. There wasn't much room. Bravo Six stood in there, gripping the inner hatch with one hand and holding Leonidas's arm with his other.

Soot smeared Leonidas's dented armor. Alisa couldn't tell if there were any rips in it. In the dim illumination provided by the shuttle's running lights—and the flashes of blazer fire still streaking between the two fleets farther from the rift—she could just see through Leonidas's faceplate. His eyes were closed, and blood smeared his face. She cursed and wanted nothing more than to hurry inside with Six so she could check on him. But Six was looking at the staff instead of cycling the airlock. If androids could gape in surprise, he was doing it.

An idea flashed into her mind. She couldn't see the rift from here and chucking the staff into it with her arm was unrealistic, but if it was still open, the shuttle's sensors would see it. And Six could fly right up to the event horizon without being affected by the radiation.

She handed it to him. "Six, this has to be destroyed, or thrown somewhere it will never be recovered."

He accepted the staff but only gave her a puzzled look, and she growled in frustration with herself. He wasn't in a spacesuit and commed in. He wouldn't be able to hear her out here.

Using exaggerated movements, she pointed at the staff, then at Six, and then to roughly where she thought the rift was—the station, having been abandoned by the mining ship, must still be close to it.

"Throw it in," she said, mouthing the words slowly, hoping he could see her lips through the faceplate.

She gripped Leonidas by the armor and waved for Six to go back inside. He let go of Leonidas but still seemed puzzled. As soon as he got back in the ship, she could comm better directions.

Hoping she wasn't making a huge mistake and risking both of their lives, Alisa pushed off the inner hatch with Leonidas in her grip. They floated away from Six—and the shuttle. He immediately closed the outer hatch, so she hoped that meant he had caught the gist.

"Mica," she commed, also hoping that the *Nomad* was still close enough to come pick them up before the radiation turned their thyroids into pan-fried glands. "Leonidas and I need a pickup."

"What? The android was supposed to get you."

"I sent him on a more important errand."

"You're an absolute lunatic."

"I know," Alisa said. "Come get us, please. I'll give you a raise. And have Alejandro standing by. Leonidas is unconscious, and we're both…" She eyed the radiation warning on her display. "We're looking forward to his radiation recovery shots."

"The ones that make you puke and piss all over the place? Did I mention what a lunatic you are?"

"Yes. Are you on your way?"

Mica did not answer, but the *Nomad* soon came into view, flying out from behind the station. They'd probably been doing their best to stay out of the fighting. Wise decision. Alisa was relieved they hadn't simply taken off for the nearest planet, leaving Alisa and Leonidas to Bravo Six.

As the *Nomad* flew closer, Alisa watched the shuttle heading to where she assumed the rift awaited.

"Lady Captain?" Six asked over her comm.

"There you are, Six. Good. Did you understand what I meant? Can you find a way to throw the staff into the rift?"

"Throw, Lady Captain?"

"Pull up close, lean out of your airlock, and chuck it in."

"I do not know if that will work precisely, but I understand your reasoning. This is a dangerous item when in the Starseers' hands—I witnessed three ships seemingly spontaneously explode during the battle."

"That was the staff—Tymoteusz."

"So I gathered. I will ensure it is no longer a threat, Lady Captain."

"Excellent. Thank you, Six."

Alisa was on the verge of switching channels—she was concerned about how quickly Mica was coming in with the *Nomad* and thought her engineer might want some piloting advice—but Six spoke one more time.

"It has been an honor to work with you, Lady Captain."

"Uh, you too, Six. We'll get your eye fixed when this is all over."

"Of course."

Alisa switched to Mica's channel and offered some advice while shifting her grip on Leonidas so she could lock her boots to the hull when the *Nomad* drew close enough.

"Any chance you're awake, Leonidas?" she asked softly, using his channel.

He did not respond.

She had no way to check his pulse or any other health statistics when he was inside his suit, and the thought that his armor might have been damaged so much that the seal was ruptured, and that he had been exposed to space all this time…She stroked the side of his helmet, wanting to touch his hair, to touch him. He couldn't be dead in there. He just couldn't.

The *Nomad* loomed close, floating into Alisa's path—she had some momentum from her push off the shuttle, but it was slight, and it seemed to take forever before she finally touched the hull of her ship. Her home.

She spacewalked along the outside to the airlock and felt almost giddy as she knocked on the hatch. She would see Jelena soon. Alejandro would be able to fix up Leonidas. Maybe she could go straight to NavCom and zip them out of local space before the Alliance and mafia people figured out that their mini war was over.

She glanced over her shoulder as the hatch unsealed, hoping to spot the shuttle. They might have been too late for Six to send the staff into the rift, but if not, maybe she could sneak away with it and hurl it into a sun or volcano. Hells, maybe a sustained blazer blast would destroy it. As far as she knew, nobody had tried to break it yet.

Alisa could see part of the station, but she couldn't see the shuttle. Maybe Six had already tried and failed to toss the staff. Or maybe the *Nomad* was simply blocking her view of the rift. Or maybe…

An uneasy feeling swept over her, and even though the hatch had unlocked, she hesitated to go inside.

"Captain?" Mica commed.

"Yes, we're here. Did you see what happened to Six and the shuttle?"

Mica didn't answer right away.

"Mica?"

"He flew the shuttle into the rift," she said. "It disappeared the same as the mining ship. The rift closed just a few seconds later. I figured you ordered him to."

"No…not exactly. I just wanted him to get rid of the staff."

"He might not have had time for anything else. Also, Yumi isn't sure if the rift will keep opening and closing now that the station has been pulled out of the door."

"Meaning…" Bravo Six wouldn't be coming back. And all those miners had been condemned to death because of Tymoteusz, and because she and Leonidas hadn't known any other way to ensure they got rid of him. She wished she'd still been at the helm when the dome blew. She might have stopped the ship before it went through the rift. "I understand. We're ready to come home."

"Soon, Captain," Mica said. "Alejandro had us stash your armor cases in the airlock, so we can hose you down and you can stick the pieces in there for cleaning. He's set up a nice decontamination zone for scrubbing your irradiated asses."

Alisa closed her eyes—she'd forgotten they would have to go through all that—but she took a deep breath and said, "I understand," again. After all they had endured, she could endure a little more.

CHAPTER TWENTY-SEVEN

After spending an excruciating amount of time in Alejandro's makeshift decontamination room—which involved sanibox curtains and buckets rather than bulkheads and fancy medical equipment—Alisa finally escaped and fled to NavCom. She *wanted* to check on Jelena and Thorian, then pace back and forth in sickbay while Alejandro examined Leonidas, but she didn't think Mica had flown the *Nomad* completely out of the battle zone yet. She needed to make sure everyone was safe before giving in to her own desires. Besides, Leonidas hadn't looked like he would be waking up any time soon. After Alejandro had brought the remote for his armor, he, Beck, and Abelardus had worked together to pull him out of it and haul him to sickbay. Leonidas had been breathing, which had Alisa sending prayers of thanks to the suns, but Alejandro had only shaken his head grimly when she questioned him about his condition.

"You sure took your time, didn't you?" Mica growled, switching from the pilot's seat to the co-pilot's seat when Alisa entered.

"It's good to see you alive too." Alisa slid into her seat and frowned at what the view screen showed—a close-up of the belly of an Alliance warship. "I thought you would move the ship away from the fighting."

"I thought I would, too, but that ugly asteroid molester swooped in and locked a grab beam onto us."

Alisa scanned the console and verified that they were, indeed, being held. The sensors showed several other Alliance ships around them. *Close* around them. If Hawk was in charge, Alisa and her crew might be able to talk their way out of the situation. But if Hawk had been on one of those warships that blew up, and that Admiral Agosti was in charge... She winced.

The mafia ships showed up on the sensors at a farther distance. Most of them seemed to be retreating. They must have finally figured out that their fearless nutcase of a leader was gone. One of the larger ships remained, Henneberry's yacht, but it was almost on top of another mafia ship. No, it *was* on top of it. The two ships must have crashed during the action. It was hard to imagine a pilot as skilled as Tomich accidentally crashing, so maybe that had been deliberate, a way to take the yacht out of the action.

"Have they commed us yet?" Alisa asked, waving at the warship dominating the view screen.

"Not yet. They just want to hold us and snuggle with us."

"We are snuggly."

Mica wrinkled her nose. "You smell like blood, sweat, and explosives."

"So...not snuggly?"

"Maybe your cyborg would think so—he has unique tastes."

"He has excellent tastes."

The comm flashed, and Alisa slapped it without hesitating. Even if it *was* Agosti, it would be better to know what he wanted than to dangle here forever.

But it turned out to be an internal channel. "Captain," Alejandro said.

"I hope you're going to tell me that Leonidas is awake, Thorian is well, and everyone else came through the battle unscathed, including the chickens."

"I was going to tell you that I have your special cocktail prepared. You probably don't want to assume that your mutated genes will protect you from all that radiation, especially if you're planning to have more children."

"No, I look forward to your cocktail."

Mica's nose wrinkled again. "Did you forget how much puking was involved with his *last* cocktail?"

"Dole them out for everyone on the ship, Doctor," Alisa said. She hoped that most of her people had been protected by being within the

Nomad, which had been within the mining ship for much of the time, but they didn't need to take chances. "And also give me an update on Leonidas and Thorian."

"Physically, Thorian will be fine once he gets rehydrated and gets some food in him. Mentally, I don't know. He's not talking about what they did to him. He's not talking at all. Abelardus said he was locked in a *box* when you found him?"

"Yeah. No idea if Tymoteusz was tormenting him in any way or was just ignoring him. They were making an android replica, presumably to replace him for some kind of scheme."

Alejandro swore. "I don't know what kind of emotional scars his time over there will leave on him. I'm not a counselor."

"That's an understatement," Mica muttered.

"He's more the reason people *need* counselors," Alisa said.

"Aren't you supposed to mute the comm when you're talking poorly about someone?" Alejandro asked.

"Why? You don't do it when you talk poorly about me. Update on Leonidas, please."

Alejandro grunted. "Better see if Stanislav is alive and can come visit him."

Alisa slumped in her seat. "That coma again?"

"I'm running tests now, and he did receive some injuries, but his armor mostly protected him from physical wounds. I don't see evidence of an actual blow to the head. Not a physical one."

"I'll see what I can do." Alisa looked at the hull taking up the entire view screen display. She hadn't heard from Stanislav since before Tymoteusz had died.

"Did you bring back the staff?" Alejandro asked. He sounded like he was trying to be casual, but he didn't quite manage. She could imagine him rubbing his hands together like a goblin anticipating hoards of gold.

"Why, will that help Thorian with counseling?"

"It might."

"Sadly, we weren't able to recover it."

"Sadly. Right."

"Even if we had gotten it, the Alliance would just take it. They're holding us right now, if you hadn't heard." Alisa frowned, realizing he had closed the channel before she finished speaking. "That man is *not* snuggly."

"No arguments from me," Mica said.

Alisa reached for the panel, intending to comm the warship herself. But an external channel lit up first.

"*Star Nomad*, this is the *Impervious*," a woman said in a clipped voice. "We are maneuvering to attach to your airlock. Prepare to be boarded."

"Well, since you asked nicely..."

The channel closed.

"Should I be offended that everyone is hanging up on me?" Alisa asked.

"War makes people cranky," Mica said.

"Keep an eye on things, will you?" Alisa stood up. "I'm going to warmly greet whoever they send over."

"With weapons?"

"I haven't decided yet."

The idea of fighting off a huge Alliance boarding party without Leonidas's help made her tired. They'd killed the evil overlord. Couldn't they be done fighting now?

Knowing she had a few minutes before the airlock tube attached and the boarding party came over, Alisa turned toward Jelena's cabin. She needed to give her daughter a hug and reassure herself that she was all right. Her cabin, however, was empty. Maybe she was with Thorian.

Alisa headed toward sickbay, but had to pause in the mess hall when she spotted Beck with mixing bowls and pans out. He still wore his armor, everything save for his helmet and gauntlets, but he'd tied an apron around his waist.

"Beck?" Alisa asked. "Whatcha doing?"

"Heard about what happened to Thorian," Beck said, grabbing a spoon from his utensil holder. "Figured the kid needs some brownies. But I'm keeping myself combat ready." He pointed the spoon at his armored shoulder. "Just let me know if you need me to shoot at any invading Alliance soldiers."

"After the day the Alliance has had, they probably need brownies too." Alisa headed for sickbay again, but paused before leaving the mess hall. "Are you sure the ingredients will be safe to use? Was anyone calculating how much radiation got through the *Nomad's* hull while we were close to the rift?"

"The ingredients are definitely safe. I put everything in the fridge as soon as I heard we were heading back this way."

"And the fridge protects things from radiation?"

"It does now. I lined it with lead after the last time we tangled with radioactive ships."

"Are you pulling my leg, Beck?"

He saluted her with his spoon. "If you're worried, just wait until you've had the brownies to take Doc's cocktail."

Alisa supposed if Thorian had Starseer genes, he could probably handle a contaminated brownie or two. Her stomach rumbled at the thought of food. She couldn't remember the last time she had eaten, but she might risk extra exposure in exchange for something chocolate.

She found Leonidas lying on the exam table in sickbay with Alejandro frowning over the monitors he'd hooked up. He had been stripped from his armor and draped with a sheet, probably because of the young guests also in the room. Jelena was on the far side of the table, sitting cross-legged on the deck next to Thorian. He sat in a chair with his legs pulled up to his chest and a blanket wrapped around his shoulders. Jelena had a netdisc out and was flipping through some display, showing things to him.

"I'm mostly liking the kittens," she informed him. "But these unicorn stickers are great. Doesn't this look like the genetically engineered unicorn in that one Andromeda Android episode? The one she freed from a lab?"

Thorian didn't respond, but his eyes were at least tracking her movements. He still needed to be washed and given fresh clothing, but Alisa could understand why Alejandro hadn't gotten around to that yet. She touched Leonidas's leg through the sheet and looked at his still face. She thought about keeping herself to that touch, since Jelena was right there, but she couldn't stop herself from moving up to his side for a hug and a quick kiss on the cheek. He'd risked so much to get Thorian out of there and put an end to this staff nonsense. In the end, he hadn't objected to the notion of destroying the artifact. After all, piloting the mining ship into the rift to get rid of the staff—and Tymoteusz—had been his idea.

"Thank you," she whispered in his ear, though she was sure he wouldn't hear her. "For everything."

She patted his chest and turned around to talk to her daughter. Jelena was gazing up at her. Alisa smiled, hoping that Jelena wouldn't choose that moment to again point out that Leonidas wasn't Dad and shouldn't be hugged and kissed.

"I'm shopping for stickers, Mom," she said.

"Oh?" Alisa asked, surprised she had a decent connection this far out. Maybe she'd loaded a catalog earlier in their trip.

"For his armor." Jelena waved toward the exam table. "To make him less scary."

Alisa's smile grew easier. "Good."

Thorian's eyebrows drew together. "He's *supposed* to be scary."

Alejandro turned at his voice. "That's the first thing he's said."

"Maybe he just wasn't interested in whatever topics you were trying to discuss with him, Doctor." Alisa ruffled Thorian's hair, not caring if it was an appropriate thing to do to a prince. He looked like he needed a hug, but that seemed presumptuous. He barely knew her. Maybe later.

"I didn't know stickers were what one wanted to discuss after escaping a harrowing life-or-death situation."

"That's because you're not ten." Alisa switched her hand to Jelena's head. "Or eight."

"I'm *almost* nine."

"In two weeks," Alisa said, surprised Jelena had kept track of the date during all the chaos of the past months.

"Can we go horseback riding for my birthday?"

"If the Alliance lets us go, we could make it to Upsilon Seven in time for that. What do you think, Thorian? Want to ride a horse? Smell some grass? Trees? Dirt?"

He looked at Jelena, and they seemed to exchange some silent communication. Then he nodded at Alisa.

"How about you, Leonidas?" Alisa patted him on the chest again. "Willing to wake yourself up to go horseback riding in a couple of weeks?"

"He's still too big," Jelena said.

"I'm sure we can find a horse that can handle him. You wouldn't mind riding with him?" She probably shouldn't push, but she found it promising that Jelena hadn't batted an eye when Alisa hugged him.

"He got Thor. Abelardus said so."

"*Abelardus* admitted that?" Alisa couldn't believe Abelardus wouldn't have taken credit for that, especially when she and Leonidas hadn't been there to say otherwise.

"Not at first, but then Thorian told us how Abelardus hid in the box with him while you and him fought." Jelena waved at Leonidas.

"Only because I didn't have armor and wasn't immune to Tiang's devil drug," Abelardus said, leaning into sickbay.

"He said he'd get Thor and he did," Jelena said, ignoring Abelardus's intrusion. "And so did you." Jelena stood up and hugged Alisa.

Alisa returned the hug, fighting back tears. She reminded herself that they still had the Alliance to deal with. She couldn't fall apart yet.

"Your buddies are knocking at the airlock hatch," Abelardus said. "Mica wasn't sure if we were greeting them with weapons or kisses."

"I'd pay quite a bit to see you greet Admiral Agosti with a kiss."

"Young-hee might get jealous if I did that."

"I doubt it."

Alisa reluctantly let Jelena go. "Jelena, will you take Thorian and show him your cabin for a few minutes? We want to make sure the Alliance doesn't know he's here."

Thorian's eyes widened, and he stood up quickly, shucking the blanket.

Jelena shrugged, probably not understanding the ramifications, but she said, "Sure. I can show him more stickers."

"Good." Alisa gave Alejandro a make-sure-they're-not-here-if-the-Alliance-comes-through look, and he nodded in return.

Once the children left sickbay, Alisa trotted down the stairs and to the airlock, certain the Alliance boarding party wouldn't be pleased about being left waiting. She peeked through the window before opening the hatch, hoping to see Hawk's face, but two big figures in combat armor stood at the front. She couldn't see if anyone else was behind them.

Sighing, she unlocked the hatch. Too bad Beck's brownies weren't done yet. She could use a bribe.

The soldiers strode in, rifles in hand as they peered around the cargo hold. Only Abelardus was down there with Alisa—she hadn't called Beck away from the mess hall—but he held his staff and squinted at them. Neither of the soldiers pointed their rifles at anyone.

"Clear, sir," one said.

Senator Hawk walked out in the same civilian clothes she'd seen him in before the battle, but they were much more rumpled, as if he'd been sleeping in them, or perhaps been thrown around his ship in them.

"Good to see you, sir," Alisa said with genuine relief. He would, at least, be reasonable.

Two more soldiers followed him out. A black-robed figure came at the end of the party.

"Stanislav," Alisa blurted, pleased since he could help Leonidas and also pleased that he had survived…just because.

He walked over slowly, using his staff for support, the lines deep at the sides of his eyes. He faced her and smiled tentatively. "I know it's no longer a horrible situation, but you can still use 'Dad,' if you like."

"Oh?" Since he looked like he needed a hug, Alisa stepped forward and gave him one. "I wasn't sure what the rules were on that."

"No rules." He sighed and leaned on her. If he hadn't also had the staff to lean on, he might have collapsed.

"I hate to ask you for help when you're clearly exhausted," Alisa said, "but can you take a look at Leonidas when you're able to? I wouldn't be here if not for him. None of us would."

"Of course," Stanislav murmured, stepping back.

"We'd also like to take the staff into custody," Hawk said. "It will be locked away so it can't be used as a weapon again, I assure you."

Stanislav's eyebrows rose slightly, but he said nothing. He had to know it wasn't here. In fact, he probably knew exactly where it had gone.

"We don't have it," Alisa said. "It was on the mining ship when it went through the rift. We sent our android in a shuttle after it to retrieve it, but I guess the rift closed. I don't know if he'll be able to come back with it or not."

Hawk frowned and looked to Stanislav.

"It may be true," Stanislav said, spreading an arm. "Or it may have been destroyed in that explosion on the mining ship. I can no longer sense it."

Alisa kept her face neutral, certain Stanislav could see into her mind and knew exactly what had happened. Yumi's drug had likely worn off by now. Still, even if he'd been working together with Hawk, he shouldn't be more loyal to him than to his own family. Or so she hoped.

"You're sure?" Hawk asked.

"Quite positive," Stanislav said.

Hawk sighed. "We'll post a ship to guard that rift. Just in case your android returns with it." He narrowed his eyes at Alisa, as if he was certain she wanted the ghastly thing.

"If Bravo Six ever is able to return," Alisa said, "please send him in my direction. I owe him an eye."

Hawk only looked puzzled at the statement.

"Do you want us to search the ship, sir?" one of the soldiers asked. "She could be lying."

Panic welled in Alisa's chest—if they searched the ship, they were sure to find Thorian.

"Oh, I'm certain she's lying," Hawk said dryly. "But I believe Stanislav that the staff isn't here."

"Er, yes, sir." The soldier eyed Stanislav, appearing puzzled by the trust.

It surprised Alisa too. Was Stanislav manipulating Hawk? Or had they come to an understanding of sorts?

"Do you know if Tomich made it, sir?" Alisa asked, genuinely curious but also wanting to change the subject.

"He's fine. We're arranging to recover him. He had an artful crash—did you see it?" Hawk smiled, but it was fleeting. "Even with his help—and with yours—we almost didn't win this one." He held her gaze. "It was close."

Though it didn't seem right to show exuberance in the face of his graveness, Alisa couldn't help but be pleased that he was acknowledging her team, that they had been useful, especially after he'd forbidden her to come. The Alliance could have chosen not to notice that the *Nomad* had fired that final deadly blow that had taken out Tymoteusz and his people.

"Yes, sir," she said. "About the future…"

Hawk regarded her warily. "Yes?"

She wasn't sure if she should press him for anything now, but when might she ever see him again? It wasn't as if admirals—or senators—spent time with freighter captains on a regular basis. "I was wondering if I—and my crew—" she thought of Leonidas, "—will be able to run freight after this. Without worrying about wanted posters and being hunted by Alliance police and soldiers."

"Ah." The wariness faded, and he looked relieved.

What had he thought she would ask? For medals? Money? Stickers? She just wanted a relatively safe life for her and her daughter. And Leonidas.

"The charges against you were already dropped," he said.

"Oh? There wasn't a memo."

"We've been a touch distracted of late."

"And, uhm, what about Leonidas?" Alisa asked.

Once, he'd said he'd allow Tiang to perform Leonidas's surgery if he agreed to join the Alliance, and there'd been the implication that any wanted posters out for him would disappear, but Leonidas had said no.

"If he doesn't make trouble for us, we don't see any reason to bother him," Hawk said.

"Excellent. I'll tell him." She was tempted to hug him but doubted that would be appropriate. "We weren't planning on it. Trouble, that is. We're looking forward to a sedate future."

"I'm not sure I believe that," Hawk said, looking at Stanislav, who smiled serenely, "but I'll withhold judgment for now." He waved at his soldiers and pointed them to the airlock. "Let's go, men. I have a dreadful casualty report to write up."

"Won't Admiral Agosti be responsible for that, sir?"

"Unfortunately, I'm responsible for everything these days. The perks of the position I thought I wanted." Hawk headed for the airlock, his limp more pronounced than usual. Someone else who was unbearably weary.

"Is he staying here, sir?" One of the soldiers pointed at Stanislav.

"I expect so," Hawk said without looking back.

"Thank you, sir," Alisa called after him. She wasn't sure what exactly she was thanking him for—showing up in time to help maybe, or for not searching her ship—but it seemed appropriate. She followed after the soldiers, so she could close the hatch, relieved that they were going to leave so easily.

"One more thing, Marchenko," Hawk said, turning in the airlock to hold up a finger and look at her.

Alisa gulped, afraid he might be reconsidering the search. "Yes, sir?"

"Tell your chef that my soon-to-be father-in-law will be in touch. Admiral Tiang is quite adamant that your man cater his daughter's wedding." Hawk's eyebrow twitched. He hadn't, after all, sampled any of Beck's offerings yet.

"I'll let him know, sir. I'm sure he would be honored. I'm also sure he would love to get an endorsement from a senator."

"Endorsement?"

"Yes, he's starting a barbecue sauce empire. If you offer him glowing remarks, they may end up on a label somewhere."

Hawk slumped against the airlock wall. "This has been an odd couple of months."

"No argument from me, sir." She smiled and closed the hatch, hitting the button to cycle the lock. Best to get them out of here before they could think up another reason why they might want to search the ship.

Once they were gone, she, too, slumped against the wall. "Did you convince him to leave without searching the ship?" she asked Stanislav, glancing at Abelardus, making the question for him too.

Abelardus shook his head.

"Not me," Stanislav said. "He's fairly certain you have the prince on board and didn't want to find him with his men watching on, because then, he would have felt forced to do something about it."

"So is Thorian to remain wanted for the rest of his life?" Alisa's thoughts of keeping him aboard, adding him to the family, and letting him have a semblance of a normal life crumbled a little. "That's disappointing."

One of the chickens squawked from its coop. Agreement?

Stanislav shrugged in answer to the question. "Perhaps in a few years, people will forget about him. Hawk didn't want to see him thrown in some Alliance prison, or worse, just because he's a kid. And he's praying he didn't make the wrong decision about that."

"Understandable," Alisa said. "Well, now that they're gone, who wants to go visit a sexy cyborg?"

"I'd rather pick lint out of my bellybutton," Abelardus said.

"A hobby that's sure to further endear Young-hee to you."

"I'm ready to visit him," Stanislav said, managing a tired smile.

EPILOGUE

The smell of hay tickled Alisa's nose, and even though she loved being in space, she couldn't help but luxuriate in the warm rays of the suns beating against her face. Thanks to its prime place in orbit around Rebus, Upsilon Seven had been designated as an agricultural world before the colony ships had even left Old Earth. The bluegrass prairies and brilliant blue-green sky stretched for miles, broken only by the cottonwood trees meandering along the river running past the stable.

The sunny, earthy air felt especially fine after the sickness Alisa, Jelena, and the others had endured on the way here, thanks to their radiation exposure and Alejandro's concoctions for cleaning toxins from the body. Alisa inhaled deeply, reminded of horse rides here as a child with her mother and also of visiting Jonah's kin on his family's farm back on Perun. A twinge of nostalgia came to her, and she lamented that he wasn't here to show Jelena the basics of riding a horse.

A thoughtful "hm" came from behind her, and Leonidas walked out of the stable, carrying a saddle. He, too, had spent long days recovering from their battle, but he had lost most of his ashen appearance. "I didn't realize this would be a do-it-yourself affair."

"It's a working ranch," Alisa said. "Thousands of head of snagor out there. The tourists come down to experience the authenticity of choosing and saddling their own horses."

"You got to choose your horse?"

"I pointed at the mild-mannered pony munching grass in the field. Henry said he'd bring her out with the others." Alisa waved to the ground where her blanket and saddle rested.

"*Henry*," Leonidas said, twisting his mouth and giving the name an odd emphasis, "said he would choose an appropriate mount for me."

"Oh? Jelena got to pick hers. Despite Henry's choking noises at the towering black stallion she picked. I was fairly certain he would object—I was certainly on the verge of objecting—but then the huge horse trotted over, stopped in front of her, and lowered his nose so she could pet it. They gazed into each other's eyes like they had an understanding. Henry said he'd never seen anything like it. I decided not to mention that my daughter is a Starseer in training and apparently likes telepathing with animals more than with people."

"Telepathing?"

"She assured me it's a word. Among Starseers. I hope she'll be all right on the big horse. It'll be a long drop if she falls off. I would have preferred a mare. Or a nice sedate gelding."

"Don't underestimate geldings," Leonidas murmured.

"No? I hear they're docile and easy to lead." She grinned at him—it wasn't as if anyone could call him one of those anymore.

"I don't know about *docile*."

"Have you seen your horse yet? That's a huge saddle Henry gave you."

Leonidas looked down at the snagor-hide item. In his brawny arms, it did not appear oversized, but Alisa would have been dragging it along behind her if she'd had to tote it around.

"He said he'd bring it out. Once he caught it. It sounded like that might be challenging." Leonidas's lips thinned as he looked around the front of the stable, perhaps searching for this challenging horse.

Ostberg and his parents—Alisa had offered to pick them up on Cleon Moon and give them a ride back to their home on Demeter—were chatting with Henry by the corral and choosing horses for the ride. Young-hee's, Abelardus's, and Thorian's voices drifted out from the stable. Alejandro and Stanislav had chosen to stay aboard the *Nomad*. Alisa kept hoping Alejandro would choose to depart, but she was beginning to get the feeling that he intended to stay with Thorian, wherever the prince ended up going. Alisa had offered to let him stay on her ship. Last she had heard, Stanislav, Leonidas, and Alejandro had been discussing Emperor Markus's dying wishes and what would be appropriate. She didn't know if anyone had asked *Thorian* where he wanted to live.

"Where did Jelena go?" Leonidas asked. "She wasn't in the stable."

"Gift shop," Alisa said. "Something caught her eye, and I told her she could charge a few tindarks to the *Nomad*. Mica's repair list will probably break my piggy bank, but I've already got some cargo lined up on Demeter. Assuming there's room in the hold." She sighed. "Yumi and Mica and Beck eschewed horseback riding and went out to purchase ducks and geese."

"The aquaponics tank is unfinished, I know, but it's not taking up much room."

"You haven't seen it when it unfurls."

"Unfurls?"

"I don't know what else to call it. Mica designed it so that it can all be sealed in when we're in a battle or in danger of losing gravity, a true tank if you will, but when everything is normal, there's an actual pool that pops out that the fowl can wade in."

"Fancy."

"I feel like my crew is more eccentric than most," Alisa said.

"Like attracts like." His eyes crinkled.

"I should slap you for that, but your giant saddle is in the way."

"It's good that I'm protected then. I was wondering if I should wear my armor for this adventure."

"For horseback riding? I'm sure even the mildest mare would shy away from a man clanking about in combat armor and looking fierce."

"I don't clank."

"No objection to the fierce part?"

"No, if imperial combat armor didn't look fierce, the designers wouldn't have had their jobs for long."

Alisa leaned companionably against him, glad he wasn't in his armor. She much preferred to be able to feel him through his clothes—or without his clothes. She grinned at the thought, though feeling Leonidas sans clothes still wasn't happening that often. Fortunately, Jelena seemed to be getting used to him, so Alisa had hopes for the future.

"How have your nightmares been?" she asked, looking up at his face, wondering if her hopes should include sharing a bed for more than sex in the future.

"They are…still present, but I do believe they've been less frequent since the surgery. Perhaps the past will cease haunting me so much in time…" He lifted a shoulder.

"In time? Such as *in time* for your honeymoon?" she asked, smiling.

They hadn't broached the subject of weddings and honeymoons much yet, and his eyebrows drifted upward. Would he object? Alisa had thought weddings had been implied when he'd spoken of having a family.

"I should not like to rush anything," he said, and she thought he meant the wedding until he added, "Perhaps by our second or third anniversary, it would be safe to share a bed for more than…recreational purposes."

"Three years after the marriage is usually about the time couples want to *stop* sharing beds," Alisa said dryly. "You don't snore, do you?"

He squinted at her. "Of course not. Cyborgs have enhanced nostrils, after all."

"That could just mean you snore extremely loudly."

"I do not."

"I guess I'll find out. In three years. That's about the time I expect to get my needlepoint battlefield."

His squint relaxed into an easy smile. "Actually, I've started on that. It's not a battlefield."

"No? What is it?"

"You'll have to wait until I finish to find out."

"I guess I should be excited that I have so many things to look forward to during my future with you."

"You should," he said agreeably and squeezed her shoulder before letting her go and stepping away.

Alisa was about to ask why he'd moved, but a cheerful cry came from behind them.

"I found some!"

Jelena ran out of the gift shop at the side of the stable, waving a stack of papers or something similar in her hand. She grinned as she came up between Alisa and Leonidas. Alisa was pleased that she didn't try to use her as a shield or otherwise put some obstacle between her and Leonidas.

"What did you find?" Alisa asked.

"Stickers," Jelena said. "For his combat armor."

Leonidas blinked slowly. He hadn't forgotten that deal he had made with Jelena, had he? She smirked at him. How fierce would he feel with stickers slapped all over his armor?

"They mostly had horses," Jelena said, starting to show them her new collection, "but I found puppies and kittens too." She paused and held up a *large* kitten sticker.

"That's bigger than I was imagining," Alisa said, watching Leonidas out of the corner of her eye, noting the stricken expression on his face. She, of course, was tickled. If he wouldn't paint his armor pink, this was the next best thing.

"Because *he's* so big." Jelena looked up at Leonidas as if she were peering into the branches of some lofty tree. "Will you let me decorate your armor?"

Leonidas stood utterly still, as if he'd gone into shock. Finally, he met Alisa's eyes, searching for some escape. A breeze whispered through, tugging at the giant kitten sticker. All Alisa did was lift her eyebrows. He had made a promise.

"*One* sticker," Leonidas said.

Jelena frowned.

"At a time," he amended. "More stickers, and I might look...uhm...evil pirates might not be scared away by me, and they'd be more likely to take over the freighter and steal your mother's cargo."

"But you can beat them up and throw them out the door if they do that. Like with the miners. I saw you on the cameras." She smiled brightly. "*Six* stickers. And I get to pick them and where they go."

"Two stickers, and that can't be one of them." He pointed at the huge one—it would take up some impressive real estate on his chest piece if he allowed it. "That one is nice." He shifted his finger toward a small puppy frolicking in what looked to be the grass in front of the stable. The top of the sticker read: Magnuson Horse Boarding and Ranch. "Maybe Henry would pay me for advertising his establishment."

"You can barely see the puppy," Jelena said, shifting through her stack. "Two stickers is so few. I don't know..."

"Two," Leonidas said firmly.

"One has to be the big one then. Look at the kitten. She's so sweet. And adorable. Look at those eyes!"

"The only place it would fit—"

"Is on your chest," Jelena said brightly. "It'll be *perfect*. And this one with the two orange kittens can go on your back. So people who *aren't* evil pirates will know you're nice." She grinned. "On both sides."

"I..." Leonidas shifted the saddle to one arm so he could rub the back of his neck.

Alisa had never seen him speechless before. Well, he *had* mentioned wanting a family of his own. Surely, this was a good preview of what that might entail.

She bumped his arm with the back of her hand. "Jelena thinks you're *nice*," she pointed out. "Surely, it's worth a sticker here and there to foster that feeling. Besides, they'll probably come off the first time you put your armor in its case for a cleaning."

"Come off?" Jelena asked with a frown.

"It's a good thing you got a whole stack." Alisa winked at her. "You can rotate them."

"Oh, good idea."

Leonidas turned toward the stable door. Thorian was walking out, also with a saddle in his arms. His face was as solemn as always, and Alisa wondered if he would ever get a chance to be a kid and perhaps learn to smile. He hadn't spoken much to any of them about his ordeal on Tymoteusz's ship—the merest hint of the topic made his lips press together and his entire face pinch in pain. At least today should be fun for him.

"Thor." Jelena waved the stack of stickers. "Come see what we're going to put on Leonidas's armor."

"Stickers?" Thorian's eyebrows disappeared beneath his shaggy hair. Alisa was going to have to take him aside for a haircut while the men debated his future. "He's an imperial cyborg officer. He should look fearsome and professional."

Leonidas's eyebrows also lifted. With hope, Alisa thought. Did he think Thorian might gainsay Jelena? And that she would actually listen to him if he did?

"He's my mom's security officer now," Jelena said. "That means he has to wear whatever uniform she thinks is best. And my mom likes stickers."

Thorian looked at Alisa. He might only be ten years old, but the hint of an accusation in his eyes made her want to squirm.

She cleared her throat and said, "I first suggested that he paint his armor pink, actually. Stickers seemed more reasonable."

"Pink?" Thorian stared at her, then at Leonidas, and finally looked at Jelena—and the stickers in her hand. "I like that one."

Leonidas rubbed the back of his neck again.

Alisa hugged him. "Just think about how humiliating it will be for the pirates to be beaten up by a man covered in stickers."

"Yes, it's the *pirates'* humiliation that I was thinking of," he said, but he managed a wry smile.

"Who's ready to ride?" Ostberg asked, heading toward their group and now leading a horse. He had lost a few pounds during his weeks in the regen tank, but he was walking without a limp or any sign of pain. Alisa was certain Beck's cookies would help those pounds return before long.

"Do you know how?" Thorian asked, regarding the brown gelding Ostberg led. It was a tall one, to match his own gangly height.

"How hard can it be? I'm a master thrust bike racer now, you know. I won heaps of money on Cleon Moon after you left."

"Did not."

"Did *too*. They know." Ostberg pointed at Leonidas and Alisa.

"He did race bikes and win money," Alisa said. "Whether horses have anything in common with something with thrusters, I guess we'll find out shortly."

The horse made a whuffing noise.

Ostberg's parents waved from the fence as Henry led several more horses toward the group, the mother with a glass of iced tea in her hand. Apparently, the senior Ostbergs weren't as adventurous as their son. Alisa hadn't spoken to them much since picking up the family, but had heard they had never developed any Starseer talents of their own and had been quite shocked when their son did after a bout with Trajean Fever. Feeling helpless, they'd let Ostberg be taken off for schooling after being approached by a couple of Starseers who had somehow learned of the boy's gifts. During a group dinner, Alisa had pointed out that Stanislav would be instructing Jelena going forward, and that they could leave Ostberg on her ship to work and learn while the *Nomad* hauled freight from planet to planet. She didn't know yet if they would take her up on the offer, but she couldn't help but feel that Stanislav would be a better instructor than those snooty tutors who'd been handling things before. Yumi, who had no plans to leave the ship anytime soon, could help with basic scholastic instruction for the children. And Alisa could use another chicken wrangler on the ship. Especially if geese and ducks were soon to be added to the flock.

Abelardus and Young-hee walked out of the stable, also leading horses. They shared quiet smiles as they walked, telepathic terms of endearment, no doubt.

"Have you two decided where you want to be dropped off yet?" Alisa asked. She assumed they would both head back to Arkadius to reunite with their people and help rebuild the temple there.

"Are there no more openings for Starseers on your ship, Captain?" Young-hee asked.

"Er, you want to run freight with me? I can't imagine how that would be interesting to either of you."

"Somehow I doubt your freight hauling missions will be *uninteresting*, Captain."

"Really? After everything we've been through, I wouldn't mind a few uninteresting months."

"And yet, it doesn't seem in your nature not to court danger," Young-hee said.

"You noticed that, did you?" Abelardus asked.

Alisa didn't know what to say. She had no trouble inviting Ostberg to stay aboard, as a ship seemed as good a place as any to grow up, and Jelena would probably enjoy having another young person around, but what crew positions would she give to Young-hee and Abelardus? Beer brewers? Duck herders?

Do you truly think we have so few skills, Captain? Abelardus asked dryly into her mind. *That we must be given such sedentary positions?*

I doubt duck herding will be a job for the faint of heart. And weren't you the brewer for your people on Arkadius?

I was, yes, but it was a part-time job. As was piloting our darts. Most of the time, I trained with the other guards to keep everyone safe when uninvited cyborgs showed up in the temple.

Did you not find that stimulating?

Not as stimulating as space travel. Even more to the point, Young-hee is enjoying being away from her mother's influence and wouldn't mind a few more months of independence while we decide what's next for us. In the meantime, I could once again work security for you.

Under Leonidas's command? Alisa asked, surprised he would volunteer for that.

Abelardus hesitated. *Perhaps I could lead the* Starseer *security contingent and be of equal rank to Leonidas.*

Contingent? Unless you're planning to command Young-hee and my father, you'd be a one-person contingent.

I could command Young-hee.

Without having your balls twisted into a knot and shoved somewhere unpleasant? Alisa looked at Young-hee, wondering if she was privy to any of this conversation.

Really, Captain. Abelardus sniffed. *Now that I'm taken by another woman, and you're taken by your cyborg, you shouldn't be thinking about my balls. As irresistible as they are.*

Young-hee snorted noisily. Alisa decided that meant she had, indeed, been monitoring the conversation. She hoped she had made some choice comments to Abelardus.

"If you want to stay aboard, you're welcome to," Alisa said. "I'm sure we can find some manner of employment for you. Perhaps you can help Yumi attend to her...garden."

"Is that truly the appropriate word for that drug manufacturing facility she has set up in her cabin?" Abelardus asked.

"Well, there are tomatoes growing in planters that hang from the ceiling."

"Thank you for coming for me, Colonel," Thorian said, standing next to Leonidas and speaking quietly, perhaps believing that everyone else was engaged in their own conversations and would not notice him. "I thought... I thought I might have to take my life to prevent him from using me. But I was scared. And I didn't know how. I thought that my father should have instructed me on that, but he never did."

The words weren't meant for Alisa to overhear, but they sent a stab of anguish through her heart.

"He never expected your brother to die and for you to become heir apparent," Leonidas responded, also speaking quietly.

Alisa couldn't believe how bluntly they spoke of such matters. She should have moved away to let them have a private conversation, but it wasn't as if they didn't know of her eavesdropping proclivities. Maybe that was why they hadn't bothered to shift away from her.

"It's true," Thorian said, "and now I'm not even that. There is no throne to ascend to one day."

"Not now, no."

Alisa frowned, not liking the implication that Leonidas still believed the empire might return someday. What had he and Alejandro been discussing back in sickbay during the days since escaping Tymoteusz? Maybe she should have been putting more effort into eavesdropping.

"Dr. Dominguez believes my place is with the Starseers for now," Thorian said.

"I know."

"Captain Marchenko said I could stay with her."

Alisa had said that no less than three times, in fact.

"I know that too," Leonidas said.

"I know my father would want me to get the best training possible... and to prepare for my future."

"Yes," Leonidas said, as if he knew exactly what that meant.

Alisa frowned again. What future? Did Thorian truly believe that he was supposed to bring back the empire someday? Couldn't he just be a boy for the next few years and then decide what he wanted to be when he grew up? The empire was gone. He could be an engineer. Or a doctor or a pilot or whatever he wished. He shouldn't have to follow someone else's program.

She opened her mouth, on the verge of saying as much, but Leonidas shot her a warning look. He didn't say anything, but his eyes seemed to be telling her that it was Thorian's decision to make, not hers.

"Would you come with me?" Thorian asked.

"What?" Alisa blurted.

Even Leonidas, rocking back on his heels, seemed surprised by the question.

Thorian looked at Alisa, his lips pinched together, and moved several steps away. Leonidas hesitated and followed him. Alisa turned her back on them, looked the other way, and sidled closer, using Leonidas's broad form as cover.

"You offered to come with me once," Thorian told him. "When you first dropped me off with the Starseers."

"Yes, I did," Leonidas said slowly, like a man deep in thought.

What was there to think about? He should tell Thorian that they should both stay on the *Nomad* and become a part of the family. After all, Thorian was a more age-appropriate playmate for Jelena than Ostberg.

"But things have changed since then," Leonidas said. "I...wish to be considered retired. I want to start a family." He glanced over his shoulder, though Alisa was sure he knew exactly where she was without looking. "And maybe even ask Alisa to marry me one day. But don't tell her that." He'd turned back, but he sounded like he was smiling.

Alisa smiled too, her toes curling at the idea of a proposal, of a promise that Leonidas would stay with her. Forever.

"I know she wouldn't mind if you stayed with us here on the *Nomad*," Leonidas added. "Stanislav will be teaching Jelena. He could teach you, too, I imagine."

For a moment, Thorian gazed wistfully out toward the cottonwoods, and Alisa sensed that he wanted to accept the offer. She silently urged him to, even if she thought it was silly that Leonidas and the others were giving him a choice. He was too young to know where the best place for him was.

"He's...not a soldier, not someone with military experience."

"Neither was Lady Westfall," Leonidas said.

"No, but they...once it was safe, they were going to take me to some other Starseers that my father trusted, people with military experience. I was to learn to become a Starseer *and* a leader." Thorian's gaze drifted toward the cottonwoods again. "Even though Father's gone now, I know that's what he wanted. I can't just spend my life on some scruffy freighter, being a nobody."

Alisa propped a fist on her hip, once again tempted to jump in, if only to defend her ship—and those who chose to ride aboard it. It was the first time she'd caught the kid saying something snobby and elitist, but she supposed that had to be in his makeup somewhere. One didn't grow up in total privilege without some evidence of the fact.

Alisa looked toward Jelena, wondering if she was also eavesdropping on this conversation—she might object to being lumped in with the nobodies. But she had drifted over to pet Ostberg's horse. More of a draw than discussing a prince's future, Alisa supposed.

"You shouldn't stay there, either, Colonel," Thorian said. "If you came with me, I know your military experience would be useful, and…" He lowered his gaze to his feet, and Alisa almost missed his next whispered words. "I wouldn't be alone again."

Leonidas rested a hand on his shoulder. "If you need me at some point in the future, get in touch, and I'll come help, but over the last few months, I've come to realize…I don't want to be a soldier anymore. I want to be a family man. As dreadful as it seems, I want little girls to put stickers on my armor."

Thorian snorted, almost a laugh.

"I've been a somebody for a long time, responsible for many lives and the execution of many orders. I've served the empire loyally for twenty years." Leonidas looked over his shoulder at Alisa. "I'm ready to retire."

"I'm sorry to hear that, Colonel." Thorian nudged a clump of grass with his foot.

Does he truly think being a security officer on your *ship will be retirement?* Abelardus asked in her head. *You've probably already got the next job lined up, something that will have pirates banging at your airlock.*

We're hauling dehydrated peas and corn from Demeter to Perun so Jelena can visit her Aunt Sylvia in the capital.

Ah, into imperial territory? Pirates will only be the beginning.

"If you get tired of being molded to be a prince and a leader," Leonidas said, lowering his hand from Thorian's shoulder, "the offer stands. You can join us on the *Star Nomad*."

Thorian met his eyes, his expression grave, as always. But a quick smile flashed across his face. "If *you* get tired of wearing kitten stickers in combat, you can join me, Colonel."

"I'll keep your offer in mind." Leonidas stuck out his hand.

Thorian shook it, his grave expression returning.

"Who's ready to go for a ride?" Henry drawled, leading the horse Alisa had picked out toward her, along with...was that a horse?

Alisa gaped at the size of the white stallion. She hadn't realized they made horses that big. Maybe it had been genetically engineered.

"Here's your horse, sir," Henry said, eyeing Leonidas with a challenging smirk. For the first time, Alisa got the hint that maybe their tour guide had identified Leonidas as a cyborg—and wasn't that crazy about cyborgs. "Already got a blanket on him. Think you can manage putting that saddle on him?"

The horse snorted, pawed at the ground, and gave Leonidas a look even more challenging than Henry's.

"Do people actually ride that horse?" Alisa asked.

She doubted Leonidas would break any of his synthetic bones if he took a fall, but she'd been hoping they would all have an enjoyable—and uneventful—outing.

"Of course they do, ma'am." Henry tipped his hat toward her. "Some of them for nearly twenty seconds."

"Pardon?"

"This here horse is for the local rodeo. He's never been truly broken. We keep him wild for the bucking bronco event. Whoever stays on his back the longest, gets a prize."

"So naturally, you're bringing him out for a bunch of tourists going on a placid trail ride," Alisa said.

"Only horse I've got that's big enough for your muscular friend here."

"I had no idea your stock was so puny that it couldn't handle a brawny rider." She scowled at him. Surely, he'd had rotund tourists here before who were heavier than Leonidas.

Holding the saddle, Leonidas took a step toward the horse, and it reared up, both legs kicking in the air. He sighed in Henry's direction. The smug handler didn't look alarmed, even though he was the one with the stallion's reins.

"Jelena," Leonidas said as the horse reared again. "I may need your assistance."

"I can help," Jelena said brightly, leaving Ostberg's horse and running over.

"Uh," Alisa said, lifting a hand, not wanting her too close to this "bronco."

But the stallion dropped to all fours, calming before Jelena was within ten feet. She squinted at the creature in some silent communication and walked forward. The stallion turned toward her, lowering his nose for scratching.

"Is it safe for me to put the saddle on him?" Leonidas asked, glancing toward Alisa as well as Jelena.

"He'll let you dress him and ride him," Jelena said, "if you let me put *four* stickers on your armor."

"The horse is concerned about stickers?" Alisa asked, since Leonidas's mouth had dropped open and he didn't appear capable of making the comment.

"Very concerned," Jelena said. "He wants what's best for me."

"He's only known you for seven seconds."

"Seven seconds of *friendship.*"

The stallion lowered his head all the way to the ground, and Jelena wrapped her arms around his neck.

"That's amazing, ma'am," Henry whispered, standing in awe as Leonidas put the saddle on—after glancing at a few other horses to see how it should be done.

Jelena stepped back from the horse hug and smiled.

Amazing, sure. Alisa wondered what kind of mental manipulation her daughter was doing to get that horse's compliance. Probably promising him carrots after the ride.

"She's definitely your daughter," Leonidas said, coming to stand next to Alisa. He bumped her shoulder gently.

"Because she's good with animals? Or because she's good at manipulating situations?" Alisa wondered how fierce he would look with *four* stickers plastered to his armor.

"I haven't noticed that you have an affinity for animals," he said dryly.

"I get along well with Yumi's chickens."

"From what I've seen, they ignore you, and you ignore them."

"That's getting along well as far as I'm concerned," Alisa said. "It's not like they're going out of their way to leave droppings in my shoes."

"I don't think chickens do that. Cats, maybe. We probably shouldn't get a cat."

Not with all those fowl, no. Besides...

"What would we need with a cat?" Alisa patted Leonidas on the arm. "We've got a cyborg who'll soon be wearing a giant kitten on his chest."

Henry led Alisa's horse over to her. She waited to make sure that Leonidas could, indeed, mount the big stallion before she climbed aboard her mare. Fortunately, whatever Jelena had promised the beast seemed to have worked.

Alisa chuckled to herself as Thorian and Jelena mounted their horses and the group rode off along a trail. She was sad that Jonah couldn't be here to see his daughter, but pleased to have another family that she could count on going forward. She wouldn't go looking for adventures, as Abelardus seemed to believe she would, but she doubted the future would be boring.

THE END

Made in the USA
Middletown, DE
02 October 2018